HIDE

Robert John Bonney

For more information, contact: http://www.rjbonney.com

For Jim

Fish gotta swim and bird gotta fly; insect, it seems, gotta do one horrible thing after another.

Annie Dillard
Pilgrim at Tinker Creek

CHAPTER ONE

Follow the Instructions

July 1, 2016. 7:01 AM

Mom and Dad:

I've gone away. I don't like hurting you and I want to be as fair as I can, but this is how it's got to be. Try to remember how smart I am. I can take care of myself. This was planned out. I'm safe, I honestly am. Try not to worry. But of course you will.

You will get other emails from me soon. You have to follow the instructions in those emails, or I won't come home. I know you will try to find me, since I'm fourteen and the police have to get involved. They won't find me.

One other thing. This email is one way, so if you reply, I won't get it.

This all must seem obnoxious. I can't explain now, but in my next message, I'll start.

Seb

1

And please don't blame the Ajahn. He never knew anything about this.

Burton Franck rolled the chair back from the desk. He had to tell his wife. Their son was gone. Gone in the middle of the night to send this incomprehensible message.

The clock on the screen showed that three hours had already passed since Seb sent the email. Burton put his hands on the armrests but did not push himself up, even though every second he sat there was more time for their son to get farther away.

What if the email was a prank or a scam? The thought of telling his wife that their child had run away made him sick to his stomach. It would be better to call the Buddhist monastery first. Seb was probably still there. They had driven him to the monastery the night before for a short meditation retreat. Everything was fine. This email made no sense.

Burton had just seen the phone number for the monastery. It was on the registration form for the retreat. He stood up and flipped through the papers on the desk as fast as he could, knocking several to the floor. Then he remembered Seb had used the monastery's phone to call his parents before going to bed. The number would be on Burton's phone.

He got the phone out of his pocket and realized he should do something else first. He clicked "Reply" to the email.

Seb, it's Dad. We love you very much. Whatever's going on we promise we won't make it worse for you.

A second after sending the message, a response appeared in the in-box.

One way account. No replies received.

The monastery's number was the first thing on Burton's recent call list. He pressed *redial*. As the phone rang, he left the office, crossed the basement hallway, and entered the laundry room.

His wife, Maddy, was using the cross country ski machine. She turned to look at him, still moving her arms and legs back and forth. The skis glided. The little wheels underneath them clicked.

"Seb ran away," he yelled. "There's a note on the computer in the office."

His wife pulled hard on the hand-grips to stop the machine from

2

moving. She hopped off and slid past her husband. He turned to follow her into the basement office. She went straight to the computer and put her face close to the screen.

After eight rings, a recorded message clicked on. "This is Ajahn Wattana. We are often meditating. It may be some time before we can return your call, but please leave a message."

"Ajahn. This is Burton Franck. Seb sent us a message saying he left the retreat. Ran away. Call me immediately."

He dialed Seb's cell next.

Their son had been quiet for most of the hour it took to drive to the monastery in New Hampshire. Viewing him in the rear view mirror, Burton had attributed his son's quietness to being preoccupied by the idea of meditating for a week. Seb had been interested in Buddhism for several months, although he was quick to say he did not want to be one. Being a Buddhist looked boring, he said. But he really liked their way of meditating and had developed an email friendship with Ajahn Wattana, the monk who ran the monastery.

Seb's phone did not ring at all. Instead, a computer voice informed Burton that its mailbox had been deactivated. He showed his wife the phone's display so she could see he had called their son. The photo on the screen was only a couple of years old but Seb looked so much younger there, smiling from the back seat of their car.

"You're not going to leave a message?" Maddy asked, while continuing to study the email on the screen.

"It's deactivated."

Burton sat on the edge of the desk, next to the computer.

She looked up at him. "No one answered at the monastery?"

"No."

"Don't people in a monastery get up early? They haven't noticed anything? Like a missing child?"

"Apparently not."

Maddy ran her finger along the text on the screen. "We have to follow his instructions?"

She sounded annoyed. Burton resisted the urge to tell her to get a grip. Their son had run away.

"This keeps getting worse." Maddy stood up from the desk and walked to the door. Over her shoulder she said, "I'll go upstairs and wake Jess. Maybe she knows something."

Burton called the monastery, got the answering machine, hung up, and called again. While it was ringing for the fourth time, Maddy walked in and went back to look at the computer. Jessica came in a few seconds later.

Their daughter moved towards the couch that faced the side of the desk, the cuffs of her pajama pants dragging on the carpet. Ever since she turned twelve, she would wear nothing that did not extend at least an inch below her heels. It had been a while since Burton had seen her in anything but T-shirts with random words and low-waisted jeans. She looked like a kid again in the white pajamas she was wearing, which had little yellow smiley faces all over them.

Jessica stopped at the edge of the couch, squinting as if pained by the overhead lamp, and swatted at the light switch several times before it clicked off. The room darkened, lit now only by the basement window near the ceiling. Jessica dropped onto the couch and folded her arms in front of her. Maddy got up from the desk and sat next to her.

"Your brother's pulled some kind of stunt," Burton said.

"I heard." Jessica said flatly, as if annoyed for being woken, but her eyes kept shifting from Burton to the computer. It was clear she knew something was pretty seriously wrong.

"He ran away." Burton continued. "That's what his email says. Do you know anything about this?"

"No," she answered.

Maddy put her hand on Jessica's shoulder. "Anything strange? Was he upset about something?"

"It's all strange with Seb."

Burton knelt down on one knee in front of her. "What about his journal? You can tell us. It's okay."

Jessica had been caught reading Seb's journal three different times. The last time, her brother had applied a coating to the notebook and, after an accusation, waiting for everyone to come into the kitchen, and turning off the lights, he made her fingers glow by shining a black light on them.

"He writes on his laptop now, with a password. Since like a year ago."

"We've got to talk to the police," Burton said. "Try to remember if you saw or heard anything."

Jessica leaned forward and began rubbing her thighs. "I don't get it. Is he staying at the monastery, like he wants to actually be a monk or something?"

Burton shook his head. "No, hon, he sent an email saying he left the monastery. That's all we know. He said he would email us again later. You know your brother. He will be into something other than Buddhism next week. He was just there for the meditation training."

4

The phone in Burton's pocket started to ring. He shoved his hand into his pocket, pulled it out and pressed "answer."

"Yes?"

"This is Ajahn Wattana. From the Kindness Center."

Their son had run away from a place called the Kindness Center.

"Did you find him?"

"I haven't found Seb, I'm sorry."

The Ajahn sounded out of breath. *Ajahn* meant teacher in Thai. He was called *the* Ajahn just as one might refer to *the* Rabbi.

"You've searched the whole place?"

"We are making another pass but, yes, we checked all the rooms before I called. We just now discovered him gone. My assistant is on the phone with the police right now. I hope you don't mind."

The police. Burton felt his entire body go hot. "Yes. Of course, the police. When was the last time you saw our son?"

"Last night, I'm afraid."

"You're only noticing now that he's not there?"

Jessica leaned her head against her mother's shoulder. Burton was not sure if their daughter should be listening to this. Maddy tilted her head and nestled her ear into her daughter's hair. The two of them gazed up at Burton. The Ajahn was soft-spoken, so they probably could not hear what he was saying into the phone.

"Your son told me before bed that he would like to miss the seven o'clock meditation. To be better able to concentrate for the rest of the day. Because he's not used to getting up early."

"He lied."

"We did not clear away breakfast."

The formality of the Ajahn's Thai-accented English used to charm Burton but he found it disturbing now. An old man from another country might not be the best person to rely on for finding a missing American teenager.

"When your son did not show up to eat breakfast," the Ajahn continued, "we passed by his room again with the bells. Then we knocked on his door. He did not respond, so I tried the door. It was not locked and he was not inside. Only a suitcase and a few clothes. Maybe he will come back."

"I don't know. He sent a strange email. I'll forward it to you. He left his suitcase?"

"Yes, although it looks like he took some of the clothes."

"I'm coming up there."

"That would be best, I think."

5

"As soon as we speak to the police. They're on their way to our house."

"They are on their way here as well," the Ajahn said.

⁂

Two police officers looked at Burton through the screen door. Big men, taller than him, and he was tall.

Burton opened the screen door and held it for them. "Thank you for coming. We can sit in here."

He motioned to the foyer, a narrow room to his right with white love seats facing each other from opposite walls.

"Thank you," said the older officer.

He and his partner sat on one of the love seats. It was a tight fit. Their knees touched and each of them immediately jerked their legs in the opposite direction. Burton stood next to the matching love seat across from them, waiting for Maddy.

She came into the foyer from the archway that led into the living room. The two officers on the love seat started to stand but she waved them down.

"Don't get up," she said. "Thank you."

She had changed out of her workout gear into jeans and a red T-shirt. The ends of the loose curls of her black hair, her "Puerto-Rican hair" as she called it, rested on her shoulders. She usually put it into a ponytail after a workout or a shower. The muscles of her jaw were clenched taut and she had the furrow between her eyes that she got when she was worked up, but the curls around her cheeks softened her appearance a bit.

For some reason his wife stopped walking a few feet before she reached the love seats. It was as if she did not want to begin what was undoubtedly going to be a painful experience. Or, she was trying to steel herself, to make sure she had a game plan. Maddy always liked to have a game plan. The officers were the experts in this kind of thing but she would be on the lookout for any missed opportunities or screw-ups.

Burton got up, walked to her, and reached to put his arm around her waist. He could feel his own arm shaking. Once he had his hand on her hip, he guided her to the love seat. They lowered themselves slowly until they were seated, at eye level with the detectives on the seat opposite them.

The two officers seemed tired, even the younger one, with puffiness

6

and dark circles about the eyes. Everyone seemed tired these days.

Their squad car was clearly visible though the bay window behind their heads. Burton noticed, further on, curtains moving in the house across the street. Dina Pintauro never could mind her own business.

"I'm Officer Quinn," the older man said. "This is Officer Masco. We're here to get your son back."

Officer Quinn certainly meant to reassure them, but his comment had the opposite effect on Burton. It sounded rehearsed. How much could a police officer who dealt with crisis every day really care about a stranger's kid, some spoiled suburban brat acting out? Burton felt sick, dizzy, as if he'd had too much coffee. He stared at the officers for a moment before telling himself these men had to care about a missing child. If anything, a runaway kid was probably not something they dealt with every day.

Burton glanced over at Maddy. He noticed a white line along the edge of her hairline. It was dried sweat. She had changed clothes but not showered or washed her face.

The younger officer flipped open an iPad. Officer Quinn glanced at Maddy. When she cast her eyes down, he shifted his gaze to Burton.

"When was the last time you spoke to your son?" the officer asked.

"Last night, around nine," Burton said. "He called us after the final meditation of the day. He's in...he's attending a week-long retreat at a Buddhist center."

"Your son is fourteen years old?"

"Yes. I know, it's a bit unusual."

"Tell us everything you recall about your conversation with your son last night."

"He said the experience was going to be interesting." Burton felt a lot of pressure to remember it all. He could think of nothing remarkable about the ride up there and Seb seemed calm but the officers might pick up on something. "It's a silent retreat. They're not even supposed to make eye contact. So 'interesting' seemed appropriate."

The younger officer smiled. This was kind but it also made him look even more like the trainee Burton assumed he was. Quinn merely nodded.

"Did he sound different?" the older officer asked.

Burton looked at his wife before answering. He saw that she had placed a pad of paper on her knee and a pen in her hand.

"The conversation was a bit awkward, but that made sense at the time. We had just dropped him off a few hours earlier and there was not much new to talk about. I figured he wanted to get off the phone and go back to his adventure. He said the food was pretty good. Nothing else significant, that I can remember. Oh, and they had to be in their rooms by ten and there was no television or Wi-Fi. But that was good, he said. It would be wrong to have Wi-Fi at a silent retreat."

Maddy's pen stopped skipping across the pad but she did not look up. Burton took this to mean she wanted him to take the lead in the conversation. He got the feeling she was on the verge of crying or rising up like a mama bear. Or both.

He was surprised the mama bear had not come out already. The officers seemed to be doing fine but she had pretty strong opinions. This was the woman who, after hearing Seb's soccer coach blare, "Goalie, come back from outer space and keep your eyes on the ball," had grabbed the bullhorn from the bench and announced, in front of both teams and all the spectators, that "coach better keep his eyes on his own balls."

"Mr. Franck?"

Burton, apparently, had missed a question. "Yes?"

"I assume you've been calling your son's cell?"

"All the time. The phone company tells us it hasn't been powered on since last night."

Maddy took a phone from her pocket, pressed a button, and held it to her ear. Burton assumed she was calling Seb's phone again.

"Tell us how he came to be at the Buddhist retreat. Was he a Buddhist?"

"It's a long story."

Quinn nodded, indicating Burton should continue. The younger officer—what was his name? Matchko? Masco. Masco just stared.

"A few months ago," Burton said. "I guess about four months ago, Seb learned about Buddhism at school and started to read things online. He found out there was a Buddhist temple not far from here. The temple had a beginner's meditation class for an hour each week. Seb went to it pretty regularly. My wife or I would go with him."

"We'll need to get the names and contact information of the members of that group," Quinn said.

"We spoke to the temple a few minutes before you got here. The group leader just emailed us the names and email addresses of the members. She doesn't have phone numbers for everyone. It was pretty informal. You can track down the phone numbers?"

"I'm sure we can."

"Two months ago a monk from a monastery in Portsmouth came to speak at the temple. He addressed the whole congregation, or whatever they're called, not just the beginner's group. The next thing we knew, he was emailing this monk, asking him all kinds of questions."

The officers were clearly intrigued by the mention of the monk. Quinn, aside from pleasantries, had been keeping a poker face, but his expression changed for a moment. Burton could not say how. Masco, on the other hand, sat up noticeably straighter in the seat. He must have realized Burton saw him, because he looked down abruptly at his iPad and positioned his fingers there as if preparing to type.

"The monk who came to speak," Burton continued, "is the same monk who's in charge of the monastery our son left this morning."

Quinn weighed this last bit of information before responding. "How long was your son there?"

"Just a few hours," Burton said. "He was supposed to be there for a week. It's a meditation retreat."

"Why do you think your son became interested in Buddhism?"

"It's sort of just how Seb is. He'll pick up on a new idea and dive in. The more obscure, the better. We never know what it's going to be. I don't know how long this will last. He says he doesn't want to be a Buddhist, that it looks boring. Other kids give him flack sometimes because they think he's showing off. I think some of them don't know what he's talking about. He shows off some times, but mostly he's just really curious and can't keep it to himself."

"I could see him getting some flack for Buddhism." After he said this, Quinn, for some reason, shifted his eyes to Maddy.

She met his gaze with a blank expression. After a moment, she said, "That wouldn't stop him. If Seb was into something, he did it, all out. Some things he takes very seriously. He can get emotional."

"What do they do at these retreats?"

"Six days of silent meditation and walking meditation," Burton said. "With a lesson each night by the monk. No speaking, even during meals."

"Do you think that upset him? Not being able to talk?"

Burton had expected this question. "I don't think a few hours of not speaking would have bothered him. Besides, it seems pretty clear he was planning on running away before he got to the monastery. The email he sent us this morning said he had things to tell us. Which is really disturbing. That he was planning this and we had no idea anything was wrong."

"You know," Maddy said, quietly.

Burton shifted in his seat to look at her more directly.

Although both officers were watching her now, she kept her eyes fixed on Quinn. Mama bear was fully awake now. It would not have been unlike her to feign meekness just to size up the person in charge. To lull him into showing his cards, if he had any to hide. Maddy did not assume everyone patronized her for being a woman or for being Puerto Rican, but Burton assumed she was really on guard now, with the stakes so high.

"I just remembered an email Seb sent the Ajahn a few weeks ago," she said. "He wrote how meditation could be scary, to realize you can't stop your brain, even if you sit quiet. The monk wrote a nice response. He said not to worry, that this was normal. The brain was built to think. We'll send the Ajahn's response to you."

"So, we have a boy who is scared of his thoughts and emotional—"

Maddy cut the officer off. "Emotional when something disturbing or serious is going on. Emotional for good reasons, but not all the time. As we said, Seb has a very active mind. He was just as likely to be excited about a new project."

Quinn nodded. If he was annoyed at being cut off, he did not show it. "Okay. Can you remember anything that made him upset recently?"

Burton and Maddy looked at each other. After a moment, each shrugged.

"Not right now," Maddy said. "I don't remember anything recent."

Quinn waited a moment, possibly for Burton to respond, then continued, "You did say he was concerned he couldn't stop his brain."

"If you read the Ajahn's response..." Maddy's phone buzzed and she looked down at it for a moment before continuing. "You'll see he explained that meditation was good for the brain, but it did require practice. Seb was really good about meditating. Every day. A half hour or so. He kept trying to get us all to do it. Although maybe not in the past few weeks."

She sighed after saying this and set her lips together. Burton could tell she was displeased. Her voice had started quavering and she did not like to appear out of control.

"I understand," Quinn said. "It's a difficult age, adolescence. But a kid doesn't run away unless he's having some pretty serious trouble. I know you said you had no idea why he left, but even a guess would be helpful. Was there anything new going on with him? Besides Buddhism."

"What about bullying?" It was Officer Masco who spoke this time.

Quinn flinched. He glanced at his partner out of the corner of his eye.

"You mentioned he got some flack," Masco continued. "For being different."

Burton never heard a word about bullying. Teasing, yes, but nothing that seemed to rattle Seb. He raised his eyebrows at Maddy, indicating he would field the question if she wanted him to. She gave a quick shake of her head to indicate she would answer.

"I don't think he was bullied," she said. "Things you would expect a kid to keep to himself, with Seb, he would tell us. Whatever was on his mind. He brought up the most personal things at the dinner table all the time. If he had a run-in with a kid at school, which wasn't often, he actually enjoyed telling us all the details at dinner. But that's what's so disturbing about his running away. He clearly has *not* been telling us everything. So, I guess it's possible he was being bullied. We should be able to find out from his friends and teachers as soon as...as soon as we're finished here."

Quinn started speaking the moment Maddy finished, as if to prevent Masco from speaking again. "Can you give an example of what you meant when you said your son used to tell you things other kids wouldn't tell their parents?"

Maddy and Burton both leaned back in the love seat to think. Mrs. Pintauro's curtains moved again. No doubt she could see the heads of the two tall men in the foyer window. Men in uniform who had emerged from the squad car parked in the driveway.

Burton looked away from the window and down at his fingers, all eight of them drumming on his thighs. He then remembered what had come to mind when Maddy spoke earlier about Seb's openness with them.

"This might not be the best example but it's what I first thought of. Seb came into the kitchen with his shirt off and asked his mother to smell his maturity. This was around the time he started to need deodorant."

As soon as Burton finished speaking, he regretted bringing up something so innocuous. Part of his motivation was to give his wife a break from the questioning, which was all being directed at her now. But it did demonstrate pretty well the kind of kid Seb was, if not the more serious issues he was ordinarily not shy about sharing with them.

Maddy nodded, but in a perfunctory way, gazing into the space between the two officer's heads. Probably not looking at their nosy neighbor, just trying to collect her thoughts.

"Here's an example," she said a couple seconds later. "Last year, they covered civil rights in social studies. He couldn't believe people would treat each other that way. We watched a movie on TV, I think it was a

11

Friday night. *Avatar* for the tenth time. He sat there, not reacting much. I don't think he was paying much attention to the movie. I asked him if he was still thinking about what he learned about the civil war and he said he was." She stopped gazing between the officers and turned her head a bit, in the direction of Quinn. "Is that what you're looking for?"

"Well, sure, yes. I know this is hard. Anything that comes to mind, really, could help us understand why he ran off and possibly where. What about his interests? You said he was into computers?"

"Into computers big time," Burton said. "He built his own. That was fun for him. Besides that, soccer and skateboarding. He definitely liked skateboarding better." He looked over at his wife. "Anything else?"

"The Green Club at school."

"What's that?" Quinn asked.

Burton frowned. *Did this guy really not know what a Green Club was?*

"An after-school program. Using magnifying glasses to demonstrate solar power, things like that. I think Seb burned his thumb. Kids concerned with the environment. The last project before school was out for the year was trying to get leftover lunches into a compost pile."

Burton was going to say the compost idea had to be set aside for the fall when he noticed Maddy looking at him.

"Duranne," she said. "How could we have forgotten Duranne?"

That was definitely something to tell the police about. What else had they forgotten?

Burton turned from his wife to Quinn. "About six months ago, his friend moved to California. Seb didn't seem too broken up after she left. But, he's obviously been hiding things from us, so maybe he really was upset."

"Unusual name," Quinn said. "A girlfriend?"

Maddy answered him. "Yes. Sort of. But they never kissed, according to Seb. Duranne didn't want to. Again, that's what I'm talking about. Who tells their parents things like that? The two of them were close but I'm not sure there's much difference between friend and girlfriend in eighth grade."

"Duranne comes from Duran Duran," Burton said. "The old pop band? Her mother was crazy about them."

The officers stared at him for a moment. His intention was to tell them everything that came to mind, in case it was useful. Seb was a pretty unusual kid with unusual friends. Most parents, he supposed, thought their kids were exceptional.

"The only thing kind of strange about Duranne," he said, "was that she left pretty abruptly. She gave us just a few weeks' notice and the family was gone right after Christmas. Seb seemed a little down at first but he only knew her for a few months and that was half a year ago. It would have been a hell of an acting job, to still be so smitten as to run off to be with her, and for us to have no idea the whole time.

"It doesn't line up with Seb's email, either. Especially the part where he said he was going to send us instructions. We never interfered with their friendship. We were always happy to have Duranne over."

"I agree," Maddy said. "Being in love with Duranne is a stretch. But what *does* line up with Seb's email?"

"I have no idea," Burton said. "We definitely need to talk to her parents."

"We have their contact information." Maddy looked at Quinn. "Should I get it now?"

"Sure."

Maddy got up and stopped in the archway that led to the kitchen. "I can talk to them in here unless you want to be the one to make the call?"

Quinn weighed this a moment. "Go ahead and make the call in here. We'll follow up."

Maddy disappeared into the kitchen. They heard a drawer slide open and pens rolling around. Quinn and Masco both gave Burton a "this is going to be okay" look. Not smiling, to indicate they took this seriously, but otherwise looking as if they were not overly concerned. Decent guys, Burton thought, but it was time to do some actual searching.

"I want you to know our son's not a juvenile delinquent," he said. "He doesn't know anything about life on the street. This is a kid who doesn't skip school. He still likes *Star Wars*, even if he won't admit it."

Both officers nodded and continued watching him with their reassuring expressions.

"He's a sweet kid, really. He seemed happy."

Maddy walked back into the foyer with her cell phone to her ear. "Hi. This is Maddy Franck. Seb's mother. I'm not sure whose phone this is but I need speak to Duranne's parents. Unfortunately, Seb ran away. We're in complete shock and really don't know what's going on. Would you please call us back as soon as you get this message? Maybe Duranne has heard from him, or might have some helpful information. Thank you so much."

She pressed the end button and sat next to Burton.

"Oh. I didn't leave my number. Just a second, I'll call back."

Maddy called again and left two phone numbers.

"We'll need the girl's phone number." Quinn said. "And the other

13

family member names, if you know them."

Maddy looked up from copying Duranne's number onto a new page on her pad. "Oscar and Lily. Ah, I'm blanking on their last name."

Burton could not remember it either.

"Rodriguez." Maddy said. She wrote down the names, ripped the page from her notepad, and handed it to Officer Masco. "I agree with Burton. This seems like a long shot. But let's not make any assumptions."

"What about his brother?" Quinn asked. "Did they get along well?"

"Whose brother?"

Burton's question caused Masco to stop typing and look up.

"Your son's." Quinn said. "Your other son."

"Our other child is a girl," Burton said. "Jessica."

The two officers exchanged glances.

"So, there's no brother?"

"No brother."

"We were under the impression the other child was a boy." Quinn turned, clearly annoyed, to Masco. "Dispatch must have thought 'Jess' was a boy." He paused to read something on his phone, then looked back at Masco. "Have them send a female."

"Sure." The younger officer stood. "I'll make the call in the squad car. I'll be back in a minute."

Quinn waited for Masco to pass in front of him before continuing. "Were they close, your son and his sister?"

"Almost two years apart," Burton said. "If you mean like friends, they used to be best buddies when they were younger, but now..." He shrugged.

Maddy shook her head. "They don't really have a lot in common. She's also at that age where she's embarrassed by almost everything, especially an older brother who should be cooler. More normal, at least."

Quinn lifted the phone he kept balanced on his knee and glanced down at it. Burton originally thought he was keeping track of time or checking text messages, but it occurred to him now that the officer had a list of things to remember on there.

Setting the phone on his knee, Quinn asked, "Did your son have access to money?"

"We just upped his allowance to fifteen dollars a week for mowing the lawn and the other chores. Loading the dishwasher. He usually spent it all, usually on computer parts. We once found eight ten dollar bills rolled up inside a soccer trophy. We've already checked. The money's gone. Maybe we should have monitored his savings."

"Let's talk about what you did after you dropped off your son yesterday afternoon. Where did you go?"

Burton glanced at Maddy. The question caught him by surprise and he could tell it surprised her, too.

"We had a meal with everybody at the monastery when we got there. We got a tour of the place and saw his little room. Then we left. We stopped at the grocery store on the way home and we've been here ever since."

"Neither of you have left the house since you got home? And when was that?"

"About six, maybe. We had dinner, watched the Sox game and went to sleep. We were all home when I found Seb's email this morning."

The sound of the front door creaking open was followed by Masco's appearance in the foyer. He walked in front of Quinn and squeezed into the space left for him on the love seat.

"This is what I'm thinking," Quinn said. "Buddhism is about dealing with suffering, right? I'm no expert on Buddhism but it seems meditation, and a meditation retreat, might be attractive to someone who was suffering. Plus, he's a sensitive guy and instead of talking to you about whatever upset him enough to run away, he didn't tell you what was bothering him."

The officer paused. Burton nodded to indicate he was following him. Out of the corner of his eye he could see Maddy make no movement whatsoever. Her way of telling the officer to get on with it.

"If he was depressed, or if you took him to a counselor or a psychiatrist, you would have mentioned that to me, right?" Quinn asked.

Maddy leaned forward. "Yes. We would have."

Quinn kept his eyes narrowed on Maddy. Masco had stopped typing. Burton leaned in closer to his wife, to make sure Quinn noticed him. He did not like the way the big man was trying to get her worked up.

The older officer continued. "Possibly he was depressed. With adolescents, they're changing, they're moody. You might not recognize depression."

Maddy interrupted Quinn as he opened his mouth to continue. "He's a passionate kid but it went both ways. One minute he's upset and the next he's running down the street to meet his friends. If he could get outdoors, he was happy. Skateboarding, hiking, swimming, whatever. Or on his computer." She held up her right hand, its palm facing the two men. "We've had our struggles when we said, 'no more computer.' But I hear the same from my friends about their boys." She paused. "Before today, I would not have said he was depressed. I can't think of anything obvious but yes, probably he was a little more distant. Like you said, he's fourteen. And he just ran away. So maybe he is depressed, the poor guy."

Quinn nodded, turning now to Burton for some reason. "Your son lost a good friend, maybe a girlfriend, not too long ago. He's obviously a thoughtful kid, joining the green club, really upset to learn about the civil rights struggle. I think we can say a smart kid, too, building his own computer. Maybe seen by the other kids as unusual. At least one time he said something about being scared at the idea of being unable to stop his brain, even during quiet meditation."

The officer glanced over at Maddy at this point, as if to underscore that she had downplayed what she mentioned earlier: Seb's comment about his busy brain.

"There doesn't seem to have been any major trauma," Quinn continued. "No evidence, anyway, of the circumstances that usually send a kid off." The officer was now alternating his attention between both parents as he spoke. "No sign of abuse or drug use. No major conflict with the parents. No trouble at school."

Maddy broke in. "So what are we going to do? We know nothing tangible. Where does that leave us? What should we be doing to figure out where he is?"

"I have a couple of ideas," Quinn said. "But you should know that most kids are found in less than twenty-four hours. We're connected with every police department in the country. Instantaneously. They've all already been notified."

"I'll try to explain what I'm thinking as briefly as I can. We have a smart boy, very curious about lots of things. But the Buddhism, from what I've heard, seems to have been important to him. At least what he got from studying it, even if he says he's not a Buddhist. He went all the way to New Hampshire to go to a Buddhist temple. He was meditating every day, even though the thoughts scared him. Sometimes. Whatever was going on with him, maybe he believed he could find his answers there. In Buddhism."

At this point, Quinn left off from looking intently at Burton and Maddy and gazed for a moment in the direction of the entrance to the foyer. Burton got the feeling the officer wanted them to take all this in and get ready for some theory of his.

The officer turned back to them. "Do you think your son might be on his way to some...ah, now I can't think of the word."

"Ashram," Masco said.

16

Quinn glanced at his partner without turning his head, only his eyes.

"I googled it here," Masco said. "While we were talking."

"Thank you," Quinn said. "Ashram. Or another temple. It seems unlikely any place in the U.S. is going to take in a fourteen-year-old, but your son may not have known that."

This idea had not occurred to Burton. He turned to Maddy.

"Maybe," she said. "I don't know." She had been solid through the disturbing list of reasons why most kids run away. This relatively innocuous scenario, though, going to be with some Buddhists, had brought tears to her eyes.

"Just something to consider." Quinn must have noticed Maddy's tears but he chose to continue speaking calmly, as if there was nothing to worry about. "I'm sure you are ready to stop talking and get your son home. We're almost through here. I just want to go back to the monk you've mentioned. How well did you and your son know him?"

The elder officer seemed to be studying Burton and Maddy particularly closely now, as if to see whether bringing up the monk again made either of them nervous. Nervous about some less-than-optimal aspect of their parenting. As in, perhaps, sending a kid off for a week at a Buddhist monastery. Burton wondered if Quinn had intentionally delayed these questions until he and his wife had let down their guard. If so, they had nothing to hide.

As he was going to reply, Maddy spoke. "Don't forget Seb wasn't planning on staying at that retreat. It was just a way to...I don't know. Buy time. Get a head start. I guess it's possible he went from that monastery to another but I don't think there's an underground railroad for Buddhists."

"They were close, though, Seb and the Ajahn. They emailed several times a week. The Ajahn always copied us on his replies and included Seb's original emails, just in case. Everything is upside down now but at the time it seemed like Seb was learning a lot and having a good time."

"The detectives up in Portsmouth have probably already talked to this monk but I'll contact him myself as well." Quinn said. "Is there anything else I should know?"

"To be honest," Maddy said, "I think Seb liked things about Buddhism but he was probably more star-struck at having a friendship with an important person. And the Ajahn got a kick out of him."

Burton nodded. "I remember one email. Seb asked, 'If there is no me, who is it that all these girls think is so hot?' The Ajahn responded

17

'I don't know' with a little smiley symbol."

Maddy shook her head. "That's what's so disturbing about this. I'm sure they had a real connection. But Seb started lying at some point. And I have no idea why."

"Was he in contact with any of the other kids at the retreat?" Quinn asked. "Maybe one of them influenced him?"

"No," Burton said. "We should have mentioned this earlier. Seb's the youngest person to ever be invited to this retreat. They have it every year at the beginning of the summer. The Ajahn made an exception for Seb. We met the others when we dropped him off last night. They're all adults. People from all over the Northeast. Seb didn't know any of them. He's a good actor if he did. Which is a terrible thought."

As soon as Burton said this, he felt a stab of regret. They might have known better than to let Seb stay at a facility meant for adults. The Ajahn did not have experience handling kids. Summer camp staff were prepared for the stunts kids pull, not a monk. The thing was, Seb had never—never—done anything like this before.

❧

Burton waited for the dot of light to travel slowly along the edge of the printer's lid. It was scanning a page from Seb's middle school yearbook.

As soon as this was done, they would crop out his eighth-grade portrait and send it to the news stations. Then they would make flyers. Burton needed a bunch of the flyers to take to Portsmouth. They needed a bunch more for around town and to send to dozens of places on a list that kept growing.

The officers had just left with their notes and several strands of hair from Seb's pillow. Being asked to search Seb's room and collect DNA samples was the most devastating part of a hour-long discussion of everything that could have gone wrong.

Maddy was sitting next to the printer making phone calls. She made a check mark on the long list in front of her and dialed another number. She had already spoken to the local news stations and the state missing persons clearinghouse.

Burton looked over her shoulder. Next on the list was a national runaway hotline, then every person they knew. There was more written on the next page.

"I have to talk to Jessica," he said.

"I've got this. I can call and get the flyers done. They'll be printed in a few minutes."

18

He had to talk to Jessica because Officer Nicole Huang was waiting in the dining room for her. The younger officer, Masco, who came with Quinn, was supposed to interview her but it was the precinct's policy to use female officers to interview female children.

He found Jessica lying on her bed, sliding her finger across her phone. The bedspread lay on the floor beside her. Burton was surprised she would play a game at a time like this. When he got closer, he saw that the screen was dark. She was merely criss-crossing grease marks made by her finger.

Jessica looked up and, upon seeing her father, reached down and yanked the bedspread off the floor. It landed in a pile over her head.

"Jess, a police officer would like to talk to you."

She did not move.

"C'mon, honey. It's Okay. She talks to kids all the time."

"What?" she asked from under the blanket.

"Her name is Nicole. Do you want to get changed out of your pajamas before she talks to you?"

Jessica sat up. The bedspread fell to the floor again.

"I have to, I guess. Can you bring me a Pop Tart?"

"Sure. We told Nicole she could come up here to talk to you in your bedroom. That's because it has to be private. Mom and I can't be here, because...we would be distracting."

Jessica stared at her father. "I have to talk to the police by myself?"

Burton did not like the idea, but Officer Huang had insisted.

"She knows what she's doing. It's better for remembering things to help us find Seb."

He sat next to his daughter and took her hand. She let it hang limp on his palm.

"I thought you were going to go up to New Hampshire and find him."

"I'm going as soon as your mom finishes printing the flyers."

Jessica nodded. He squeezed her hand.

Officer Huang had cautioned Burton against discussing Seb's disappearance with Jessica before she had the chance to interview her. Huang did not explain why but Burton knew the reason. She did not want him to coach his daughter. He, the father, was automatically a suspect.

While Burton sat with his daughter, waiting for Maddy to yell to him that the flyers were ready, more disturbing thoughts ran through his mind.

He was disgusted that there were enough men who harmed their own children that the father was always the prime suspect. Afraid, a little, that he might be falsely accused. The word "accused" itself was awful. Accusations happened when someone was harmed. Seb was in danger.

According to Officer Quinn, most children were home in twenty-four hours. The police had a vast national network to draw upon but Burton was not about to wait for them. He was not going to find out what it meant when a child was gone for more than twenty-four hours.

CHAPTER TWO

Portsmouth, New Hampshire

Burton's Subaru shuddered as an eighteen-wheel truck passed him on the right. The truck had to be going more than eighty, because Burton was going seventy-five. He would be driving faster but he was trying to read his phone. He gripped the steering wheel tighter with his left hand and brought the phone's screen closer to his face until the text message was legible.

"Meet you at the bus station in Portsmith. Terrie."

His sister never could spell. It was not just her thumbs hitting the wrong letters. He was so grateful she was coming. She ran a business with her partner and she knew how to get things done. But mostly he was glad he would not be alone during the search.

He pressed the voice-dial button on his phone and held it near his mouth. "Call work."

After four rings, the recorded voice of his assistant, Mina, answered. He left a message.

"Hi Mina," he shouted over the road noise. "I won't be in tomorrow. Please clear my calendar. Thanks very much."

Tomorrow, Monday, Mina would listen to the message and go straight to the sequencing lab. She would gossip with his technician Morgan about the strange message the boss left while driving on the highway. After that, she would probably take a half-hour break in the old library. Nobody in his lab would blink at a single unscheduled day off. Seb would be back today. After taking Monday off to recover, Burton would be back at work on Tuesday and never have to tell anyone. No one at work would ever know that Seb ran away.

He tried phoning his sister, got her voicemail, and hung up.

A car containing blonde people, a woman with two boys in child seats behind her, passed on the right. Their blonde heads made him wonder if there were a lot of Latinos in Portsmouth. Seb was half Portuguese and half Puerto-Rican, with light brown skin from skateboarding in the sun, and a head of black curls. He might stand out more if there were not a lot of Latinos in town. On the down side, he was tall for his age, the tallest boy in his eighth grade class, at five-foot-nine. Strangers might not realize how young he was. It would take more than a cursory look to recognize Seb's earnest-kid body language. Eyes wide, going everywhere in a near-run, immersed in his activity, oblivious to how he appeared.

The phone rang, bringing up Maddy's photo. Burton pressed "speaker" and set the phone on the seat next to him.

"Jessica's interview is over." On the crappy phone speaker, with the road noise, Maddy was hard to understand. "Officer Huang ... a few minutes ago. Jessica said it went okay. She ... all right."

He picked up the phone and put it to his ear. "Did they figure out anything?"

"I don't know."

"What do you mean you don't know?"

Maddy hesitated. He had been a little short with her.

"I mean," Maddy said a second later, "they're still following this procedure of withholding what they're thinking in case one of us is... involved."

"That needs to stop. They need us. We know what to make of whatever Jessica told them more than they do."

"I agree."

"We just ask Jessica what she told them."

"I already did. There's nothing we didn't know already."

"Did we hear from Duranne's parents?"

"No. I think that might have been Duranne's cell phone. I just remembered that kids don't listen to voicemails. Let me get the other phone and send a text."

Burton could hear Maddy breathing as she walked.

"I talked to the manager at the bus station in Portsmouth. She seemed pretty confident nobody with Seb's description took a bus out

22

of there. I'd like to believe there are not enough degenerates out there to worry that a fourteen-year-might actually be picked up hitchhiking. And Seb's not stupid. But if someone did pick him up, I'll make sure they regret it for the rest of their lives."

Maddy was not violent and not prone to revenge. So her comment hit Burton pretty hard. Not just his wife's fury. He had not considered Seb hitchhiking. They needed to get him home ASAP.

"Did you get Seb's phone records from the website?"

"He hasn't made any calls or texts to California or anywhere outside of Massachusetts in a couple months. Except the call he made to us last night from the monastery. His cell hasn't been turned on since midnight last night. The phone company said the website is updated almost instantly. Though he could have used a computer to make a call to California or wherever. Oh, hold on. The other phone is ringing. I'll be right back."

Maddy hung up. In the absence of her voice, the Subaru's wheels on the highway and the cup rattling against the cup holder seemed even louder.

Seb met Duranne at a "March for Safe Streets" that the whole family participated in the previous fall. Burton had been impressed when Seb asked this very cute girl how she dared wear a New York Yankees cap in Boston.

They started texting each other all the time. A week later, she had Seb tutoring Latino immigrants in basic English at an agency where Duranne's mother volunteered. Her parents had emigrated from Mexico and were active in things like that. Duranne also started skateboarding with Seb and his friends in the evening and had eaten dinner with his family several times. The two of them did spend a lot of time together.

Seb seemed down the night he told them Duranne was moving away but not distraught. They texted each other for a while after she was gone. He moped for a week or two. After that, he seemed fine. If he really was trying to reunite with Duranne, it would be quite a trick to travel incognito for 3,000 miles to California. Not to mention that he and Duranne would then have to live like outlaws on the run. Her parents were not about to let Seb stay with them. Burton was sure of that.

He was baffled by everything else. He had no idea when Seb started lying. When did his interest in Buddhism become an act? He certainly sent misleading emails to a monk nice enough to keep up a correspondence with him and invite him to the retreat. Not to mention sitting immobile for twenty minutes a day. Was he capable of meditating after he started cooking up this scheme? They could see him with his legs crossed and eyes closed out there in the yard. The little brat must have been pretending to meditate.

The brake lights on the car ahead got close very quickly. Burton had to jam his foot on the brakes. In a few seconds he had slowed to a complete stop. It was really bad timing for this amount of toll booth traffic.

He stared at the rows of red lights before him and the long line of roofs shining in the sun. He could not even see the toll booths. Stupid humanity sitting in traffic jams for dumb reasons. Shopping for crap they did not need. Taking their kids to music and dance and baseball every day. Some place where they never disappeared from their view. Some safe place with walls or a fence around it. They should stay home once in a while and let their kids run in the neighborhood.

Burton inched the car forward. He refused to allow himself the luxury of cursing. Besides, he was in no position to complain about anyone else's parenting. He and Maddy had taken Seb to a place without a fence around it and now he was gone.

Maddy called back.

"That was Seb's soccer coach. First time I've talked to that hot head in a year. He was actually really good about it. He's contacting parents from Seb's team to meet the rest of us next door, at the Guptas." She paused. "The Becks and Ignatellos are coming. Talina from my work. Oh, another call. Hold on."

Neither he nor Maddy had big families to build a search party from. The only local relative was Maddy's mother. His brother was in Texas with his wife and son. His sister, Terrie, was not too far away, in Vermont, where she lived with her partner, Missy. She was already on her way to Portsmouth to meet him. Their parents were gone. That was his family.

Maddy was an only child from a single-parent family. Her father had gone to Florida before she reached kindergarten, leaving her and her mother in California. He had two other children with his second wife but Maddy had not met them. Her father never once came back to California to see her. He called from time to time but Maddy never called him. When Burton and Maddy started dating she told him, "I have no use for my father."

There were times when Burton thought she might benefit from talking to a therapist about her father. If she had little reaction to something Burton thought was clearly disturbing, he wondered if the way her father had treated her was the reason. He did not know exactly what abandonment issues were but they had something to do, he thought, with avoiding pain by not getting emotional in the first place. He never mentioned this to his wife because she had let her father go. That, to him, seemed reasonable. He was not sure opening old wounds would be a good idea.

Burton knew this was not the time to think about Maddy and her father, but her reaction to Seb's email that morning felt strange to him. The first thing out of her mouth was exasperation over Seb's statement that they had to "follow his instructions." She could be so pragmatic. Her jaw had been trembling, though. He remembered the terrible sight of that.

She loved Seb deeply. This, he never questioned. He should not have been surprised by her toughness. It was her way. It would probably help them catch Seb even sooner.

He inched the car forward. Jams at the tolls happened more often this time of year because of vacationers, but it was still totally infuriating.

Maddy still had him on hold but she managed to get a text to him. Her mother, Rosa, was on her way to the house.

Rosa lived a few towns over. She would no doubt show up with bags of groceries. Burton cared about his mother-in-law but preferred to care from a distance. She either did not have a filter or did not see the point in using one. It was a rare visit when she didn't annoy Burton or outright piss him off. She had to know he did not want to hear her ideas about parenting. Ideas she had acquired during a rough childhood in Puerto Rico. As in the time Seb did a cartwheel and she told him boys should not do "girl wheels."

Maddy came back on the line. "Burton?"

"I'm here," he said.

He could at least see the toll booths now. It was really bad timing for his E-ZPass to be broken. It would have gotten him through the tolls a lot sooner. He realized, only then, that he should have gotten into one of the much shorter lines for E-ZPass holders and just paid the penalty when it came in the mail later. This really pissed him off.

"Your brother called," Maddy said. "He told me you didn't answer."

"I didn't get a call." Burton held the phone out and saw the voice message symbol at the top of its screen. "Oh. I have a voicemail."

"Do you think Seb could have gotten a motel room? A motel room with Wi-Fi?"

"I don't know. It's possible. We'll get flyers to the motels after we hit the parks."

"Another call," Maddy said. "Hold on."

Burton thought he could not be more agitated than he already was, but he was wrong. He and Terrie now had to search every motel in Portsmouth in addition to the bus station, shelters, and all of its coffee shops and parks.

He and Maddy both thought the same thing. Most likely, Seb was hiding in a park. He probably knew he should not hang out in public places for long if he did not want to be discovered. A park not too far from a coffee shop or library where he could send email. They were monitoring his phone with the help of the police and the phone company but it seemed unlikely he would risk turning it on, since it had GPS. Their son made it clear in his email that morning he believed he would be untraceable. He could have borrowed a phone from a friend but he was too smart for that. He had to know kids would not hold up to questioning by Dr. Jordan, the school principal. The students loved Dr. Jordan. Not to mention questioning by the police. If Seb had somehow obtained a new phone, he could be anywhere. But a fourteen-year-old could not get a phone by himself, right?

Besides needing a place to go unnoticed, if Seb was free to go where he liked, it would be a park. He was always for going to parks. Even in the winter, Seb would wander off to the county park a mile from their house. Bundled up, he would be there for hours, whether he could get a friend to go with him or not. Seb could have secretly purchased a little hiker's tent and sleeping bag and hidden them under the clothes in his suitcase before he left home. Such a low-profile tent could easily be hidden in a clump of shrubs or in a shallow depression between a few trees. If Seb was not able to get a tent in advance he could have taken a plastic tablecloth and blankets from the monastery. Burton needed to ask the Ajahn if any blankets were missing.

After they searched the parks in Portsmouth, Burton and his sister would check places in town with internet. First, though, Burton would meet Terrie at the bus station. The police had already been there, but Burton wanted to have a look and talk to whoever was there. From the bus station they would go to the biggest wooded area in the city, the Urban Forest. Ajahn Wattana was bringing some of the Buddhists to meet them and split up into search parties to cover the rest of the parks in town.

This plan had been shared with the state and local police. They were assured that all officers were on high alert and had a photo of the missing boy. The dispatcher promised to reiterate the suggestion to check parks and places with internet access. Burton did not get the feeling that officers were canvassing all the wooded areas of Portsmouth.

Driving through, probably, but that would not be enough.

Maddy came back on the line. "I have to get ready to go next door." She sighed. "It doesn't make a lot of sense for Seb to go all the way to Portsmouth and then come back here, but putting his photo around town could remind people of something he said or bought. Unless he's so devious he went all the way up to Portsmouth just to come back here, to throw us off his scent."

"He was devious enough to pretend to want to go to this retreat in the first place."

Burton gunned the Subaru around a car in the fast lane and passed it on the right.

After the engine quieted, he said, "Were you able to ask the Ajahn to look through the emails he and Seb sent?"

"I talked to him. He said he was in his office reading them. We trust this guy, right? If he and Seb were cooking up some scheme, all they would have to do is use different email addresses."

Maddy sounded annoyed. Burton was pretty sure she did not believe the Ajahn was involved, just aggravated that the man had not noticed their son leaving his monastery in the middle of the night.

"If there were emails they hid from us," he said, "the police should be able to find them pretty easily. Seems really unlikely a monk would help a kid run away."

"They should scour his computer anyway. We need to make sure."

Neither spoke for a couple of seconds. Burton let his view of the cars between him and the toll booths get a little blurry. He was tired already.

"I'm looking at Seb's email right now." The trembling in Maddy's voice was clear, despite the phone's crappy little speaker. "He's basically saying, 'I'm gone, you won't find me, I'll email.' So cold. We aren't the greatest parents in the world but I never expected anything like this from Seb. It just doesn't make sense. No sense. One day we're talking about his school paper on the guy who invented the skateboard and the next day he's left home and tells us he's not coming back until we do what he says? Am I missing something?"

"We're both definitely missing something."

"And I'm wasting our time getting my feelings hurt." She paused. "He's in trouble. He's the one who must really be hurting. Something bad must've happened to drive the poor guy to such extremes. And to live with it for who knows how long. He must have been planning this for a while."

"Seb is fourteen," Burton said. "And not that brave. I bet he calls us before it gets dark."

Burton drove while eating a mashed granola bar. Jessica had run up and stuffed it into his back pocket as he was walking out the door. He counted the cars between him and the toll booth. Ten, and a toll collector in no hurry.

He had just told Maddy that Seb would be home that night, but Burton did not believe it. After all their son had done to prepare for this, he would try to make it at least one night on his own. Officer Quinn said something about most kids returning within twenty-four hours. Maybe one night would be enough to convince Seb he needed to come home. If he called at six in the morning, Quinn would still be right about twenty-four hours.

The car in front of him let a big gap build between it and the car in front of it. Burton let out a long, annoyed breath and tossed the granola bar wrapper on the floor. He reached over to get the printout of Seb's email from the seat next to him. He held it against the steering wheel and glanced down to read while keeping the road in the upper periphery of his vision.

Two phrases stood out.

"This is how it's got to be."

"You will get other emails from me."

Burton scanned further down and stopped at the words that stung Maddy so badly. They had to follow his instructions? Since they did not know why Seb was upset, they had no way of knowing what he thought they should do. At least he planned on communicating with them. If he were successful in staying away for more than a day, which was clearly his intention, they should be able to trace his emails. The police ought to be able to do that.

In the meantime, Burton would drive from one place to another. The idea was to catch Seb on his way to or from sending an email, or getting food. Then Burton had a disturbing thought that had not occurred to him before. Seb could already be far from Portsmouth. He had promised to explain by email but he did not say when.

Burton found himself thinking the best scenario would be for the police to find their son trying to hitchhike. The trouble with this idea was that there certainly were, to use Maddy's term, degenerates out there who would prey on a fourteen-year old. Burton switched to hoping Seb would avoid hitchhiking. Their son had to know the police would be looking for a young man of his description on the roads in and around Portsmouth. Better their son stick to parks. Seb knew his way around a park and could run, as opposed to being stuck inside a strange adult's car.

Seb's lying was hard to take, but kids lied. The thing that really scared Burton was the tone of finality in his email. Email, without exclamation points and smile icons, easily came off as cold, but smiles or punctuation could not disguise the plain fact that he wanted to separate himself from them. That's what it was: separation. That's what hurt and all the more because it came out of nowhere. Seb against them. His own family.

None of the common scenarios listed on the missing persons websites seemed likely: Seb befriending an adult, drug addiction, running away from bullying, kidnapping. Burton hoped his rejection of these scenarios was not just wishful thinking. In any case, they were looking everywhere and considering everything. And they had to accept that Seb had been more dishonest than they imagined he could be. He was not, at least not entirely, just a sweet and fundamentally innocent kid.

Burton could not think of a significant example of Seb being dishonest. Once, when he was around ten years old, Seb put a password on the family computer and tried to extort a trip to the roadside ice cream place with the tiny roller coaster out back. Being a child, Seb did not have much patience, and gave his parents the password after five minutes of waiting for them to give in. He was learning, as all kids do, his limitations. What may have been significant about that event was how he and Maddy responded. They were amused, and probably a bit proud, of their son's precociousness. There was some mild reprimanding.

This was not the first time he and Maddy wondered if they were too indulgent. What parent did not? Had they gone too far with their strategy that Seb operated differently than most kids his age and needed less conventional parenting? Until now, though, there had never been any consequences to worry about. Nor did it seem like they had been particularly indulgent. Letting Seb stay up late to watch PBS documentaries, or letting him join a Buddhist group where he was the only child? The problem may have been cumulative, a growing belief on Seb's part that he was an equal to adults. This was certainly not his parents' intention.

There was the time Seb hacked into his school's PA system to play a recording spliced together from war movies. According to his sister, who was the first to tell them the story, laughter had erupted in classrooms all over the school as a choppy sequence of voices identified students who had been harassing Seb's cousin Sasha. Sasha's mother was Russian. Her husband, Burton's brother Jake, might have saved their son some grief by intervening on the name choice.

Maddy and Burton were certain their son was the culprit, but they let it be. He had been protecting his cousin. If Dr. Jordan, the principal, had called them into his office, they might have agreed to some sort of consequence. The principal never did, though. Dr. Jordan had a soft spot for Seb.

It was hard not to have a soft spot for him. This was a boy who left the room when commercials showing hungry children aired on the television. The day Sasha and his family moved to Texas, Burton found Seb lying on his back out by the garden in nothing but his swim suit and a pile of bird seed on his stomach. He lay there until each seed was eaten by sparrows and chickadees. Maddy was not home that day. Seb ended up with a mild sunburn and Burton wondered if he should have intervened but it seemed at the time more important to let him be.

Seb's email tried to give the impression he was safe, but what did he know? He was just a kid. Preferably a kid in a park, not a motel. The thought of a motel made Burton's skin creep. What motel would take in a fourteen-year-old and what sort of people would be staying in that kind of motel?

They had to rely on the authorities to intercept Seb if he was on a bus, train, or, somehow, a plane. His photo was all over the local television news so Seb being on foot might be the best scenario of all. Someone would see him and call the police.

As for Quinn's idea that Seb might be on his way to an ashram, there was nothing called an ashram within a hundred miles of Portsmouth. Maddy was checking with local Buddhist groups to see if he had contacted them for suggestions. She would also call the ashrams, even those that were far, far away from Portsmouth. Her list of places to call was enormous and growing.

Burton finally pulled up to the toll booth. He did not look at the toll collector, just held out a ten dollar bill. As soon as the woman on duty deposited change in Burton's hand, he hit the accelerator. He went straight for the passing lane, which was now completely clear.

What Seb needed to do was send another email now. Then the police would be able to triangulate his location or do whatever it was they did to track people down.

It would be stupid, though, to wait for that. Burton drove up the interstate going ninety miles an hour, organizing his thoughts around what they had to do next.

Ordinarily, they had no worries about their son going off to a park.

30

This was a city park, though. Most likely there were others who needed a secluded area like a park to hide themselves or their stuff. Most homeless people were harmless but there were probably some who would see a kid as an easy mark.

They never worried about Seb's solo trips to the park near their home. That was him all over. As soon as he was old enough to be allowed out of his parents' sight, they found him happily talking to himself behind a tree in the back yard. He had hiked and climbed every inch of the park near their house, twice ending up with poison ivy rashes on his entire body, including his face and groin. The unspoken rule amongst kids that you could not be seen out and about alone did not bother him. If nobody wanted to go to a park, he went by himself and had a good time.

The closest thing they had to a clue was the Continental Divide Trail. Officer Quinn had asked them towards the end of the interview if there was a place Seb might want to go, however far-fetched it might seem. Kids, he said, often did not understand how difficult actually getting to a certain place might be. Maddy and Burton had answered, at the same time, "The Continental Divide Trail." The CDT, as Seb referred to it.

It would be no easy task for him to get to the CDT. They had just left him the day before in Portsmouth with nothing but a carry-on suitcase and a small backpack. The northern trailhead of the CDT was in Montana and the southern one in New Mexico. Each had to be two thousand miles away. Hiking the CDT was a dream of Seb's, but he knew it could not be done without specialized climbing gear, high-altitude supplies and a big, expensive backpack. Burton supposed Seb might try to buy this equipment on his way west. He really hoped their son was not that desperate or delusional.

Neither of the detectives had heard of the CDT. Burton had yet to meet someone who did. It was a hiking trail along the Rockies all the way from the border of Canada to Mexico. Seb had tried on several occasions to convince the family to go there for summer vacation. There were entrances all along the trail, he said, so they would not have to hike the whole thing. Mountain climbing up and down the Rockies did not sound like a good vacation to any of them but Seb. The ideal vacation for Maddy, Jessica and Burton was a cabin on a small lake in New Hampshire, although Jessica occasionally suggested Cancún. Not that she knew the first thing about Cancún. She probably saw it on a television commercial.

Seb used to talk about hiking the entire CDT. There was a poster of the trail in his room, a photograph of a stone peak in a sea of trees with a diagram of the trail underneath. He had come to accept it would not be possible to hike the CDT before he was out of high school, as it took a good part of a year, even for the most experienced hikers.

Burton could feel the blood thumping in each of his temples. Did Seb really understand the CDT was too dangerous to hike by himself? Parts of it were freezing cold and other parts were best traversed with a team, or a least a buddy, with expertise in rock climbing. One thing consoled Burton. If his son's email was essentially honest—even with Seb's recent manipulations, Burton believed it was honest—he was not in a position to manage hiking the Rockies. He had an agenda, things he wanted to tell his family. Emails and instructions to send. Burton picked up Seb's email again. It was possible Seb would try to get to the CDT after he'd given his instructions.

On the other hand, Jessica had reminded them not too long ago that Seb was into Hindus now ("Buddhists, honey"), not the CDT. He had two new posters in his room, one of the Tibetan Himalayas and one of a temple in a jungle, with a monkey on its front steps. Even so, they would send Seb's picture to park offices all along the CDT and to the CDT hiking club.

Whether Seb was headed to a park or trying to get west to the CDT or to California to be with Duranne, only eight hours had passed since he sent his email that morning. He could not be far. It was possible he snuck out of the monastery shortly after the Buddhists went to bed and sent the email from a different location, but that meant sixteen hours, max. There was also the fact that Seb probably knew better than to be roaming the streets of Portsmouth in the middle of the night. A teenager on his own at two in the morning ran a big risk of being stopped by the police.

Burton noticed, just as it was curving away, the Portsmouth exit he wanted to take. Looking over his shoulder, he saw he had enough space to get in ahead of the car exiting behind him. He gunned the engine and yanked the steering wheel to the right. The Subaru lurched across the triangular area you're not supposed to drive on and into the exit lane. Several rocks shot out from beneath his wheels. The car he cut in front of laid on its horn.

His first stop was the first gas station he saw after the exit. It had no maps of Portsmouth. The next station had six maps and he bought them all. He arrived at the bus station a few minutes before Terrie was due to get there.

The sky had been clear when Burton left home, but clouds had moved in. It looked like rain was coming.

In the cloudy light, the bus company sign in the window of the station looked sad. You could see white scratches all over the black letters. This scratched sign that should have been replaced years ago reinforced Burton's idea that a bus station was the place desperate people came to. It still had this beat-up old sign because most people who took the bus were struggling and the bus company was not able to charge enough to buy a new sign.

Burton wanted to get a good look at the station and talk to the people that worked there. He hoped Terrie would get there soon. There were a bunch of city parks to get to afterwards, before it got dark. He had not gotten a chance to find out how many parks there were in Portsmouth or what they were like. He might have to push through brambles and barbed wire. That would not have stopped Seb at all.

He leaned over to get one of the Portsmouth maps that had fallen onto the passenger-side floor. He spread it out on the seat next to him. There were more blocks of green, signifying parks or forests, than he expected. The map showed some of the region surrounding the city and there were even larger blocks of green there. He knew that these forests extended far beyond what could fit on the map. He wanted to cry but nothing happened.

The phone rang again. Burton twitched every time the thing rang. How great would it be to hear Seb was home? To turn the car around and head back before having to enter the bus station? As he picked up the phone, he saw "Dallas TX" on the screen. His brother.

"You okay?" Jake was the most matter-of-fact person Burton knew. He had been a lawyer and was now a judge. Constant exposure to b.s. in the courts had shortened his already short patience.

"We're hanging in there," Burton answered. "No clues, other than the fact that he's some place where he can send us emails."

"What can I do?"

"Nothing right now, unless you know of a secret legal resource that could help us track down Seb."

"Lost kid? No. Sorry, bro."

Burton could not recall the types of cases Jake worked on these days. He and Burton were six years apart, with a sister in between, and had never been very close. When Jake's son Sasha and Seb became friends, Jake and Burton saw more of each other, but now that he lived in Texas, their relationship consisted of check-ins over the phone every month or so. In the five years since they moved to Texas, Jake had not been back to New England. Burton had invited them up to spend Christmas several times, noting that there might be snow and their sister could come down from Vermont, but it had not happened. Jake's ties were with his wife's family now, and they spent Christmas in Georgia.

"I did ask around after I couldn't reach you," Jake said. "It's usually state police. FBI for young kids if kidnapping. Hire your own, I say." He had a bit of Texas in his voice already although the Rhode Island accent was still in there, too. His pronunciation of "hire" had turned into something like "hah."

When they were kids, Burton was the little brother Jake and his friends did not want around. By the time Burton was more than just a kid, his brother had gone to college in New York. After that he went to Connecticut for law school. They never got to know each other.

But it wasn't just that. His brother had social skills issues. Possibly he was just boring. Burton would do his best to make conversation and it would land with a thud. Once he said the Patriots were the best football team ever known to mankind. Jake said, "True." Then silence. His son, Sasha, wrote a play with Seb, some years earlier, about cucumber-shaped aliens. All Jake had to say was that he didn't understand a word of it.

"I should book a flight then," Jake said.

"If you could talk to your cop and lawyer and judge friends, we could really use some insider information."

"You must need manpower, though. Right?"

"A lot of things are in the works. You'll be the first to know."

His brother wanted to help, that was clear enough, and it was really sweet of him. Here he was, a smart guy, a judge, offering to fly up from Texas and Burton was turning him down. The truth was, Burton did not want his brother around, trying to communicate and having to think of things he could do.

"Seb'll be back real soon," Jake said. He sounded a little hurt.

"You're probably right."

"Okay. Just call."

"I will. Thanks, Jake."

"Sure. Hi to Maddy. To Seb when you see him."

Jake's phone number disappeared from the screen and a text from Terrie popped up.

"Ten minutes."

Burton's sister ran a home renovation business in Vermont with her partner, Missy. Burton and Terrie were close, and the kids loved to visit their place. She lived on a country road great for biking, and there was a lake nearby for swimming. They met several times a year for day trips to the beach.

They might have seen more of each other, though. Burton was pretty sure Missy was the reason. She did not seem to be a big fan of kids. Burton and Maddy's kids, anyway. The first time she and Terrie came to stay at the Francks' house, Maddy overheard Missy in the stairway to the basement calling their kids spoiled. Missy then said something Maddy could not hear very well but it sounded like a complaint about having to sleep on the pullout couch in the basement. When Maddy told Burton what she heard, he at first wondered if they should have let the guests stay in the master bedroom. Recalling the spoiled kids comment, he changed his mind.

It was true that during dinner, Jessica had crawled under the table and refused to come out. Seb could not stop laughing. Jessica had never gone under the table before. It occurred to Burton that his daughter sensed Missy's critical vibe and was acting out. The Francks had recently been seeing more of Aunt Terrie. Maybe Missy just took a long time to warm up. In any case, Terrie seemed to love her.

Through his windshield, he could see, above the bus station building, long, narrow clouds, dark at the center. They stretched across the sky in regular row after row. Burton could not recall seeing clouds like this before. He was not a believer in omens, but their strangeness disturbed him. The thought of rain did not help.

He had no qualms about searching for Seb in the rain. He would not even notice the rain. It was the thought of Seb caught unawares, or overly confident, huddling under an umbrella, shivering, forced to take the assistance of a stranger with a dry car, and only a scumbag would take a kid into their car. Maybe that was not true, a kind soul might give a cold child a ride, and hopefully take them to the police. Seb had to know, in any case, that he should not get into a car with a stranger. If he was in danger of hypothermia, would Seb be forced to take the risk of accepting a ride from a stranger in a car? Burton found himself hoping it would be a little old lady that helped his son. The pathetic-ness of this hope pissed him off. He slammed his fist against the driver's side window. Fortunately, it did not shatter.

The entire day so far had been an unbroken series of one bad thought after another. The only relief came when Burton said to himself it did not matter. Whatever came up, they would deal with it, and keep dealing with it, and Seb would be home.

Terrie's old pickup truck veered into the parking lot, too fast, tires squealing. She always drove like that. She crossed the lot diagonally across the vacant spaces.

At the same time, a "ding" sounded on Burton's phone.

It was a text message from Ajahn Wattana: *"We participants in the retreat are heading now for the urban forest and will wait for you in the parking lot."*

Burton typed, *"Thank you very much."*

For some reason, Terrie parked her truck three spaces away from Burton's car. She hopped out and strode towards him, pumping her arms. She was at his window before he had rolled it all the way down.

"Brother."

He looked up at her through the car window. "Thanks for getting here so soon."

"Of course. Have you gone inside yet?"

Burton shook his head. "Just got here. I was texting the Buddhists."

Terrie opened her mouth to respond. He held up a hand.

"We can talk on the way in."

She stepped back and he got out of the car.

"These Buddhists aren't like, cultish, or brainwashy, or anything like that?"

Burton gave her a sideways glance to see if she was joking. She looked serious.

"I'm not ruling anything out but I really don't think so. The police talked to all of them. It's possible they were infiltrated by some predator, but that doesn't explain Seb's email."

They stopped outside the glass door to the bus station. The sky, although cloudy, was still light enough to reflect off the glass door, making it impossible to see inside.

"You're sure it's from Seb? The email?"

Burton wanted to get inside the bus station but Terrie seemed to want to ask these questions before they got inside.

"I'm not sure of anything."

His sister closed her eyes momentarily upon hearing this, then nodded her head a few times rapidly. "It's got to be from Seb."

Burton did not know whether she believed this or was just trying to make him feel better.

"We'll find him," his sister continued. "A fourteen-year old...he's fourteen now, right?"

"Yeah."

"People are going to notice a kid on his own once it gets late, if not before."

"That's what everybody says."

He held the door for her. They were immediately greeted by a strong pine scent, deodorizer fake pine. Burton assumed it emanated from a restroom. No one was in line at the ticket window. In the front row the connected plastic chairs opposite the window sat a white woman with a dark skinned girl next to her. Each held a phone near their face, watching a video of some sort, and did not look up. There was no one else in the station.

Burton walked up to the ticket counter.

"Hi, can I help you?" The woman behind the glass at the ticket counter squinted at him out of dark eye sockets, under rows and rows of wrinkles. The air conditioning did not seem so cold as to warrant the maroon turtleneck she wore, but she was quite thin, and probably close to seventy.

"Yes. I was wondering if you've seen a boy here, possibly alone? He looks like this."

Burton took Seb's eighth grade picture out of his wallet and lay it on the counter. Terrie leaned in closer to look at it. Seb was wearing an orange short-sleeve shirt with a collar. His hair was a little shorter in this picture so his black curls were less obvious. Burton took from his wallet another, more recent, photo. In this, Seb's hair was about as long as it was now, curled under his ears. This photo was much smaller, though, having been cut with scissors out of a group gathered around Jessica's birthday cake. Burton placed this photo next to the school portrait.

"You mean him?" The ticket agent pointed to Burton's left. He turned to look at the wall. There, on a white sheet of paper, below the words *Have You Seen Me?* was a flyer with a black and white version of the school portrait. Below the photo were the words "I may be in danger" and the phone number to call.

A truly awful sight.

Burton nodded slowly, scanning the flyer. He had a fat pocket folder full of the flyers under his arm but he had not seen it displayed in a public place.

"The police gave it to me," the ticket agent said. She seemed proud of the fact.

Dumb woman, Burton thought.

Terrie had moved around him to get close to the flyer. She put her glasses on. The image at the center was the same school photo of Seb in the orange shirt but it was gray and grainy from the black and white printer the bus station staff had used to print it.

"Have you seen him?" Terrie asked, without looking away from the flyer.

"No, I'm sorry." The agent looked in the direction of the flyer, as if she could see it, even though it was on Burton's side of the wall next to the window. "But I've only been here since noon."

Burton glanced at the digital numbers above her head. *3:15*. He felt slightly better hearing that someone else had been working the ticket counter earlier. This person could have seen Seb.

The agent hunched her shoulders and shook her head slowly. "The police already talked to the man who was here this morning. I'm sorry."

"You have a copy of the flyer in there, with our number?" Burton asked.

The woman smiled weakly.

"Take a few of these," he said, reaching into his folder.

Ajahn Wattana shuffled across the urban forest's parking lot towards Burton, who was standing by his car. The monk was quite tall and lean, not at all the image of the round-bellied Buddha statues Burton was used to seeing.

His head was completely bald and he wore a marigold-yellow robe, so he still looked very much like a Buddhist. His skinny knees were exposed below the hem of his robe, probably because he was so tall. The white tennis shoes he was wearing looked odd with this getup, but he had certainly not been prepared to be searching parks this morning.

The rest of the Buddhists remained near a large van painted white and red. Most of them wore sweat pants or baggy jeans and sweat shirts, which they had undoubtedly expected to be wearing during a day of meditation. They watched as Terrie pulled her truck in next to Burton's. A number of their sweat tops matched the bottoms, which made them, with the little bus nearby, look like a group from a senior center on a field trip. Two of them appeared to be in their twenties but they could have passed for staff.

"Mr. Franck," the Ajahn said as he came to a stop in front of him.

Burton felt a tug on his hand and looked down to see the Ajahn squeezing it between his two palms.

"Burton. Call me Burton."

"What can we do? We've told the police everything. Should we all look in here, in this forest?"

The monk's Thai accent was harder to understand than usual. The poor man was clearly rattled.

Terrie emerged from her truck and stopped a few feet away from them. The Ajahn looked over at her.

"Your sister?"

"Yes. Terrie, this is Ajahn Wattana."

His sister bowed as if greeting a royal dignitary.

"Hello, Terrie," the Ajahn said, bowing to her in return.

"I haven't had time to mark up the maps," Burton said. "Let me get them."

He retrieved the six maps of Portsmouth from the car and brought them to a picnic table at the side of the parking lot. The Buddhists started coming towards him, en masse. They gathered around the table with similar looks on their faces: disoriented, cowed by the responsibility of finding a missing child, and trying to look as upbeat as possible.

Terrie took the maps out of Burton's hands and distributed one to every other person around the table. There were twelve people in total, ten Buddhists, Terrie and Burton. Burton spread out his copy of the map on the table. He took a pen and circled the bay-front park.

"If someone could search this park, that would be great."

After a pause, one of the twenty-somethings, a guy with a bushy beard, said, "I'll do that." He turned to the man next to him, a much shorter man with a close-trimmed gray beard. They nodded at each other.

Burton circled the green areas on the map with a red marker and numbered them. He then passed the maps around. He had not drawn a circle around the urban forest. It seemed to him the most promising of the parks in town. He and Terrie would search it themselves.

After distributing the last map, he realized he did not pay attention to who got what park to search. In any case, they had received copies of the flyer with the phone number to command central. Maddy was carrying that phone around with her in a little fanny pack.

"Thank you," Burton said. "So much." The last word came out as a croak. "Feel free to look anywhere else that occurs to you. The more minds the better."

After a chorus of "we'll find him," and "yes" and "absolutely," the Buddhists went back to the van. The Ajahn stayed with Burton.

"We will go back to the monastery first," he said. "Some have cars there. We will check in later. You will call my mobile phone as soon as you find him?" The Ajahn's English was so formal.

"Yes," Burton said, shaking the Ajahn's hand. "Thank you. Seriously. This is a huge help."

"Hopefully we will speak soon." The Ajahn put his free hand over Burton's and squeezed back. He turned to Terrie, bowed, and turned to join the others who were taking their places in the van.

Burton and Terrie got trail maps from a wooden box outside the park office. The office was closed on weekends.

"I'll take the part without trails," Terrie said.

"No. I will."

"I live in the middle of the woods, right?" She owned several acres in Vermont, surrounded by a state or national preserve. "I'm not going to get lost. Besides, it's a field of some sort. That's what these symbols on this map mean. I should be able to tell where I am. Oh, and that reminds me. Missy is walking around our property right now. Just in case. Too soon for Seb to get there probably, but she'll do it again tomorrow."

"Thank her for me?"

Terrie nodded, gave his shoulder a squeeze, and turned to walk in the direction of the area she had pointed out on the map. Burton headed for the main forest trail.

The trail cut into a forest of old oaks and pines, and all sorts of smaller trees and bushes. Burton could still identify not only oaks and maples, but beech, sycamore, and ash, by their leaves, although he had forgotten how to distinguish the different types of pine. He had spent hours as a boy looking through the old set of encyclopedias that used to belong to his father. An early stage in his development as a nerd. He almost laughed out loud, right there on the trail, at the thought that he had pushed his son into nerd-dom by giving him his old encyclopedias and his love of identifying plants and animals. Seb never used the books but he did read a lot of the same information on the internet.

This place, all its variety of life, would definitely appeal to Seb. In a matter of minutes the terrain had changed from sand to moss to ferns. A little further on, Burton could see a salt marsh through a sparser section of trees. Several of the pines were quite old, with puckered wounds where branches had once been. A squirrel commented on Burton's intrusion with a long stream of annoyed chatter.

Seb would be able to hide a tent in here. But even a camouflage-colored tent, if he had the means to get one, would be found through a proper canvassing effort. Unfortunately, the police were not yet on board with organizing a large-scale search of the city's parks based on Burton's hunch that Seb would be drawn to trees. They were confident that their process, distributing Seb's photo to the entire force, scouring the city in squad cars, and doing whatever else they typically did, was the best way to find a missing child.

The Buddhists were the only people Burton knew in Portsmouth, and he didn't really know them. Still, having them was a huge help. At the same time, he felt like the job was too big. He began jogging, trying to make as little noise as possible. If Seb was near, he might duck under cover.

Ten paces in, he slowed down. He could run until his heart gave out and not cover every place in the city where Seb might be hiding. After a few steps, he started running again. Seb could be around the next bend. He would run through all the parks if necessary.

The trail ended abruptly at the parking lot. Terrie arrived a few minutes later. She stopped across from Burton, who was leaning against the hood of his car. She put her hands on her hips, leaned forward, and breathed heavily. Her running shoes and socks were caked with mud and her legs were spattered up past her knees.

"It's actually a swamp over there." After another deep breath, his sister continued. "I had to walk around part of it, but you can see across the whole thing. There's a big lake or estuary in the middle. I looked there, too, thinking he might be on boat or a raft. I guess I was thinking of *Huckleberry Finn.*" She glanced down at her legs and stared at the splattered mud.

"There's a towel in the back of the wagon," Burton said.

Rain began to fall in slow, fat drops. Burton hoped it would be a quick summer storm.

Terrie looked up from her muddy legs and gave her brother a brave smile. "What's next?"

"Coffee shops where Seb might have gone to send his email. He might be going back to send his next one before they close. You read his email?"

"Yes."

"He thinks he's going to be gone long enough to send us at least another. Sounds like he has more than one planned." Burton glanced down at his phone. "Maddy texted me a list of coffee shops. And motels. We'll do those last."

The list included addresses. They would use his phone's navigation app to guide them to each one.

Terrie opened her mouth to speak just as a loud rumble of thunder came from nearby. They both looked up. The sky had become quite dark.

"I'll leave my car on the street outside this park," she said. "In case it closes. That way I can navigate while you drive."

"Okay."

"What about McDonald's? They have internet."

"That's good. I'm so glad you came."

She stepped forward, hugged him, and immediately stepped back. "I've got mud on me."

"I didn't notice."

⬧

Rain started pouring down just as Terrie went back to her truck to get a few things. She returned to Burton's car soaked. He put on the heat for her. She rubbed her hands through her hair, sending water flying, then found a baseball cap in the back seat and put it on her head.

"It might be better if Seb did get on a bus," she said. "Dry and captive. I'm sure Maddy's got every bus station in the country checking in with their drivers."

Burton was not so sure a bus would be better. Soaked and chilled in a park, with his clothes and blanket or sleeping bag wet for the night, Seb might be forced to give up. On the other hand, he could be awfully stubborn.

He and his sister leaned over the cup holder with the town map between them. They tried to put the coffee shops, *McDonald'ses* and motels in an order that would minimize backtracking. They laughed, for a brief moment, when Burton said *"McDonald'ses"* out loud.

Their experience at each place was remarkably similar. The person at the cash register first greeted them cheerfully. Then their smiles faded, possibly sensing from Burton and his sister's body language that they were about to get some unusual, possibly difficult, request. When Burton explained that his son was missing, the manager was summoned. The managers all treated them very kindly. Not one refused to let them put up the flyer. Unfortunately, nobody recognized Seb's photograph.

It rained for a full hour while they drove and got in and out of the car. When the sky cleared, Burton saw the sun was about to go below the horizon and felt a surge of panic. It was looking more and more like Seb was going to be out there alone, at least for part of the night. Perhaps worse, not alone. The Buddhist search party had yet to call, which meant they had not found Seb, but it also meant they still had places to search.

Burton's phone rang. Startled, his foot reflexively pressed on the brake. Terrie lunged forward. She handed him his phone without taking her eyes from the road.

"Burton. This is Thomas Wattana."

"Hi...Thomas." Burton had not remembered the Ajahn's first name, nor had he ever spoken it out loud.

"We finished our searching. We stopped by some of the church youth groups that were meeting this evening. I am sorry we have not learned anything about Seb but we are going to search the parks again tonight."

Burton was planning to do this himself. "That's really good of you."

"We thought he might return to one of them as it got dark."

"I thought the same. That he might be...doing something, I don't know what, during the day and then go to the woods to sleep."

"You just passed the McDonald's," Terrie said. "Never mind. We'll go back. Just keep on this road."

"Ajahn." Burton had forgotten the Ajahn's first name already. "Would you mind if we stopped by first to get Seb's suitcase? I'd like to look through it."

"You'll have to go to the police station, I'm afraid. The state police. They took it."

The police station was on Burton's list already. They probably should have gone there sooner, but it was open twenty-four hours and he kept putting it off. Besides, Maddy and Officer Quinn were keeping close contact with the local and state police in Portsmouth. Terrie obviously knew they had to go there now. She was tapping at her phone to get directions.

Downtown Portsmouth was not a big place. When they pulled up to the police station, Burton was surprised to find it was a new, homey-looking brick building. It looked like a suite of doctors' offices.

They asked the receptionist for Detective McDermott. Instead of using the seats in the waiting area, they remained leaning on the counter. The receptionist ignored them.

A few minutes later, a door at the side of the waiting area opened and a woman walked towards them. She was wearing a white polo shirt tucked into tight green chinos that came up high on her waist. Her hair, cut in a bob, was very orange, in stark contrast to her rather pale face. She carried an iPad under one arm.

"Mr. Franck?" the woman asked.

"Yes."

"I'm Detective McDermott."

"This is my sister, Terrie."

"We can use the conference room. Follow me. It's a little convoluted to get there."

Detective McDermott reminded Burton of Maddy, except for the hair. And the pants worn too high. Really, it was only the way she moved like a tennis player, each step a bounce onto the other foot.

When they reached the conference room, Detective McDermott said, "Have a seat, please. I'll be right back."

She returned with Seb's suitcase and set it at the other end of the table. It seemed to Burton she had placed it as far away from him as possible.

They already knew from Ajahn Wattana that Seb had left the suitcase behind. The old carry-on did have wheels but it would have slowed Seb down. Still, seeing it on the table was a new low. It felt as if Seb had separated himself from everything to do with his family.

McDermott sat directly across from Burton. "You've been searching the parks?"

Burton lingered on the bag a second before turning to McDermott. "Still are."

"All our officers have his picture and they patrol every inch of the city. If your son is here we'll find him."

"Could he have gotten on a bus?" Terrie asked.

McDermott narrowed her eyes at Burton's sister. The officer would have looked rather young were it not for the pronounced crow's feet at her eyes. Detective's eyes, Burton thought, just like Officer Quinn's. Staring at you to the point of discomfort in the hopes of pushing out a comment that might have been repressed.

Terrie was having none of it. She stared at McDermott, waiting for an answer.

"None of the bus lines had any solitary children traveling," McDermott said. "We can't rule out that he passed himself off as an adult. He is tall enough."

Burton nodded.

"The local police in neighboring towns have been notified," McDermott continued. "And I'm keeping in touch with Officer..." She looked down at her iPad. "Quinn."

"When does the FBI get involved?" Burton asked.

This was something he and Maddy wanted to research but there was not enough time before he left to come to Portsmouth. He supposed Maddy would tell him if there was anything he should know.

"They've been informed. At this stage we rely on essentially the same resources. The shared databases, the missing children agencies. The FBI only takes over an investigation for..." McDermott paused for a second. "For a kidnapping of a child twelve or younger. Which is fine, because the State Police are going to find him before they would."

Burton would ask Maddy to make sure this was true. She probably already knew.

He had been thinking that Detective McDermott spoke in a strange way and now he realized what it was. She spoke slowly. He wondered if this was something she had been trained to do when dealing with people under stress. Some kind of calming method. She probably dealt with people under stress constantly. He appreciated this but they had things to do.

"What else?" He asked, curtly. There was still a lot to do.

Terrie shot a glance his way, then looked down, She could be brash but this was to disguise that she was basically a big softie. When they were kids, she cried any time Jake teased Burton. Even arguments about what re-run to watch on TV would bring her to tears.

McDermott responded to Burton's question with a slow smile, annoying him more. "We work with the runaway shelters, youth services, the homeless shelters," McDermott said, with a bit of a smile, annoying Burton more. "We have a full fleet combing the city twenty-four hours a day."

Burton wondered if he was being treated like a suspect by McDermott, too. At this point, he did not care. They would do what they were good at and he would take care of the rest. He looked down at his notepad. There was something else he wanted to ask.

"What about the Ajahn's computer?"

The detective paused for a moment, staring at him. "We have it."

Burton waited a second for the detective to continue. When it was apparent she was done, he said, "I'd like to look at my son's suitcase."

"Of course."

McDermott leaned over to pull the suitcase towards them but could not reach it. She and Burton stood at the same time. She let him walk to the end of the table. He unzipped the case and let it fall open.

It was empty except for two brown loafers and one pair of neatly folded blue slacks.

The Subaru reeked of fish and grease. Burton had suggested they eat in his car. Everybody in the fish-fry place looked tired and annoyed. Too tired to wash their hair. The light from the bare fluorescent tubes on the ceiling only made everyone in the place look more disheveled. He and Terrie had been sizing up park-goers, coffee shop people and fast-food-eaters all day and Burton needed to retreat to the only private space they had: his car.

"Pierce Island?" Terrie asked.

"Seb would love it. A park on an island. Bridges you can walk over."

Terrie, who was using both hands to hold her sandwich, pointed at the map between the seats with her elbow. "He could definitely walk there from the Buddhist place. It's kind of small, though. Don't you think the Ah-Ja and his crew would have seen him? They searched that park twice already, right?"

Burton did not correct her mispronunciation of Ajahn. "Maybe Seb was waiting until the park emptied out. Where he could have been all day...I really don't know."

"Maybe it's closed now." Terrie stuffed the remaining half of her sandwich into a bag on the floor. She wiped her fingers on a napkin before picking up the map and squinting at it.

Burton shrugged. "Let's find out." He took his phone off the dash-board and pressed the compass icon. "Pierce Island."

"Getting directions to Pierce Island," his phone answered.

He followed the spoken prompts through a series of turns through the narrow streets of the old part of town. They passed a waterfront park, lit in patches where there were lampposts. A little further on, a graveyard came into view. Only the tips of ancient crosses and curved headstones were visible above a short stone wall.

When they reached the end of this street, the phone announced, "Arriving at Pierce Island."

Burton pulled over. The map on his phone showed that the lane that forked off to the left, up an incline, was the park entrance.

"There's a sign," Terrie said.

She leaned out the window to look at the sign's smaller print. "It closes at eleven. So it's legal for a few more minutes. To whoever would go in there at a time like this."

Terrie spoke the last few of these words in a whisper, no doubt re-gretting how it would sound to her brother.

They gazed up the incline. It was not apparent but this had to be the bridge onto the island. They were minutes from downtown and yet this place, dark and lined with weeds and trees, looked something you would see out in the country. Burton hated the thought of Seb in there. Portsmouth was a decent-sized town and there were certainly violent and depraved people within its borders.

"I'd rather not take the car in there," he said. "Seb will recognize it."

"He'd recognize you walking, too. Maybe sooner."

"We don't have all night to walk around the park, anyway. But if he sees us before we see him, he could get away."

"How about this." Terrie pointed across her brother's chest, in the direction of his open driver's side window. "I could wait in the shadow of that tree. This bridge is the only way out of the park. If Seb comes out, I'll text you and follow him. Or follow him while texting. You could call the police as you were driving out of there."

Burton turned to see where his sister was pointing. It was a stand of trees on a grassy plot that seemed to be a continuation of the graveyard behind the wall beside it.

"What a nightmare."

"It's going to be okay."

"Let's do it." He held his phone out in front of him. "My phone's still got power. Yours?"

"It's good." She got out and looked down at him through the window. "Take as long as you need."

He drove onto the bridge. At its crest, he could see, for the first time, the water that surrounded the island. There was a river or narrow inlet from the Atlantic on his right. To his left, a tidal pool of sorts with boats moored to a dock. The road sloped down from the bridge and continued onto a narrow, grassy strip of land with water on both sides. Ahead, he could see that it curved out of sight into trees. The trees looked giant, stretching above the scant light in the park, disappearing into the darkness of the sky.

His phone rang.

"Where are you?" Maddy asked as soon as he put it to his ear.

"Pierce Island."

"What is that?"

"It's a park on the edge of town."

"My God. Oh my God. A dark park on the edge of town?"

The car's headlights moved over the road and the narrow strips of grass on either side of it. Everything else was dark. You could not tell where the water began. He passed two cars parked on the shoulder. There were people in the park, somewhere.

"Any news?" he asked.

"I keep checking our email every few minutes for the explanation he's supposed to be sending. It's driving me crazy."

"I know. I know. Have you come up with anything else?"

47

He heard her tapping at her computer keyboard. "His phone still hasn't been turned on. He obviously doesn't want to be tracked. I thought he might try to get a new phone. That way he wouldn't have to venture out for internet to communicate with us. I don't know how he would get a new phone, though. The stores check ID. I called a few and they said they would never give one to a fourteen-year-old without a parent involved. The only thing I can think of is if he offered money to someone for their phone."

If someone gave Seb a phone, Burton would come down on them *hard*. Maddy did not need to hear that right now, though. Instead, he said, "I think he's going to get scared once it gets late and give this up."

"Probably you're right."

For a moment, neither of them said anything. It felt good to have her on the phone with him while his car crawled in the dark across the park.

"There's a wooded section coming up," Burton said. "I think he could be there. I better get off the phone."

"Be safe."

"I'll be fine. Love you."

"Love you."

He set the phone on his thigh and guided the car slowly around a bend. A row of very tall trees came into view, their bare branches stretching high into the sky. They reached so high, they appeared to bend and loom over the car. It seemed impossible their roots could hold such tremendous, leaning weight. A wave of profound fear swamped him. The world was a dangerous place. At night, very dangerous. Seb was at its mercy, or rather, its lack of mercy.

When the car entered the wooded area, Burton began looking for a place to park. In a minute, the squat, white towers of a water treatment facility came into view. The road looped around in front of the chain-link fence that contained the water towers. He had reached the far side. The park was smaller than he thought it would be. If Seb was in this park, he was not far away at all.

Burton drove around the circle, past the water tanks, and headed back in the direction from which he had come. He was back in the wooded area a few seconds later. He parked on the side of the road and felt around on the passenger seat until he the found the map. All it showed was a roughly circular trail inside the perimeter of the woods. He put the map in his back pocket and got out of the car.

It was very dark. There were no lamp posts at this end of the island. Burton took this to mean the area was not meant to be used after daylight. He considered leaving the flashlight off, to catch Seb unawares, but he really couldn't see much without it. If Seb saw the light and took off, Burton would either hear him or see him and Seb could not outrun his father yet.

He went straight into the woods, following the circle the flashlight made on tree trunks and the sandy earth. Everything outside the circle was black. He realized he was ascending an incline when one of his feet slipped in the sand. His old running shoes had no tread remaining. A minute later, he sensed pebbles grinding under his feet. He shifted the beam down to reveal a gravel trail. He opted to cross the trail and keep going in what he hoped was directly through the middle of the woods.

Bushwhacking in the dark suddenly seemed desperate. Ludicrous. Was he prepared for this? How could anyone be prepared for this? At any moment, he might come face to face with his son. He imagined Seb blinking in the bright light with an expression of profound disappointment on his face. It was a bad feeling.

In five minutes, the woods ended at a little inlet off the bay. Burton could smell dead fish somewhere nearby. The water lay still. The only noise was a rising and falling chorus of creaking bugs. Instead of trying a different route back through the woods, he began walking along the shoreline, keeping the trees to his right. Since this part of the island jutted out into the bay, he could see much of the park now, including the thin grassy strip he had driven across. Tiny lights off in the distance swayed back and forth. They were probably boat masts. Farther beyond these, dots glowed low on the horizon. Windows of homes or warehouses on the shoreline.

Where was Seb in all this darkness? Where in the world was he?

Burton returned to the car. He drove off without looking in his rearview mirror. It was, he realized, petulance, and nothing else, that had stopped him from looking. *If Seb shows himself only as I'm driving away, I don't want to see him.* As soon as he realized this, Burton checked the mirror. The spot where he had parked, empty, of course, grew darker and darker as he left the wooded area.

The road curved left and then to the right. The car's headlights played across a lawn with a few small trees here and there. Just as the headlights swerved away, he thought he may have seen a shape that could be a person slumped up against one of the trees. Burton slammed on the brakes and twisted the steering wheel hard to move the lights back to where he thought he saw the shape. The car lurched to a stop perpendicular to the road, blocking both lanes.

The shape jumped up and began to run. It was a woman in a long tan raincoat, which was split so far up the back that white shorts showed through. Her long greasy hair kept flashing in the headlight beams as she ran towards some low shrubs near the shoreline. She fell into them and disappeared.

Burton's heart pounded. He stared at the empty lawn for a few seconds before backing up and setting off again for the exit. On the down side of the bridge, the headlights picked up Terrie walking in his direction along the side of the road. He stopped beside her and she got in.

They drove in silence. If she had news, she would have told him.

"I'll stay in Portsmouth tonight," she said a minute or so later. "I'll get the Buddhists early tomorrow. Buddhists wake up early, right? If Seb's in town, one of us, or at least one of those police cruisers will see him. He can't hide in the woods forever. You go home. We don't..." She paused. They gazed forward as he drove. "Maybe he's heading home. Right now."

"Thanks, sister."

CHAPTER THREE

THE RODENT

SOMETHING WAS MAKING Burton's face warm. He could see orange light through his eyelids. It felt nice. He opened his eyes just enough to see the weathered barn beams on the living room ceiling. His chin itched. He lifted his head and saw, stretched out over him, the baby blue afghan his mother knitted for him decades ago. Maddy must have placed it on him. She shouldn't have. How long had she let him sleep? The brightness of the room told him it had been hours.

It was four in the morning when he got home from Portsmouth. He had intended on closing his eyes for only a few minutes.

Ka-knock-ka-knock-knock knock!

The sound was an alert that a new email from Seb had arrived.

Burton bolted upright. He turned and swung his legs off the couch. Maddy slammed into them as she was running between the couch and the coffee table. She did not even look down to see what happened, just kept straight on for the laptop, which was sitting on a TV table next to the recliner. When the woman was focused, she did not bother herself with trivialities like getting in someone's way. Burton hopped up and ran to join her.

He had programmed the computer to announce the arrival of messages from the strange email address Seb had used for the first time yesterday morning. The *knock-ka-knock* sound was a file Seb once

51

found online, a recording of a woodpecker smacking its beak against a tree. It was set to the highest volume possible and placed in the center of the living room on a TV tray-table.

Ka-knock-ka-knock-knock knock!

The alert repeated just as Maddy reached down for the laptop. Burton could see her shudder with surprise. It was really loud.

She slid her hand under the computer. Burton shouted as her knee hit one of the table's legs and the thin silver computer slid off the edge of the table. She managed to grab the laptop with one hand and keep it, wobbling, in the air, as the table crashed to the floor She got her other hand on the laptop, turned, set it carefully on the coffee table, and lowered herself to the couch. Burton sat next to her. He could feel her legs trembling through the couch cushion.

A voice behind them asked, "What happened?"

They turned to see Jessica at the top of the two stairs that separated the dining area from the living room.

"An email," Maddy said. "From Seb."

Jessica walked quickly down the two steps and bounced onto the couch, to the left of her mother. Burton, with Maddy between them, leaned forward and smiled at their daughter. A very small, it's going to be okay smile. Jessica shifted her eyes to the laptop so quickly, he could not tell if she noticed. Before Burton could look at the screen himself, Myro, their dachshund, ran his little claws across his bare feet. Burton knew the dog would go straight to Jessica, his favorite.

The three of them scanned the series of messages on the screen. The most recent of them, the one at the top, had the same email address Seb used for his first message the day before. A nonsense jumble of numbers and letters with *.net* at the end.

Burton double-clicked the message. It opened to fill the screen.

I really don't want to hurt you.

This message, and other ones I send are for Mom and Dad but you can show Jessica so she knows what's going on.

I need you to read something and think about it. There's a folder at the bottom of the cedar chest in the upstairs hallway, under the extra blankets.

Read what's in the folder and think about it. Talk about it.

Since I'm not around to see whether you did what I said, please make a video to tell me what you think and post it on YouTube. Be honest.

Name it the Franck Family Video.

Seb

"How long does he think he can keep this up?" Maddy held her hand to her forehead and closed her eyes for a moment. "And why does he keep saying he doesn't want to hurt us? He obviously does. Does he really expect us to believe he can be out there on his own? He can't even remember to close the refrigerator door."

Jessica stared at her mother for a moment then leaned down to scratch Myro behind the ears. Burton gave Maddy a dirty look. She took a deep breath, then she turned to their daughter.

"Hon?"

"Yeah?" Jessica said, weakly. When she stopped scratching Myro, he climbed up her leg and clung to it, his way of asking to be put in her lap.

Maddy wiped tears from her eyes. She was not able to respond right away. Burton could see she was trying not to start crying outright in front of their daughter.

She put her hand on Jessica's knee. "I'm upset. I'm upset that your brother would play games with his safety like this. He knows better."

Maddy gasped. It looked for a moment like she might break down.

"It's okay, Mom. Seb sounded like a jerk in that email."

Jessica was crying herself at this point. Maddy wiped a tear from her daughter's cheek. To Burton, it looked like their daughter was more upset about seeing her mother cry than about what Seb had done.

The dachshund was still clinging to Jessica's leg. She tried to pry him off and he pressed his body hard against her. She left him with his little legs wrapped around her calf.

Maddy leaned back against the couch and looked at the ceiling. "I know we're not perfect, but I'm obviously missing something. What did we do that was so bad?"

"You're, like, the best parents." Jessica said. She pushed at Myro again. He growled. She pushed harder and he rolled onto the floor. He let out one of his fake "you hurt me" whines.

"Somebody doesn't think so," Maddy said.

Burton stood. "I'll get the folder from the cedar chest."

"Okay. The sooner we get a video on YouTube, the sooner he'll reply."

"And then the police can trace where he watched it, if he's not home already." Burton believed this was possible when he started speaking but by the time he was finished, he was not so sure.

"I'm forwarding this to Officer Quinn." Maddy leaned forward and started clicking at the keyboard.

Just as Burton was about to turn the corner to the staircase, Jessica said, "I'll help you look for the folder, Dad."

"Let me do it, hon."

Jessica said, "Uh," with disgust.

Burton turned around in time to see his daughter pull her legs up and roll over to face the back of the couch. As soon as they got the chance, they had to come up with some way for her to help.

Maddy started stroking Jessica's arm with her hand. Their daughter flinched to make her mother stop. After a second, Maddy put her hand on Jessica's arm again. This time their daughter remained still and let her mother stroke her arm.

Seeing this, Burton felt a little frustration of his own about Seb. Their son did not seem to care what he was doing to his sister. This was too much for a twelve-year-old. But that was all the more reason for her parents to stay strong. At least in front of her.

He turned, went out of the room, and up the staircase two steps at a time. The upstairs hallway, with the three bedroom doors closed, was completely silent. Ordinarily, all kinds of noises made it up to the second floor. Television, Jessica's video calls on her phone, slamming kitchen cabinets. Such quiet only amplified the fact that Seb was not around.

He went straight to the cedar chest at the end of the hall, just beyond the master bedroom, and lifted the lid. The chest was stuffed with blankets. He pulled them out, one after the other, and tossed them onto the floor. Finally, with the last blanket under his arm, he saw, on the bottom of the chest, a manila folder. The blanket fell from under his arm as he leaned into the chest to get the folder.

He used his thumb and forefinger to pinch one corner of the folder and withdraw it slowly. Just as he was about to set the folder onto his other hand, a sheet of paper slipped out and hit the bottom of the chest with a clack.

It was a single, yellowed sheet of text. At the top of the page, in large pink letters, were two words. "The Rodent."

Ah, *The Rodent*. The newsletter that Burton and some graduate school classmates inflicted on the student population every week or so. It was just one page, double-sided if they had enough material. Burton had been Associate Editor or something like that. They gave each other titles, resisting the urge to include things like "King" or "Alchemist" for the sake of credibility. They really did hope to do good with that little newsletter.

He opened the manila folder. There was nothing else inside. Burton tossed the folder in the direction of the pile of blankets and stared down at the page at the bottom of the cedar chest. What was Seb up to?

He got down on one knee to carefully remove the newsletter. Its top right corner was missing and it looked insubstantial, almost crispy. He used two hands to lift it out of the cedar chest, as if a twenty-year-old piece of paper would fall apart in his hands.

He had not thought about the newsletter in years.

The pink letters of *The Rodent* had been red when it was originally printed. This reminded him of an argument amongst the six or so regulars who wrote and distributed the newsletter. Was the red text intended to symbolize blood? Should they change the color? Non-violence was one of the newsletter's underlying principles.

"Is *The Rodent* supposed to gnaw away at the truth but not draw blood?" one of them complained.

This set them to laughing, and they fell back on the frayed furniture of the graduate student lounge. Disgusting, stained couches and chairs that smelled like body odor and spilled beer. Probably because they had soaked up generations of sweat and beer. It did not seem like twenty years had passed since those days.

After they stopped laughing, Oliver Pitts asked, with a mouthful of pizza, how nonviolent any of them would be if their mother was being attacked.

"Violence only when necessary," someone suggested.

Burton said the word "necessary" was too vague a term.

"Rodent is a vague term," someone else said.

They really did have a lot of fun back then. Scrambling to create a newsletter each week before the gathering dissolved into a party. They printed it late at night, when no one was around, on Political Science or Biology Department photocopiers. Stacks of the newsletter were placed next to the official campus publications in the cafeteria, the student center, and the library, along with the usual crap: bands looking for singers, flyers for tutoring by students who might or might not be qualified to tutor.

The issue of *The Rodent* that Burton now held in his hand must have been in one of the boxes of old photos and yearbooks in the attic. Seb used to like going up there to marvel at how goofy his parents used to be.

Burton saw now that he had written the cover story of this particular issue. He lowered himself to the floor and leaned against the cedar chest to read it. What had his twenty-year-younger self gone on about this time?

The title of the article did not clue him in either: "Future Generations – by Burton Franck."

Burton did not recall ever writing an article with that title, but he had churned out a hundred stories over the three-year life of *The Rodent*. Half the stories were passed over for pieces written by the others.

He read on: "You might have heard the term global warming. If you haven't, that's because there are people who want to make sure you don't."

Now, he remembered. This had been one of his more vehement tirades. He never imagined his own son would read it.

A photo of flares shooting high above a desert came next, with the second paragraph beside it.

"Why would anyone want to keep this information from you? Because the way to stop global warming and the damage it will inflict is to cut down drastically on burning fossil fuels. As in gas and coal. Burning less fossil fuels means less profits for the fossil fuel industry. Keep the public ignorant, and the profits keep rolling in."

A long, boring paragraph about the science of greenhouse gasses followed. Burton had included this explanation because nobody knew what global warming meant back then. He had to ask his prof a number of questions in the course of writing the article.

Burton stopped reading. His gaze drifted beyond the top of the newsletter to a framed painting on the wall. A duck or some kind of bird Jessica made in kindergarten.

Why did Seb have to find this, of all the articles Burton had written?

He skipped the science and skimmed over the next paragraph. Failure to dramatically reduce the amount of greenhouse gasses we were creating was going to do a lot of bad things. Half the world's population displaced by flooding. Wars over food. Snow and ice that used to be permanent would disappear and then, even bigger trouble. A feedback loop which humans could not stop, even if they didn't burn so much as a match. The planet would continue to get hotter and hotter and hotter.

Burton was furious the day he submitted the article to the rest of Team Rodent. Half of them flat out did not believe what he had written. Fortunately, Dawn Donnelly, who really was some kind of genius, said it was true. So the article got printed as the full-page cover story.

"Burton?" Maddy called from the bottom on the stairs.

"I'm almost done," he yelled back.

"What is it?"

"I'll show you in a minute."

"All right."

There were two paragraphs Burton had yet to read. Maybe they would clarify why Seb was having him read this article now.

The second-to-last paragraph began: "Will we do what needs to be done? Will we make addressing global warming Priority Number One? (each word capitalized, to mimic a large scale effort like *Operation Desert Storm*). Every person has to contribute. Just like we did to put a man on the moon and to win World War II."

The newsletter was wrinkled badly at the bottom. Burton had to place it on the floor and smooth it out to read the final, short paragraph.

"I hope, if I see this article some day in the future, I will be proud of how we responded to this challenge."

Jessica's voice floated up from the kitchen. She was pressing Maddy for information about what was in the cedar chest. Burton let the newsletter drop to his lap.

Seb could not have understood the context in which this article was written. Global warming was a vague idea to most people back then. Burton would not have known much about it himself, were it not for one of his professors in the biomedical PhD program. He tried to remember the professor, but all that he could recall was a perfectly shaved head.

One morning before his usual lecture, the professor turned the lights off. A buzz went around the room as the students wondered what was going on. Next, a video appeared on the huge screen behind the podium. Burton remembered something else about the professor now. When not lecturing about things like the function of microorganisms that lived inside the body, he conducted research on the impact of humans on the ecosystem. Tourism in the Galapagos was one of his pet topics.

Burton had not thought about the video they saw that day in many, many years. Which was surprising, because at the time, it bowled him over. He remembered how strange it was to be in biology class watching footage of U.S. Senators in a semi-circular row, looking down their glasses at witnesses.

With the room so dark, the white text at the bottom of the video stood out starkly. It gave the name of the witness who was speaking, a scientist from NASA or the National Institutes of Health or some other government agency. No, it was definitely NASA. Burton remembered because he thought they were going to hear about signs of life on the moon or something like that.

Instead, the scientist described global warming. The footage they were watching was a Congressional Hearing about global warming specifically, if Burton remembered correctly. The hearing had occurred in the late 1980s. Burton was certain about the date, because he had been shocked to learn that eight years had passed since this NASA scientist hold Congress what was going on and he was only now learning how dangerous the situation was.

The scientist told the senators that he was 99% certain that air pollution was making the atmosphere of the entire planet warmer. He was pretty adamant that humanity had to sharply reduce the burning of coal, oil and gas. We also had to stop cutting down forests that absorbed the carbon dioxide we were creating. One statement Burton thought he would never forget was that humans had already altered the climate in a way that would affect life on earth for centuries. Very dangerous, irreversible effects would happen if we went on with business as usual.

Burton was infuriated that such an important topic could have been pushed aside. After class, he went back to the tiny bedroom in the house he shared with five other students and wrote the article he was looking at today.

Afterwards, he looked into changing the focus of his PhD program. He needed to follow through on the call to action he wrote about so forcefully in the article. The University offered degrees in things like geophysics, environmental science, and meteorology. He actually took scissors and cut from an issue of *The Rodent* the words "Will the apathetic lot of us do what needs to be done?" and taped this line of text on the wall above his desk.

How long did he try? He could not remember. Deep in his PhD program at the time, he was working in the lab seven days a week, sometimes getting home after midnight. Time passed. He and Maddy got married, got jobs, had two kids.

Burton was also in a real minority back then. Global warming was news but not like it was today. Back then, the dire predictions in Burton's *Rodent* article must have looked paranoid. A tree-hugger resorting to scare tactics. But they were not scare tactics. He was reporting what he heard. How could it have happened that such a huge problem did not remain at the forefront of everyone's priorities? His own priorities! Seb had to have understood on some level that his father became one of the "apathetic lot" he railed about in the article.

Diabetes research was not slouching. It was a huge problem that needed to be addressed. He and Maddy had a family to support. But who did not have jobs and other family obligations?

He and Maddy bought fuel-efficient cars. Environmental issues were a big factor in choosing who they voted for. They tried not to be wasteful. Was that it? Burton could not think of anything else they had done. How was that possible?

He could blame the very bad people who put a lot of effort into suppressing information and intentionally confusing people about global warming. It was right there in the *Rodent* article he wrote all those years ago. He was a scientist, though. An investigator. He, of all people, should have known that you had to stay vigilant and keep digging. It was depressing to think how easily the whole thing slipped away from him. How he forgot the lesson of cigarette companies who got away with lying about the effects of smoking until motivated people and brave journalists and scientists finally put an end to that.

Now, though, was not the time to sit on the floor, dwelling on his mistakes. They had to find their son. Unless that was precisely what Seb wanted them to do. Feel guilty. If so, why had he made clear in both emails that he did not want to hurt them?

Maddy was no doubt unhappy that Burton still had not come downstairs but he needed a few more minutes to organize the thoughts racing through his mind before he lost them.

Seb had been concerned about environmental issues for some time. Besides the Green Club at school, he would do things like insist the family not order more food than they could eat at restaurants. But the dire predictions in Burton's article must have shocked him. He suspected Seb had not known that the problem of global warming, instead of being improved, had been allowed to get considerably worse for decades.

The article had obviously hit their son hard. He would not have asked his parents to read it right away otherwise. And now they had to make a video about it. Responding to such a complex issue could make for a very long video.

Burton then wondered if it would help for Seb to hear that the newsletter he found was the link that brought his parents together.

The six members of *The Rodent's* editorial board, all self-appointed, were sitting in their usual corner of the student lounge the night Burton first saw Maddy. That night, insults were going back and forth about the merits of contemporary art. The majority opinion was that "greatness" was determined by looking different, self-promotion, and being financed by the right people. Dennis Stutz countered that a genius should not be penalized because smart art sellers and collectors recognized talent when they saw it.

Dawn Donnelly got so annoyed she left the room saying, "Genius? All you have to do is go look at that big square of black plywood on the wall of the theater lobby. It looks like a piece of scenery that fell off the stage." She nearly bumped into Maddy and her best friend Silvia on her way out.

The Rodent group had commandeered nearly all the box-crate furniture, as they called it, in this corner of the lounge. Silvia walked right into the center of the space. Burton and the rest of them stared at her expectantly. She merely smiled. Maddy told Burton later that Silvia had overheard their conversation about contemporary art and wanted to get in on it.

"For sure, a lot of contemporary art is crap," Silvia said. "But that's part of the game. Did the artist have a good eye for color? Or did they knock over a can of paint, glue their passport photo to the canvas, and just get lucky?"

"Like Rothko," someone said. "Rothko is a first class lucky bastard."

"Definitely some luck involved," Maddy chipped in, surprising Burton. She had been standing a half step behind Silvia, looking like her friend had yet again dragged her into something.

"It's easier to fool people about abstraction," Maddy continued, "especially the really abstract stuff. I can stand there and think, do I like this? What does it mean if you have to ask if you like something? And do I really, or am I trying to guess what's considered good art by the experts, so I don't look unsophisticated?"

Burton used Maddy's comment as an excuse to smile at her. He had never heard of Rothko before. She was cute. Athletic, in a light blue baseball jersey with white stripes down the sleeves. He liked sporty women. She smiled back. He was not sure if she was playing with him, having figured out he was only trying to score points with her.

Silvia sat down in the only empty chair left in this corner of the student lounge. Maddy had no option but to sit on a couch next to a couple of guys she did not know, directly opposite Burton.

She and Silvia remained talking with Burton's gang until the lounge closed for the night. Burton decided Maddy was making enough eye contact to indicate real interest. When they all got up to leave, he chickened out on asking if he could see her another time with the pathetic excuse that he would study in the student center every night until he saw her again. Three nights later, she came in wearing running shorts and a sweat shirt. She looked good and he was intimidated.

She stopped near the soda machine and picked up a copy of *The Rodent*. He never found out if she had noticed him and stopped to read the newsletter solely to encourage him. He wanted to keep on believing it was true.

When she set the newsletter down, he lunged out of his chair. Maddy noticed his awkward movement and a smile broke out on her face. He came very close to pretending he had not noticed her and was going to get a drink.

But he would have hated himself if he did that, so he went to her and told her she had just doubled their circulation. He could not hear her response over the blabbing in the student center, but she smiled again. He nodded, pretending he had understood her. She frowned and he panicked. Possibly he was not supposed to have agreed with whatever she said. At this point, he had nothing to lose, so he shouted an invitation, including Silvia as a buffer, for them to come to the next newsletter planning meeting. She accepted.

Not long before they got engaged, they came upon a Rothko in an art gallery.

"Not his best work," Burton said and Maddy laughed.

It was already noon. A day and a half had already gone by since Seb sent his awful email and they still had no idea where he was.

Maddy was at the basement desk typing up a script. They would use it for the video Seb asked them to make. She was the faster typist, thanks to many hours doing consulting work from home for different local charities. This had been a good gig when the kids were little. It became pretty lonely after they went off to school. It was now summer vacation but neither kid was interested in hanging out with Mom any more.

The script they had written was not perfect but time was getting away from them. They had to stop agonizing about the ideal way to react to Burton's article. Their son could not be out there another night.

While Maddy clicked away at the desk, Burton sat on the couch and reviewed the missing persons websites again. He read about one family's candlelight vigil. Just the thought of people standing around in the dark with light flickering on their sad faces made him sick. They were not going to do that.

The websites did have excellent suggestions, many of which they were following, but nearly every good idea conjured up disturbing images. When Burton read a bit about kids hiding out in areas of cities that were not well policed, he stopped reading and closed his eyes.

He allowed himself a minute to sit that way. His eyes felt better, but his mind, of course, kept right on going.

Officer Quinn seemed competent. Entire police departments and all the relevant agencies concerned with runaways were on the alert. A multi-state canvassing effort was in full swing. As soon as Maddy finished the script, they would make the video and post it for Seb.

One of the websites had recommended keeping a journal of their thoughts as a way to capture information that might prove useful. Information they might forget later. Burton and Maddy were both keeping a journal. They were not hiding their journals from one another, there just had not been an opportunity to share them. They should do that soon.

He opened his eyes and found the document he used for his journal on his laptop. He had not done anything like this since before he was a teenager. The closest thing to a journal in his current life was keeping lists of what he had to do at work. He was doing the journal about Seb the same way:

July 2, 12:30 pm

Continental Divide? Quinn asked - Seb's ideal place. Checking bus plane hitchhike. Would he really try? If yes will get caught in transit.

Left messages Duranne in Calif. No response.

Terrie in Portsmouth again today. How could nobody see him? Did not go far?

Seb email. Wants to know what we think about my global warming article. Wants reassurance? Apology? What does this tell us about where he IS?

Burton set the laptop on the end table.

They were not letting Jessica see the old *Rodent* newsletter. It had clearly upset Seb, and they did not want to risk the same with her. At least not until they knew better how to talk about it. But they wanted her to participate in the video so they settled on telling Jessica it was an article her father had written a long time ago about the need to work on global warming. Jessica responded by calling Seb a freak and then going to the couch to read one of the Harry Potter books for probably the tenth time. They left her there and went down to the office to plan the video response Seb had requested.

"Come see what I've got," Maddy said.

He got up from the couch and leaned in next to her. She scrolled through the document, pointing out where she made edits. Her elbow kept poking Burton in the biceps but he kind of liked it. He suggested a couple more changes and then they emailed it to Officer Quinn.

While waiting for Quinn to reply, Burton went back to the couch with his laptop and pulled up his email. So much crap to rifle through. He could see Maddy's index finger banging at the keyboard, no doubt erasing message after message, just as he was. In less than five minutes, a response from Quinn appeared in both of their inboxes.

"Looks good. I like the way you emphasize your willingness to meet your son's terms. Copy me on the YouTube link when you upload the video. Quinn."

"I guess that's it." Maddy said.

They got their stuff together and left the basement office. Burton retrieved a tripod from the storage closet. He had to go up two flights to their bedroom to get the camera. Maddy was standing at the sink gulping down a glass of water when he carried the equipment across the kitchen and down to the living room. He attached the camera to the tripod and trained it on the couch. Jessica was curled up in one corner of the couch, staring at him.

"I can't believe you're not going to let me see the thing that was in the cedar chest," she moaned.

"I'm sorry, Jess, really," Burton said. "We'll show you, just not now."

Jessica tilted her head, stared at the ceiling and let her mouth drop open. "Uhhhh," she said. She shut her mouth quickly and narrowed her eyes at her father. "Then why should I even be in this video?"

Burton focused the camera on her. She made an ugly face then looked away.

Maddy walked to the couch and sat next to their daughter. Burton saw she had printed out the script and was holding it in her hand.

"I'm sorry, Jess," she said. "Things are a little out of whack now. We have to stay on top of things to make sure Seb gets home today."

"I know," Jessica said. "Damn it."

Burton looked over the top of the camera at her. The curse, he figured, was meant to show she was mature enough to read what was written in the newsletter.

"C'mon Jess." Maddy reached a hand towards her daughter.

Jessica pushed it away, scrambled off the couch, and ran out of the room. Maddy opened her mouth as if to call after her. Instead, she took a long, audible breath, got up and followed the sound of Jessica's feet pounding the stairs to the second floor.

Burton checked the settings on the camera. They needed to do the video now, so Seb could be satisfied and make his way home before it got dark. At the very least, respond to their video and give them a clue as to where he was.

From his position near the fireplace, Burton could see the entire living room and kitchen. The dining table was covered with books, note pads, two laptops, several mugs and a bag of corn chips. To his left the backyard was visible through the sliding glass doors. A lime green cap lay in the grass. Jessica's, from her lyrical dance class.

The house fit them well. Burton liked in particular how the kitchen was connected to the sunken living room, separated only by a couple of steps. During the day it was bright with natural light from the south-facing glass doors. They could do all sorts of things here and be near each other. Seb would read in the living room, even if others were watching television, just to be around them, occasionally looking at the screen if they laughed loudly or it got really quiet.

Besides the house, there was a park less than a mile away and Seb was there all the time. He had friends within walking or skateboarding distance. The ocean was not far, and they went often in the summer, and to ice skating rinks and state parks at other times of the year. It was easy to park the car at the train station and go into Boston. They had it good.

Burton supposed it was normal for a kid to take these things for granted and to fantasize about leaving. The article about global warming was upsetting, no doubt, but to actually leave? What else happened and how had they missed it? Worse, what was this about starting to explain later? How long did he think he was going to stay away?

Jessica entered the kitchen and marched down the two steps to the living room, keeping her eyes on the floor the whole time. She dropped onto the couch and looked up at the camera with a bored look on her face. Her mother came in and stopped next to the kitchen table.

"What about filming a discussion in here? Just like at dinner time, when each of us tells how our day was. Sitting on the couch looking at the camera is going to feel strange."

The front door slammed. A few seconds later, Grandma Rosa walked into the kitchen with several bulging plastic grocery bags in each hand. She had her own key to the house.

"No camera for me," she said. "Nobody wants a movie of my big *culo* in front of the stove. You tell me when it's time so I can get out of the way."

Burton had informed Rosa over the phone that they were about to make a video for Seb and would explain later. She was fine with that because she was coming to cook meals and keep Jessica occupied. She was in for a challenge because her granddaughter no longer wanted to play Yahtzee or do much of anything with adults.

Burton could not deny having Rosa around would really help them focus on getting Seb back but he did not relish the thought of going through this with her around. *El Mosquito* got on his nerves. She said what was on her mind, and most of the time what was on her mind rubbed him the wrong way. Her religious invocations in particular, which he took to be a deliberate attempt to inject some faith into their church-less house.

"Hi, Grandma," Jessica said from the couch.

"You come up here and give me a kiss," Rosa said.

She held the grocery bags behind her as if she was going to heave them onto the kitchen counter. At a little over five feet tall, she would have to swing back far to get them up there. She hesitated long enough for Burton to come up and put his hand on her shoulder.

"Let me." He kissed her cheek and took the bags from her.

"Hi, step-son." Rosa never tired of this joke. Her English was fine.

Jessica got up from the couch and jogged over to her grandmother.

Rosa wrapped her arms around Jessica, pulled her against her soft body, and squeezed. "Hi, Jessie." She released her granddaughter. "You're too skinny. I'm going to cook something good."

"I'm a vegetarian, remember." Jessica said.

"But you can have one pork chop?"

"Just the vegetables. Cooked in a separate pan, okay?"

"Why?" Rosa asked. "Oh, all right. Go make your movie." She turned towards the counter, lifted the bottom of a bag, and dumped garlic, onions, tomatoes, frozen corn and a parcel wrapped in white paper onto the counter. "Tell your brother I said his butt should be beat good when he gets back."

"Mom," Maddy said, shaking her head.

"Your uncles Felix and José both ran away when they were boys." Rosa said as she chopped the end off an onion. "They came back the next day. And they learned who was in charge when they got home, I tell you that."

Burton could not believe she had started on this already. He knew what she believed about her brothers. How they learned from the "school of hard knock" (Rosa still dropped the *s* on plurals from time to time) to appreciate what they had back at home.

"Seb is not street-savvy like your brothers were," Maddy said. "And this is not Puerto Rico in the 1960s."

Rosa stood for a moment with the chopping knife in the air. Her face went blank and she brought the knife down, chopping an onion in half. If his mother-in-law had offered up any more parenting advice, Burton may have told her to shut the hell up.

Maddy and Burton once had a very effective method of discipline. The threat of withholding video games would set the kids groaning like they were chained in the basement without food. It worked for years, until recently. Seb did not care much about video games anymore. Jessica still spent hours with her games, but she seemed to be willing to suffer without them out of sheer stubbornness.

They had moved on to the talk method. This was infinitely trickier. Both children firmly believed they could reason their way out of things.

"Seb," Burton once said. "Do you understand why you shouldn't tell Mr. Baumgartner that his nose hairs are sticking out?"

"Yes."

"Why?"

"Because it hurts his feelings." A pause, and then, "But he doesn't care that it makes me sick and I can't eat because his nose hairs are so long and gross."

Sending the children to their rooms was not a major deterrent. In there they could read, draw, or write in their journals. Neither child was going to lie in bed and honestly assess why they had been punished. The parents tried requiring an essay on why they had been sent to their room, but all they got was a regurgitation of obvious answers.

Burton went back to the camera by the fireplace and adjusted one of the tripod legs. He was about to announce that they had to start filming when Jessica appeared at his side.

"Can we please do this video, now?" she said. "I'll behave."

Maddy came into the living room and sat on the couch. Jessica joined her, leaving space between them for Burton. Rosa leaned against a countertop, out of range of the camera.

Burton pressed the record button and hurried back to the couch.

Jessica whispered in his ear. "This is weird."

Burton nodded. He turned to face the camera and made a quick wave with the palm of his hand.

"Hi, Seb. We want you to remember one thing before we get started."

Maddy placed the typed script in his hand. He glanced down at it.

"If you need help," he said, lifting his eyes to the camera, "no matter what, we will help you. Me or your mom or both of us. Email or phone or meeting in person. No strings attached."

He paused to check the notes again and was surprised to hear Jessica begin to speak.

"Hi, turd," she said. "They wouldn't let me read the mysterious article, so I don't know what's going on, except that you're upset about global warming. Which I already knew."

She folded her arms, cocked her head and looked bored again.

Burton turned from watching his daughter to face the camera. "Since I wrote the article, I want to say a few things about it. You probably think I'm a big hypocrite. Well, I did drop the ball. I try not to be wasteful, and recycle, and it's a big issue for me when I vote, but you had no way of knowing that. Anyway, it's not enough.

"So here's an offer. I'll give you every free minute I have to work on a plan to get serious. We can do great things together. Your mother and I should have been doing more of this before, but we've already learned some new ways we can really make a difference, and we want to get started with you. If you are thinking something else, let us know?"

After a pause, Maddy added, "Seb, I'm sorry you read that article alone."

Burton realized that he had not called Seb by name. The police had encouraged them to use Seb's name as much as possible.

"I hate to think of you being upset and alone," his wife continued. "To be honest—you asked us to be honest—I was upset, too. You didn't give us a chance to talk to you. To help you before you left. But you must have good reasons and you've asked us to help you in your way. I'm your mother, so of course I'll help you."

Burton was not sure what expression to put on for the camera while Maddy was speaking. He thought perhaps a hint of a smile while looking confident yet also concerned. He forced a smile, realized the grin was not doing it, and decided to squint his eyes, to show thoughtfulness.

"Seb, honey," his wife continued. "About your dad's article. That's what you asked us to discuss. It made me, both of us, realize how we've been hoping the experts, the scientists and engineers, would figure it out. We expected they would coming running down the street with red flags long before things got this bad."

Maddy paused, probably to let Seb digest what she had just said.

"That was wishful thinking. We need experts but they can only do so much. They need us to support them and we haven't.

"I can't help saying we could have a better conversation about this if you were here. Yes, I'm biased because I'm worried sick about you, but ...well, I just love you, okay?"

Burton had lapsed into staring at Maddy. He was supposed to conclude with saying "I love you, too," but he thought of something that might be useful to say. He raised his hand.

"This is just an idea. I was thinking of all the people I see walking around the research center in the summer with sweaters and fleece jackets on. Meanwhile, outside, it's ninety degrees. Just last week, I saw two different people with space heaters under their desks. There's probably a million, literally a million, office buildings in the world chilled like refrigerators every day while people are wearing sweaters inside. I have no idea why. Maybe employees are more productive when they're kept cold. Maybe it keeps them awake. Whatever the reason, it's unacceptable. Anyway, maybe you and I could go talk to the big boss about it."

Jessica leaned in front of her father to occupy the central focus of the camera. "Just come home, Seb. It's not funny anymore."

CHAPTER FOUR

DETECTIVE OF TECHNOLOGY

JESSICA, MADDY AND BURTON scarfed down peanut butter on toast for a late lunch. They were getting dangerously close to a second night of Seb out there alone.

Jessica finished first. She moved to the couch and flicked through channels on the television, settling on a movie with David Bowie dressed as an elf. In minutes, she was asleep. Burton went into the living room, unlaced her sneakers, and slid them off. Sleeping a lot until Seb came home was probably a good thing.

Maddy pointed her finger at the ceiling. Burton nodded. They picked up their laptops and carried them upstairs. Rosa was quietly washing dishes and could keep an eye on Jessica.

They closed the bedroom door and climbed onto the bed. With so much to do, it felt wrong to be sitting on the bed. Too much like the Sunday morning years ago, when they would read and sip lukewarm coffee for hours. They used the bed because they could easily look back and forth between each other's laptops as they went through their long list of calls.

Also, in the bedroom, they could be more frank with each other. They whispered the most disturbing things (*who could have hurt Seb?*) just in case Jessica had creeped on her stockinged feet to listen outside their door. Their daughter was supposed to be writing letters asking for help finding her brother. These would be posted on the runaway websites and anywhere else they could think of. She insisted on writing these on the couch in front of the TV, though, and kept falling asleep.

Maddy and Burton had the handwritten list of contacts on the bed between their legs. It was already marred with smudged ink and coffee spills. To hear better during calls, they turned away from one another and covered their free ear. Maddy called Officer Quinn first and Burton, Detective McDermott up in Portsmouth.

The list now contained every Buddhist group and center in New England. There were dozens, though most were tiny operations, weekly gatherings in yoga studios, and if they had phone numbers, there was no one around to answer. Mostly they had web pages or emails. The only places where someone did answer the phone were the temples run by Tibetans or Sri Lankans who could barely speak English. Some could not speak English at all. They had no idea what was being asked of them. "Please, come visit," they would say.

Every place Burton or Maddy contacted was emailed the flyer with Seb's picture. Anyone who had a mailing address was sent a snail mail as well. Rosa was stuffing envelopes, hand-writing addresses, and putting on the stamps. Jessica helped here and there. The monasteries within a few hours drive of Portsmouth were or would be visited in person by Terrie or Ajahn Wattana. Maddy or Burton wanted to go but they were already in over their heads.

Burton finished the second-to-last number on the list. Maddy was on the phone with the last. The list had grown even as they were calling. Some of the people who actually answered the phone had suggested other places to call.

When she ended her last call, Maddy did not say anything to Burton. She just began clicking away at her laptop. Was she mad at him? *Was she blaming him for this?* He really wished he would stop thinking about his wife's behavior and focus on Seb but, well, at least he had not vocalized any of the insults that came to mind.

He readjusted his position against the headboard, and brought up the map of Portsmouth on his laptop again.

Pierce Island looked rather small. The Urban Forest would not be easy for Seb to get in and out of. They had persuaded the police to pay particular attention to the parks. Burton zoomed out to include parks outside of Portsmouth. There were a bunch and some of them were big. He sat there staring at the big chunks of green on the map. Very big amounts of green.

Maddy, he realized, had grown very still. He glanced over and saw a tear rolling down her cheek. On her laptop was a photo, the kind of photo they had already seen too often. A rectangular close-up of a child, with her name underneath, and a date. The date she disappeared. This child had been missing for three years.

"Why are you looking at that?" he asked. His intention was to spare her pain, to get her to stop looking at the child's photo, but his question came out sounding rather harsh.

Maddy wiped the tear from her cheek with the back of her hand and blinked at the screen.

"Our situation is completely different," he continued, more quietly. "Seb is keeping in touch. And that girl was kidnapped."

"How do we know Seb wasn't kidnapped? They could be orchestrating this whole...thing."

"I really don't think so. What kind of kidnapper wants to send messages like that?"

"A sick one. An eco-terrorist."

The idea of a kidnapper pretending to be their child made Burton furious. Any person who would do something like this should be destroyed. It was hard enough to concentrate on what they had to do without getting furious as well. If anyone else was involved in Seb's— the word disappearance came to mind and he pushed it away—they needed to calmly and methodically find this person.

"The emails sound like Seb," Burton said. "The way he thinks and the way he talks."

"If that sounds like Seb," Maddy said flatly, "then we really failed. Because the person who wrote that email, the fourteen-year-old who ran away to another state, should have been seeing a psychiatrist." She closed the laptop and continued to gaze where the screen had been.

It felt as if his wife wanted to get away from him. As if he was impeding her, she who was willing to look at hard truths.

Yes, they had failed their son. He must have been struggling and putting on a good face for a while and they missed it entirely. Something serious must have happened to him. But nobody, no doctor, no teacher, no guidance counselor, not Maddy herself, had suggested a problem or a mental health issue. The time Seb lay in the back yard with birdseed on his stomach after his cousin Sasha moved away, they considered sending him to a counselor. They did not. Being upset at losing your best friend seemed like a normal reaction, even if it was expressed in Seb's unique way. Burton wondered if all children in modern society, with access to so much information about the wild and scary world on the internet and a thousand TV channels, should see a psychiatrist.

Maddy's hand lay limp on the bedspread. He put his hand over hers, partly to test if she would withdraw it, but also because he hurt for her. She smiled faintly. He massaged her hand by sliding his over top of it, pressing his fingers between hers, applying a bit of pressure with his palm. Her eyelids fluttered for a moment and came to rest, closed.

Burton kept his hand over hers. It felt good. At least they were okay. Crazy-thinking was understandable in this situation. He hoped Maddy would fall asleep so they could just be still together, if just for a few minutes.

Maddy began to snore.

With his free hand, Burton brought up the YouTube page where they had uploaded the video assignment they did for Seb. He had been checking it several times an hour. The title, and the word "assignment" in particular made him feel more than ever that something terrible was going on. Being held hostage by their own child. Being given assignments. It heightened the feeling that they were not only failing as parents but now completely out of control. He was stuck in these thoughts until he noticed comments under the video he had not seen before.

He nudged Maddy. She opened her eyes and gave him a questioning look. He pointed at his laptop screen. She leaned in to see what was there. They had seen the first two comments already. Prayers and hopes that Seb would be home soon.

Under these was a new message from someone identified as 22TRUTH. It stated: *"Sure. Stop burning fossil fuels and see the world fall apart. These are just estimates by scientists. Let's not freak out."* The comment directly under this read: *"You believe in the science behind the medication you take, don't you?"*

The next comment under the video said, *"Parents begging a child—it's shameful."*

Burton started to grind his teeth.

The final comment stated: *"The girl is cute."* Burton clicked "reply" and typed *"jump off a cliff."* He then erased those words and deleted the reply he had started.

Still no comment from Seb.

Maddy squeezed his biceps.

"I'm losing it," she said.

He put his arm around her. Her body felt hard, tight.

"The police said most kids turn up by the first day and most of the rest by the second." Her voice cracked. "We're halfway through the second day and we don't know anything."

Burton waited. Maddy did not continue.

"It's waiting that's killing us," he said.

"Two days. I really, really, really don't understand."

"He's keeping in touch. He wants to be in touch with us. That means something. A lot."

Maddy nodded. "That *is* good. But he's also not giving any clues. Now that California is out, we don't have anything specific."

Mrs. Rodriguez, Duranne's mother, had contacted them, finally, that morning. She apologized for the delay. She used the phone Maddy had called only to communicate with her husband and daughter. The three of them had been together all weekend and the phone had been in a drawer the whole time.

Burton was not surprised Duranne knew nothing about Seb's disappearance, but it was still disappointing. He had been harboring a little hope they would intercept Seb at some bus station in New York or Ohio, trying to get to California.

Mrs. Rodriguez confirmed that Duranne had not heard from Seb for nearly two months. Maddy asked her if she would mind checking her daughter's phone records. Mrs. Rodriguez agreed to do this, which was good of her. She could have taken offense at the implication her daughter might be lying.

Burton supposed there was still a chance that Duranne and Seb had communicated some way. Perhaps she would get nervous and confess later. He was not counting on it.

Maddy slid down the headboard until she was on her back. The laptop on her stomach rose up and down with her breathing.

"Where could he be?" she asked. "A campground by the side of the road in a tent from Walmart?" She turned her head towards Burton and shifted her eyes up at him. "Be patient with me, okay?"

"I will," he said. "You do the same with me."

She looked back at the ceiling again. "It's just...I sometimes have these negative thoughts about him. I'm scared to death and I'll probably be nauseous until he's home, and that's fine, I'm his mother. But I can't shake this awful feeling that he doesn't seem to care about us. These demands and this cat and mouse game, making us wait for his emails? What could we have done to deserve that? I feel totally guilty we were oblivious to what was going on with him and yet... I don't know. It's just not a good feeling."

"Did you expect to feel good right now?"

"No. I'm... surprised, I guess. Disappointed that Seb, of all people, would be doing this."

She was not merely disappointed. She was angry.

Burton was not sure what was going on with his wife, but it annoyed him. He needed to figure out how not to waste time trying to understand her right now. He decided he would stick with his most recent theory that she had been dropped on her head as a baby and the pragmatism switch had been knocked into the permanently "on" position.

He could feel the warmth of her body, an inch away from his on her bed. Now he felt guilty. She was a human being and she had just asked him to be patient with her. Still, the comfort he had felt being close to her was gone. He told himself it was not realistic to expect to feel any pleasure in these circumstances.

⟨≈⟩

Burton woke with a snort to find he had fallen asleep sitting upright on the bed, with his back to the wooden headboard. Maddy stood in the doorway, on her way out.

"I'm going to help with dinner," she said.

"Just order something."

"Rosa is already cooking. I can smell it. I'll go down and set the table."

He nodded. She closed the door. Meals were depressing, reminders of how stupid life was, that you had to keep feeding yourself even when you did not want to. And each time a meal had to happen, Burton was further aggravated by the reminder that time was passing. Seb was gone two days now. It was a truly awful thought, his son out there alone all that time.

He picked up the phone and called his boss, Dr. Bob, the director of biomedical research at the university. Seb's photo was on the news. People at work knew or would know soon.

Dr. Bob told Burton not to do anything work-related, not speak to his lab or anything, just go find his son. He would take care of everything. Burton started to ask how things were going but his boss would not let him speak.

"Don't think about this place," Dr. Bob said, and hung up.

His boss called back a minute later. "Except let us know how to help. We sent Seb's picture to the umpteen thousand emails here. He'll be home soon."

"Thank you," Burton said just before Dr. Bob hung up again.

The scent of frying garlic and onion came in through the gap under the bedroom door. Burton looked at his wrinkled T-shirt in the dresser

74

mirror. He briefly considered putting on a new one, then went downstairs.

Maddy and Jessica were sitting side by side at the kitchen table, with a plate of rice and beans in front of each of them. They seemed to be in the middle of an intense conversation and looked up distractedly at him when he came in. The food on their plates was untouched.

Rosa lifted the huge iron skillet she brought with her from home and held it out towards Burton. He shook his head to indicate he did not want any. There seemed to be a lot of food still in the pan.

Jessica looked away from her father and back to her mother. "I don't have any summer reading."

Maddy blinked at her a couple times. "I know you do. Your teacher gave me the list."

"I mean I don't have any summer reading I have to do right now."

Her mother interlaced her fingers and set her clasped hands on the table. Burton recognized this trick, which Maddy employed to remind her to pause and take a deep breath before speaking. "Please get the list and the next book you are supposed to be reading."

With a glance at the clasped hands, Jessica got up and left the room.

Rosa dropped the nearly full pan on the stove, loudly, opened the basement door, and clomped down the stairs to the laundry room.

"Thank you, Rosa," Burton called after her. "Big baby," he said to himself. He felt a pang of regret afterwards. Did he really think his mother-in-law had dropped the pan loudly because nobody ate her food? He had managed to keep the thought to himself, at least.

A minute later, Jessica walked into the kitchen and dropped a wrinkled piece of paper and a copy of *Watership Down* onto the table. She sat next to her mother and Burton took the seat around the corner from them.

"Mom, I don't care about this book. I can't read it right now. I'm preoccupied."

"Okay," Maddy said. "I just..." She blinked a few times.

Jessica's frown started to wobble. "Why is this happening? Why can't we find him? Is Seb smarter than you guys?"

"He's more clever with computers," Burton said. "But we've got the police with their networks and technology."

To himself, he wondered how much energy the police could put into one kid. He had no idea how many kids were missing in Massachusetts and New Hampshire. His wife and child turned to look at him. He tried to figure out how to say what he wanted to say in front of Jessica.

"Maybe there's more we could do," he said. "To track down his email."

Maddy tilted her head to the side. "Hire somebody?"

Burton nodded slowly. "Yes. We need to hire somebody."

"There must be such a thing," Maddy said. "A computer detective. How do you find a detective? Google 'detective?'"

"That's how to find everything," Jessica said.

"Maybe Officer Quinn can recommend someone," Burton asked.

Maddy bit her lower lip. "How about we try to find someone ourselves. Do this part our way, without their limitations and their rules? Meanwhile, the police can keep on with their own search and we double our chances of success."

Jessica stared at her mother, probably trying to understand what she was talking about. Then she reached for the laptop at the center of the kitchen table and pulled it over to herself.

"It'll take forever if you guys do it," she said.

Burton and Maddy leaned in to get a better view of the screen. Their daughter typed "computer detective" into the search field. The page filled instantly with results.

"See." Jessica clicked on a small arrow. A list of options opened up. "You can search for things that were changed, like in the past year. That way you don't get something old."

After selecting several options quicker than Burton could follow, Jessica hit enter, and different results filled the screen. The rapt expression on her face pleased him. She really needed to be able to help. He noticed she was wearing the black т-shirt with a gorilla she had worn the day before and was wearing when he woke her up in her bed that morning. This was uncharacteristic of her. Unlike her brother, she followed social conventions very carefully.

He wondered if they should have sent her to stay with a friend after all. What a fuss she would have made, though, if they tried to make her go. Since they opted to keep her with them, they needed to do a better job of making sure she was okay. As okay as possible given the situation. Helping them find a detective was relatively innocuous, he hoped.

"There's hundreds of detectives near Boston," Maddy said.

Burton stood up and started pacing behind Maddy and Jessica. He looked down over their heads at the screen. "The person who knows how to do this might not live around here."

"It's not like we can get a recommendation." Maddy said. "Who do we know who has hired a detective?"

"All these detectives are great," Jessica said. "According to their websites."

"Yes, everyone has excellent reviews, so that means nothing. Except for this guy. He should check his website, because there's some angry people on there."

Jessica pointed. "What about that one?"

"Internet detective—finding your lost loved ones, human and otherwise." Maddy read out loud.

"What does that mean, human and otherwise?" Burton asked. "Finding a dog on the internet? Veto."

Jessica looked hurt for a moment, then returned to scanning the computer screen.

"That one sounds reasonable," Maddy said, pointing at the screen. "Robert Washington, private detective. Specializing in locating missing persons. It's clear and sounds professional." She reached for her phone and typed in the phone number listed on the screen. After listening for about a minute, she hung up.

"So?" Burton asked.

"An old man's voice. He should at least clear his throat before recording a message. Anyway, I think we need somebody young, someone who really understands technology. Who grew up using computers."

Myro barked at the sliding glass door. Burton let him out. A gust of lilac blew in. They were blooming. He did not care.

"What about this one?" Jessica asked. "Detective of Technology. Trace anonymous communications, locate missing people. Call Phillip Geer."

"The job title's unusual," Maddy said. "Does he fix computers? Can I see, hon?"

Jessica pushed the laptop back to her mother.

Maddy scrolled down. "He has a degree in Physics from Harvard and a Master's in Computation for Design and Optimization from M.I.T." She looked at her daughter. "That's the Massachusetts Institute of Technology. Pretty impressive. There's the logo of a private detective association on here. No address but a Boston phone number."

Burton stopped pacing and got closer to the screen to see what they were looking at. His hand hit a pile of papers and one sheet fell off, flipping over.

It was their flyer for Seb. His eighth-grade photo reminded Burton that he had been voted "most likely to succeed" that year, which was a surprise because he got a bunch of c's. Most of his classmates did not know Seb's grades, though. They knew him as the guy who talked about things they never heard of.

"He looks like a baby," Maddy said.

This photo had been chosen because Seb looked particularly boyish. They hoped this would engender more sympathy and inspire people to try a little harder to remember to look for him.

Burton looked away from the flyer to the website for the "Detective of Technology." It was nothing more than a black background with white text on it. The only information on the screen was his credentials, phone number and email address. Bare bones but to the point, with a nice, legible font.

"You want to try this one?" Maddy asked.

"Okay." Burton took the phone and dialed.

A voice answered during the first ring.

"Phillip Geer."

A British accent. Interesting.

"Hi," Burton said. He had a bad habit of trying to lighten things up at the wrong time. "I'm inquiring about your detective services."

"Oh. I see."

This response made Burton wonder if Mr. Geer did not get a lot of business. His prejudices started flowing. Detective bum in a basement apartment with piles of clothes everywhere and nothing hanging on the walls. An overfed man with bad posture. Several days' beard highlighting translucent British skin.

Mr. Geer spoke again. "How may I help you?"

"Are you available for a missing person case?"

"Let us make sure it's appropriate first."

"We're trying to find a person who is using an email provider we can't trace," Burton said. "The email address is just a long string of letters and numbers."

Maddy drummed her fingers on Burton's forearm and whispered, "Just tell him the truth. The whole story. He's a professional. He has to keep confidences."

Burton nodded. "It's our son. He's fourteen years old and is communicating only through this email. Two messages so far. He's promised to send more.

"We were completely taken by surprise by his disappearance. There weren't any conflicts in the family, or any sign he was unhappy. What we're looking for is someone who can locate the email company our son is using and obtain permission, or otherwise trace the location the emails were sent from."

Phillip did not answer for a couple of seconds. "These things are possible. It can be tricky if he's using a foreign email re-router that won't answer questions. They're all over, Asia, Africa, South America.

Your son would have to be rather knowledgeable to accomplish this."

"Oh, he's knowledgeable," Burton said.

Knowledgeable since they weaned him off *Star Wars* with a refurbished laptop. They were fed up with *Star Wars*. Seb watched the movies and the cartoons based on the movies over and over again. He read the crappy books created for the fanatic fan market and refused to sleep in anything other than *Star Wars* sheets and pajamas. His mother was constantly pulling action figures from under the mattress. The space between the mattress and the box spring was *the deep core of Tattooine*.

The beginning of the end occurred the day Seb came down to breakfast speaking *Yoda*. The annoying backwards vernacular of *Yoda*.

"Secret, shall I tell you? Yummy they are not, bananas."

"Just eat your fruit."

"A teacher, *Yoda* is. Show you all forms of light-saber combat, I can."

It was cute for a day. Jessica, six years old at the time, laughed and laughed at his *Yoda*-isms. She followed him everywhere, trying to do the same, and failing. Her attention only encouraged Seb.

Maddy tried empathy. "It's hard to understand you, Seb, when you speak like Yoda. Would you do Mommy a favor and speak like *Luke Skywalker?*"

"Understand, you will, with time."

"No television, you will watch tonight." Burton said. "Unless you give us a break from the *Yoda* talking. In fact, why don't you take a little break in your room."

Seb reminded them, halfway up the stairs to his bedroom, "Cry, *Yoda* does not. *Grand Master of Jedi Order*, he is. Afraid of the *Dark Side*, think you?"

"No *Dark Side*," Burton said. "Read a book up there. Not a *Star Wars* book."

The refurbished laptop worked like a charm. Seb could not get enough of it. At first, he wanted only to download *Star Wars* games. Burton insisted they try other things. The cool programs available on shareware and freeware websites soon trumped *Star Wars*. They both became hooked.

Seb found a program that recorded his voice and played it back as Donald Duck, which made him and his father both laugh until they had trouble breathing. He installed a screen-saver that morphed his face into African animals. Together, Burton and Seb learned a bit of programming and developed a game where little Seb and little Burton heads rammed each other.

With more free time, and a child's resilience, Seb's computer skills surpassed his father's. It was cute, and probably stoked Burton's ego to have his talented child teach him things. He never imagined his son would use this superior knowledge, knowledge they had such fun building together, against him. It was a real slap in the face.

Burton could elaborate on Seb's talents later, if they decided to hire Mr. Geer. For now, he condensed the story into, "Our son is pretty talented with computers. It's a hobby he and I shared. And then he surpassed me. He has a lot more free time than I do."

"Young people are very familiar with technology. They often do their own troubleshooting and learn a great deal this way."

I know that, Burton wanted to say. Mr. Geer sounded awfully young. Being close in age to Seb could be an advantage, as long as he knew more than how to get around a computer.

"Ask him if he's tried to find children before." Maddy said.

"Have you tried to find children before?"

"I have."

Mr. Geer did not say whether he found them.

"A Master's in computer science from M.I.T. is impressive," Burton said.

"Thank you. How long has your son been gone?"

"Two days."

"I'm sorry," Phillip said.

He sounded genuinely concerned, which was a good sign.

"Will you help us?" Burton asked.

He flashed a look at Maddy. She assented with a nod, even though she had heard only what Burton spoke into the phone.

"At this point, I have yet to fail," Mr. Geer said. "I will send my terms and rates for you to review and give you instructions on how to download the proprietary software I developed to assist in deciphering communications."

"I should send my email address to the one on your website?"

"Yes, please. Also forward any emails you received from your son since he left. What is his name?"

"Seb. Sebastien Franck. He goes by Seb."

"Please also forward an email from the address that Seb normally uses. Any email addresses he uses."

"Sure."

"Do you have any leads on where he might be?"

"Not really. Parks. Coffee shops. Ashrams. To be honest, we really can't imagine where he is. He disappeared from a Buddhist monastery in Portsmouth, New Hampshire the night before last. He was just there for a short retreat. I'll send you the press release we did and a few more facts."

"Okay. Good."

"Can you let us know soon if you'll take the case?"

"I would like to check a few things first. I know time is critical so I will respond within the hour."

Myro started another slow lap around the kitchen table, grumble-moaning as he did when he sensed things were not right.

Seb was going to be alone now for the second night in a row. Around eleven that evening, Burton took the laptop down to the basement office. He felt like shouting at the top of his lungs. No particular word, just noise, but he could not with others in the house.

His legs started to feel weak, as if they might actually give out from under him. It was like his body was punishing him for not getting some release from shouting.

He lowered himself to the cold leather couch, holding the laptop tightly under his arm. He was afraid he would drop it. The coldness of the couch felt good. He set the laptop on his legs and closed his eyes. The light-headedness passed in about a minute.

He opened his eyes. The room was dim, lit only by the glow of a street lamp through the small basement window near the ceiling. He opened the laptop and blinked at the bright screen. A few emails had arrived since he last looked. One of them was from Phillip Geer.

I will take your case. There is something strange about it, though. I assume your son is using one or more companies or individuals to take his email, disguise it, and send it on. These parties are often not in the US. What is strange is that I can usually find some features of the re-routed email that link it to whomever might be re-routing it. At least what country they are in. This is a new wrinkle, but I welcome the challenge. It's just a matter of time before we will have an answer.

Please click on the link below to download my software and follow the prompts to grant me access to your computer.

The software will collect data. This will reveal what is going on.

I will contact you after your son's next message arrives.

Yours,
Phillip Geer

"My software." Well, la-de-da. A challenge? How jolly good and a bottle of rum.

But maybe cocky and confident were good qualities in a detective. Burton clicked on the link, granted permission to download, and watched the progress bar move across the screen.

Maddy opened the door to the office, giving Burton a start. She began to yawn and put a hand over her mouth.

"I'm so tired I might actually sleep tonight." She yawned again. Her eyes went to the computer on Burton's laptop. "From Seb?"

"Phillip. This might not be so easy."

She knelt next to the couch. Burton moved the software download indicator out of the way and turned the laptop so she could see Phillip's email. She frowned at one point and put her finger on the screen next to the paragraph describing how Seb's messages had thus far stumped the detective.

"Unbelievable," Maddy whispered.

Rosa appeared in the doorway with a basket of laundry in her arms. "Boys are sneaky."

"And girls aren't?" Burton asked.

Rosa screwed up her chubby face, looking a bit like a confused pug. White socks and shirts bulged up to her chin from the laundry basket as she squeezed it harder.

"Nice, Burton," Maddy said.

Rosa's face relaxed. "You're right, step-son. Seb is your boy, not mine."

The joke she never tired of, calling him *step-son*, melted Burton's irritation. "You were trying to make me feel better," he said. "I'm sorry. It's been a long day."

Rosa shook her head. "I'm sorry, too. Poor Seb—" She closed her mouth, widened her eyes and glanced to the side. A warning. Jessica appeared next to her grandmother in plaid sweat pants and a white tank top.

"What happened?" she asked.

"Mr. Geer just discovered how tricky your brother is. He said..." Burton decided not to tell his daughter that Geer had referred to the case as a challenge. "He has software to catch Seb at his own game."

CHAPTER FIVE

Garbage

Day three and no closer to knowing where Seb was. Unbelievable. Unbelievably bad.

Burton's legs burned from the laptop on his thighs. It had been resting on his legs all morning while he called and emailed and scoured the internet. He must have glanced up at the phone on the desk a thousand times. It was the line they were keeping open for incoming calls. Any sound within earshot, a creak in the walls or footsteps upstairs, would send his eyes immediately to the phone.

The only thing worse than waiting for the phone to ring was when it did ring and the caller had no news about Seb. It rang twice that morning. The dentist's office and Jake.

Jake had offered again to come up. Maddy and Burton still thought it would be better if he stayed in Texas, working his judge connections down there. If they had a clue where Seb might be, they might have something for Jake to do up in Massachusetts. Perhaps they would soon.

Maddy had left Burton in the basement a half hour earlier to see if Jessica wanted to go to her swimming lesson while she made phone calls from her car. Burton was surprised when he heard the garage door rumble open. He thought Jessica would decline for sure. It was possible her mother may have offered something more enticing than swimming lessons.

Burton's back ached from hunching over the computer. He rested his head against the couch. It was time to go back to Portsmouth. His sister Terrie had to leave the night before after spending a second day searching. Ajahn Wattana had been with her for a good part of the time. He had decided to cancel the retreat. Burton told the monk he would reimburse him for the lost revenue. The monk said no. Burton decided to just write a check after all this was over.

The idea of driving the streets of Portsmouth made Burton feel even more tired. He had slept an hour tops the night before. He would not tell Ajahn Wattana he would be up there. The man had things to do. Burton could drive around parks and libraries by himself. If the entire police force had not seen Seb in Portsmouth, it seemed unlikely he would. But he had nowhere else to look.

Before leaving he checked the most promising online discussion boards for parents with missing children. There was nothing new. The advice about coping annoyed him. They would cope. What they needed was insider information on how to get their kid back.

He came upstairs to find Jessica in the kitchen with a gym bag reeking of chlorine. Her grandmother was bent over a newspaper at the kitchen table.

Rosa peered over her glasses. "How was swimming?"

"I froze my nuts off," Jessica said.

Her grandmother frowned.

Jessica squinted at her. She apparently did not recognize the problem with her own metaphor. Burton leaned over and kissed his daughter's cheek. He set his laptop on the kitchen table. He went nowhere without it and carried it with the cover open, so he could hear the Seb-alert, should a message come in.

"We saw Mrs. Meyer and Mom got mad," Jessica said. Her mother came into the kitchen with a canvas tote bag.

"Liesel Meyer came up to the car as the kids were getting in," Maddy said, dropping the bag on the kitchen table. "Stay home, you feel like you're hiding. Go out, and you have to endure people who are happy their kid would never do such a thing."

"What did she say?" Burton asked.

"'Hi' and 'I'm so sorry.' It was the look on her face. I didn't want to see that from her."

Jessica went to the refrigerator and took out a bowl of Rosa's home-made rice pudding. She got a spoon and leaned against the counter.

"I think Seb is going to like the video we made," she said. She stuck the spoon in the pudding and twirled it around. "Unless he wanted us to come up with a plan to end global warming." She stopped stirring the pudding. "No, I know what he wants. He wants us to see we *don't* have a plan."

"You might be onto something," Maddy said. "We—"

A loud series of knocks interrupted her. The woodpecker alert on the laptop. An email from Seb had arrived.

Jessica's spoon fell from her hand, clattering against the edge of her pudding bowl.

"Speak of the...boy" Burton said.

All four hurried to the end of the kitchen table where the laptop lay. Rosa got there first. She stepped back so the others could get closer.

A small window at center of the screen displayed the subject of the message: *"Assignment Two."* This was the third message in three days. Burton wondered how many assignments Seb intended to send, and if he planned to wait a day for each. He told himself it did not matter. They would find him today.

He clicked the "open" box and an email message filled the screen. It said:

Please do this:

Each of you get a heavy-duty trash bag. Jess can do it too.

Put anything you would throw away in your bag. Wherever you go, take the bag with you, even if it's to work or the store.

Myro's dog food packages, shopping, food you're going to throw out, boxes.

Put recyclables in there too. Even newspaper or mail unless you really have a reason to save it.

Tomorrow night make a video about doing this.

Post it on You Tube as "Franck Family Video 2."

Seb

"I heard of this one already," Jessica said, condescendingly. "At school."

Burton's trash bag contained two granola bar wrappers, an apple core and a yogurt container. Everything he had eaten while in Portsmouth. He had combined his "assignment" with another day of showing Seb's photo and hoping to catch him trying to get internet service somewhere. Burton had eaten the yogurt without a spoon by squeezing the cup and pushing its contents into his mouth.

He dropped the bag next to the dishwasher and washed his hands in the sink. Searching the city this time without Terrie was rough.

It was ten o'clock. Seb would be spending a third night out there on his own.

The trip to Portsmouth had revealed nothing new. None of the park staff noticed a teenage boy on his own. Burton drove up and down the streets, pulling over every time he saw a cop. If they were in squad cars, he waved and pointed until they pulled over. They were all well aware of Seb, what he looked like, and seemed genuinely motivated to find him. Some of them jokingly let on that they had been warned Burton would harass them in the street if he crossed paths with them.

Burton was almost certain Seb was no longer in Portsmouth. There was a chance he had made friends with someone in the city who was hiding him. The cops, at least, had to keep looking there.

He went upstairs and found Maddy sitting on the bed with her back to the headboard and her computer on her lap. She was dressed in a white short-sleeve v-neck and red running shorts. An oscillating fan turned on the dresser opposite the foot of the bed. She did not like air conditioning unless it was really hot.

Her legs looked great in the satiny shorts. Burton climbed onto the bed and kissed her neck. She set her laptop on the end table, then slid down until she lay facing the ceiling.

"What is he not telling us?" she said. "And why isn't he telling us? I don't get it."

Burton propped himself up on one elbow and looked down at her. "It's like he's trying to prepare us before he says what's really on his mind. To soften the blow. I'm not sure he realizes that's only making things worse."

Maddy studied him for a moment. "He had us read your old college newsletter first for a reason. This has to have something to do with global warming. We knew it was a huge issue twenty years ago and did crap about it.

"He may say he's not angry with us, but I think he *is* punishing us.

Otherwise, if the point is wasted time, you'd think he'd get right on it. It doesn't make sense to stretch this out and put himself in danger at the same time."

"He's a kid," Burton said. "He probably doesn't think he's in danger. And obviously he had a plan that he worked out in advance, so he's just following that plan."

He was losing his patience with Maddy again. He did not want to get bogged down with things that should be addressed later, but it kept happening. He certainly could not say anything about her father or "abandonment issues." Besides being an oversimplification, it would make her furious.

He wondered for a moment if they should just get it out and over with. All this *not* being angry was a suck of energy. Seb said he was not mad at them, Burton was trying not to be angry with Maddy, and she was frustrated with Seb.

It was possible his wife was just a blunt person. Some people were built that way. Less than a month after they first met, his future wife told him his breath smelled, not all the time, but definitely that night. Doritos and beer. He thought it was funny. Not a year into their marriage, after more blunt comments, he began to think she might just be bad at assessing the impact of her words. Once she returned an article he asked her to proofread, with the word "NO" written in half a dozen places, underlined three times in each case. He asked her if she really thought it was necessary to write *NO* in all caps and underlined it three times. She said she didn't want him to miss them.

His wife remained lying on the bed, staring at the ceiling while they spoke.

"You're probably right," she said. "He doesn't know what he's doing. He does know how to hide, doesn't he?"

"Look at me," Burton said, slowly.

She rolled her head slowly on the bed to look at him, a blank look on her face.

"We're all confused," he said. "Of course we want to know why he's doing this, and we've got to try to figure it out, but we might not figure it out before he gets home. Even if he's acting strange, he's still the Seb we know. And that's how we're going to find him."

Burton was going to press the point harder but something occurred to him. He did not want to lose the thought just to win an argument.

They had been focusing on how Seb's emails could be used to find him. They would do the chicken dance if that would work. But they had to be very cautious about trying to manipulate him with their videos, because Seb wanted them to be honest. Burton was certain that Seb needed to know, above all, that he could trust them. Which did not mean that they should tell him everything. He did not need to know Maddy thought his garbage assignment was childish.

Burton had been lying on his side, looking at Maddy, throughout the conversation. He lowered himself to his back and rested his head on the mattress. They were now both staring at the ceiling. This was tough. They had to stay on the high road and keep a laser focus on their son's best interests.

"What Seb is talking about is serious," he said. "Email can sound cold, too. Maybe that's why his messages feel so hurtful."

"You're right," Maddy said softly. She put her fingers on his biceps and gave it a gentle squeeze.

They lay there for a couple of minutes not speaking, which was a relief. The house was silent. Burton wondered what Jessica was up to. Rosa was most likely in her bedroom doing whatever she did in there. She had stacks of paperbacks, so he assumed she was reading. One day, when things were back to normal, he would start up a conversation about books or something. Rosa was a big reader.

Maddy broke the silence. "What do you think it means that he didn't mention our video?" She must have sensed her earlier comments were a bit hard, because she said this quietly, so quietly that Burton could barely hear her.

It was true. Seb had not said a word about the video he asked them to post on YouTube.

"I don't know," Burton said. "Why have us do this and then not respond?"

"Do you think he wanted us to say something else? Maybe he was hoping we'd say what you wrote wasn't true."

Burton thought about this for a moment. "Or that we were doing environmental work we just hadn't told him about."

"Probably it's what you said before. He's got a script and he's reading from it."

They were still staring at the ceiling. Looking at nothing but white helped settle, a little, the jangle of thoughts in his mind. It had been their hope that Seb's reaction to their video would provide a clue to his whereabouts. But he only gave them another assignment. Hopefully the police or Phillip Geer would see, in his last email, something his parents could not see.

Burton wondered why Geer hadn't called yet. How long could it take for his software to work? It had been running when Seb's most recent message came in. Burton made sure of that.

He rolled onto his side and rested his cheek on the mattress. A strong floral scent filled his nostrils. Rosa must have brought her own detergent, washed the sheets, and put them back on the bed.

"I thought for sure Seb would be tired of this by now," he said. "Or that he would be scared and come home. Or we would find him. I never thought a fourteen-year old could go undetected for three days."

"The downside to having a clever child," Maddy said. She squeezed her eyes closed. It looked like she was fighting back tears. She opened them and said, "What if he's not ready to come back?"

"Meaning?"

"Seb seems to think he's on par with adults. If we force him to come back, what's going to keep him from going off again?"

"Us. The police." Burton said, his annoyance coming out this time. "He wouldn't get far."

"Don't jump on my back. I'm only trying to consider all the possibilities. I'm not saying we should call off the search."

"It's probably not even legal. Call off the search for a child."

Now Burton wanted to tell Maddy she was cold-hearted. Genetically cold. He turned to face the ceiling again.

"I never said anything about calling off the search. I just thought our son was kinder," Maddy said, her words trailing off. "What are we going to say to him when he comes home?"

That's not exactly the kind of question to ask when you don't want me to jump on your back, Burton thought.

"When he comes home," Burton said. "We tell him we love him."

"Of course we say that. Because we do and he needs to hear it more than ever. I'm not going to talk about this if you're going to give me that tone."

"We'll figure it out," Burton said with a sigh.

"I'm just saying we have to be prepared for when he gets home. He could walk in the door in fifteen minutes. We indulged him and he abused it. We have to assert our authority. Maybe not the minute he walks in the door, but we're going to have to deal with it pretty soon. I'm not saying we don't take some of the blame. And we will do everything possible to help him. Maybe there's no way to be prepared. I don't know."

Burton could tell his wife he agreed. She was right. They did need to be prepared to talk to Seb. But he said nothing. After a couple more minutes of staring at the ceiling in silence, she rolled over, this time with her back towards him.

This was not good. He and Maddy needed to be good.

He placed his palm at the center of her back and rubbed in a circular motion. This was a massage she liked. She did not stop him. With a pang, Burton remembered he was going to sit down with Jessica and see how she was holding up. Now it was too late. Hopefully she was asleep.

As Burton worked his hand between Maddy's shoulder blades, he wondered if she could sense a subtle difference in the massage. He was not sure if he was doing it for their children's sake only.

❧

The box of doughnuts Rosa got early on the morning of day four was still on the kitchen counter. Jessica must have left the lid open. Burton picked up a glazed one and took a big bite. It was stale but not bad. It was well past lunch and the first thing he had eaten all day. An audible gurgle emanated from his stomach.

He stuffed the rest of the doughnut into his mouth and pushed four styrofoam cups and the pink and orange box into his bag. They did not need to antagonize Seb by advertising styrofoam in the background of the video. Rosa was not participating in the garbage assignment.

A door upstairs slammed shut. Next came thumping on the stairs. After a final thump, Jessica came into the kitchen with a giant white bag. Not one of the smaller bags they each started out with. It clanked on the tile like a string of cans behind newlyweds driving away from the church.

"Let's put them on the coffee table," Burton said.

They carried the bags into the living room and sat next to each other on the couch. Her bag made a wide ball, while Burton's lay on its side, less than half full.

Jessica's bag was covered with words and images drawn in permanent marker. Red-petaled daisies, rectangles that were probably supposed to be laptops, blue butterflies. Long snakes wound in and around the words. "Trashy Trash" was written in thick black letters. Below that, in green, read: "Forced to be green by Seb Franck, eco-terrorist."

"Are those snakes?" Burton asked, suppressing a smile.

"Worms."

Maddy walked in to the kitchen and down the two stairs into the living room, holding her bag out in front of her like it smelled bad. She noticed Jessica's decorated bag, blinked, and a little smile crept onto her face. The first real smile Burton could recall seeing since Seb left.

90

Jessica jumped up. "I forgot something." She banged up the stairs to her room.

The dryer in the basement started to hum. Burton decided to buy Rosa some flowers. Wasn't doing a nice thing for someone how you got over resentments? She really deserved a token of appreciation for taking care of them.

"Nothing from Mr. Geer?" Maddy asked.

"No, and it's stressing me out. Could Seb have outwitted an M.I.T. computer scientist?"

"Maybe he's working on another case?"

"I don't get the feeling he has another case."

Jessica returned with a paper bag clinking as if there were marbles inside. She stuffed it into her big plastic bag.

"I guess I shouldn't call Seb a liberal poseur?" Maddy set her bag on the coffee table.

"What do you think?"

"I'm blowing off steam, Burton. You really think I would say that on a video that's supposed to make Seb want to come home?"

"I'm sure Jessica appreciates you saying things like that in front of her."

Jessica shrugged. "I don't know what it means, 'liberal poster.'"

"Your Dad's right," Maddy said. "I shouldn't have said it."

"What's a liberal post-errr?" Jessica squeezed her mother's forearm. "Poseur."

Jessica frowned and turned to her father.

"It comes from French," he said. "To pose. It means faker. I've thought about it too, Maddy. Whether Seb is just looking for something to make a stink about, to justify running off. But the fact is, he did run off."

"I think he really is upset about global warming," Jessica said. "Not faking."

"I do, too, Jess," Maddy said. "He asked us to be honest but that doesn't mean telling him every idea that pops into our heads."

Burton wished Maddy would stop talking. They had a video to make.

Rosa came up from the basement and seated herself in a chair by the sliding glass door, out of camera range. Burton went behind the tripod to make sure the line of the camera cleared the garbage bags on the coffee table. Jessica's was so high he could only see her head from the mouth up.

"What's that big thing in your bag, Mom?" Jessica poked at it with a finger.

"The box from a shirt I got delivered. I was kind of glad my bag was really empty. It made me look very green. I thought about leaving the box in our bedroom but Seb asked us to be honest, so in my bag it went."

"Dad's got a donut box in his." Jessica leaned back against the couch. "Seb wouldn't run away just to teach us not to get take-out, would he?"

"I hope not," Maddy said. "Why is your bag so full?"

"You'll see."

Jessica and her mother watched as Burton jogged over to the couch. "Camera's on," he said.

Burton sat between his wife and daughter. He set note cards he had prepared on the table behind his bag and glanced at them before beginning to speak.

"It's been four days, Seb," he said. "You've gotten our attention. We're listening, but we ask that you listen to us, too. If there is some reason why you can't come home, please at least let us know what it is, so we can do something about it.

"You can see how much we love you by the piles of garbage before us."

He held up a stack of index cards for the camera.

"I made notes. Our thoughts after the garbage experiment. We were surprised at how much garbage one person can throw out in a day. Also, what exactly it was we were throwing away. Creating garbage every day that is going to sit on the surface of the earth or float in the ocean for maybe a hundred years. Every day, seven billion people." Burton lifted his bag. "Making this much trash. At least in the wealthy countries."

He tilted his head towards Jessica. "Your sister reminded us we live on a huge planet. We realized finding a place to pile up our garbage is not our biggest issue. It's the pollution created to make this garbage, some of which we use for maybe five minutes." He lifted from the top of his bag one of the coffee cups Rosa brought back from the coffee shop. "Like this cup."

"There's the gas burned to cook the food, the fumes from the car to get the doughnuts, the heat or air conditioning in the factories and our own house. I'm sure you know we are in serious trouble if we don't start reducing the amount of fumes, like carbon dioxide and methane, that we put into the atmosphere. That's why we think you had us do this..." Burton could not recall the word for a second. "Assignment. To see how easy it is not to realize how much impact each of us has and even harder to see what all of humanity is doing."

Burton's hands were shaking. He dropped the next index card he was about to read. Jessica bent to get it.

"It's okay," he whispered and let the card lie there.

Burton stared at his notes. There were too many. Turmoil over food shortages in the Middle East linked to global warming. Dark earth and sea water that had been covered for thousands of years by snow and ice was now absorbing heat instead of reflecting it away. That was on top of the greater amount of heat being trapped due to air pollution. Which lead to more melting and more heat and so on. He should have read them out loud beforehand.

He shuffled the cards, looking for the one that listed countries already reducing their greenhouse gas emissions in a significant way.

Jessica jabbed him in the ribs. "Dad!"

"Sorry, Seb. Overboard on the notes. One thing we wanted to point out is that using energy and creating waste is unavoidable. It's a natural part of life. Three little people are not able to understand how much this world can sustain. Which is why we have to listen to the experts. Why we should already be listening to the experts. And they're saying there's no time to waste. The good news is—"

The garbage bag on the coffee table directly in front of Burton began to move. He looked down to see his bag sliding to the right of the table. His daughter was pushing it out of the way with her bag.

"Wanna know what's in my trash bag?" she asked.

Jessica pressed her body against her father's until he shifted to the right and squeezed up against Maddy. His daughter took his place at the center of where the camera was pointing. She grabbed the bottom of her bag, lifted and tipped it upside down. Its contents banged onto the coffee table. Several objects and papers fell onto the rug.

"Stupid hobbit books. Necklace with a soccer ball charm." She wiped her nose with the top of her hand. "Venus fly trap. I killed it. Killed the killer. Who gives a Venus fly trap to a vegetarian?" She punched her fist into the dry earth. The plastic pot cracked and dirt spilled onto the table. "Oh, and my birthday present." She felt around inside the bag and produced what looked like stained glass: a metal-lined circle of translucent blue with the marks of a peace sign on it in red. "Shrinky Dinks." She held the peace sign closer to the camera.

"Jess." Maddy put her hand on Jessica's thigh.

She pushed the hand away. Her hair kept falling in front of her face each time she leaned forward for emphasis. She thrust it out of the way impatiently.

"You ass. You didn't even do the project right. It's supposed to be a week that you carry your trash around with you. It's supposed to be like a big, heavy, smelly Santa sack over your shoulder. One day, who cares? Mom eats like a bird. Her bag's empty except for that shirt box and we didn't even go out shopping, 'cause you've got us all messed up, waiting for you."

Burton and Maddy leaned back to look at each other behind their daughter and raised their eyebrows at the same time. Burton decided Seb wanted honesty and he would let his sister say what she had to say. Maddy must have felt the same. They did not interfere.

Jessica pushed her bag and its remaining contents off the table. It hit the floor with a crash. She pretended not to notice. "I'm so schizo right now. I don't know if I'm mad because you went away or because of what you're doing to Mom and Dad or because you didn't take me with you."

Rosa, from her chair by the sliding glass door, said, "No, baby. Don't talk like that."

"I mean," Jessica continued, "I get it. I get what you're doing. Well, some of it. Being an activist." She blinked in the direction of the camera, as if waking out of a spell. "I just don't understand why you ... why you're making us feel like you're better than us. What did *you* do about global climate..." She noticed the Shrinky Dink in her hand and tossed it over her shoulder.

It shattered on the kitchen floor.

Burton waited a few seconds until it was clear Jessica was done.

"That's not exactly how we thought this was going to play out but it was honest, right? I don't think we could have planned it better. We want you to come home. We're a family. We love you like crazy. And we need your help with this climate stuff."

He left the couch to turn off the camera. Maddy followed him.

"Can you edit out Jessica's part?"

"I could."

"Maybe Seb should hear it all?"

"I say leave it."

Rosa walked to the couch and leaned down to wrap her arms around her granddaughter.

"Sorry, Grandma."

Rosa, with her arms still around Jessica, turned to look at Maddy. "How old is this girl?"

"She's twelve, Mom," Maddy said. "You know that."

"How can she say such things?"

"She reads a lot. She's smart."

94

"I think I don't like what she reads."

Burton did not feel like being a part of this conversation. He left the room. As he passed the bay window, the sky lit up with a flash. A boom followed a second later. It was the Fourth of July.

CHAPTER SIX

Inside the House

Day five was more of the same agonizing dead-ends until the phone rang a little before noon. The caller id showed "Phillip Geer."

Burton answered. "Hello, Mr. Geer. Would you mind holding on a sec? I want to get my wife."

"Of course. I mean, I don't. Mind."

He found Maddy at the table on the patio, talking on her phone.

"Phillip Geer just called," he said. "He's still on the line."

"Ah, I've got to run. Thank you so much."

She clicked off the call and looked up at him. The desperate hope on her face was painful to see.

"Let's go downstairs where we can talk," Burton said.

He went back into the house and down to the basement office. When Maddy joined him in there, he locked the door. Burton switched the phone to speaker and lowered the volume in case Jessica stationed herself outside the door.

"Okay, we're ready."

"I called to tell you the results of my analysis. It took longer than expected. My apologies."

Burton felt wobbly again. He leaned his elbows on the desk. Maddy assumed the same position beside him. It was dark in the basement office, because neither of them had turned on the light and not much of the morning sun made it through its one small window.

"Go ahead," Burton said.

"It's coming from within the house."

Maddy gasped.

"What does that mean?" Burton asked. "What are you talking about?"

"I mean..." Phillip faltered. "It's a figure of speech."

"What's inside the house?"

"I didn't mean...to alarm you."

"It's fine," Burton said.

"I'm so sorry. My friend likes to use this phrase."

"It's from a horror movie," Maddy said. "The police tell the babysitter the murderer is inside the house. The murderer is calling from the children's bedroom."

"Oh, no," Phillip said. "I'm so sorry. I didn't realize."

"Can we please stop talking about the frigging figure of speech?" Burton said.

"Yes, of course. I'm....yes. What I mean is the email is being routed through equipment in your house."

Burton stretched over to turn up the volume. Maddy caught his eye. Her bewildered look matched how he felt.

"What do you know? About routing through our house?" Burton asked.

"I believe there is a phone or a computer hidden in your house."

"You're sure?" Maddy asked.

"I'm sure. I don't suppose your son left his computer running?"

"No." Maddy and Burton said at the same time.

"I have to tell you, he is quite clever. Or has clever friends."

Burton did not appreciate the admiration in Phillip Geer's voice. He leaned closer to the speaker phone, tipping over a cup of pens in the process. He waited until the sound of rolling pens ceased. "How do you know this?"

"It's a proprietary process, I'm afraid."

"Please, Mr. Geer," Maddy said. "Help us understand what is going on."

A pause. "I sent various types of messages to the email address of your son's messages. I analyzed the automated responses that bounced back. I assumed the responses were coming from the person or company who was disguising and forwarding the messages. Eventually I realized that there was no person or computer re-routing his messages. The email address is junk. It finally came to me that your son was not using traditional email at all.

"He, or someone he knows, must have written a program to send messages with a fake address by way of the wireless internet network you use at home. This could only be done if the computer sending his fake emails was in the house, or at least within range of the wireless router. Possibly in your yard. That way he could avoid any possibility of being traced to where he is."

"And why?" Maddy asked. "Wouldn't stripping his identity through a foreign re-router be enough?"

"He may have suspected whoever was re-routing the email could be persuaded or forced to cooperate with the authorities because a child was involved."

Mr. Geer paused. They could hear him breathing through the speakerphone. He seemed agitated or excited by what he discovered. What he claimed to have discovered.

"I'm not sure how you know all this but if you're hacking government websites, just don't tell us," Burton said.

"My arsenal of tools are all legal. And I use technologies not limited to the internet. There, I've said more than I intended."

Arsenal of tools and a cup of tea and some scones.

After a pause, Phillip said, "This is a very sophisticated setup we are dealing with."

"I can see that," Maddy said. "It's a knife in the heart, too."

"Let's just find this computer," Burton said. "Obviously we need to find this computer, right?"

"I think so," Mr. Geer said. "My sense is that it's an actual computer, not a phone, because of the complex programming required. This is something to be grateful for. A phone could be hidden anywhere. Another thing in your favor: it is most likely connected to a power source. A very powerful battery might be used, but it would have to be big, and have a timer to turn it on and off. To last for days and days."

A thought occurred to Burton. If it were true, he would go to pieces. What if Jessica was sending the messages on Seb's behalf? Would she be willing to put on such an act? Looking scared and getting angry? Or was she so emotional precisely because she was involved? No, he decided, this was not possible. It was just a nightmare and not something that Maddy needed to hear.

"Should we tell Officer Quinn about this?" Maddy asked. "I can call him now."

Burton put his hand over the phone. "Let's find the computer and let Phillip examine it first. The cops might not let him touch it once they find out about it." He removed his hand from phone and said to the detective, "Do you think you could solve this mystery if you had access to the computer we're looking for?"

"Well," Phillip said. "It would certainly help."

❦

Maddy would search the basement. Burton the attic. Rosa the first floor. Jessica, the second. Rosa had the pots and pans cabinet open before the others were out of the kitchen.

Burton accompanied Maddy back down to the basement. Seb, or an accomplice, was not going to pop out of a closet, but the mere thought of such a thing prompted him to follow her down there.

The bottom of the steps presented three options. The workout/laundry room, the office, or the storage room.

"I think the storage room," Maddy said, stopping in front of its door.

The storage room was a huge, unfinished area spanning half the length of the house. They kept all sorts of infrequently used things in there, like Christmas decorations, luggage, camping gear, old furniture and all sorts of stuff Burton could not remember.

He came up behind his wife and put his arms around her. "I'll trade you the attic if you want."

She let her head fall back to his chest. "It's okay."

"You have your cell?"

"Uh huh. You?"

"Yes. We can use the walkie-talkie feature."

"Burt?" She asked, looking up at him from below, pressing the crown of her head into his chest as she arched her neck.

"Uh huh?"

"Do you have any better idea why he's doing this? Slowly revealing things? Giving us environmental lessons?"

"Only that it's definitely related to environmental issues. He's hit that hard in both assignments. Maybe you're right and he's mad at me for knowing so long ago and not doing very much about it. We'll find out as soon as we get that computer."

"I hope so." She let the weight of her body rest more fully against him. "This is too awful. What would make him do this? It can't just be about that article you wrote. I'm...I'm..."

Burton could feel her body shaking. He kissed the top of her head. "He clearly thinks he's justified but that doesn't mean he knows what he's doing."

100

"I feel guilty for feeling scared."

"Why?"

"I should be stronger?"

"Nothing's going to stop you. You don't have to worry about that."

His wife turned to face him. "We've got to get moving."

She kissed him on the cheek and headed for the storage room door. He started up the basement steps. Just before he reached the top, a crash sounded below. He flinched, but kept on. Maddy, he guessed, had grabbed a suitcase and shoved it out of the room, working her way in.

He passed the kitchen on his way to the second floor stairs. Rosa had already covered the kitchen table with cereal boxes, jars of food, dishes, and plastic containers. The empty cabinets with their doors open resembled a giant, empty dollhouse.

"I'm nervous," she said. "I don't know what I'm going to find and I might break it."

"Me too, Rosa. Me too."

When he got to the second floor, Jessica ran up to him.

"I'm searching my own room. Wouldn't it be messed up if he put the computer in there?"

"It would be his sense of humor."

He tickled her side and she giggled.

She watched him as he pulled on the string they used to open the stairs to the attic. One end of a rectangular cut-out in the ceiling descended while the other end was held in place by a hinge. A folded staircase was mounted on the other side of it. Burton pushed down until the hinge locked with a click. A wave of hot air poured down onto him. He unfolded the stairs and set their bottom edge on the floor. It was not much more than a ladder.

"Seb, are you up there?" Jessica whispered into the attic space above.

Burton put a foot on the first of the narrow slats that served as steps. The stairs creaked and bent at the hinge. He waited a moment before taking a couple more steps.

He looked down at his daughter.

"Your Mom and I can take care of this," Burton said. "Why don't you let Gramma take you over to Dorrie's house? It's only two blocks away. We can come get you any time."

"You guys can stop trying to protect me. I would feel strange not knowing what was going on, even though you won't tell me everything. I'm not too worried, anyway. Seb always gets away with things."

He and Maddy had concluded that Jessica would be more upset being separated from them than she would be by being around while they dealt with getting Seb back home. She did not have to be there, though, while they searched the house for something she did not really understand.

"How about just a little break until we find this machine?"

"No, I don't want to. Please? I want to help."

A grin creeped over Jessica's face.

"What are you smiling about?"

"I was thinking about Grandma Rosa trying to spank Seb when he gets home."

"You know that's not going to happen." He paused. "Promise me you'll let me know if you need a break. Dorrie's mom said you could come over whenever you wanted. Even late at night."

"Okay. I will."

Burton climbed the rest of the steps and looked around. The underside of the angled roof above him was nothing more than exposed beams and boards with nails sticking through. The floor was a series of plywood sheets laid end to end. Yellow fiberglass insulation showed through the gaps between the plywood. There was dust on everything and specks of it floated in the air.

He found a light socket affixed to the beam at the apex of the house and pulled its chain. At close range, the light was painfully bright, but it barely lit the far ends of the attic.

There were boxes everywhere, except at the front and back of the house, where the sloping ceiling was too low. The attic at its highest point was not high enough for him to stand erect. His back was going to kill him, unless he found the damn computer soon.

It was so dry and hot up there Burton's nose itched. The insulation below the floor kept the heat in and prevented the house's cooler air from penetrating. The only thing separating him from the sun was the thin roof.

He lifted his shirt to take it off. When he saw how his stomach was pushed into folds by his jeans, he decided to keep it on. A washboard stomach on a man nearly forty was not to be expected, but he did not want to keep seeing the folds.

The attic contained what they were not ready to throw away and what Maddy called "museum pieces." Jessica and Seb loved to dig through the boxes. They especially loved the photos of their younger parents and relatives and the crazy clothes they wore. Once in a while they would come downstairs laughing at a lopsided, leaky clay cup or some other work of art they made as toddlers.

Some boxes had gone straight from the attic of their previous house to the attic of this house. At least they had been smart enough to leave the heavy boxes of textbooks at the curb during the last move. Too bad *The Rodent* newsletter had not been in one of those boxes.

Burton took a step back and hit his head on a beam. "Dammit."

"Dad?"

He walked over to the attic hatch and looked down.

Jessica's peered up at him. "What happened?"

"Hit my head. What are you doing?"

"I'm going to your room to look."

"Okay."

Burton went back where most of the cardboard boxes had been placed. He opened the folded flaps of the box nearest to him. His mother's cut-glass punch bowl lay inside, on top of a pink, flower-printed curtain. It had a noticeable crack near the top rim. She was gone five years now, his mother, and his father, what was it? Nine years already. Burton and Maddy had never used the punch bowl and neither had his mother. She just wanted to have fun with her family, serving iced tea from a giant glass jar with a spout that she brewed by placing the jar in the sun.

He remembered the day she gave him the punch bowl. "We don't socialize with people who need to be served from a punch bowl, do we? I think you're just being nice, taking it off my hands."

She would want him to get rid of it. "The thing is cracked, Burtie, cracked."

He set the box with the punch bowl away from the other boxes. All things that needed to be tossed would go there. Maddy could look through them if she wanted to. Most likely whatever Burton set aside would remain in the attic until the next time they moved to a new house.

A muffled shout came from below. Burton thought he heard the words "clothes in your closet." He suddenly remembered the tiny pink panties with the strategic smile he gave to Maddy a few months ago. Jessica did not need to see them. He knelt near the attic hatch and shouted down. "Don't worry about the clothes, Jess. You can let Mom go through our stuff."

"Ha, ha. Okay, Dad."

"Why don't you see what's in Seb's room?"

"Oh, all right."

He heard her giggle as she passed underneath, on her way to her brother's room. He was glad to hear her laugh, that she could forget, for a moment, what they were dealing with.

Inside the next box was the *Lazy Student's Cookbook*. He picked it up. A dog-eared page contained the advice "Adding a slice of ham will make boring grilled cheese totally radical." The book went to the "useless" area with a toss. And, he told himself, no more reading.

He pushed his hand deeper into the box, feeling around for a computer-like shape. A toy quacked. His finger struck something hard. He grabbed a hold and pulled it out. A child-sized bicycle helmet.

Another thing they would never use again, but it was good to see. Seb used to be crazy about biking. Maybe he was off on a bike somewhere now. He had dropped biking for skateboarding, but you could not skateboard very far.

A red sticker caught his attention. He turned the helmet around. It was the logo of the local Down syndrome association. Next to that sticker was the remnants of another sticker which had enough of it remaining for Burton to recognize "Tour de France."

When Seb was ten, he decided to be the youngest person ever to compete in the Tour de France. A week after he learned what kind of training the Tour de France required, he announced he had signed up for something else. He was going to be the honorary co-person (he meant chairperson) of the Down syndrome association bike-a-thon. His friend Charlie's sister had Down syndrome and her mother was the leader of the local DS association.

The DS bike-a-thon would be ten miles long.

They were at the dinner table that evening. Jessica had already gone upstairs. His parents used to require that everyone stay at the table until all members of the family had finished eating, but Seb just took too long. He ate slowly and talked a lot.

"I'm sorry," Burton said. "It was nice of you to offer to help with the DS bike-a-thon, but you know you can't have any new activities until the 'needs improvements' on your report card go away."

"But I told Mrs. Williams I would do it. It was my idea, to have one kid with DS and one kid who doesn't because that's include...inclusion. That's how I got to be co-person."

"Don't they already do a Buddy Walk?" Maddy asked. "Anyway, your father's right. You'll have to tell Mrs. Williams you can't do it."

"This isn't an activity. This is special work." Their son meant social work.

"Your grades are your special work right now," Maddy said, walking towards the phone they kept on a little shelf near the kitchen thermostat. "I'm going to call Lisa Williams."

Seb looked down at his plate. Burton could see he was trying not to cry.

"Hi Lisa? It's Maddy Franck. Oh, good. We just heard about the bike-a-thon."

Their son began to get up from his seat.

Maddy put her hand over the mouthpiece. "Stay put, Mister."

Seb lowered himself slowly into the chair, slumping all the way until his chin rested on the table.

"Just today?" His mother said. "Ordinarily we'd be happy to do it, but we have some restrictions due to the last report card."

While Maddy listened to Mrs. Williams's response, she shrugged her shoulders at Seb. He slid completely under the table.

"It is sweet of him. Thanks. We'd be happy to. If we're still into biking next year."

They thought that was the end of it. A few days later, Maddy found Burton in the basement office.

"Seb left his journal open on his desk," she said. "I meant to look away, but the letters were so big."

"Uh huh?"

"*Mean Parents* was written across the top of the page. *A novel and a true story.* And get this, the next line says, *Coming Soon from Random House.*"

They both laughed.

Maddy shook her head. "Oh, but he goes on. There's a byline, too. *The story of the parents against disabilities.*"

"Are we going to talk about this?"

"No. Let the little bugger write it. I don't think we have to worry about Random House."

Burton realized he was kneeling with the little bike helmet in his hand. His knees hurt from pressing against the plywood. He set the helmet back in the box and covered it with the toys and books he'd taken out. He switched to squatting with his forearms resting on his thighs.

The next two boxes he looked through contained nothing but children's books. He pushed these into the potential trash area. The squatting position hurt even more than kneeling. He sat on the floor. His T-shirt was soaked through with sweat.

An hour later, the phone near him began to beep.

"Hello?" Maddy's voice echoed.

He picked up his phone but could not remember how to use the walkie-talkie mode. He tried a couple different buttons.

"Hi. Hi?"

Maddy started speaking over him. "I didn't find anything."

"Me neither," he said.

"I can't hear you. I'm going to the kitchen for a quick coffee if you want to meet me. Maybe we're not doing this in the most efficient way."

Burton climbed down the ladder. He looked in at Seb's room. Jessica lay on her stomach on the floor, reading an old notebook of Seb's. The wooden box Seb built to store private things lay next to her, the latch and padlock pried off. A hammer lay next to these.

He went downstairs to the kitchen and found Rosa with the refrigerator door open. She hid a wet rag behind her back when she saw him. She had been cleaning the refrigerator. He smiled. She shrugged.

"Is it coffee time?" Rosa asked. "Sit down. I'll make it."

"Thank you."

Burton sat at the kitchen table. Rosa leaned in front of him to remove a bag of coffee from the mass of food and dishes there.

Maddy came up from the basement.

"Did you finish in the storage room?" Burton asked.

"I think so. There's nothing plugged in down there."

"Huh." Burton had forgotten what Phillip Geer told them about the equipment needing to be plugged in. Pretty stupid to waste all that time going through boxes in the attic. He supposed a cord could have been run through a hole punched into the side of a box and Mr. Geer did say it was possible Seb was using a super-battery. Burton was starting to lose hope. Maybe there was no computer in the house.

Rosa poured water into the coffee maker and poked her finger at several buttons before the machine began to gurgle.

"Maybe Seb put solar power on the roof," Rosa said.

"Good thinking," Burton said. "We should look up there."

Maddy got up from the table and skipped over the two steps to the living room. She went out to the patio through the sliding glass door. She disappeared from view and reappeared at the door minute later.

She returned to the kitchen.

"I didn't see anything."

Burton set his elbows on the table and leaned forward to rest his chin on his clasped hands. "This is unreal."

Rosa had apparently emptied the refrigerator during her search of the kitchen. She came to the table and took a pickle jar and a milk jug back to the refrigerator. Maddy and Burton watched her as she emptied the table of food. The coffee maker hissed. They were taking a coffee break and Seb was getting farther and farther away.

Rosa closed the refrigerator door and said, "I'm going to go look in the garage. I got a feeling about the garage." She stopped in front of the door to the garage and made the sign of the cross. The door swung open and she disappeared.

Maddy got up, poured coffee, and delivered two cups to the kitchen table. She went to the refrigerator next, took out a container of cottage cheese, retrieved two spoons from the drawer and returned to the table. She and Burton ate out of the container.

"I never asked you what you heard from your clients," Burton said.

"They're using a temp agency and put the rest on hold. They can wait. This can't go on much longer."

They took a sip of coffee at the same time and found themselves eye to eye over the rims of their mugs. Maddy's eyes were bloodshot. Insomnia had been a problem for her since she was a teenager. On occasion, when Burton woke up alone in bed, he found her in the living room with a book. She had learned to get by on less sleep but they had hardly slept at all since Seb disappeared.

Burton thought of Maddy's father yet again. Although it was worry about Seb that was keeping her awake, her intensity and her drive probably made it worse. At least some of this had to do with being left alone with Rosa when she was just a kid. When this was all over, Burton was going to call that man and give him hell.

"What are you thinking about?" Maddy asked.

Before Burton could come up with an answer, a door slammed upstairs.

"Dad! Mom!"

It was Jessica.

Burton and Maddy dropped their coffee mugs. One tipped and poured coffee onto the floor. They left it and rushed out of the kitchen. The door between the garage and the kitchen slammed just as they hit the stairs. A second later, they heard Rosa breathing heavily behind them.

Jessica was standing in front of the closet in Seb's room. Its sliding door was pushed all the way to the right so that the left half was completely exposed. The closet was empty.

Burton, Maddy and Rosa all looked towards Seb's bed at the same time. It was covered with clothes, shoes and soccer gear.

"I got a little excited and just took everything out."

Jessica's face shone with perspiration.

107

Maddy, Rosa and Burton all turned from looking at the mound of stuff on Seb's bed to face her.

"I noticed the smell. That's why I cleaned out the closet. Can you smell it?"

Rosa went into the closet sniffing. "Oh, yes. Paint. And something else."

Burton and Maddy stuck their heads in. The paint smell was accompanied by a bit of cologne.

"He left a stick of deodorant in there," Jessica said. "With the cover off."

"Want me to get a flashlight?" Rosa asked.

"We don't need one," Jessica said. She pointed to the side wall of the closet. "You see?"

Maddy leaned closer to the wall. "What are we looking at? Oh..."

"The color on this wall is different from the others." Jessica said. "Right? Or cleaner. Except for these pieces of tape." She tugged at a strip of transparent tape on the wall.

"His Yoda poster used to be there," Maddy said.

The Yoda poster had hung above Seb's headboard for years. It came down two years ago, to avoid embarrassment when friends came over, but he had not been able to get rid of it, and taped it up in his closet.

"I took the Yoda poster down," Jessica said. "After I noticed the paint smell. That's when I saw the line in the wall."

All eyes followed Jessica's finger to where it pointed at a razor-thin indentation running horizontally across the wall of the closet. It then became clear that the indentation formed a three-foot square in the middle of the newly painted section of the wall. The indentation was very subtle. It was right where Seb's Yoda poster had been since the day it was relegated to the closet.

Maddy ran a fingernail along the indentation. "Oh, Seb."

Burton recalled smelling paint coming from Seb's room a few nights before he went off to the Buddhist monastery. Seb was always constructing something. How could they have known about this? A few months earlier, Seb had built and painted a two-level lounge for Myro, although chubby Myro never went onto the second level.

"Should we call Phillip?" Maddy asked.

"We might as well see what's behind this wall first," Burton said. "I think I should cut through it, right now."

"Be careful," Maddy said.

Burton smirked before he could stop himself.

"I know you will," she said.

Rosa, Maddy and Jessica stepped backwards to let Burton pass out of the closet. He went to the basement to get a box cutter and his toolbox. The three watched in silence as he re-entered the room and stooped in the closet. He set the toolbox on the floor just outside the doorframe.

"Jess, will you be my assistant?"

She nodded, knelt, and opened the toolbox.

He pressed the blade of the box cutter into the top of the right-hand vertical indentation and pushed until it broke through with a pop. Burton could feel sweat trickling over his temples. He pushed down on the blade and it sliced through easily. He no longer doubted one bit that they had found what they were searching for.

After the right-hand side was cut, Burton brushed white dust off his fingers, then continued across the bottom, up the left side, and across the top. The newly cut piece of wall board remained in place.

"Screwdriver? Regular, not Phillips."

Jessica knelt again and chose the perfect screwdriver, thin with a broad head. He placed the tip of the screwdriver at the top-center, pushed it in, and pulled back. The piece of sheetrock began to detach from the wall. When an inch of space opened up at the top, he stopped. Rosa tugged Jessica backwards.

"Mad, would you please turn the light off?"

A second later, the room darkened. A glow appeared in the strip of space exposed at the top of the square.

"*Dios mío,*" Rosa said.

"Okay, light back on."

Burton came out of the closet with white powder on his hands, chest and thighs.

"This might be a little messy so you might want to stand by the bed."

The group of three moved back a few steps.

Burton resumed his position in front of the cut. He slid the fingers of both hands inside the opening and pulled hard. The top half came loose and fell against his chest. Another tug and the whole piece came completely free. Dust and chunks of sheetrock fell around him. He took the square of sheetrock out of the closet, carried it into the hall and leaned it against the wall.

"Come on out here with me," he said. "Let's wait for the dust to settle for a few minutes."

They left the room, Maddy following close to Burton. He could tell she was trying to read from his eyes whether he was upset by anything he saw in there.

He closed the door and went to the bathroom to wash off the dust. He came back to three scared-looking people standing next to Seb's door. Maddy put her hand on the knob and he nodded. They went straight to the closet with Maddy in the lead. The four of them squeezed inside.

A small laptop computer was in there. It rested on a wooden board in between two vertical studs. A piece of paper had been taped over the computer's screen. The paper was white but appeared light blue due to whatever was being displayed on the screen behind it. In the space between the next vertical stud to the right a flat, silver box rested on another wooden board. Several wires extended behind these machines and down the wall behind them.

The board on which the computer rested was held up by two columns of red bricks. Burton recognized the white PVC pipes underneath this equipment as plumbing for the bathroom. The bathroom was the room next to Seb's.

A change in light caught his attention. The glowing paper taped over the screen had turned green. A screen saver, it seemed. The computer; the strange flickering, silver box; the wires and the whole assembly looked like something a terrorist would put together.

Burton tapped Rosa on the shoulder. "Excuse me, mother-in-law."

She gave him a faint smile and stepped aside.

He stuck his head inside the hole. Its cave-like smell, probably from bathroom moisture, made his nose itch. Maddy's head appeared in the hole next to his. She held herself there by leaning a shoulder into Burton's biceps.

The paper covering the screen turned yellow. Handwriting became visible. Burton reached for the paper but Maddy stopped him by placing her hand over his.

The words, written in black with marker, he recognized immediately as Seb's handwriting:

> *I figured you might find this eventually. Please don't touch the computer. The emails are coming from here. Doing anything with the computer will make them stop. I might as well tell you now. I wrote the messages and assignments before I left. They are set up to come out on a schedule. I know you want to get in and see the messages but please don't try that. If you mess with the computer, the messages will be deleted, and this is my only way of talking to you. Seb.*

Maddy turned away, her eyes wet. "Who the hell hurt him?"

"We've got bigger problems than that," Burton said.

Jessica squeezed in between them. The paper turned light purple as the screen changed color again. She lifted the note over the screen. The screen showed only a solid purple color, no text or images.

"He's not really emailing us." Jessica said, letting the paper drop over the screen.

"It's sickening," Maddy said. She sounded on the verge of sobbing. "He could really be in trouble and we'd have no idea."

"Let's go," Burton said.

Jessica was taking air in little gulps and blinking away tears. They should not have let her see this. It was strange and scary. What choice did they have, though? She had been the one who found the computer. They should have at least calmed her before going in and staring at the machines.

Maddy put her hands on Jessica's shoulders and gently turned her around. "C'mon, hon. This is actually good. We solved one big mystery and now we can focus on looking in the right place."

She led Jessica away from the closet and out of Seb's room, with Rosa close behind.

Burton was nearly out of the room himself when it occurred to him to check something. He switched on the flashlight and ducked back into the closet. The others seemed not to notice, their feet shuffling down the steps. Burton scanned the interior of the hole with the flashlight beam. Only when he stuck his head in as far as he could without hitting the laptop, did he find what he was looking for. A bare metal electrical box with a white plastic cover was suspended by a screw from one of the wall studs near the bottom of the space. Two cords were plugged into it.

Burton watched a piece of lasagna fall off his fork. "I hope Mr. Geer didn't get stuck in traffic."

Mounds of lasagna sat uneaten on all four plates. Jessica chewed on the corner of a piece of garlic bread.

Maddy set her still-clean fork down. "Did he say anything about what we found in the closet?"

"He said he wants to look at it first. "

Burton lowered the fork slowly, trying not to make any noise when it touched the plate. The equipment in the closet bothered him, for reasons that may not have occurred to Maddy. He was not sure what to do.

"What?" Maddy squinted at him. "What else?"

"I've got to talk to you."

"Don't fight," Jessica said.

Burton got up from the table. "Let's go to Seb's room."

Maddy gave Jessica an "it's okay" smile before standing. Burton heard her precise, hard footfalls on the steps behind him and she was not even wearing shoes. He went into Seb's room and waited for her to meet him by the closet.

"So Mr. Geer was right," she said. "This time."

"He was right. To be honest, I had my doubts, especially after he was wrong about the emails being relayed through a foreign country."

"Who knows when we would have found this thing if he wasn't helping us."

Maddy slipped by him, into the closet, and leaned in near the note taped over the computer screen. Burton bent down to fit under the clothes pole that ran overhead and squeezed in next to her. They read once again the note's cold warning not to do anything with the computer.

He slid a finger under the paper and lifted it up. The screen changed from purple to blue and he flinched, thinking for a moment that he had accidentally caused the computer to do something.

"It's not like the thing will self-destruct if we take this paper off," he said. "It's held by scotch tape."

"No, but we should leave it for Mr. Geer." Maddy turned to him. "What did you want to talk about?"

They were less than a foot apart. He could smell her orange-scented skin lotion.

"Let's get out of the closet so I can stand up."

Maddy walked over to Seb's bookcase and he followed. A picture frame on the top shelf had fallen over. Burton lifted it and set it upright again. It was a photo of their dachshund dressed in a penguin costume with Seb and Jessica, on either side of him, each holding one of his front paws so he stood, awkwardly, like a penguin. A wave of sadness hit him and then, dread.

"Seb ran wiring in there," he said, looking directly Maddy's eyes. "Electrical wiring. He could have burned the house down and us with it."

Maddy had been gazing at the photo, too, but switched abruptly to meet his eyes. He thought she would respond. When she did not, he figured she wanted him to be the one to deliver the tough love this time.

"I don't know about you but I feel like making a video and telling him he could have burned the house down and killed us all by running electrical wires in there. That might get through to him. Or, it could backfire."

Maddy nodded and waited for him again.

"Just now I was wondering if the police might not look as hard for him, thinking he's a spoiled brat. They have abused children to save. That's crazy, though, right?"

"Everything's crazy right now." She put a hand on his shoulder. "My feeling is we don't want to give him more reasons to feel uncomfortable about the thought of coming home. But let's see what Officer Quinn says."

Her hand on his shoulder felt good. Really good.

"Something could happen to him," Burton said. "Could have already happened to him, and these messages would keep coming."

Maddy nodded and stepped closer. She put her arms around him and rested the side of her head on his chest. He put his arms around her and held her tight.

Phillip Geer called from his car an hour later. He had missed two of the three shortcuts they advised him to take to avoid the worst of rush hour. Burton ended up on the phone with him for twenty minutes before they heard the muffler of a car in the driveway.

"I'll go meet him," Burton said. "Let's not surround him on the front steps."

He opened the door to see a young, dark-skinned man standing on the welcome mat. The man appeared to be Indian or Pakistani. He was wearing a blue, short-sleeve polo, which was tucked into khakis, and a brown belt to match his brown loafers. A backpack dangled from one shoulder and his hands were in his pockets. He looked like a teenager.

Burton felt stupid. "La-de-da" and a cup of Dar Jeeling and all his other pathetic jokes. He had been to M.I.T. many times. There were a lot of Asians there. Millions of non-white people spoke English with a British accent. He had assumed Phillip was a white, scone-eating stereotype. Nice.

He held the screen door open. "Hello, Mr. Geer. Come on in."

Mr. Geer stepped in. Burton began the process of atoning with a warm handshake and a pat on the back.

"Thank you so much for coming on such short notice."

"It's not a problem. I understand. Please call me Phillip."

"Phillip, come back and meet the rest of the family."

They passed through the foyer with the opposing white love seats. The staging area that Jehovah's Witnesses, girl scouts with cookies, and other strangers never got beyond. They had only known Mr. Geer, Phillip, by way of a few phone calls and emails over the past four days, but he did not feel like a stranger.

Burton led him to the kitchen.

Phillip cleared his throat. "It was a laptop?"

"Yes," Burton said. "An old laptop we forgot about. It used to be in a box of phones and computer things in the basement."

Maddy, Jessica and Rosa were in the final stages of putting the kitchen war room materials into neater piles.

"Everybody, this is Phillip. Phillip, this is my family. My wife Maddy, my daughter Jessica and Maddy's mother, Rosa."

"Hello," said Maddy and Rosa in unison.

A beat later, Jessica said, "Hi."

"Hello everybody. Nice to meet you. I'm very sorry I'm so late."

"Don't worry about it," Maddy said. "Can I get you something to drink? Or maybe some lasagna? You had a long drive."

"No, thank you. It looks delicious, though."

Jessica seemed to be trying to hide a smile. Burton assumed it was Phillip's British accent.

"We should get to it then," Burton said. "Come see...come see for yourself. It's upstairs."

He walked to the staircase and Phillip followed. When Maddy, Jessica and Rosa clomped up the stairs behind him, Phillip must have known he would be working with eight eyes watching.

They stopped in front of Seb's room. For some reason, no one moved or said anything. Phillip took this as a cue to go in first. They had not intended to spook Phillip with the eerie glow from the closet, but there it was. Maddy flipped the switch to turn on the ceiling lamp in the bedroom.

Jessica and Rosa moved towards Seb's bed. Burton and Maddy stood to the side of the open closet.

"That's it, Mr. Geer," Burton said. "Phillip."

The young man walked in and stooped before the hole in the wall. The paper turned from yellow to red as if sending a signal to the new visitor.

"There's a note on the paper. You'll be able to read it in a minute, when the screen saver color changes."

"Here's a flashlight," Maddy said.

"Thank you."

Phillip moved closer to the hole. He studied the interior for several minutes before coming out of the closet.

Lines of white dust marked the young man's blue polo. His eyes had watered up. Burton could see this was a person who was not good at disguising his feelings.

"I'm sorry," Phillip said.

"What's wrong?" Maddy asked.

"What I told you originally was not correct. I've not seen this before."

Burton nodded. "Do you know anything more, now that you've seen it?"

"I'd like to check something first. It won't trigger any response from the computer."

"Of course."

Phillip removed a gadget from his backpack and rested it on his thigh. It appeared to be a hand-made miniature computer the size of a paperback. The front half was glass and the back, gray metal. The glass screen looked like a little car dashboard, with a dial and red digital numbers. Phillip tapped and slid his finger on one side of the screen. Letters and numbers flickered.

"We can sit if you like," Burton said.

He pulled the rolling chair away from the desk and moved it near Seb's bed. Phillip lowered himself into the chair while continuing to move his finger around the little gadget's screen. Maddy motioned for her mother to sit in Jessica's desk chair, which had been brought in earlier. Maddy sat in a folding chair. Burton and Jessica lowered themselves into the only space on Seb's bed not covered with clothes. Phillip was now surrounded.

He moved his finger over the screen for another minute and then looked up.

"The small, silver box is a backup battery. There is a battery in the laptop, of course. The primary power source, however, is electricity through the power cord. Have you noticed the outlet underneath the plumbing?"

"We did," Burton said. "It has to be new. There would be no reason to have a plug behind the wall, between the tub and the closet."

"Yes, the outlet is new. It appears someone with knowledge of electrical systems made a connection to existing wiring. Did your son have this kind of knowledge?"

"Who the hell knows?" Burton said.

Burton wondered how many mistakes in parenting they had made. Should they have monitored Seb's spending more closely? His allowance always went to computer parts or skateboard stuff but just as often he salvaged computer parts from old machines people left out on garbage night.

"To quote a professor of mine," Phillip said, "what we have here is robust and redundant. And that was at M.I.T."

Phillip may have said this at one time with admiration in his voice but he had been chastened. It seemed likely he mentioned his qualifications now purely to reassure them. He scanned the four strangers in front of him briefly before continuing.

"This setup can withstand most contingencies and keep going. Your son is good. I'm sorry." He looked down for a moment before directing his gaze to Burton. "I did not expect being here to be so difficult. Please excuse me. I'm sure it's much more difficult for you."

Burton shook his head. "Don't apologize."

"You see, I left England when I was twelve years old to attend school in the U.S. I was miserable being separated from my parents, and they were unhappy, too. We survived. I called them via computer every day. Children are resilient, if that helps you. But I do feel bad about letting you down. You have such a nice family."

"You did not let us down, Mr. Geer." Maddy said. "You've done a wonderful job. We would never have guessed about..." Her eyes went to the closet. "We really appreciate what you've done."

She leaned forward and squeezed Phillip's hand. He looked a little uncomfortable. She let his hand go a couple seconds later and straightened up.

"Do you think he's communicating with this computer?" she asked. "To confirm that it's working? Or maybe to add something he didn't think to say?"

Phillip did not answer right away. "Based on his note, knowing the computer might be found, I don't think he would risk leaving a record of his location by communicating with it. That's the whole point of scheduling the emails in advance. To leave zero traces."

"Can you get into the computer without setting off Seb's booby trap?" Burton asked. "Or is this a bluff? Do you think it's possible our son could have programmed this to permanently erase his messages if someone tried to read them?"

"It's possible. Such a thing would require very sophisticated programming, though. For the time being, I would recommend leaving the computer alone. Your son has been very thorough so far."

Maddy waved a hand in the direction of the closet. "If the booby trap is real, and the messages got deleted, could you recover them? My understanding is that it's hard to erase something completely from a computer. The reason I ask is that we might be able to find him, to intercept him, if we could see the future messages."

"You are correct that merely emptying the trash is not enough to keep information from a professional. I once recovered information from a computer that was set on fire. I set it on fire myself, actually." Phillip shook his head, as if to shake off his bragging. "We have to consider that your son could be clever enough to delete information completely. If he has indeed boobied the computer."

Burton smiled a bit at Phillip's mangling of "booby-trap." The smile faded quickly. Here was a young man completely devoted to his parents. Their "internet detective" would probably never do what Seb had done. If their son was not in such grave danger, Burton would be embarrassed.

"We wanted to make sure you got a chance to examine this...setup before we contacted the police," Maddy said. "They might not let you have access after this. Since you're not going to touch it, I'd like to give them a call."

Phillip stood. "Of course. I can still continue to work on this case if you like. It's a first for me so I'd need to do some more research. You can call or email me any time. I won't charge. Unless it takes more than half an hour. Then I will need to charge. My father would be unhappy otherwise."

"We'll pay for any time you give us," Maddy said.

CHAPTER SEVEN

WHAT?

THE WOODPECKER EMAIL ALERT sounded from downstairs. Burton glanced at the clock on the nightstand. Eight in the morning. He ordinarily woke up earlier, without an alarm clock, and was annoyed. They had forgotten to bring the laptop to the bedroom. The woodpecker Seb-alert was coming from downstairs.

He jumped out of bed and made for the door, hoping to retrieve the computer before the alarm repeated a minute later and woke Jessica.

"Is it Seb?" Maddy called from the bed.

"Yes. New message."

She tossed the bed covers off. Burton ran downstairs dressed in his pajama bottoms only. He found Rosa in the living room, curled into a ball on the recliner, asleep. He leaned over the computer on the coffee table and hit the mute button. Maddy came up behind him.

"I can't believe she slept through that," she whispered.

"We should have woken her before we went to bed."

Rosa's lip trembled. A snore passed through her open mouth. If she was not asleep, she was a very good actor.

Burton took the laptop with him to the basement office, with Maddy following. They sat on the cold leather couch. He rested the computer on one of his thighs and one of hers.

The subject of the new message, in bold, was *"Assignment number*

119

three—not for Je..."

The column was not wide enough to show the full subject. The date shown, July 7, marked exactly one week since Seb's first email. One week completely out of touch. Prior to learning these were canned emails they had the consolation that he was doing well enough to keep in touch. They had no such consolation now.

"I don't think I'm ready for this," Maddy said.

Her leg trembled, making her side of the laptop rise up and down. Burton clicked to open the message. It filled the screen. They could now read the full subject line: *Assignment number three—not for Jess.* Below this was something that looked like a poem.

What?

I will just disappear?
Some day lose everything?

At first I thought, that's bad news
Then I wondered if it really was
Because here is getting crazy
And
Heaven sounds boring

What can I do?

Pandora's box
Brain cracked
Now I know
Why adults lie

The End
(of the poem)

I'm trying not to go crazy.

The reason I had you do the garbage collecting assignment was so you could see what's going on with my brain. It won't stop. I know garbage is normal but there seems to be so much crap. I can't stop thinking about global warming every time I see all our crap. Which is all day long. Not just garbage at the side of the road. I know it's a little crazy, but every time I see plastic, especially some stupid plastic toy that gets broken right away or dumped in a closet, I think this plastic crap is going to last forever. Is that worth it? And then there's cars. You can't get away from them. If I can't see them or smell them, I can hear them. And there's only one person in most of the cars. All making global warming worse.

Global warming is in the news, people talk about it, they recycle maybe, they have big meetings, but we still seem to be going down the tubes. People aren't taking it seriously. Just like you said way back when, Dad. Our whole country should be getting into it big time, like they did in World War Two. But that is definitely not happening. Why? I don't get it. Even the pope said we are committing suicide. How scary is that? I think maybe I'm already crazy and it's too late.

Sometimes I think I'm just trying to get back through the crack in my brain. Back to the kid who didn't know about this stuff. I wish we studied the myth of Pandora in English before I ever went on the internet.

For the YouTube video, just say you got this message. Please don't talk about my crazy mind and how it's not crazy or that I have good reasons or any of that.

Call it Pandora's Box and the Kid, so Jess doesn't find it when she searches for Franck Family Video, which she will do. I don't want her to know about the poem. And you shouldn't leave this laptop where she can find it, since you're probably saving my messages. For evidence or whatever.

Seb

The message on the screen was still moving up and down in time with Maddy's shaking leg.

She let out a long breath.

"I know," Burton said. "I know. At least there's some hope in there. He's trying to get himself back to the kid he was before. The one who was not so upset."

"That's true. But I get this awful feeling he thinks it's going to take a while."

"He might," Burton said, "but we're going to find him first. Then we can help him."

They could not respond, as Seb asked, with only "we got your message." To not respond to such struggle, to such pain, would be irresponsible parenting. And they needed to say more than just "We love you." The trick would be to convince Seb he could cope better with their help without patronizing him.

Burton and Maddy remained on the couch staring at the email. The nervous bouncing of Maddy's leg had stopped. It was a hell of a lot to absorb.

She forwarded the email to the detectives. Then the two of them sat there re-reading it. There was nothing specific about where Seb was or what he was doing, as had been the case with his previous emails. This message was particularly hard to deal with because they now knew it was at least a week old. They had to consider that their son might be somewhere different than where planned to be. He may have run into problems.

"I see at least two clues here," Burton said.

Maddy nodded. "He felt so overwhelmed in his own home. In our neighborhood. I hate the idea that he felt that way and couldn't tell us. But clearly he did. Are you thinking the same? He's gone somewhere pretty different from a Suburban Massachusetts house?"

"Yes. At least somewhere without the reminders he gets here. Near the ocean could work, because the sound of the waves is all you hear. If he went to one of the state parks on the coast, someone would have found him by now, though. They're not that big. I don't know. Maybe a house near the beach where he could hide out?"

"I don't like the idea of that at all," Maddy said. "A stranger letting him stay with them or an abandoned building. What was the other clue?"

"What do you think it was?"

His wife let her head rest against the couch. "Trying to get back to the kid who didn't know about global warming."

"Yes," Burton said.

Seb had grown up in this house. There was no other childhood place for him to go back to.

That there were actual clues in this last message had excited Burton, but the feeling was already starting to slip away. They knew Seb did not want to be here, in their home, or any place like it. That still left half of North America and nowhere in particular. It did give a little more credence to the idea of Seb heading for the unspoiled areas of the

Continental Divide Trail. All three thousand miles of it. The CDT had been pretty far down their list of possible places because of all the gear that would be required.

Burton told himself to get it together. They really did know more. And he hoped their son had found some relief as long as it did not encourage him to stay out there longer. The trouble was, Seb clearly did not understand the kind of danger he was putting himself in.

A new disturbing idea came to him then. Seb wanted to be away from the triggers of his home life so that his upsetting thoughts would stop. If he was off by himself, though, he could be in for a rude awaking. Thoughts could be relentless when a person was all alone. Would he understand that his family was his best hope if it all became too much?

⁕

The sound of cloth sliding on steps caught Burton's ear. Jessica was on her way down to the basement in her slippers.

He glanced at Maddy. She grabbed the laptop and slid it under the couch. Sometimes a parent had to lie. Besides, the message had been addressed to him and Maddy alone.

The door creaked open. Jessica came in wearing a Patriots jersey that came down to her knees and black slippers from Chinatown. She held a book out in front of her so they could see the title.

You Can Build Your Own Computer

"I took this from Seb's room a long time ago. I don't know why. It made me fall asleep in like three minutes." She grimaced. "I forgot I had it in my room."

"Thanks, hon," Maddy said. "It's actually good timing. We didn't know there was this special computer involved until now."

Jessica flipped to a page and displayed it to them. "It has notes too. Like this."

There were words in tiny pencil print in the margin.

The note on this page said, "I don't want to buy computer parts. How do you make it from junk?"

Jessica took a step forward and dropped the book on the couch. "You guys look funny. What's going on?"

Her eyes lingered on Burton.

He realized he was sitting there in his pajama bottoms with no shirt, because he had run downstairs when the Seb email alert went off.

"We have to call the police about the computer in Seb's closet." Bur-

123

ton stifled an impulse to glance in the direction of the laptop they just slid under the couch.

"I hope they have a good computer guy," Jessica said.

"They have a whole network of computers connecting all the police departments in the country. It's pretty amazing, actually."

Jessica inched forward. She looked torn between climbing in between her parents and saying something witty and tough.

"Seb's gonna come home on his own, probably before we find him," Burton said with confidence he did not feel. His second lie to Jessica in less than a minute.

"Would you go wake your *abuela?*" Maddy asked. "We left her sleeping in the living room last night. I feel bad."

"She's cooking."

"Go help her?"

"Ya, I get it. Scary phone call to the police."

Jessica spun on her slippers and left.

Burton recognized the book. A member of the computer club at the community college had given it to Seb when he was in sixth grade. The club did not last much longer, which was a big disappointment to Seb, who clearly liked hanging around the high school boys, a couple of college students, and the "old man" (the man was about thirty years old). He was learning a lot from them. Burton was, too.

Maddy scooted forward on the couch. "I'm going to get dressed. You want me to get you a shirt?"

"Okay."

Maddy turned in the doorway. "What about Mr. Geer? Should we tell the police about him, too?"

"I think so. They won't be happy. We can just say it made us feel better, like we had to try everything possible. Maybe they'll even put more resources on the case to try and show him up."

"Or not," Maddy said and went upstairs.

Perhaps it had been a mistake to let Mr. Geer, Phillip, do his thing independently of the police. This very thin, earnest young man, who looked like he was still in high school. One reason they had not yet told the police was that they were not sure if all of his methods were entirely legal. There was also the possibility the police would not allow them to share all they knew with Phillip. On top of this, they did not want Phillip to get cold feet knowing the police were monitoring him. The fact that the police had not been able to discover the computer might be their saving grace. They could not deny Phillip was good.

With a thud in his stomach, Burton remembered that Seb had *not* sent them an email that morning. He had forgotten, for a few minutes, and then felt the shock of it all over again, that Seb was not in a conversation with them. He had been out of touch since he left the monastery a week ago. He could be lying in a ditch.

Burton leaned forward and rested his forehead on his hands. He pressed the bottoms of his palms into his eye sockets until his eyes hurt. They had no idea if Seb was okay. No way to help him if he needed help. And, surely, he needed help.

They also had zero information about what Seb thought of their videos. What if he wanted them to start actually doing something about global warming? How were they supposed to take on global warming and search for their son at the same time? But not enough time was the excuse people always used.

There was no winning in this situation.

Fine, Seb, Burton said to himself. *You win. We get it.*

On top of all the other agonizing decisions they had to make, they had to wrestle with the idea that following Seb's "instructions" was encouraging him to stay out there longer. His scheme was working. Even worse, Jessica might end up feeling emboldened to do some similarly dangerous stunt herself. That was just crazy-thinking but Burton knew it would inspire him to keep an even closer eye on her.

The book their daughter just delivered, *You Can Build Your Own Computer,* lay one cushion over from Burton on the couch. He picked it up and turned to the table of contents. There might be something in there about programming a computer to send messages on a schedule. He flipped through looking for notes in the margins. One said, "I don't think so!" A few pages later, "Hi Jess, you little spy," with a smiley face. After page twenty, the notes stopped. Seb had lost interest in this book. Burton flipped through all the pages anyway.

There was one last note on the blank page at the very end of the book.

> *Cave man to other cave man: Ug. I make computer.*
> *Ug? What it do?*
> *Count rock.*
> *That dum.*
> *You dum.*

In the span of a couple years, Seb had gone from silly jokes about cave men to the painful poem on the laptop under the couch. Adolescence was a time when kids became more self-conscious and secretive about what was happening to them but how could they not have noticed such a profound transformation?

❧

The phone on the basement office desk rang, loud at close proximity to the couch where Burton sat. It startled him, as it did every time these days. He tossed Seb's computer book onto the couch and jumped up to answer it.

"Mr. Franck?"

"Hello?"

"This is Thomas Wattana. Do you have a minute?"

"Oh, hi, Ajahn. I mean Thomas. Of course."

"You can call me Ajahn. Most people seem more comfortable with that. But no matter. I was looking at the messages your son and I exchanged. I do every day. However, the email he sent you this morning struck a chord. I thought you would want to know. I'm sorry I did not think of it before."

"Maddy and I were copied on all of the messages and we've read them many times ourselves. We can't expect you to know our son better than us."

A click sounded on the line. Maddy—hopefully not Jessica—had picked up the phone in the kitchen.

"In any case," the Ajahn continued, not pronouncing the letter "s" in "case." A week later and he was still not composed, still less careful about his English. "I don't fool myself to believe I am smarter because I am a monk."

"I bet you are."

The Ajahn paused for a moment. "I will read you the email exchange with your son I am referring to. Your son wrote to me:

"'Ajahn, if the way to end suffering is the eight-fold path, how do you get the world to follow the eight-fold path when they're not doing it and they really need to?'"

"All his emails were like that," Burton interjected. "Impatient to learn Buddhism."

"Perhaps," the Ajahn said. "But the answer I gave concerns me. It sounds rather stiff. I replied:

"'The Buddha told us to follow the eight-fold path when these questions arise. He did not say our specific questions would be answered, simply that following this path will ultimately end suffering.'"

Burton could hear papers being shuffled

126

"I now think this answer was not appropriate," the Ajahn said.

Burton was not happy with his son for the harm he had done to this kind man who only wanted to help him. He and Maddy kept blaming themselves for letting Seb get to the point where he ran away but times like this left him wondering if their son had a mutation.

"Ajahn, we blame you for nothing. My wife and I read the exchange you just read. It didn't seem especially important to us either until Seb's most recent email."

The Ajahn took a loud breath and let it out. "I must accept what happened. However, it is difficult not to wish I did not say something more encouraging to a fourteen-year old. There is a reason the Buddha smiles. We can be at peace in each moment."

"I think your answer was very good. I think it helped Seb understand. That it's okay, no matter how big the challenge."

"This would please me greatly. I wonder what I can do now? I meditate but I also believe in service."

"I think having you meditate is exactly what we need. We certainly can't do it nearly as well as you."

He and Maddy never meditated, actually.

"I am certainly meditating about Seb."

"Thank you."

"When it is convenient, may I ask how things are going? I know you are busy."

"Any time. We'll let you know as soon as Seb is back with us. Thank you again, Ajahn."

"Take care, Mr. Franck."

CHAPTER EIGHT

MILES AND MILES

BURTON WAS ENCOURAGED by the clouds. Full sun in the summer took a lot out of him and he wanted to run fast.

The McCreerys were both at work so he cut through their property. He entered a break in the weeds at the back of their yard and pushed his way through tall stalks of Queen Anne's lace and thistle. It was the thinnest of paths, trampled down by deer, kids, and himself. Stalks flapped against his legs for a quarter mile until he came out onto a packed gravel trail. The county park.

He focused on his form. Hips forward at all times. One knee and the opposite shoulder forward, then switch. Breathe into the belly. Short, quick steps. Feet raised a minimal amount from the ground.

For a moment he thought he might lapse into his runner's trance.

As if. Seb was gone more than a week now. His last email was incredibly painful. There would be no runner's trance until their son was home.

Burton felt guilty for running at all, but he had a reason. A redirection of energy from his tightly wound brain into his body might force his brain to relax and finally think a bit differently. They had tried everything else.

Maddy may have had something similar in mind when she suggested they wait a day to respond to Seb's email. A delay might change the way Seb was thinking, too. Trigger some fear and send him home. A little time to think might underscore how truly separated from his family he was.

He hopped over a creek and stutter-stepped up the steep bank on the other side. When the trail leveled off again, he had a surprising thought. Maybe the running was having an effect on his brain. The thought was this: he was behaving the same way as Maddy. She directed her frustration at Seb. Burton directed his frustration at her. Maybe a person just could not endure this much stress without blaming somebody.

He knew the run was altering his state of mind for sure by the time he passed the big birch. The two mile mark. It was an effect he had dared not wish for. A bit of relief. His shoulders and upper back felt considerably less tight. But the relief was not only physical. He and Maddy were—big surprise—different. And those differences were only exacerbated when their family was in jeopardy. What was important was that his wife wanted Seb to be safe and happy as much as he did. Knowing this, feeling this, was the biggest relief of all.

Burton was tempted to let go and relax into his run for a bit but he could not lose the clarity of thought he had gained.

Seb had gone from reading his father's article to checking the facts on the internet. He had confirmed this in his last email. He probably hoped to learn what progress had been made in the twenty years since Burton wrote the article. His last two emails made it clear that what he found was another punch in the face. He learned how pathetic the response had been. Instead of rallying and making sure this potential threat to every person's life did not happen, people went around burning more than ever.

How demoralizing and infuriating this must have been. No wonder Seb felt like he was losing his mind. But why had he chosen to process such difficult information without at least one of his parents by his side? It could be Maddy. She was innocent of writing the article.

Instead, Seb looked for answers on his own and found very disturbing things.

Burton wished his son had confronted him directly. It was true that he had fallen down on the job in a major way but he did know a fair amount about the current state of global warming. He tried to imagine, as best as he could while in the middle of a run, how he could have convinced Seb that his father was an ally.

Their son's last email made it clear that he was traumatized by humanity's unwillingness to face a critical problem. He had left them with the task of presenting a plan and gaining his trust by way of a short video.

This would not be easy. Climate science was complicated and human behavior even more so. The nations of the world had been trying to get an effective plan together for decades. Al Gore's *Inconvenient Truth* movie made big news for a while and then global warming pretty much disappeared from the news. Action by the U.S. Government fell apart. Global warming finally re-emerged as a major concern in the U.S. but few people wanted to talk about it and hardly anybody seemed to know what to do.

This was a lot to consider for a video addressed to a fourteen-year-old.

Exactly how much Seb learned before he left home they did not yet know. He gave no indication he was done explaining himself by email so it seemed likely more was to come.

He was now running at a good clip and felt strong. More focused, too. He knew this could be a placebo effect, since he had the goal of being in a steadier state of mind when he set out on the run, but it was still true. He felt different. What they had been doing so far was not working, so he had nothing to lose by going with this.

For some reason his mind went to the possibility that Seb had taken an adult into his confidence. Every person who had been in contact with Seb had been considered. The retreat participants and the Ajahn had been cleared by the police, not that Burton ever suspected him. They had no leads. He hoped the detectives were not still wasting their time investigating whether the culprit was him.

Maddy was the one with the social services background but Burton knew enough. Kids who were manipulated by adults were often afraid to say anything about it. It was also bad timing that Seb found *The Rodent* article as an adolescent. Had it happened earlier, he would certainly have confronted his parents right at the dinner table. Without his parents to talk to, it was possible he had turned to someone else.

Burton then thought of something he had never thought of before. Could their son be sick? Animals hid when sick. But this had to be a ridiculous idea. His heart, already going fast, pounded harder and he was gulping breath.

Breathe, he told himself. *Breathe deep, all the way down to your stomach. Breathe fast but take it in deep.*

The rapid fire of his thoughts had gotten him running too fast and with bad form. He cut his pace in half.

Seb had no obvious illness. A hidden illness could only be diagnosed by a doctor and a doctor would be required to inform the parents of a minor about a serious health condition. To feel you were going crazy was a sort of illness. Seb had mentioned more than once that he thought he might be crazy. And so? Where specifically would he go to protect his vulnerable self?

The big hill at the center of the park came into view. It was always a challenge for Burton to pace himself on this hill. As he worked on taking shorter steps, he was reminded of the steep, rocky trail on Mount Mansfield. The family had gone there for a hike a month earlier. Seb spent half the time waiting for the rest of them to catch up. He had to be healthy. An illness unknown to the rest of the family was not why he went off by himself.

A couple months prior to the hike on Mount Mansfield, Burton and Seb had driven to a trail in New York State for an overnight hike. This was the third year in a row they hiked with a tent and sleeping bags in their packs. They stayed up late into the night talking by the fire. Jessica was not interested in hiking for more than an hour and Maddy stayed home with her. Sweating on a sunny climb, making eggs on a cool morning, swimming in a chilly pond, they always came home from those trips feeling good. He and Seb never said it out loud, but these trips made them feel strong and at peace with the wild world. The real wild. Not a place with rest rooms and showers. Not only could they survive there, they thrived there.

That was it. That was it!

Seb was in a remote place. Not in a park, not even an urban forest. Most of the state parks would not be remote enough. He was in the deep woods. This would be the only place that could offer Seb a chance to dodge the avalanche of disturbing information coming at him, like the sounds and smells of cars he described.

What they had to do was focus much more on the biggest, least travelled areas, like national forests. Their belief that the Continental Divide Trail required too much gear and travel had missed the point. The point was not that Seb really wanted to experience the CDT (although he did). The point was that the CDT was his vision of the natural world at its most unspoiled.

Why had they not realized sooner that Seb would be compelled to somewhere as remote and pristine as possible? This was why he set up emails to be automatically generated. He would only have to journey out of the forest once in a while to watch his parents' videos. It did not matter if he had to travel a long distance to view the videos. There was no need to watch them right after his parents posted them. His emails were not responses. They were canned. Weeks old.

Burton nearly yelled out loud from frustration over not making the connection before. He was running too hard again. His whole chest was heaving and he was not to the top of the hill yet. He was ordinarily too proud to switch from running to walking but he had a good excuse. He slowed down to a walk.

Proud fool will kill himself during a run one day, he thought.

He still had a couple of miles left to go. Once he caught his breath, he would jog the rest of the way home. He was eager to tell Maddy and Jess what he had realized. It was probably not going to be easy to make them understand, though.

Once he reached the top of the hill, he started to jog slowly. A thought occurred to him that he had not considered in a very long time. There was a family precedent for going into the wilderness. An odd precedent involving Seb's grandfather and great grandfather.

Seb's great grandfather (Burton's grandfather) was a first-generation Portuguese born in Providence. Everyone called him Avo. Avo and Burton's grandmother moved in with Burton's family after Avo lost his job. He had worked for years in a factory that made yarn or thread. Burton was seventeen at the time. He imagined Avo working in a loud place with a lot of loud spinning machines. It seemed like it would have been hard work and not fun. Jake was already away at college so Avo and grandmother slept in his room.

Avo had a permanent scowl on his face said next to nothing to Burton. Burton took it personally. As a self-centered kid, he did not realize his grandfather smiled at no one.

He avoided Avo as much as possible. This was not easy. Their little two story house in East Providence had three small bedrooms and one bathroom upstairs and a bedroom, kitchen and a living room downstairs. Avo was always downstairs. Burton either went to a friend's house or read books in his room.

One night his parents took his grandmother and Terrie to see the road tour of *The Phantom of the Opera.* They asked Burton to keep Avo company and left the two of them at the kitchen table. The clock radio on top of the refrigerator was giving a play by play of the Sox game. Avo was drinking Muscatel out of a jelly jar glass. Burton was reading a book at the other end of the kitchen table.

Things were going okay until the radio announcer launched into a commercial and Avo said something Burton could not understand. He set down his book. The bottle of Muscatel was already half gone.

"Sorry, Avo, I didn't hear what you said."

"Did your father ever tell you about his trial by fires in the Berkshires Mountains?"

"I don't think so."

Avo made mistakes in speech all the time. He was born in the U.S. but probably had to learn English on his own, since both his parents came over from Portugal. His poor English was further obscured by a wicked bad Rhode Island accent and Muscatel. Berkshires came out as "Buhrshuzz."

"I gave him sardines, peanuts, crackers and a water canteen," Avo said, rubbing the jelly jar with both palms. "Drove him up there and told him he needed to appreciate the wild. Because we lived in the city since he was a boy. I drove him up to a place I know and dropped him off, told him go straight in a mile, there's a lake. Left his bike with him, too, in case he needed an emergency. Told him to hide the bike near the road and said I be back in a week."

Burton did not know what to say. He wondered if his grandfather was joking but dared not ask. There was no remorse in his voice. Avo glanced over at him and almost smiled. He was bragging.

The announcer came back on the radio. Burton could still remember the promotion being announced, seat cushions awarded to the first so many people at the next game. He remembered because he hoped his grandfather would want one of these cushions and stop talking. After all these years of nothing to say, Burton did not want to get friendly with Avo now. He would be off to college in a year.

"I showed your father how to use a compass before we went up," Avo said, reaching for the bottle of Muscatel. "Told him don't sleep with your food, bears, you know, and don't wipe your ass with poison ivy."

This bit about the poison ivy left Burton thinking the story was not true. He still did not know what to say. His grandfather poured more muscatel and Burton took the opportunity to start reading his book again. Only years later did he connect his father's complete lack of interest in going anywhere outside the city to Avo's story. Being unprepared and abandoned in a dark forest for a week might make anyone uncomfortable outside of an urban setting.

Other families picnicked in state parks all the time. The closest Burton's family ever came to a remote place were state beaches near Providence. His father often stayed at home. Burton once got happily lost in Colt State Park. This one afternoon of wandering amongst the scrub pines and dunes may have been the reason he, a city boy, ended up introducing his family to camping. It was not from Maddy. She was a city girl, too. Avo's interest in "the wild" seemed to have been passed like a recessive gene through his son to Burton. He and Maddy took the kids camping and picnicking in state parks all the time.

The tale Burton's grandfather told him that night, which Burton once found too extreme to believe, became something he did believe. Probably because it was such a great story.

Seb never met Avo but he went fishing a few times with Avo's son, his grandfather. The Providence River was just a few blocks from his house. It was possible his grandfather told him, while they fished, about the time Avo left him at the edge of a forest with a bike and some sardines to fend for himself. If Avo really did do such a thing in the first place. Hearing a story like this could have contributed to Seb's belief that he could survive alone in a remote place. Burton wished he had asked his father if the story was true. If his father had spoken to Seb about the ordeal, he better have made it clear that it was a very dangerous thing to do.

In the course of thinking of Avo's crazy story, Burton missed his turn-off. His intention was to return by way of the deer path. He was now at the far entrance of the park, on the rich side of town. Hundred-year oaks, big lawns, and the tall peaks of Tudors lined the street. It was great for running but he ignored his surroundings. He had finally had a real lead and he needed to work on it before he got home.

Massachusetts had big expanses of forest. The family had visited parks all over the state. New Hampshire had even more forested land and some of it was not far from Portsmouth. There was probably just as much wilderness in Vermont. And there were massive tracts of woodland just across the Piscataqua River that separated New Hampshire from Maine. Seb could have gotten to forests in any of these states by bus. Even Quebec could be reached in a day. Burton remembered Seb once mentioning that Quebec contained places more wild than anywhere in the whole U.S., including Alaska.

The matter of access to the internet to watch YouTube videos would be Seb's main limitation. Since he did not drive, Seb could not go too deep into the woods. Had he rented a cabin with Wi-Fi using cash and a fake ID? Even a tiny cabin in New England was expensive in the summer. Seb should not have that kind of cash, but he had surprised them several times already. Could he have charmed his way into the protection of a hermit, living on the side of a mountain?

Burton stumbled on an uneven section of the sidewalk. He managed to stay upright but decided to walk the rest of the way. He could cool off and not be sweating profusely when he got home.

Seb had to know adults would be required by law to contact the police and give him up. And he had to know that any adult willing to keep his secret was dangerous. For him to think otherwise would mean an utter failure on the part of his parents. Still, *someone's cabin* needed to go on the list of possible scenarios that he and Maddy kept locked in a drawer in their bedroom. That list was one thing Jessica was not going to see.

❧

After a hot shower, Burton wrapped a towel around his waist and walked into the bedroom. A run was better than a drink. And he knew, finally, what to do to find Seb.

Maddy was sitting at the foot of the bed, looking in the dresser mirror and doing something with her ponytail. He came over and blocked her view. She looked up at him.

"I'm sorry about taking off. My head was starting to hurt."

"It's okay," she said. "We all needed a break. Jess and I fed the squirrel with the mohawk."

She removed a black elastic ring from the ponytail. Her hair fell over her ears and onto her shoulders. In a quick motion she gathered it up to create another ponytail. It looked the same to Burton.

"I should have stayed with you after his poem. It was rough."

Maddy squinted at him. "Maybe you can make it up to me tonight."

"I could make it up to you right now."

"You could try."

He placed his hands on her shoulders and leaned down to kiss her.

❧

Burton lay with his face against Maddy's shoulder, sweating. Sunlight streamed in from the skylight. The television blared downstairs. It sounded like dialogue from a movie. Jessica watched only movies on television, not shows. She had probably turned up the volume because she wanted her parents to come out of the bedroom.

He rolled onto his back. "Have you heard from your jobs?"

"They're not calling me and I'm not calling them," Maddy said. "They know I have to do this. It's fine."

Being together this afternoon was the best thing to happen to them since Seb disappeared. Quick but intense. It was a relief to feel good together. And now they had work to do.

"There's something I want to talk about," he said, running a finger

136

down her back. The rumpled bed sheets had formed a sort of paisley pattern there. "I think we need a family meeting."

Maddy sat up and swung her legs off the bed. She picked up the top sheet, wrapped it around her body, stood, and looked down at him. "You don't want to run it by me first?"

"It's just an idea. Nothing scary. I want to tell you and Jess together."

He glanced around the room. There was something they were forgetting. Maddy padded into the bathroom. She shook out her ruined ponytail before closing the door. The shower began to run.

A moment later, the door opened and she stuck out her head. "I just remembered. Jess doesn't know about the last message. The *What?* poem. Are we going to pretend that never happened? Are we going to do a video without her knowing?"

"We can't let her think Seb has stopped communicating with us. Even if it is all pre-recorded. We could tell her that Seb asked us not to share his last message with her. She won't be happy, of course."

Burton stood up to scan the bedroom. There was definitely something they were supposed to do. He was still thinking about what they would say to Jessica when the answer came to him. The laptop.

"What are you looking for?" Maddy asked.

"I just realized we left the laptop in the basement, under the couch. Seb's poem was still on the screen."

He slipped on shorts and snuck down to the basement. He got the laptop from under the couch and then took a quick shower in the tiny bathroom at the back of the laundry room.

Jessica frowned at her father when he walked into the kitchen. He was reminded of the time he had been upstairs with Maddy for a couple of hours in the middle of the afternoon and came downstairs to catch Seb whispering to his sister, "Mom and Dad are acting weird again."

A plate of fried plantains sat steaming at the center of the table. Rosa's specialty. Burton poked two with a fork, dipped them in ketchup, and ate them standing by the table. Amazing. Jessica ate one with her fingers.

Maddy came in wearing shorts and the same white T-shirt Burton wore. It featured a cartoon frog and the words "Mad Scientist" underneath. It made no sense but they had laughed when they discovered the shirt in both of their sizes at the university bookstore's annual clearance of things it could not sell.

"Where's Grandma Rosa?" Maddy asked.

Jessica finished chewing. "She went to the store."

Rosa went to the store every day.

Burton noticed little clumps of grass clippings stretching out behind Jessica, down the two steps to the living room, and over to the sliding glass door. He recalled the drone of a lawn mower while he and Maddy were upstairs. Jessica had cut the lawn.

"So, I had a revelation on my run," Burton said. "And Jess, you're a sweetie for doing the grass."

Jessica grinned.

"Seb's in a forest. Not a park, a big forest, without people around."

A few seconds passed.

"That's it?" Jessica asked.

Maddy sat next to Jessica. The two looked up at him, waiting for an answer.

Burton took a seat across the table from them. He pushed back to balance on the chair's rear legs, holding on to the table for support. "Well, that's what we need to work on."

"He's in the woods watching YouTube videos?" Maddy asked.

He could not tell if she was being sarcastic. In any case, it was a good question. He leaned forward and let the chair go back to resting on all four legs. "He only needs to hike out to get internet to watch a video once in a while. It doesn't matter when he watches them, right?"

He looked over at Jessica. She blinked at him. How could he explain this well?

"That tone in your voice," Maddy said. "I know it. You have no doubt."

"Yes, you know me."

"But, what...I mean..." Maddy glanced at Jessica for support.

Jessica nodded a couple times in agreement with Maddy's struggle to understand.

"I guess," Maddy said, "I'm not sure where this gets us. It's not exactly a new idea. We're in touch with every national park, hiking club and state forest in the Northeast. They all have his flyer."

Burton held up a hand. "You've also been in touch with every Buddhist group, ecology club, Boy Scout troop, runaway center and commune in the Northeast and—."

"Uh oh," Jessica said.

The expression on her mother's face made it clear she did not appreciate where Burton was going with this.

"Wait," he said. "That is one hundred percent the right thing to do. And we need keep doing those things. We know more now. We just shift more of our focus onto the big parks and national forests. Redouble our efforts there. That's what I'm suggesting, anyway."

"Because you have a hunch?"

"I haven't explained everything yet. Yes, some of it's a father's intuition, a very good hunch, but it also makes complete sense. He loves nature. That last garbage assignment we did? The garbage you find in the woods is natural, it's no problem. Rain washes it away, bugs eat it. A dead tree turns into a gray sculpture. Then there's the 'What?' The existential questions."

Burton avoided looking directly at Jessica but he could see her eyebrows knit.

"If Seb could go anywhere he wanted," he continued. "If this was his chance, don't you think he would want to be in a quiet, unspoiled place? It doesn't have to be the Continental Divide. He had to be at least somewhat pragmatic."

Maddy stared in his direction. She seemed to be trying to formulate a response.

"What are you thinking?" Burton asked.

"You can't just live in the middle of a forest. You need food. Besides, he's so social. I guess I'm not sure what new information we have. We know he likes the outdoors. What exactly was revealed to you on your run, that's new?"

"The revelation is that I know it. The deep woods. I just know it. You weren't with him after our weekends, when the two of us did primitive camping. No bathroom, no showers. I was always happy to get home and get a shower, but there was this thrill. We felt strong. I think he needs to feel strong right now. Why alone, we still don't know."

"All right," Maddy said. "No one else has a better theory. Or feels as strongly. We focus on more remote places. Have you had time to figure out how we do that?"

"I have a few ideas."

"I think he's on a bike." Both parents turned so quickly to look at Jessica, that she threw her head back in surprise. "When Dad asked what Seb would do if he could do anything he wanted, I pictured him riding his bike. Isn't that what a revelation is? Seeing something? You know he can't sit still. He could still have his nature and ride through forests."

"You mean riding and riding?" Maddy asked. "Not staying in any one place?"

"Maybe."

"He did love to bike," Burton said. "Does love to bike. Maybe he mapped out a bunch of back roads. Maybe if he was heading in the direction of the Continental Divide he would feel better."

"So what can we do differently?" Maddy asked.

"How about showing his picture around bike stores in Portsmouth?" Jessica said.

"That's an excellent idea," Burton said.

Maddy picked up a plantain with two fingers and dipped it into the ketchup. "There's got to be maps with roads recommended for biking."

Burton nodded. "Without you two, I'd be walking around with my thumb up my...nose."

Jessica smiled, but just for a moment. None of them felt comfortable smiling for long.

"And we have Phillip Geer," Burton said.

"We could have Phillip pull data on places with public internet access that are near big forests."

Maddy picked up a note pad and pen and began to write as she spoke.

"Maybe Phillip Geer could find out if someone near a big forest watched our videos. One of us could go with Jess to visit rangers in the Massachusetts forests, see if they will let us onto the roads not open to the public. I guess we'd have to rent a Jeep. I don't know about Maine. That's one big forest. Your Aunt Terrie would probably be willing visit all the places with internet near the big forests in Vermont. And then there's New Hampshire. Oh, this is impossible!"

Maddy set the pen on the pad and turned to look across the living room and out the sliding glass door. Burton wondered if his idea was not quite as solid as he originally thought. He may have been light-headed during the run and lulled into his own fantasy in the midst of the quiet of the park.

"Can't they ride a helicopter over the forests to look for him?" Jessica asked

Her mother shrugged. "Maybe once we have a better idea which forest he's in. We should at least see what Phillip Geer thinks."

This comment of Jessica's, besides making Burton's revelation feel even less useful, produced the disturbing image of a loud chopper and a high-powered beam of light sweeping across treetops, and Seb running like a fugitive.

◛

The lump moving under the covers of Maddy and Burton's bed was Myro. Burton reached his arm in to get him. He had to climb halfway across the bed before he was able to catch the dog by its hind leg. The little paw slipped loose and Myro squirmed away, fabric rippling. Burton pulled the covers all the way back. Myro, to change the subject, rolled over, exposing his stomach. Burton stroked it for a minute before carrying him out of the room.

The light was off in Jessica's bedroom. It was not yet ten. Asleep early again. Burton deposited the dachshund next to the closed door to her room. She usually left it open a bit so he could sleep with her.

Myro stared at Jessica's closed door for a moment, then turned around. He begged Burton with his eyes to understand that they were obliged to let him sleep with them, since he was locked out of Jessica's bed. Myro, though, was not a considerate user of the bed, sleeping on heads, moving around all night, and wriggling his legs as he ran in his dreams. Burton left him in the hallway and closed the door.

Jessica's dark room and Myro moping in the hall had Burton rather agitated. He needed to end this ordeal for everyone's sake. And he and his wife now had the impossible task of filming a video that would convince their son to come home when he expressly told them not to do that.

Maybe waiting a day to respond really would make Seb more inclined to listen to them.

They had decided not to say anything about Burton's big "a-ha" on his run. They did not want to incite Seb into doing something unplanned and even more dangerous. He would probably not be surprised or too upset that they felt compelled to say more than "we got your message."

Maddy carried a few books from the night stand and placed them in a pile on the dresser opposite the foot of their bed. Myro scratched at the door. Lazy scratches like a branch against the house. Burton sat on the bed so Maddy could place the camera in the right spot atop the pile of books. She looked through the viewer to see if it was focused on the right place. Burton waved from the bed. Maddy removed one of the books. Myro's claws scraped against the door again.

The dog's scratching gave Burton an idea. He opened the door to the hallway. Myro inserted his nose and sniffed the doorframe, taking his time, now that he knew Burton would not shut the door on his little face.

"Get in here," Burton said.

Myro walked in.

Seb might or might not recognize the sentimental card Burton going to play with the dog his son loved, but Seb wasn't playing fair, either. He lifted Myro by the belly, sat on the bed and put the dog on his lap. Myro sighed happily. It was a major coup to be accepted into the parents' bedroom. A bed with two warm bodies.

Burton's intention was to manipulate Seb into homesickness. As Maddy focused the camera, he realized there was another good reason to have Myro there. What better way to counter existential confusion than the "Hi, I love you, what more could anyone want?" expression on a dog?

"Myro and I are ready," he said.

Maddy looked at the dog in his lap and gave a knowing smile. "It's late and we look like hell, but maybe Seb should see that, too."

She pressed the camera's red button and hurried over to the bed. They waited for the mattress to stop bouncing up and down before beginning.

"We read your poem," Burton said. "We're glad you shared what you wrote." He was surprised at the coolness of his tone. He supposed his intention was to allay Seb's fears that they were going to make a big deal about his traumatic poem and email.

Maddy followed. "It hurt to read the poem and what you shared afterwards but a parent wants to hurt with their kid."

They had gone back and forth about whether they should say child or kid. They opted to avoid implying they thought Seb was immature. They had considered using the word child to sow seeds of doubt in Seb's mind. That he really was not old enough to be on his own.

"We're sorry we didn't make you feel comfortable enough to share those thoughts." Maddy tilted her head to the side, in Burton's direction. "With us before."

Burton found himself wanting to ask Seb if someone had hurt him. To tell him that they would protect him. To tell him that they were sorry they had not protected him well enough and that they would never let something like this happen again. He hesitated because Seb was already fragile and it might make things worse to bring up someone hurting him if it had not happened.

Then it came out anyway.

"We are here to protect you Seb. Always." Burton paused to let that sink in before continuing with the part they had planned on saying.

Maddy did not flinch. She would certainly have asked Burton what the hell he was doing if they were not being filmed. She waited for her husband to go back to the planned script.

"We'll respect your wishes and not discuss what you wrote about yourself in the last email," Burton said. "We're going to talk about ourselves instead. We're going a bit crazy, too, your mother and I. Not just because you ran away. This world needs help bad. We think you could be an awesome advocate for taking care of this planet. And, of course, we want you to come home. Safe. You told us what you want. You didn't say we couldn't tell you what we want. As if you didn't already know."

Maddy went right into her part. "Big surprise, we talked more than you wanted us to. Maybe we couldn't let you have the last word. Speaking of which, we have another thing to tell you. We found your computer. We're not going to touch it."

Officer Quinn had instructed them to say this and nothing more about finding the computer.

"That's all, I guess," Maddy said, then put on a brave smile. Burton wondered if she knew how pained she looked. "Be safe, honey."

"Or come home," Burton said. That was supposed to be a joke.

Maddy got up, turned off the camera, and returned to the bed.

They sat gazing at the camera, its red "recording" light now dark. Myro yawned. Burton's focus shifted to the dresser mirror behind the camera. He realized he had not once looked at his reflection during the recording. Maddy, he saw, had shifted her focus to the mirror as well.

"You're crying," she said.

"I see that."

Then a tear rolled out of her eye.

Man, they looked tired.

They sat there. Burton remained hazily focused on the mirror. Maddy looked away. She was probably self-conscious after looking at herself for so long. Burton did not know where else to look.

For some reason, Burton thought of his father again. Who may or may not have been taken from the city for the first time to be left at the side of the road with a bicycle, miles from civilization. Then he thought of the cigarette and oil companies and all the people with their heads in the sand. Seb should count himself amongst the most sane.

"How do you track down a teenager who's not using his phone?" Maddy asked. Her eyes moved slowly back to the mirror to meet Burton's eyes there. "Whose computer is talking to us instead of him?"

"Don't use technology?"

CHAPTER NINE

In a Field

THE BOY SWERVED HARD to keep the bicycle from dropping into a pot-hole. This road was more pothole than road. He jerked the handlebars violently from side to side, slaloming between the holes. You had to ride kind of fast to have enough momentum to pull out of each turn. At the next pothole he had to wrench the front tire to the left so sharply he just about went over. It was exhausting. He must have looked ridiculous, jerking his way down the road.

About as ridiculous as he looked being left in the middle of nowhere with two packs and a bike. When he got dropped off on that road the other day he felt so scared he almost left his bike and ran after the van, waving his arms for it to stop.

He must have been biking up a hill without knowing it because he could now see much further beyond the stalks of whatever crop was growing on either side of the road. Fields of these crops went on for miles in every direction. The rain must have flowed quickly off this elevated part of the road because there were a lot less pot holes here. The boy could glide easily between the dips and bumps. For the first time he did not have to stare constantly at the ground and could look around. Just as he did, a powerful gust of wind forced him to go right back to gripping the handlebars and staring at the road. The wind calmed down a minute later and he tried looking around again.

The massive mountain on his left was incredible. It had always been in the corner of his vision, even as he stared at the road, because the thing was so big. The mountain was maybe twenty miles away but it felt like it was right on top of him. A shiver ran down his spine. It felt as if it might at any moment fall over and crush him.

The huge mountain made him feel small at first, like a little nothing. But then, as he kept riding, the thing always to his left, he suddenly felt strong. He was surviving in the middle of fields and woods with this giant beside him. The wide open sky told him he could go forever, powered by his own body.

It was easy to believe this was the biggest mountain in the state. Nothing near it had such a wide peak, such a long ridge of rock that made all the other mountains look like they were this mountain's children. Dozens and dozens of children filling the horizon to the North and West. Between every pair of peaks you could see more peaks behind them. And between those, even more peaks. Layers upon layers that reminded him of the plywood scenery they used for plays at school.

Small islands of birches floated here and there in the green fields. Pale blue cornflowers waved from the side of the road as he rolled by. Grasshoppers shot out in all directions. One hit him squarely on the chest, making him laugh. Birds called. Insects creaked. Wind whooshed in his ears when he pedaled harder.

He began to sing, to shout, a punk-rock song about war. It felt so good to sing as loud as you wanted. It did not matter that he only knew the words to the chorus and mumbled the rest. He shouted "glor-ee-ee-ee" and weaved in wide turns down the road. Halfway through the next "glor-ee-ee-ee" he saw a cowboy hat above the head and shoulders of a man in the crop field ahead.

The boy stopped singing and coasted. There was no way the man in the cowboy hat had not heard, and probably seen, the spectacle he had been making. The man turned to look at the him as he approached. The boy could see now that the man was sitting on a tractor in a space cut into the field at the edge of the road.

"Hi there," the man said.

The boy, his heart pounding, squeezed the brake under his left hand. As soon as he did, he knew he had made a mistake. With only the front tire immobilized, the bike's rear tire spun out, shooting rocks into the field. Several banged off the tractor. By the time the bike came to a stop it had done a 180 degree turn and the boy was facing the direction from which he had just come.

"Whoa," the man on the tractor said. His face was brown and wrinkled all over. He was holding a sandwich in his hand near his mouth. He took a bite and stared down, chewing.

Although the man sounded friendly, there was not a person around for miles. The boy did not know what to say.

The man on the tractor swallowed and said, "You're out early."

"Yes."

"Musta gone by in the dark. It was dark when I started out this morning. What did you go that way for anyway? Nothing there. You lost?"

How to answer that question? The farmer—the boy decided it was safe to call a sunburned man on a tractor in the middle of a giant cropfield a farmer—stared down at him. He was not smiling but his squinting eyes seemed amused.

"Fishing a pond," the boy said. This was mostly a lie.

"Past where the road ends? Bunch of ponds closer. Must be looking for something special to traipse all the way in there. Clearing out some muskies for us?"

"Well..."

"It's all right buddy, I'm just jabbering."

The boy turned the handlebars back and forth, making an 'X' under the front tire.

"You want some tomatoes? I got tomatoes comin' out of my ears."

"A couple." The boy did not like tomatoes, but it was free food, and better to leave the farmer pleased. "Thank you."

"Just go up to the barn on the left. They're on a table. Probly five hundred. Don't take 'em all."

No laughter, just a wide grin from the farmer. His teeth were brown. The boy smiled back.

"If your Mom wants more, tell her to come back and get."

"Okay. I will. Bye."

The boy pushed off, rolled, hopped on the pedals and accelerated. But not so fast as to look scared.

How stupid, to have broken his *binoculo-glasses*. Sat on them the night before and snapped them in half. Now he had to ride more than twenty miles, one way, until he found a place that had glue. With tomatoes in his pack.

CHAPTER TEN

The Good People of Boston Public

Burton waited for a break in traffic so he could exit the town library parking lot. Ashton Dombrowski's mother pulled in to his left. Both their windows were rolled down and their eyes met. She waved and he waved back. He resisted the urge to look over his shoulder to see if she had turned back to look at him with pity on her face.

He clicked off his left blinker and switched on the right. He was late for relieving Maddy but he did not want to go home yet. A drive past the horse farms first.

As soon as he reached cruising speed, his eyelids started to lower. He let them go almost all the way closed, hoping this would make him feel less tired. He let them close a little more. At thirty-five miles an hour, he could coast. He was tired of not sleeping and tired of getting nowhere. Everything they had done to find Seb had failed. This trip to the town library was the latest.

They had a lot more hope two days ago. He and his daughter had been excited on the drive to Portsmouth to check the outdoor gear stores. They enjoyed each other's company for the first few stores and by the last, their good cheer was mostly an act. The day ended with soggy fries at a diner and just wanting to go home. At home, they found Maddy with bloodshot eyes, working on a long list of internet cafes and libraries near big forests in New England.

"I called every one," she said. "Half of them just rang. A bunch of the numbers were bad. Anybody with email got a flyer. It's done."

Except they were not done. The next day the three of them had gone on a road trip to visit places near state and national forests. Rosa looked scared at the prospect of being left behind. To occupy her, and because it needed to be done, Maddy gave her a stack of flyers to mail to all sorts of businesses in the vicinity of these state and national parks, including all the places that did not answer their phones. Not only internet cafes, coffee shops and park offices. Grocery stores, bait shops, senior centers, churches. Any and every public place.

That day they drove to the mountains on the border with Connecticut, beginning a route that would take them through Massachusetts and into New Hampshire. The first place, a coffee shop, was closed and would not be open until five that night. They taped a Seb flyer to the front door. The next place had printed and posted the flyer Maddy emailed them the day before. They thanked the owner and bought coffee. Maddy cried. A couple dozen coffee shops and libraries followed. Much sympathy and no leads.

That night was spent in a motel. Their unit had a patio looking straight at an overgrown and wet hillside too steep for hiking. The foothills of the White Mountains. People in lawn chairs sat smoking cigarettes on the patios to the right and the left of the Franck's room. Everybody sat there staring into the woods. Lights flashed through sliding glass doors further down. Families watching television. The Francks went to bed.

The following day was the same, driving from coffee shop to general store to park office. Whoever was not driving was on the phone with the police, Phillip Geer, everybody. Jessica slept or tried to read in the back seat. All that time in the car was hard. Trees flew past the windows for hours on end as they sat there alternating between worried and exhausted.

This was why Burton fell asleep on his way to drive past the horse farms after leaving the library. The rumble strips at the side of the road jarred him awake. He shuddered and sat up straight. Going for a drive was obviously a bad idea. Maddy would wonder what he was up to. He realized he just wanted to be alone. That could not happen, of course.

He found his phone and gave Maddy a call.

"Any luck at the library?" she asked. It was probably supposed to sound cheerful but it didn't.

"I tried first for an unbiased answer. 'Do you recall a teenaged boy looking for information about national parks, or forests last month?'

The answer was no."

"Did she let you see what books he checked out?"

"After I showed her the police report. The only book he checked out this year was *Fight Club*. I have a printout for the past three years. Nothing helpful as far as I can see. He doesn't do books any more. *Fight Club* surprised me, though. Buddhism and *Fight Club*?"

"Maybe the violence drove him to Buddhism."

Maddy the analytical one. She should be the scientist. Burton's latest hypothesis was more simple. Seb was mentally ill.

"All his skateboard friends were into that book, you know," Maddy said.

"Were they? I thought the only reason they went to the library was to skateboard around it."

"What about book stores?" Maddy asked. "Books about forests. I don't know. Foraging. Bike routes."

Burton closed his eyes again. He could drive for a bit with them closed. Maddy would keep him awake.

Not getting an answer, Maddy continued. "What about that kayak place near Lexington? He could have gone there for some outdoor thing."

The rumble strips again. Burton opened his eyes and jerked the car back into the center of the lane.

"I could go there now," he said. It was something. Not a bad idea, really. "He wouldn't risk having things like that delivered to the house. Maybe he rode his bike over there and bought a topographic map of a national forest or something."

The car passed along a split-rail fence. Three horses stood together in the enclosure, under the shade of a sycamore. One of them, a black mare, stood out against the tree's pale trunk. The children used to love driving down this road, hoping to find a horse near the fence, so they could stop and feed it clover.

"Hon?" Maddy asked. A strange tone in her voice. Fear?

"Yes?"

"What about the big library in the city? Boston Public."

Boston Public would have topographical maps for the entire world. The U.S., for sure. Any kind of information about biking, life in the woods, or whatever else Seb had on his mind.

"It would take him all day to get there, get what he needed, and come back," Burton said. "I think we would have noticed."

"Five or six weeks ago. The day we went to that bluegrass festival. We were gone all day. Jess slept over Grace's house."

"I'm going."

"Okay. That was fast."

Burton knew part of his motivation was just to do something. The alternative would be to go home and spin their wheels some more. "Unless you want to go? Get out of the house?"

"Ah, thanks. I'll go if you want me to."

He could tell from Maddy's tone that she did not think driving into the city would be any kind of respite. "I'm not far from Route Two. I'll just keep driving."

"All right. Burt?"

There was no one approaching from the other direction. He slowed the car and did a U-turn.

"Yes?"

"I don't know." Maddy paused. "Call me when you get there?"

Burton tipped his head back to take in the building's facade. Huge, really huge, rectangular blocks of smooth gray stone. They had been piled together to form a giant mass on the corner of Boylston & Exeter. Three crescent windows cut into the stone looked down from an upper floor.

Not everybody liked this entrance to the Boston Public Library, at least not this facade. It was the country's oldest library. Shouldn't it look old? Burton loved the modern facade. He had good memories from back when he used to come here as a graduate student. This immense modern structure had seemed so urban and his younger self really liked that. His older self still did. Those who wanted the Americana feel could use the traditional entrance down the street towards Copley Square.

They had been to the city many times but never brought the kids to the library. Burton liked having a private memory anyway. Hours wandering, flirting, reading, doing a little homework. Enjoying being a young man on his own.

He bypassed the main information desk and headed for the courtyard at the center of the complex.

It was as impressive as ever. A square pool with a fountain surrounded on three sides by a colonnade. The fourth side seemed to be the back of a building unrelated to the library. It had a stone balcony which seemed as strange and out of place as it always had.

The colonnade around the courtyard supported a roof wide enough to cover tables for two. These were the best seats in the library. You had shade for your book and a view of the fountain. Burton used to sit there for hours in the spring. When it was cool he wore a jacket and winter hat just to stay out there.

Back inside, he stopped to ask a young man pushing a cart of books where to find the map collection. The young man never completely stopped pushing and told him to take the steps to the second floor and go left.

The woman at the desk for maps and other collections said, "May I help you?" Her expression was blank except for the hint of wariness most people acquired when Burton approached. Urgency and anxiety were apparently obvious in his face or his posture.

"Hi. I have an unusual request. Do you remember a young man looking for maps of national forests or wilderness areas in the past month or two? Possibly topographical or highly detailed maps or guide books?"

The librarian tugged absent-mindedly at a necklace of little silver spheres as she processed this information. Burton held up a copy of Seb's school portrait for her to see.

"My son. He's disappeared and I think he might have...he might be hiding in a forest somewhere."

She studied the picture for a second and then glanced at Burton. This was common, too. Checking to see if he resembled the child in the photograph. He actually did not look much like Seb. They shared a thin face and high cheekbones. Not Burton's straight, dirty blonde hair. Certainly not his receding hairline. Seb, with his dark curls and light brown skin looked much more like his mother.

Before the librarian could reply, he removed the police report from his backpack and held it out to her. "He's been missing for nine days now. His name is Seb." Burton lay the report on the counter.

A woman carrying a canvas bag crammed with books came up and stood a couple inches off to Burton's right. Too close.

"I'm sorry." The librarian said. "I don't recognize him."

The woman next to him got even closer and switched her canvas bag from one hand to the other. He expected the librarian to look over his shoulder and say, "I'll be right with you."

Instead, she said, "Please wait here."

The librarian walked away from the desk and disappeared into a wall-colored door Burton had not noticed before.

The woman with the canvas bag turned and walked away.

The librarian returned five minutes later. "No one in the map stacks recognized him. There are others who work this desk but they aren't here today."

"Do you—"

"My supervisor asked if you wouldn't mind waiting a few minutes longer. She was going to look into something."

"No, I don't mind at all. Thank you so much."

The woman went back inside the door.

He scanned the counter for Seb's photo. The librarian had taken it and had not brought it back. Burton realized he had no other copies with him. He had plenty of flyers but not another color photo. This was not good.

The librarian returned to the desk, nodded at Burton, and started typing onto a keyboard.

"The maps," he asked. "Do all maps have to be retrieved from storage? Or is there a place where you can go look through them yourself?"

"All maps, except for those that are in regular-sized books, have to be retrieved by library staff." The librarian kept her gaze on him while she spoke but her fingers never stopped tapping at the keyboard.

The hidden door in the wall opened and an African-American woman with close-cropped hair came out. She strode towards Burton, her long gray skirt kicking forward at the knees and the sleeves of her white blouse flapping. If she wanted to look like a missionary school teacher, it was working.

Her posture only added to the effect. She held herself so erect Burton was concerned she might tip over backwards. He thought she would go behind the desk with the other librarian but she walked up to him. He was surprised at how young she looked. In her mid-twenties.

"You're the man whose son is missing?"

"Yes. Burton Franck."

"I'm Jessica Landry. Manager of..."

A loudspeaker overhead announced a children's book reading somewhere in the library. Burton was unable to make out what she was manager of.

"Hello, Jessica."

She held up a large cell phone.

"I scanned your son's photograph." She gave him a gentle smile, showing the tips of bright, white, perfectly aligned teeth. "I sent a message with the photo to all building personnel and asked anyone who may have seen your son to contact me. I also mentioned he may have been looking for maps."

Without writing anything down, Burton's request had been passed on twice, perfectly. The one and only Boston Public Library. And this woman with the same name as his daughter.

"That is so, so nice of you. I'm...thank you."

"You're welcome. A fair number of our staff are not here right now and might not respond right away. May I have your contact information?"

She took a piece of scratch paper and a miniature pencil from a wooden box on the counter and slid it towards him. He wrote down his contact information. She slipped the piece of paper into her hand with a neat flick and lay her business card and Seb's photo in its place.

Her kindness affected Burton. He needed a moment to compose himself. He pretended to search for something in his backpack. A couple of seconds later, he said. "I was hoping there would be a way to see if my son had a card and what books he checked out."

Jessica Landry gave her head a little shake. "That, I'm sorry, I can't do. I can find an administrator to speak with you about that."

"Don't you dare apologize. You've been so tremendously helpful. I'll talk with the administrator in a bit. My guess is that Seb didn't check anything out. He's been very careful."

"I'll be sure to contact you right away, should we hear anything."

"I'm going to be here for a while. I want to check your collection of books on wilderness survival."

Seb liked to make notes on pieces of scrap paper and insert them as bookmarks. Even if he had not been careless enough to leave a note behind, the survival books might give Burton some ideas.

"Would you like any help locating them?"

"No, thank you. I'll start with one of the computers and make a list."

"Best of luck to you, Mr. Franck."

With a nod, Jessica Landry turned and strode away, her backwards tilt more prominent when seen from behind. He thought he understood her old-fashioned clothes, now. An effort to look more authoritative given her young, and female, face.

Burton commandeered a shelving cart for the books he was amassing. He passed several library staff. None of them said anything, although one did give him a borderline dirty look. He parked the cart next to a wooden table with sturdy wood chairs in an open space between metal bookshelves. The library, for all its elegance, still had some surprisingly plain areas. Plain was totally fine. The space was nicely empty, although air conditioning poured from the ceiling directly onto his head and gave him goose bumps.

He flipped through each book as he transferred them from the cart to the table. He put books that circulated on one side of the table. He could take those home and go through them later.

He found no notes. Without a system to guide him, he chose to study more carefully the titles that intrigued him most.

Don't Eat That!, *My Side of the Mountain*, *Finding North*, *Barehands Fishing and Other Ways to Stay Alive*, *A Walk in the Woods*, *Shelters and ****holes*.

The books all had potential but Burton could find nothing concrete in them. He pushed them to the side and pulled the next stack towards him. He tilted his head sidewards to read their spines.

His cell phone rang. He dug for it at the bottom of his backpack and pressed the answer button as soon as he found it.

"Mr. Franck?" A woman's voice asked.

"Yes?"

"It's Jessica Landry. Are you still in the library?"

"I am." He stood up.

"There's someone here I think you should talk to. At the counter where we met earlier."

"I'll be right there."

He piled everything onto the cart as fast as he could and pushed it as fast as he could down the corridor. The cart was not made for speed. The front end wobbled from side to side and clattered loudly.

A slim man with a head of bushy gray and red hair was standing in front of the help desk with his hands folded over his belt buckle. Jessica Landry was standing next to him.

Burton abandoned the cart several feet from them and said, in his final steps, "You heard something?"

The man glanced over at Jessica.

"My associate, Gerome, saw someone last month he thinks may have been your son."

Gerome pulled down at the points of his shirt collar and began speaking. "Someone who looked like the boy in the photograph spent an afternoon going through a large number of topographical maps of the northeastern U.S." He pronounced "northeastern" with a deep-south twang.

"Jessica." Burton said. "Did I tell you that's my daughter's name?"

She smiled. "No."

"You're wonderful." He turned to Gerome. "Here's a hard copy photo of my son."

Gerome took care to hold the photo at the very edges.

"His name is Seb. Did he mention his name?"

Gerome looked up from the photo. "No. He spoke very little. I retrieved materials based on a long list of call numbers he wrote out by hand. I remember because most people print these out when there are so many. He asked for the list of call numbers back, now that I think of it."

Unbelievable, Burton thought. Seb wrote the call numbers by hand in case a printout could somehow be traced back to him. Even more unbelievable, they had a clue. A real clue. Burton felt woozy, like he should sit down, but he kept it together.

"Other than asking me to retrieve the materials," Gerome continued, "the boy seemed uninterested in talking. I remember because I do tend to make conversation when I'm assisting patrons." He glanced sidewards at Jessica.

She gave him a little "get on with it" smile.

"There are so many interesting stories. The reasons why people seek out information are fascinating. Especially when they are looking for maps."

"The photo," Burton asked. "You're certain that's him?"

"I'd be hesitant to say for certain but this looks like the boy I helped. Of course, there weren't any other teenagers looking for lots of maps in the past month, so perhaps that's biased me."

"Did he happen to mention why he was doing this?"

"No, sir, I would have remembered that. Because I was curious myself."

"And he asked for topographical maps of New England?"

"The Atlantic states, actually, and Pennsylvania I believe. Is that an Atlantic state? I think it borders the Delaware River not the Atlantic. Your son, I mean the boy, asked not only for topographical maps. Highway maps and oversized books, too. He was at the photocopier for hours." Gerome held up a finger. "Oh. I recall getting him quite a few books and maps for the Appalachian Trail. Come to think of it, most of the maps I retrieved would have included the Appalachian Trail."

"What about the Continental Divide Trail?" Burton asked. "Or states not on the East Coast?"

Gerome squeezed his chin with his forefinger and thumb.

"Not that I recall. I didn't want to be intrusive. He really wasn't making eye contact. I hope I didn't seem too intrusive. It's not as if I plagued him with questions." Gerome cast another glance at Jessica. "I think I asked if he was going on a trip. Something like that. I don't remember what he said. To be honest, I thought something might be... amiss. Mind you, it was only the vaguest of thoughts. I couldn't have known..."

"Of course not." Burton said. "I'm grateful you're so observant. And have such an amazing memory."

He had just scored a point against Seb at his own game. Technology. Although it was not Burton's idea to scan Seb's photo and distribute it to all of the library staff's hand-held devices.

It was also unsettling to feel like you were in a battle with your own son. Trying to keep a step ahead of your children was normal, but they were at real odds here. It had taken a non-stop hunt by the whole family, not to mention Phillip, the police, a bunch of other people, and the Boston Public Library, just to get this one clue.

"If you like, I can gather materials of the sort I brought your son," Gerome said.

"That would be great. Let's start with Appalachian Trail maps."

Gerome nodded, turned, and went to the door in the wall. There had to be a skyscraper's worth of book and maps in there.

"As for me," Jessica said. "I've got to return to my office in the catacombs."

Burton pressed his hand into hers. "My whole family thanks you."

"Come back together some day. I think they'll like it."

"We will. We will."

Gerome returned twenty minutes later with an uncommonly wide cart. It was full of materials. A number of the maps and atlases were two feet long and nearly as wide, unopened.

"Your son—the person I helped, I mean—spent the majority of his time copying maps like these here." Gerome gestured to one of the piles on the cart. "New England topographical maps and Appalachian Trail maps."

The Appalachian Trail. When Seb was much younger, he heard about the Appalachian Trail on Massachusetts public television. It was he who suggested the family make their first visit to the trail two hours west of their home. Seb loved the Massachusetts A.T. but other parks around the state were stiff competition. State forests with lakes to swim in. Small, fast flowing rivers for canoeing. Swamplands with boardwalks where they searched for skunk cabbages and jack-in-the-pulpits. Nature preserves on the coast with their sand dunes and scrub pines. But Seb did love the idea of the A.T.

He was not yet addicted to computers and still used books at the time. He set off to the town library to learn more about the A.T. From this research he learned about the Continental Divide Trail. This trail had bigger mountains. It had animals like bighorn sheep you could not see on the A.T. or in any New England park. That day in the library, Seb abandoned the Appalachian Trail like a friend who wanted to play embarrassing little-kid games.

The Continental Divide Trail captured his attention like nothing before. Burton figured Seb's ego was a factor here. The CDT (Seb had the entire family calling it the CDT before long) was a trail no one had ever heard of. The idea of the Continental Divide itself was impressive, sending its rain to a different ocean depending on which side it fell.

Seb used his allowance to buy two CDT posters and he asked for a film series about the trail for Christmas. Then he started pestering his parents to spend their summer vacation on the trail in Montana or Colorado.

But Seb did not study the CDT at the Downtown Boston branch of the library. If he had been willing to try traveling two-thousand miles incognito, the task of acquiring the extensive equipment required to survive on the CDT had probably persuaded him to let go of the idea. So he settled on the good old A.T. and set about charting his course with help from the map-man himself, Gerome.

Burton had to adjust his assumptions. He had envisioned Seb sitting by a stream, meditating on the deep thoughts he had been sharing with them in his emails. With the Appalachian Trail, however, you stayed in a shelter one night and had to move on. You were not allowed to camp as long as you liked in a shelter or in a tent off the trail. It often took most of the day to get from one shelter to the next. Seb would also need to leave the trail to find an internet connection to watch the videos. This would not be a problem. The A.T. crossed roads and intercepted trails that led into towns throughout its length. Seb could have his deep woods experience, periodically check videos in town, and keep moving. As his sister said, he was not good at sitting still.

Dwelling on possible scenarios would need to be done later. Burton had stacks and stacks of materials to go through. He pulled a pad from his pocket to note his train of thought for further reference.

Seb was definitely on the Appalachian Trail. He would not have spent a day photocopying A.T. materials just to throw a red herring out for his family and the police. Especially considering what a long shot it was that Burton had connected with Gerome at all. He certainly could not have counted on Jessica Landry broadcasting his photo. He would have at least left a clue to lead them here if he was trying to send them on a wild goose chase. Luckily, his mother was a genius. It was her idea to check the main branch downtown.

Gerome was still waiting by the cart with his hands folded over his belt buckle.

"What time do you close?" Burton asked.

"Nine. I'll be off soon, but Cyndi at the desk should be able to help you. Would you like this cart somewhere near the photocopier?"

"Yes. That would be great, thanks."

"I know of a copier that will work well for you. It's less busy."

Gerome began pushing his wide cart down the hall. Burton followed with his own cart.

There was a table not far from the copier. They parked the carts on either side of it.

Burton took Gerome's hand and kept it for a moment. "Thanks. Really. You may have saved his life."

"You're quite welcome. I hope your son is home soon." Gerome bowed, just his head and neck, and then looked embarrassed for bowing.

Burton unloaded the materials onto the table carefully. Gerome had grouped them by state. There was hope for mankind in Gerome. And Jessica.

Some maps were folded, some in rolls. One, depicting the entire A.T., was laminated and five feet long. The topographical maps were the real finds. Burton spread one out on the table. It showed a section of Vermont. The entire map was covered with symbols and concentric lines indicating elevation. Blue for streams. Dotted lines for trails. Little pine trees for forests. Numbers for altitude.

There was not enough time to look through these things. Burton was going to have to photocopy them. If he didn't get through all of the materials, he would write down their names and come back again. Maddy and Jessica, with her fluorescent sticky notes, could come along to help.

The Massachusetts materials alone occupied two shelves of one cart. Burton decided to start there and continue northward. It seemed unlikely Seb would go south in July. It would be hot enough in New England with a pack full of camp gear and supplies. If necessary, Burton could get information about the southern part of the trail later.

He felt cautiously vindicated about his "revelation" that Seb was in the deep woods. There were no books about bicycling. Burton had intentionally not mentioned bicycling to avoid putting suggestions into Gerome's head. Gerome would have remembered.

A tiny, five by three inch book sat at the top of one pile. Its navy blue cloth binding was frayed at the edges. *The Appalachian Trail in Maine* was printed in faded gold embossing on the cover.

Burton picked up the little book and flipped through it. Published 1960. Every step of the trail was described inside. Folded maps were tucked in and attached at the start of each chapter, showing the section of trail described on the following pages. Each attached map unfolded to nearly two feet square. Many of the maps were torn along their folds. Burton would be photocopying until the library closed.

He paused for a moment to consider if Seb was actually quite far from the Appalachian Trail. Riding his bike, perhaps, on the Natchez Trace in Mississippi, or some other place he had never mentioned, feeling guilty but amused by the thought of his father photocopying away in the wrong direction.

CHAPTER ELEVEN

HUMANS OR NOT

BURTON WATCHED A CHICKADEE on the feeder hanging from a shepherd's hook at the edge of the patio. It chirped and flew to a spruce branch nearby. Another chickadee zipped to the same perch on the feeder where the other had been. He thought of Seb on a mountain ridge watching a great bird, an eagle. Feeling enough peace to keep him afloat until they found him and helped him make his way in the mixed-up world.

The second chickadee flew off and Burton looked back to the laptop on the wrought-iron patio table in front of him. He waited for his eyes to refocus. The cup of coffee had not done much to counteract another night of shattered sleep. It seemed to have made him feel more tired.

The map on the screen featured a number of bold icons: "P" for parking/trail access and "F" for spots along the Appalachian Trail where you could get off and not have to go too far to buy food. He located the last stop in New Hampshire, wrote its name and GPS coordinates on a pad of paper, then switched to a similar map of the A.T. in Vermont.

Ten days. Ten agonizing, preposterous, incredibly screwed up days. They had pestered every ranger, club and blog connected to the Appalachian Trail and still knew nothing. Except for things like the fact that the Appalachian Trail went on for more than 700 miles in New England alone.

The sliding glass door slid open with a bang. Jessica came onto the patio in gym shorts rolled down at the waistband. Burton thought she was too young for this look but opted to say nothing. His daughter jogged over to Maddy, who sat with her legs folded to one side, pulling weeds from a flower bed, and plopped on the grass next to her.

Burton loved his wife for how she continued to try to make their daughter feel safe and not consumed by anxiety. They were doing their best to distract her.

Myro came around the side of the house. He saw his two girls by the garden and ran to them, his stomach swaying. He leapt, stumbled over Jessica's legs, and landed on his back. The dachshund remained there, barking to be scratched. Jessica reached over and ran her fingers along his stomach, but she kept her eyes on her mother. After a few seconds of her half-hearted scratching, Myro flipped over, clamped his mouth on a trowel, and ran a few feet away.

"Hey mom. Did you just set the timer on your watch?"

"Uh. Yes?"

"It's okay. I know you can't sit in the garden with me when Seb's in trouble."

"We have to take some breaks." Maddy kissed her daughter on the cheek. "You're a good kid."

Myro dropped the trowel and fell to the grass. He lay there with his head between his paws.

"Have you guys noticed how many people are making comments about our videos?" Jessica asked. She looked over her shoulder to Burton at the patio table. "Some of them are really getting into it."

"Some are trying to help." Maddy said, without interrupting her weeding. "But there's a surprising number of scums."

Jessica laughed, apparently amused by her mother's terminology. "And people that are, like, *go Seb!*"

"Yes, that's what I'm talking about."

Ka-knock-ka-knock-knock-knock! abruptly sounded from Burton's laptop.

Jessica gasped.

She and Maddy hopped up and jogged to Burton's side. They leaned in towards the computer. He brought up the email program. There was a new, unread message there. He opened it just as he remembered that the last message had been intended for Maddy and him only.

The new message's title read: *"Video for Mom, Dad & Jess. Next one just for Mom and Dad."*

"Huh," Jessica growled.

The only text contained in the body of the message was an underlined string of letters and numbers. A hyperlink. Burton clicked it.

A video player opened. Seb was sitting cross-legged on a bed in track pants and his soccer jersey. Burton recognized the blue and green plaid comforter which was still on Seb's bed. The web cam was picking up too much light. Seb's face appeared exceptionally pale atop the dark blue of his soccer shirt.

"He's in his room," Maddy whispered.

Seb held up a hand as a greeting. "These messages are starting to get personal, and really it's between me and Mom and Dad. So I made a second video just for them. This video is for Jess."

Ka-knock-ka-knock-knock-knock!

They all flinched at the same time. A small window appeared in front of the video, covering Seb's face. It was the notification that the parents-only video Seb just mentioned had arrived. Burton closed this newest announcement window just in time to see Seb open his mouth and begin to speak again.

"Jess." Seb narrowed his eyes, in what looked like an attempt to appear more big brother-ish. "Be awesome and don't worry about me, though you probably hate me and I don't blame you. I may be confused but it's gonna be okay. This is my way of dealing with, well, whatever. You know how strange I am. But I need to keep the messages just for Mom and Dad from now on. Forgive me, okay? I hope to make it up to you some day. Love you."

Seb picked up a remote control, pressed his thumb on it, and his image froze.

Burton closed the laptop.

"That was useless," Jessica said.

"You want to talk about it?" Maddy asked.

"I'm okay. I want to see the next thing from Seb."

Maddy lay a hand on her cheek. "I don't blame you."

"I saw the YouTube movie you made about Seb's poem," Jessica mumbled.

Burton's and Maddy's eyes met for a moment. With nothing to communicate to one another, they looked at Jessica.

"The one he told you to give a secret name. So I couldn't find it. Well, I found it. Pandora." Jessica backed away from the table and bumped into the handle to the sliding glass door.

Burton did not know what to say. A couple seconds passed. Maddy stared at Jessica, waiting.

"How?" Burton asked.

"I did some searches and used the time, eleven o'clock, when you were in your bedroom. And then...I had to see the email from Seb. The one with the *What?* poem."

Maddy glanced at Burton. "We didn't leave the laptop out after that, I'm sure."

Jessica spoke without looking directly at either of them. "I logged into your email using my laptop. The messages stay on the website for your email, if you don't delete them from your computer. I guess Seb didn't think of that."

They may not have explicitly forbidden her from reading the *What?* poem, or searching for the video they made in response to it, but Jessica had to have known she was going against their wishes.

"What could be in Seb's new message that's worse than his poem?" Jessica asked. "And he says he 'hopes' he can make it up to me? Like he might never see us again?" She looked confused at this point, uncertain if she was doing a good job of getting permission to see the parents-only video.

"Come here Jess," Maddy said.

Jessica hesitated, then stepped forward.

Maddy reached her arms around Jessica's waist and pulled her in. "I'm sorry. I'm sorry about all of this."

"Can I see Seb's video? That little one we just saw doesn't count. I've seen everything else so far and I'm still okay."

"Your Dad and I are going to look at it first. We'll decide then."

Maddy set the laptop at the foot of the bed. She lay on her stomach in front of it with her feet towards the headboard, and propped herself up on her elbows. Burton gazed out the window at the driveway. When Seb got home they would put their laptops under the wheels of the Subaru and crush them.

He closed the curtains to block the glare from the sun and stretched out next to Maddy. On the screen was a still shot of Seb on his bed in half-lotus, wearing the same clothes as in the video for Jessica. Maddy clicked on the translucent triangle at the center of the image to begin playing the video.

Seb sat quietly for a second. Then he asked, "Why don't we drink water?" His voice sounded thin through the laptop's small speakers.

He looked towards the ceiling, as if to gather his thoughts, or, perhaps, to gather his courage.

"What's up with all these people that go around saying they don't like the taste of water? Are we *that* out of touch with reality? Is there any other animal that doesn't like the taste of water? And that's just drinks. Is it because food used to be hard to get and people didn't know when they would be eating again, so they gobbled up what they could? It makes me think of Myro. He never says no to more food.

"Are we only as smart as that fat dog? Can't we tell we're destroying the world? But we *do* know we're destroying the world, right? And we still don't stop? How is that possible?

"Do you remember the Buddhist meditation we went to where they talked about the danger of desire? That's another idea that got stuck in my head. I started to feel like an out-of-control animal trapped with other out-of-control animals doing stupid things constantly.

"It scares me. My own species scares me. I think I might hate my own species."

Seb smiled here. He seemed surprised to have smiled. He tilted his head forward and ran his fingers through his hair. When he looked up again, the smile was gone.

"I mean, most people don't want to hurt themselves or anybody, right? So maybe they're just screwed up. And maybe the world would be better off without them.

"You know some people say I think too much, right? Well, ever try to stop thinking? That's another Ajahn question. Anyway, I kept thinking about humans and I wasn't feeling any better about them. Like, even if burning coal wasn't causing global warming, we still knew it made a lot of people sick. And you know what? We burned it anyway. Because we don't care. Because people suck. That's what I kept telling myself. Not fun.

"I asked myself if I went to a place not messed up by people, would I stop going crazy? That would mean doing exactly what Dad said in his article, being selfish and not helping to deal with the situation. But I didn't know what else to do to stop going crazy.

"If I told you what I wanted to do, you wouldn't let me do it. Not to really be alone like I needed to be. You would watch me like a hawk and I couldn't get away. And the thought of being trapped made me feel even more crazy. I had to get away really soon, before you realized I was going crazy and stopped me.

"One day, I don't know if you remember, the day I stayed home with a stomach ache, that was the worst day. This idea kept coming back to me. Maybe the world would be better off without humans. But I'm a human. I didn't want to think about it anymore but I couldn't stop."

Seb took a deep breath. He uncrossed his legs and rearranged them into a half-lotus again, this time with a different foreleg on the bottom.

"I got all tough in the first messages, to show I was serious. Since I've been gone this long, I guess you know I am.

"So there's only one more assignment. I have a question: would the world be a better place with or without humans? The global warming that's happening wouldn't be happening if it wasn't for humans. A lot of animals and plants are going extinct for stupid things that humans do and we could be next. And it's our own fault.

"Just tell me what you think." Seb pulled a piece of paper from behind himself, glanced down at it, looked up again, and said, "Call the video 'Humans or Not?'"

He smiled a smile that looked forced. Intended to ease their worry. "Got to go."

Seb waved and pressed the remote. His image froze, hand in the air from waving, and then shrunk down until it was one of a dozen small, still images of videos in a grid on the YouTube page.

Burton and Maddy re-ran Seb's video. They did not speak as they watched, just took notes and played the video again.

After the sixth viewing, Burton asked, "I'm done. You want to see it again?"

"No. Thanks."

Seb had called it his last assignment. Burton hoped, it felt like an ache, the feeling was so intense, that the video response they were about to make was the last thing their son needed to hear and he would come home. How likely was it he would find their videos so unsatisfactory that he still would not come home? Burton felt panic surge when he realized how all their previous videos, with their emphasis on Seb's well-being, could have reinforced his fear that they would watch him like a hawk, and possibly trap him in his house or a hospital.

Maddy suggested they try to think of times they themselves had wondered about the human species. She and Burton did some free writing on their own, then talked, and then taped notes to the wall. The pressure to get this last assignment right impinged on every thought, every word they spoke. Previously they had managed to run with their ideas and even ended up feeling optimistic they would connect with Seb. They did not feel so optimistic about this video. Seb had asked a question that was not easy to answer.

They decided to focus on the best examples of people taking on global warming and having success. Seb needed to hear this, even if he did not ask for it.

These notes were taped onto the wall next to the others. They had notes all around the perimeter of the bedroom. Next, they made a first attempt at ordering the pages of notes by writing a number on top of each in blue highlighter. Maddy would type them up and see what they had.

She sat on the bed typing while Burton retrieved notes and paced back and forth in front of her. When she was done, Burton pointed to the clock at the bottom of the laptop screen. They had been at it for two hours. It was time for decisions.

He sat next to her. They deleted most of what they had, moved the remainder around, and added a few new thoughts. Finally, Maddy changed the font and broke the notes into sections so they could refer to them during filming.

"Do we need a dress rehearsal?" she asked.

"I think we've waited long enough."

"I'll go downstairs and print it."

Maddy put her hand on his thigh and gave him her "we can do this" smile. Burton returned the coaching with an affirmative nod. He wondered if she felt as anxious and incompetent as he did.

He went downstairs to see what was going on. The clock read noon. Rosa was not preparing lunch for the first time since she had arrived. The only sign of life down there was a pair of hands protruding from a pile of cushions on the couch. The hands held an open copy of *Watership Down*. Jessica had been trying to do some of her summer reading but never got far before falling asleep.

"Where's Gramma?" her voice said from behind the pillows.

"Home somewhere," Maddy said, coming in from the doorway to the basement. "We would have heard her brakes if she went out."

"C'mere Jess," Burton said. "We need to talk about the video we're going to make."

Pillows moved and Jessica's face appeared. She looked scared. She pushed the pillows off of her, onto the floor. Her father motioned to one end of the kitchen table and the three of them sat there.

"Does that mean I get to be in the video?" Jessica asked.

"Maybe we could do a two-part answer, just like Seb did a two-part video for us." Burton said.

"Whatever. He should hear he's not so clever. Like I found his secret poem."

169

"I'm not sure that's a good idea." Maddy said.

Jessica tossed *Watership Down* to the other end of the table. "Maybe my big brother should know I saw the video, too. The video I wasn't supposed to see. About bad humans." The paperback teetered on the edge of the table, and then fell off and hit the floor with a loud slap.

"Jess." Burton stared at her. She had disobeyed them, again. "I wish you hadn't. I really do."

Jessica looked away.

Maddy watched him. It was his turn.

In a calm voice he asked, "Do you want to tell me how you were able to see the second video?"

Jessica's mouth twitched. "The web version of your email."

"Oh, that's just great," Maddy said. "Same as before. Are we stupid?" She leaned away from the table and gave Burton a "do something" look.

They should have known Jessica would check their email but they were too busy trying to get a video response to Seb as soon as possible. They would not forget to change their password this time.

"Jess," Burton said, "we have to stick together. We've got our hands full trying to get Seb back home. Each of us to has to try our best. I know it's hard. We have to trust each other, and that includes trusting that we, as adults, know better about some things." He placed his hand over hers. "Okay?"

"I'm supposed to trust you when you're lying to me?"

"What are we lying about?" Burton asked.

"Putting things on YouTube with secret names. Like *Humans or Not.*"

Maddy's chair squeaked on the tile as she slid closer to Jessica. "Please get your laptop."

"No."

"Get your laptop."

"I won't." Jessica jerked her hand out from under Burton's.

Maddy calmly said, "Then I—"

Jessica stood. "Nooooo!"

"It doesn't matter," Burton said. "We're changing our email password."

Jessica used her computer to keep a diary, play games, listen to music, and communicate with friends. To take away her "sad old laptop" (most friends had smaller, newer gadgets) when she was stuck at home, with Seb's absence hanging over them always...Burton did not think they should do it.

"Please sit down, Jess," he said.

She sat.

"If you disobey us again, we're going to lock up your laptop. You'll only be able to use it when one of us is around."

"You didn't say I couldn't watch the video."

This last wisecrack was probably intended to avoid appearing too happy over retaining her laptop but it could have pushed her mother over the edge. Maddy sat there with her eyes closed and her hands folded under her nose, trying to re-focus on what they had to do.

"Actually," Burton said. "We *did* say not to watch the video. We said we were going to watch it and let you know."

The three of them sat there at one end of the table, their eyes cast down at its surface. Jessica started chewing a thumbnail.

"I'm going to check on my mother," Maddy said.

She got up and walked down the hall. They heard a knock. A few seconds later, "Mom?" The door creaked open and closed.

Maddy returned to the kitchen five minutes later. "She won't talk. Just kept saying to do what we had to do. That I should go back to be with my family. I don't know what's gotten into her."

"I'll make her a card," Jessica said. "With owls on it. She loves the owls. I wonder if she knows I draw owls because I can't draw anything else. An oval with two big circles for eyes and a beak between them and you're practically done."

"That's exactly what she needs." Maddy said.

Jessica stood. "I could make eggs for lunch, too."

"We're not going to feel like eating until we do the video, don't you think?" Burton asked.

Maddy followed his lead by asking, "How about making some notes for your part of the video?"

His wife had apparently come to the same conclusion as him. They had to give Jessica an opportunity to express her feelings about Seb's videos. They could always edit out her part afterwards if necessary. They might indeed have to monitor all use of Jessica's laptop once they were done with the video, but they would deal with that later.

The kitchen table was never without an assortment of pads and pens. Jessica reached for one of each. She bit the end of the pen and looked down at the paper.

Maddy got up and stood in the doorway, looking down the hall in the direction of her mother's room. Burton picked up the script and scanned it. Jessica began writing.

He set the script down. "What music does Seb like?"

"Nothing new." Jessica gouged out what she had written, leaving blotches of ink on the paper and getting some on her hand. "The Clash.

So prep school."

Burton did not understand this comment. Seb went to public school. The Clash seemed cool enough. Although, if your father thought they were cool...

He had been thinking to suggest they play some kind of music Seb liked during the video, something optimistic, but that probably would not be cool, either.

"I'm done," Jessica said.

Maddy came back to the table and sat down. Jessica did not offer her notes to either of them to review. Burton decided to let it be. He handed the script to Maddy.

"Will you do the reading?"

She scanned it, set it down, and crossed out a couple of lines.

Burton looked over her shoulder to see what she had done. "Why did you cross that part out?"

"It's maybe too intense. Too...I don't know. Maybe he won't get my references?"

"These are our gut feelings. That's what he wants. He'll know what you mean."

Maddy lifted up the script and said, "All right, I'll read it."

Burton drummed his fingers near Jessica's pad of paper. "You ready, sweetie?"

"I guess so. Can I go first? I want to get it over with."

"Sure."

Burton went over to put the camera onto the tripod by the fireplace. He came back to the couch to sit in the space Maddy and Jessica had left for him.

Jessica slid forward and looked down to read, without looking up, from the note pad she had placed on the coffee table. "Not to brag but I found the email and the video you didn't want me to see. You're not the only computer genius in the family."

She made no attempt at inflection, reading like it was a homework assignment she resented. "For your humans question, how about you make a list of people you know. Then you can go talk to the sucky ones about how maybe they could suck less. Instead of complaining. That's all I have to say. Bye."

She thrust herself back and squeezed in under Burton's arm.

Maddy held a set of note cards out in front of her. "Your Dad's and my thoughts. We humans have our flaws, but we are also good like no other species is good. Most cats will torture a mouse until it dies, perhaps out of instinct, but not caring at all about the mouse's pain.

Humans don't do that, except for a few very messed up ones. Dogs are loyal to their family, but not to strangers. Humans are sensitive to the suffering of strangers and to other animals. They care even when there's nothing in it for them. They care about people on the other side of the world. Not all the time, of course. We do think about ourselves first. But we are the only species that cares about people we never met. That's what gives me hope.

"As you've pointed out, humans have the biggest problem they've ever had to deal with and they need to act like it. Your father and I were going tell you about some of the big successes that are already happening, but, well, your sister had a conniption about the garbage homework and we never got around to it. Maybe you know already. There are entire countries that have figured out how to be strong and not make global warming worse. A carbon fee is one way some people are already having success. People are talking to each other. Like your sister said. Sort of."

Here Maddy glanced over at Jessica and winked, then turned to face the camera again.

"We are anxious for you to be here with us. There's so much to talk about. How we are part of nature, not controlling it, and how that's a good thing. How knowing this can give you real joy and peace."

Maddy set her note cards down and looked into the camera.

"There's another thing about humans, though. We have a lot in common, but we all have to find our own way. You're young but we understand that you need the freedom to deal with what you're going through in a creative way. In a way that doesn't make you feel trapped. Because what you've had the courage to face is not easy. We can't promise no pain, or no fear, but we can promise to be creative along with you. Maybe you could make a deal with the school to do part of your freshman year in an ashram. Or some other quiet place. Who knows? A laboratory up in the Arctic Circle.

"If it makes you feel any better, you are asking the same questions that people have been asking for a very long time. Everybody from Shakespeare to rappers to Robert Frost. Remember that poem about looking into dark woods on a freezing cold night and wondering why he wants to go in there? That's the hard part about being human, I'm afraid. There isn't an easy answer book. But we do a lot better when we try to figure these things out together.

"We hope that's a decent answer to your question. Thank you for being honest with us."

Burton was about to make a joke about giving Seb a longer answer than he wanted when a strange noise, a rapid clicking, distracted him. It was coming from the hallway beyond the kitchen and growing louder.

He, Jessica and Maddy turned to look over the couch. Rosa strode into the kitchen and marched down the two steps to the living room. She came around the front of the coffee table stopped in front of the camera. She was wearing a black dress with a red rose pattern and black high heels. Burton could no longer see the camera, only Rosa's rump.

"God will help you," she said. Then she bent at the knees to get her face in line with the camera. The edge of the coffee table hit her calves but she managed to rather gracefully sit on the coffee table. She steadied herself by placing her palms on its surface.

"Wherever you are, ask him for help. His plan is too big for you to understand. Even too big for Doctor Einstein to understand. God loves you and will not forsake you." She twisted her body to glare, with wide, scared-looking eyes, back at Burton. The expression changed to surprise at her own boldness. She turned around and looked into the camera once more. "It's about time someone told you that."

With both hands, she pushed herself up and stood. She smoothed out her dress before walking away without looking at anyone on the couch. A citrus perfume remained in her wake. As her heels clicked away, slower than they had during her approach, Burton imagined her hips moving with extra sway. A last waltz before entering her room and packing her things. The door opened quietly and closed without a sound.

Goodbye El Mosquito, Burton said to himself. *La* Mosquit*a*?

The camera had filmed them sitting there on the couch, listening to Rosa walk away.

"You got a very diverse response, I think." Maddy said with a hint of a smile. "If you take away one thing, though, let it be this: we will find a way. A way for you to not feel trapped. To not feel watched like a hawk. We'll have to talk to you about how to do that but I promise you we will."

CHAPTER TWELVE

THE PLACE WHERE THE PEOPLE FALL OFF

AFTER THEY FINISHED AND POSTED the video for Seb, Jessica scrambled eggs and started to cook them in Rosa's giant cast iron pan. A few minutes later, Rosa strode into the kitchen. She swept her eyes across Burton and Maddy, doing her best to keep a poker face, and joined Jessica at the stove.

"I'll make toast," Rosa said.

Grandmother and granddaughter worked silently at the counter together. Burton and Maddy remained at the table, staring off into space. A few minutes later, Jessica brought a tray of juice and cups to the table. Rosa sat next to Maddy. She may not have realized this would mean she would be directly across from Burton. The two of them managed to put food on their plates without looking directly at each other.

Not more than a half hour ago, Rosa had explicitly criticized his parenting. His failure to comfort Seb with reassurances about God's protection. She blamed him exclusively, which was obvious from the way she turned to stare at him, and him only, in the middle of her unscheduled appearance in the video.

Burton decided to put an end to this crap now, with sugar instead of venom. He looked up from his plate. "Thank you."

His mother-in-law blinked at him several times. Her mouth fell open a bit.

"Thanks for loving our son."

Burton meant it this time, which he realized only after the words came out of his mouth.

"Yes. I do."

Maddy placed her hand over her mother's. "We're going to have a talk, Mom. Burton found a clue in Seb's video. He wants to hear what we think."

Jessica interrupted them by plunking down a large platter of scrambled eggs smelling strongly of Swiss cheese. Toast slices, cut on the diagonal, encircled the eggs. The meal resembled a lumpy sun with fat brown rays. It was past two in the afternoon and the family was finally hungry.

Burton picked up a piece of toast, buttered soggy the way he liked it.

"Did you notice anything?" He took a bite of toast and chewed before continuing. "Did you see or hear any clues in Seb's video about where he might be?"

Forks that had been scraping into eggs stopped at the same time. Rosa had not seen either of Seb's videos and looked from Burton to Maddy and Jessica, waiting to learn more.

"His video lines up with the A.T. pretty well," Maddy said. "Lots of time without people around. And the people that he would meet aren't wasteful or litterbugs. You can't hear cars up there, either. I would guess that a lot of the hikers are environmental activists."

"There's that," Burton said. "I agree. I was thinking of something even more specific. I should just tell you, because I'm not sure there's any way you could have caught it."

He waited for Rosa to finish spreading raspberry preserves on her toast. "Rosa, you know about the A.T.?"

She squinted. "Is it like the FBI?"

"No, Grandma." Jessica suppressed a grin. "A. T.—As in Appalachian Trail. As in the Appalachian Mountains. A hiking trail. Dad found out that Seb was looking at a bunch of maps and books about the A.T. before he...ran away."

"Yes, of course I know about the Apple..." Rosa said. "Trail."

Jessica covered her mouth with her hand.

Her grandmother gave a light smack to her granddaughter's wrist. She dropped the knife she was holding into the preserves jar. It clacked loudly against the glass. "I pay attention to what's going on. I see all those maps. It's far away from the world that scares him."

"Yes," Maddy said.

"Props to you Grandma," Jessica said.

Maddy turned to Burton. "Okay. Tell us what you heard. Or saw."

He stood, feeling the urge to pace, but decided to keep still. His wife, mother-in-law and daughter stared up at him. They were curious, of course. Convincing them would be another matter.

"I'm thinking of the part where Seb talked about a place not messed up by humans."

Burton paused to make sure they understood what he was referring to. Jessica and Maddy nodded. Of course they knew. Seb's parents-only video, the one Jessica found on her own, had arrived just the day before. Rosa had not seen the video but she nodded to let Burton know he should continue.

"Before we made the video, I thought of a time Seb and I were walking in Fisk Park. He was probably nine years old then. We had looked through a book about the Appalachian Trail and he was so excited. I don't know what he saw in the book but he was under the impression that you could see the whole United States from the top of the trail. Thinking about it now, it makes sense why he moved on so quickly to the Continental Divide Trail. You can't see the whole country from the A.T. if the CDT has a taller mountain range that blocks your view of California."

"But we already think he's on the A.T.," Maddy said.

"I'm getting to that. When Seb told me he would be able to see the whole U.S. from the A.T., I didn't correct him."

Then he said, "Except I'd be scared to go to Mount Katahdin."

"I asked him why he would be scared."

"Because that's the end of the Appalachian Trail. I might fall off into Canada."

"I couldn't help laughing a little. Then I asked him what he meant."

"Where the trail ends is Canada, and there's no people in Canada. Because it's too far down from the top of the Appalachian Trail."

"The trail ends in Maine, not Canada," I told him. "And there are people in Canada."

"But not many?"

"Depends on what you call many. Not many compared to the U.S."

"And they're stuck there because they can't get back up onto the trail?"

Burton smiled. "Seb looked really concerned for the Canadians. It was pretty cute. I told him, 'No, I think they could leave Canada if they really wanted to.'"

"That is really cute," Jessica said.

"I wish I'd remembered that story before. But Seb hasn't talked about the A.T. in years. Remember how he used to walk all the way to the library? How they had to request books on the CDT to be sent from the main branch because they didn't have anything with maps?

"Who knows where he would have gone if he had enough money and the ability to travel incognito? Possibly the CDT. He might have tried to get to Tibet.

"But I think we really have to go with what the man at the library found. Gerome. Seb would not have used the one full day he had on his own to review materials about a place he was not going to. The types of books and maps he studied really point to some remote part of New England.

"I was thinking again about the story I just told you about Seb worrying he would fall off the A.T. into Canada. Suddenly I knew that's where he would go. We're talking about the very first place he associated with the frontier. The land without people. And it's not that far from Portsmouth. He may not remember our talk but the idea is still there, down deep. One of those events in your childhood that sticks with you. I forget what that's called. Stronger than an impression. Burned into his young mind, for lack of a better way of saying it.

"On top of that, there's what he said about getting back inside Pandora's box. Recapturing his childhood. Plus, as we've said, going somewhere without noisy, garbage-making humans."

Maddy, Jessica and Rosa just stared at him. No one gave any indication he had convinced them. Rosa took off her glasses and cleaned them with a paper napkin.

"So, what you're saying is that he's on Mount Katahdin," Maddy said. "Near where the trail ends."

"I'm saying he went to Mount Katahdin. You can't stay there. Maybe he camped on the side of the mountain for a day or two, but you're not supposed to stay in the same spot day after day on the A.T. Besides, Katahdin is in Baxter State Park.

Burton walked over to the collage of maps on the kitchen wall. It was four feet high and six feet wide. He and Jessica had scotch-taped photocopies from the Downtown Boston library to create a map of all the New England States together. The information there was mind-boggling. Elevation levels, trails, roads, tracts of forested land. The green areas that denoted forests took up half the map.

"That's Katahdin." Burton pointed to the center of a large green rectangle in the middle of Maine. "The big green rectangle is Baxter State Park. We've had the Baxter Park rangers looking for him since he left. And those guys are serious rangers. Baxter is a big place and you don't want to get lost in there. If Seb was hiding in a cave and not coming out to watch videos or do whatever else he wanted to do, he might be able to stay in Baxter. But I think one of the rangers would have seen him if he moved about the park."

"Then where did he go?" Rosa asked.

Eyebrows went up. Rosa had stayed out of these conversations after she and Burton tangled the first couple of times. Was her appearance in the video, and now this question, a sign she would be injecting herself back into the conversation? Burton did not begrudge her desire to contribute.

"Seb must be hiking south on the A.T., probably somewhere still in Maine."

Burton pointed to Baxter Park on the wall again.

"He would have started on Katahdin. He's been thinking for some time he was on the verge of losing his mind. What could counteract his impatience with humanity more than standing at the top of the place where humanity ends? To see all the way to Canada. To have made it to Katahdin and to the very top of the Appalachian Trail?"

"I don't get it," Jessica said.

They waited.

She cocked her head to the side. "He's going to go all the way up there and then hike back to the same place he came from?"

"Not the same place."

Burton avoided looking directly at Maddy. He was certain he was right, but not confident he could explain much better. She still had her poker face on.

"Katahdin is pretty much due north of here. The trail heads southwest away from the mountain."

The stillness in the room indicated the others were considering the idea. It was a little complex.

"I know," he said. "There's no hard evidence. But you heard the urgency in his messages. He's not even sure he likes human beings. He needs to sort out his thoughts. And I know him. He would go some place special to do it."

Rosa began gathering plates of uneaten eggs. "I think we need coffee. No, Jessie, you can't have any."

Maddy was staring at Burton. He stared back at her.

She shook her head as if shaking off a trance. "Okay. Let's say you're right. Let's think this through. It would take a whole day, maybe two, for him to get to Katahdin. I bet it's three different busses."

"If that's where he really wanted to go," Jessica said, "he could do it,

Mom."

Maddy nodded but she had not taken her eyes off Burton. "Well, your feeling that Seb went to really deep woods looks like it was right." She gestured with a tilt of her head towards the big green spaces on the maps taped to the wall.

"If I'm following you," she continued, "Seb takes his chance to see Mount Katahdin and hopes to get some inspiration there. That's where it all begins."

"Ends, actually," Burton said. "Not to be obnoxious. Just for future reference, if we're talking to other people about the A.T."

"Okay," Maddy said. "He heads south on the trail because it ends on Katahdin and doesn't go any further north. Are you saying he's making his way along the A.T? Using it as his oasis?"

"Exactly."

"At least we have a theory to try. We'd have to figure out how far he could have gotten."

"I have an idea. It's a fairly big range, though, not knowing how long it took him to get to Katahdin or when he started hiking. Or how fast he's hiking."

A grin broke out on Maddy's face. "Of course you know that already."

Burton was not sure if his wife's smile was sarcastic. He would not blame her if it was.

"I was testing my theory before talking to you. It's a lot to explain."

"Let's get tape flags for the map on the wall," Jessica said.

"Well," Burton said. "There's one more thing."

The smile disappeared from Maddy's face.

"I've got to go up there."

"C'mon, Burton."

"It's already late," Burton said.

"Why bother having this discussion with us if your mind is already made up? You realize you will be out of commission once you're up there, right? You're going to chase him down the Appalachian Trail? How long does it take to hike through Maine? Weeks? And if you're wrong? I agree the A.T. seems like our best lead but you have to admit the Katahdin thing is just a hunch."

"Mad—"

"We have to talk upstairs."

"Fine."

They walked out of the kitchen.

Burton closed the bedroom door and leaned against it. Maddy sat in the armchair they kept next to the bed. The chair they used only for the laundry basket.

Outside, a basketball smacked the driveway. There was a hoop over the garage door, just below their bedroom window. Rosa's voice drifted up. Jessica's sneakers squeaked, probably running to retrieve her grandmother's shot from where it rolled into the yard.

Burton remained leaning against the door. "I was honestly just trying to see if there was anything to this idea before getting your hopes up. Or mine. Once I checked things out, I was convinced."

"I don't believe you."

"What don't you believe?"

"You're not interested in my thoughts on this. You just want to hear that I'm not going to get in your way."

"That's not fair."

He went over to the bed and sat. They were only a few feet apart, at right angles, looking past one another. He had screwed up, he knew it, the way he presented things as a foregone conclusion. His conclusion. It was true, that he started out only wanting to look deeper, to see if the Mount Katahdin idea was worth bothering them about. He had reservations at a motel already only because time was short and he was checking for vacancies. He was not about to tell Maddy this. Not now.

"You're right," he said. "I am doing an imperfect job of dealing with the situation but it will be two weeks soon. I've got to try this."

Maddy looked a little bit more in Burton's direction, but not quite eye to eye, which he only noticed because he had done the same.

"You made up your mind without me. That's what hurts. You hoped I would agree, but you had already made up your mind. That's not how this is supposed to work. But, never mind that, you can't just run off to the Appalachian Trail."

"I know I told you in a screwed up way, but I still think I need to go to Maine. Right away."

Maddy sighed. "I'm tired of being the bad guy. But I don't have some grand theory about where Seb is, either." She closed her eyes and shook her head a few times before opening them and looking at him directly. "I do think your idea is worth pursuing, but...something feels wrong."

"What, you doubt my motives now?"

Her expression darkened. He had not intended on antagonizing her more, but it looked like he had.

"I guess if one of us has to stay home with Jessica, it should be me. At least I'm willing to parent."

"You really want to start that now? You want to look at my parenting, right now? Great idea."

"You want to look at what I'm dealing with? Both of the Franck boys running off to the woods because they want to believe that's going to make things better. Life doesn't work that way, Burton. You think I like sitting around here waiting?"

Burton told himself to keep his next thought to himself. But he didn't. "You know, your mother is out of touch."

"What the hell is that supposed to mean?"

"This idea that tough love means letting your children go and fend for themselves. Children. We're talking about a child."

Maddy put her hands on her knees. Burton thought she was going to push herself up and walk out of the room. She did not. She merely sat there looking at the floor as if she was at her wits end. Possibly they both were.

After staring this way for a few seconds, she turned in the chair. Their knees knocked. Burton slid over on the bed to make room for her leg.

"Here's a news flash," Maddy said. "I love our son. But we have to keep our heads clear and deal with the painful facts. We will find him but we have to keep cool."

"You think I'm playing into his hands."

"I think we need to be very careful about...trusting him right now. There, now I sound like the bad guy again. Well, sorry, it's reality."

It occurred to Burton that he should stop the conversation right now and suggest they at least breathe for a minute. He got up from the bed, walked to the window and looked out onto the driveway. Rosa and Jessica had finished shooting hoops. He spoke again, sooner than he intended, and with his back still towards Maddy.

"I'm aware that he's manipulated us. But I also know pretty well how he thinks."

"You think you know Seb so much better than me."

This comment really annoyed Burton. What was her problem? And then he knew. It went way back.

He turned and leaned against the windowsill. Maddy watched him from her chair on the other side of the room.

"I know what this is about."

Maddy tilted her head back. "What is this about? Tell me."

He should not have gone down this road but he knew he would not stop now. Maybe they needed to be blunt. Their fourteen-year-old son was gone. Completely gone. Nothing was working. Maybe they had to say what was really on their minds.

"You're jealous." Burton tried to show in his expression and tone of voice that he had not said this with malice. "You've been jealous for years of the bond Seb and I have."

When Seb was a toddler, Maddy and he were best pals. How he loved her, and ran to her when she came into a room. While Burton was at work, they spent every day together. The happy pair, making trips to the zoo, the playground, the arboretum. Lying on a blanket in the back yard playing with Myro when he was a puppy the size of a cucumber. Making coasters and gluing pebbles to picture frames at the YWCA.

Things started to change when Maddy's best buddy entered the first grade. The adventure days, just the two of them, stopped. Later, Burton and Seb started exploring computers. One night, she quietly asked him why she no longer had anything in common with her son.

"You're officially out of your mind," Maddy said, flatly. "Jealous? Why don't you keep going? I'm also a bitch. Deficient in motherly instinct. Is that why you let Seb slide? Because you needed to compensate for my harshness?"

Burton pushed off from the windowsill and walked over to Maddy. Her face wrinkled up, a combination of anger and confusion as to why he was approaching. He lowered himself onto one knee. Closer now, he could see she was trembling.

"I let him slide?" He heard the pleading in his voice. "As in slide out of this house?"

She looked away. He sat on the bed again, close to the chair where she sat. He was careful not to knock her knees.

Did he let Seb slide right out the door? By letting him join groups where he was the only kid, like the Buddhists and the computer club? Maddy had gone along with these. Burton had not twisted her arm.

There was the time Burton's father gave Seb fifty dollars in a white envelope. This might not be the best example of what Maddy was talking about but it was the only thing that came to mind. His father gave no instructions on what was to be done with the money, nor did he say why he was giving his grandson the money at that particular time.

The very next day, Seb announced he wanted to use the money to buy a Yoda statue being sold through an online auction. Maddy pulled Burton aside. Seb did not understand money, she said. Parents invested money for their children until they were old enough to understand it.

Burton claimed Seb would learn more from the consequences of his actions. It was not a lot of money. Maddy gave in because it was Burton's father who gave the money.

Seb won the auction, not too smartly, bidding all fifty of his dollars before they could at least give him advice on how to handle an auction. The statue turned out to be lopsided, hand-made ceramic which did not look much like Yoda. Seb was so mad he threw the statue in the garbage. All Maddy did was give Burton a burning look. He said nothing either, because he was so angry. Angry that she would take this as evidence that Burton was a pushover. He knew what he was doing. But here they were, years later, in deep trouble, and she blamed him. Of course he was partly to blame. No one was perfect. But he was not going off to Maine with this hanging over his head.

"Are you saying I've been such a wimp that I emboldened Seb to go out on his own?"

She stood, suddenly, surprising him.

"I can't say that. I can't say anything. I'm speechless." She strode to the door and left the room.

A minute later, the bedroom floor began to vibrate. It was the garage door rumbling open.

Burton told himself to get off the bed and go down to her. Tell her through the car window that he knew she cared for Seb and wanted with all her heart for him to be safe. He remained seated on the bed.

The car's engine revved and then grew quieter as she drove off.

Opposites attract and they bring opposite points of view with them. He and Maddy had learned to make things work. This ordeal with Seb was pulling their makeshift system apart.

Vibrations from the garage door under the bedroom woke Burton up. He had fallen asleep on top of the bed without turning on the fan. The room was hot and sticky and he felt like crap.

Would Maddy come directly up to their room?

He switched on the lamp.

She came in five minutes later and sat in the chair next to the bed. Her thin smile revealed she had either forgiven him or put matters off for another day. He propped himself up on his elbow and waited for her to say something.

"I'm sorry." She leaned forward and kissed him on the cheek.

Burton thought about kissing her on the lips but he did not want to show her up. He kissed her on the cheek.

"I'm sorry, too. For, well, we probably shouldn't get into it."

"We're both sorry and we both think we're right. But we're both also winging it. We're good parents. I suppose we'll have to talk about the unresolved stuff at some point. When all of this is done."

"No doubt we will talk," Burton said with a smile.

Maybe they would talk about her father then. Or not. In any case, he had wasted precious time on the man, even if he was to blame. Burton could not believe he had missed the parallel until now. A father to blame, just like himself. And a mother. The creators and the ones to blame. It was not an easy job.

Maddy put her hand on his knee. "Do your thing. Go up there to the end of civilization."

"Thank you."

Burton stood up and looked down at his wrinkled T-shirt and jeans. He took a few steps and stretched.

"What else do I need to know?" Maddy asked.

"I'm going by myself because we need you to keep doing what you're doing. It's just as important. More important. I was thinking you might want to check out Jessica's bike theory. There might be something to it."

"You'll have an itinerary?"

"Yes. There's a town close to Katahdin. A lot of people go there before heading up to the A.T. I'll start there."

"You already have a place to stay lined up? I assume you're not counting on finding him the day you get there."

"Well, yeah. I have a reservation."

Maddy smiled and shook her head. She walked to the dresser, opened a drawer, and threw a few pairs of socks on the bed. "You need to pack."

"I'll leave you my itinerary but basically, I'll scour this town where I think he must have started, find out if anyone saw him. He will be hiking south. I've already calculated the furthest he could get if he was the best hiker in the world. It's sort of slow going in Maine, and the blogs say it's even rougher because of all the rain in June. Parts of the trail there are very steep, too.

"I'm thinking to drive a little beyond the farthest possible point Seb could have reached, hike north, and intercept him."

"Jessica's talking about going with you," Maddy said. She started to laugh and then cut it short. "I don't think we need to talk about that."

CHAPTER THIRTEEN

WATER

WATER POUNDED THE BOY'S FACE like a fire hose. He took one hand off the rope, holding tight with the other, and paddled with all his strength to keep from flipping onto his back.

There was a loud crack. The rope and the branch it was tied to bent down. His body plunged deeper into the water. His entire head was swallowed up by the water.

He used his free hand to reach higher on the rope and pulled himself up until his head and mouth were above water level. Mad water plowed onto his neck and streamed over his shoulders. One current pushed his body down while another lifted it up. Both tried to drag him away.

Water pressed every part of his body. He was receiving the most complete, simultaneous full body massage possible. He bent his head down so that his face was in the water. The cold current pressed hard against his scalp. His body was flapping like a flag in a gale.

And then he let go. The creek washed him backwards like a fallen tree in a storm. The water widened, grew deeper. The currents dissipated. His legs dropped and he kicked to keep his feet from hitting bottom. He was carried off to the side of the creek. The water became slower and shallower until his toes touched a flat, slimy piece of shale. He pressed both feet down, bent into a crouch, and came to rest in that spot. Water glided around him, his wild massage ending with a gentle cool-down.

The boy walked back to a towel and gear which lay on a boulder upstream. His body smelled of creek. Wet leaves, mud from its basin and its banks, algae, and all kinds of tiny creatures that had been pulled, swirl by swirl, from pools and eddies into the rushing water.

He stretched out on a sunlit boulder to dry and warm. He could have fallen asleep, but his pale body had yet to grow its own protection, and he did not want to get fried.

There was dinner to get, anyway. Hopefully it was not too late in the day or too warm for fishing. He had woken up early this morning but allowed himself to drift back to sleep until it got too warm to stay in the tent.

He grabbed his fishing pole and a bag of worms and looked for a spot to fish. The creek got wider not far from there. One side of it was still. Bugs skittered across the shadow of an alder tree.

After ten minutes with no bites, he moved upstream. He crossed a shallow rapids, the water splashing up his calves. The creek was bordered here by a cliff. With his back to it, he cast sidearm, shooting the line out with a whip of his wrist. He reeled in steadily to keep the hook from sinking and snagging.

His ass itched from the wet shorts. After the fourth worm drowned, he made another resolution. Fish before doing anything else.

The guy at the bait and tackle shop said a spoon lure was the best bet for brook trout. The boy tied a spoon lure to the line, casted, and waited. He tried to think of a way to get frogs without a net.

He started reeling in. His pole bent and he yanked on it to set the hook. He reeled in a snagged weed, minus the spoon lure. He had a bunch of the lures and tied another one on. He kept casting into this pool because he could see the fish. After a half hour of casting, the line jerked taut again. The boy reeled slowly until an undersized trout was drawn onto the rocks at his feet.

He used his foot to hold the eight-inch fish. It might be another night of dried rations if this illegally small dinner squirmed away. He removed the hook and began to gather river rocks as best he could while keeping the fish pinned to the ground with his foot. He made a circular formation with the rocks until there was a small enclosure at the edge of the creek. He set the fish inside and quickly covered the space with a thin slab of slate. For insurance, he set a heavier rock on top of the slab.

This was to be the only fish of the day. He cleaned the little trout and then headed back to camp. He stopped to examine mushrooms he would never dare to eat. Twice he had to get out the compass and map to reorient himself.

A baby blue rag dangling from a pine branch came into view. It was an old T-shirt he had taken out of a ditch on his way back from town. Although it was dirty and half-rotten, it was still clearly blue amongst the green and brown of the trees. A stranger would see only an old shirt blown into a tree by the wind. Not a marker.

The boy stopped first at the camo-print tarp with pine needles strewn across it. His bike still lay in the hole underneath. Before moving on, he checked to see if he could pick out his tent amongst the underbrush and trees ahead. It took a minute, which thrilled him. He walked over to the tent. It was only obvious that he was looking at the brown camouflage pattern of a plastic tent when he was a half-dozen feet away.

The tent was long and wide enough for his body and nothing else. Its roof sloped from two feet high at the front to barely a foot high at the end. He had hammered the stakes on the left side of the tent right up against a downed tree. If you looked quickly, the little brown and tan tent could not be distinguished from the tree. A thick, narrow-leaf variety of dogwood obscured a good part of the tent's front door. To complete the concealment, the boy had buried a thick hemlock branch upright at the back of the tent to simulate a sapling.

He walked to the cedar tree where he had stashed his food and supplies. He chose this particular tree because its first branch was eight feet above ground and might not be noticed, should anyone happen to be looking for a tree where a bear-bag might be stashed. There were tons of more easily climbed trees all around.

The boy had to jump to get a hold of the lowest branch, hoist himself up, and climb several more branches to reach the rope that was keeping the bear-bags in the air. He untied the double square knot and lowered two green, waterproof bags to the ground.

With the thickest parts of the neighboring trees below him, he could see pretty far. Clouds striped with pink hovered at the lowest edge of the west horizon. Another sunny day tomorrow. Chatter passed from tree to tree, squirrels, he supposed, discussing the invader.

He looked down. Except for the bags he had just lowered, the forest floor appeared the same in all directions. No sign of a person. The boy varied the routes he used to get around his camp and tried to remember to lift his feet when walking, so as to leave needles and twigs where they lay.

The first time he released the bags he forgot to re-tie the rope and it fell to the ground with the bags. He had to climb back up with the rope tied to a stick in his pocket, so he could throw it over the limb, far enough out so that no big creature could hang on to the trunk and grab it or chew on it.

This time he tied the rope with a double square knot. He climbed down and swung as if on a trapeze from the lowest branch, let go and had to run several steps because of the forward motion before coming to a stop.

One bag contained "fragiles" and the other, "not-fragiles." Of course, the not-fragiles had landed on the fragiles, but the fragiles weren't that fragile, and the most important things were protected in a metal box.

The metal box was one of the coolest things he bought. It could be folded flat by undoing latches on each edge so it did not take up too much space in a backpack. The metal box stayed in the bag because it was only for emergencies. His phone with the battery taken out was in there. He did not know how long the charge would last. That was okay. He nearly left the phone outside the forest, in a plastic bag, under a rock, just to be totally separated from it but decided to take it along, in case he never went back in that direction. Everything else in the metal box was backup stuff in case he lost anything. A first aid kit, matches, water purification pills, fish hooks, fish line, a forest map, a highway map, a compass, and his old fold-up knife from Cub Scouts.

He had a system already. The first step was to remove a tarp from the not-fragiles bag. He then took from each bag what he needed for the night and piled these things onto the tarp.

On top of the pile was a waterproof plastic bag with a stack of papers inside. The papers had books he copied from the internet and converted into a tiny font. This was to avoid the weight of actual books. You could find almost any book on the internet if you looked hard enough.

The boy built a contraption so he could read the tiny text. He knew it was geeky but he called them binoculo-glasses. And then he went and sat on the damn binoculo-glasses just after he set up camp. He had to spend a whole day on his bike to find a place with superglue and get back before dark. It was a gas station that sold everything, including all kinds of junk food. The boy ate three packs of peanut butter cups before the long ride back.

Under the tiny-print books was a giant plastic bag of turkey jerky. There were two hundred sticks of turkey jerky in there. Just in case. Piled around the turkey jerky bag was everything else he needed for dinner and sleeping.

There was quite a big mound of stuff on the tarp. All of it carried a long, long way on the boy's bike. Up and down mountains. He had to push the bike over plants that were too thick to ride through for the last mile or two.

The boy decided to get his journal and make a record of what was on the tarp before it got too dark.

The Bear Bags
- *World's biggest bag of turkey jerky*
- *Bag of micro-books*
- *Foldable shovel*
- *Gallon paint can filled with wax*
- *Metal pot*
- *Pan*
- *Plate*
- *Cup*
- *Bowl*
- *Snap-together utensils*
- *Empty plastic bags for collecting berries*
- *Super-light, super-compressible sleeping bag*
- *Rain poncho*
- *Self-inflating pillow*
- *Sneakers*
- *Bottle of* DEET
- *2 duffel bags of clothes*

The clothes and sleeping stuff he kept in the tree so he could leave the front door of the tent unzipped. That way, if an animal thought his body odor inside the tent meant food, they would not have to chew or claw their way into the tent while he was gone. He never brought any food in there. Of course.

Something was missing. The boy looked inside the bear bags at the stuff he had not taken out. A bottle of olive oil, one of two quart-sized bottles of DEET, a half-gallon jug of water. That was the backup water. He groaned. That's what was missing. He forgot to stop by the spring to refill his canteens after fishing. All he had to do was fill this backup bottle tomorrow. No big deal but annoying.

The wax-filled paint can made him smile every time he saw it. Not just because it was a cool invention (not his own). He smiled because he remembered the day he got dropped off at the side of the road with his bike. There was too much weight in the left saddlebag compared to the right and he nearly ended up in a ditch at the first sharp turn in the road.

He picked up the paint can and the cooking stuff and carried it to a third spot. A spot about fifty feet away from the tree where he hung the bags and away from the tent. He knew where it was because of a birch tree with a big piece of white bark hanging off. The cooking hole was next to this tree, under a log. He rolled the log away, set the paint-can in the hole, straightened the wick at the center of the wax, and went off to find two green-wood branches. The branches were for holding the pot over the fire.

In a minute, the fish, minus head and tail, lay sizzling in the pot. He ate red raspberries and watched his tiny catch crackle and fry. A fire would have been easy. There were dead branches within arm's reach of most of the pines, but fire could be seen from a distance. The paint-can-stove's flame burned below the lip of the hole, and gave off nearly no smoke.

The boy heard another crackling sound different from the one made by the frying fish. A light rain had started to smack the leaves above. The angled branches of the canopy channeled the drops out beyond him.

CHAPTER FOURTEEN

MOTEL, MAINE

BURTON FRANCK WAS VERY CLOSE to the end of the world, where the Appalachian Trail stopped and (eventually) Canada, the hinterland without people, lay beyond. It had taken a drive to Portland by car, long-term parking at the airport, getting a taxi, and renting a jeep.

His room at Pete's Motel "In the Shadow of Katahdin" smelled as if the previous owner had been there a while with a cat. He had taken a short tour of the premises the night before. Of Pete's ten units, two had name signs on their front doors.

Burton was eager to go see Erin Casimir, the ranger near the trailhead in Baxter Park, but he had to check a few places in town first. Maddy had already spoken with her several times. The ranger, they learned, had a PhD in ecology and knew the area extremely well. Burton wanted to meet her in person, to put Seb more prominently in her mind.

His first stop in town before heading up to Baxter Park would be the Sunflower Cafe. Both an A.T. guidebook and a website had identified the cafe as a favorite amongst hikers.

His phone rang just as he pulled out of the motel's parking lot. He answered without looking at the number.

"Hi, brother. Maddy said you are in Maine?"

"Hey, Terrie. I think he's here. Somewhere on the Appalachian Trail.

In Maine." He rolled up the window to hear her better. The super-jeep's tires made a lot of noise.

"Oh, wow. Did you find a note or a map in his stuff?"

"Sort of. A librarian at the Boston Public Library remembers someone like Seb looking at maps."

"Of the Appalachian Trail?"

"Yes."

"That's awesome! Oh my God. So now what? I can't believe you found that. Did they have a record of his library card? I can't believe they remembered he was looking at the Appalachian Trail. In Maine!"

"The materials weren't just about the Appalachian Trail. And not just Maine. Seb had them bring him about a hundred books and maps, all kinds of trails and national forests along the East Coast."

"Oh. Okay." Terrie's voice lost a bit of its enthusiasm. "But most of them were about the Appalachian Trail? Or Maine?"

"A bunch of them were. But it reminded me of something Seb said about the Appalachian Trail when he was really young. I'd forgotten all about it. We've been looking into the A.T., but not as much as we should have. The thing is, he hasn't been interested in it in for years. His thing was the Continental Divide Trail. Bigger, more awesome. You know what a dreamer he is. He actually got rid of all his stuff about the A.T. years ago ... Damn!"

"What?"

"I took a wrong turn."

Burton picked up the map he'd gotten from the motel lobby. It was a sheet of printer paper showing the four blocks that made up downtown. The crooked and blurry map looked like it had been copied and copied again multiple times on the crappy old printer behind the front desk. Burton would have to wait until he was off the phone to make sense of the thing.

"You want me to call back?" Terrie asked.

"No. No. This is a very small town. I can't get too lost. Anyway, the Boston library really solidified something. The books and maps Seb got were all about the Northeast, and mostly about wilderness areas. They triggered some memories about conversations I had with Seb when he was younger. And we realized that he probably had to rein in his dreamer side if he was going to pull off...whatever it is he's doing. No cross-country trips or anything like that."

"I guess," Terrie said. "I haven't seen what you saw. Or the talks you had with Seb."

"Focusing on Maine is a little bit based on intuition. A theory. But

I'm pretty sure. I have to try."

"All alone?"

"It's hard to explain. Not even Maddy completely understands. Just trust me, okay?"

"Sure." Terrie did not sound so sure. "So where in Maine are you?"

"Just south of Baxter State Park. I got in last night."

Burton could hear Missy's voice through the phone but could not make out what she was saying.

"Appalachian Trail," Terrie said in a muffled voice, to Missy apparently. "I trust you, brother. Just tell me what I can do."

"Let's see how things go. This is just one part of the whole search, um, strategy."

"Our brother keeps calling, you know. I talked to him last night. He still wants to come up. He says it would be no problem to delay things on his docket or get someone to fill in for him."

"I wish I could think of something he could do up here, but..."

Burton had considered asking his brother and sister to help him search the Appalachian Trail. The truth was that he had not told anyone exactly what his plan was. Not even Maddy. He did not want to be told the plan was absurd. It might be, but it might not, and he had to try.

"Sorry," Terrie said, after a pause. "I thought you were going to say something. So what's your plan?"

"I'm going to see if anyone around this town has seen him first. Then go to the trailhead in Baxter Park."

"Oh."

Burton's mind was in overdrive. Terrie seemed to want a little more of an explanation but he could barely explain what he was doing to himself. They had been trying everything that every expert recommended. If he thought about what he was now doing, it seemed crazy, but it was time to go with his gut.

He had considered hiring a tracker. The problem with that idea was that the tracks of every hiker on the A.T. overlapped. A tracker would only be helpful if Seb went off the trail and they would have to know approximately where he left the trail. The trail passed through thousands of square miles of woods in Maine alone.

Burton did go so far as to call a tracker, a rough-sounding guy who answered the phone, "yeah?" This man was a professional who lived a couple hours away from Baxter. He said he would be ready to go at any time, for the right price.

Burton had also seriously considered organizing a posse to canvass the A.T. but he hated the idea of Seb being brought in by a stranger. He could not even imagine how such a thing would be done. Being "brought in." A short period of trauma might be worth getting Seb home but, the truth was, Burton wanted to be the one to meet his son.

He kept thinking how Seb, in his current state, might react if confronted by a stranger. Even meeting someone like his Uncle Jake would probably not go well. Seb liked Jake all right but Burton was pretty sure he would turn and run the moment he saw him.

At this point, they had park rangers, police officers, hiking clubs, detectives, runaway organizations and everyone who saw his flyer looking for Seb. Still, if someone was to come face to face with his son on the trail, to take him away from the oasis he believed he desperately needed, Burton wanted it to be himself. He hoped, he really hoped, he was doing the right thing.

He was about to apologize for leaving Terrie hanging on the phone when he saw that their call had already ended. He pulled over to the side of the road, dialed his sister's number, and made a u-turn while it rang.

"Spotty service up there?" his sister asked.

"A bit, yeah."

"I'm not sure how much you heard of what I was saying. I think I should go sit in a beach chair in one of the parking lots on the A.T. in Vermont. I was thinking the one in Peru. There's always cars there. I could question everyone that leaves and enters the trail."

"Terrie—"

"I'd rather do that than worry. I could go to Portsmouth again but we know he's not there."

Terrie had searched Portsmouth three times since her first stint with Burton and the Buddhists the day Seb disappeared.

"Missy and I are a little slow with jobs right now anyway. We need to get caught up on our accounting and taxes. I can use my tablet in the trail parking lot. I don't need Wi-Fi."

"Well, yes, that would be great."

Ahead, halfway down the block, a sign with a yellow sun on it was swinging in the breeze. This had to be the place Burton was looking for. He slowed the all-terrain-vehicle he had rented and looked for a spot to park.

"I need to do something now," he said. "You can always check with Maddy if you can't reach me up here. My signal is probably only going to get worse."

"Take care of yourself, okay?"

"I will. You're the best."

"Oh, yeah."

⁊∿⁊

The Sunflower Cafe's walls may have been sunflower yellow at one time but they were orange now. Stained, perhaps, from the days when smoking was allowed inside. Every table in the place was different. Round, square, Formica, wood. There was a long plank held up by stumps with benches on either side. All the chairs were mismatched as well. It looked like a well organized flea market.

Burton headed towards a little pine table with a red plastic-leather chair at its side. The only other diners in the place were four white-haired people in short-sleeve polos, sitting at a table on the other side of the room. Burton pegged them as bed-and-breakfasters. Anyone heading out on the trail would be long gone. It was too soon for anyone to have finished hiking. Locals, he assumed, would not be dressed preppy on a weekday. Probably not on any day.

At the back of the place, a woman was tugging at the cash register. A quilt featuring a sunflower at least four feet in diameter hung on the wall behind her. Light streaming through the two plate glass windows out front made the silver threads outlining quilt-flower's seeds glow.

A cylinder of paper rolled out from behind the counter into the dining area. It was the cash register tape. The woman ran over to grab it.

"Damn!"

She bent down, with one hand on her lower back, and picked up the register tape. When she stood, she noticed Burton and frowned.

"Oh, hi. I'll be right with you."

The woman passed behind the counter, picked up a menu, and appeared at his table with a pen and pad. Had she not been blonde, Burton might have assumed she was Native American. Straight hair halfway down her back, a reddish-tan, and a poker face. He wondered if the thing about a poker face was a stereotype.

She had a sunflower logo on the left of her T-shirt and a name tag that said *Maureen* on the right. Burton guessed her to be around fifty, not from wrinkles, because her round face didn't have many. It must have been the way she held herself.

"Good morning," the woman said in a tone much friendlier than Burton expected from her unsmiling face. "I bet you could use a cup of our delicious coffee."

"It shows, huh?"

197

"Ah, no." She looked confused for a moment. "I say that to every-body in the morning. Boring old me. Except to the mean old bastard who told me I needed to get a new line."

"I would love a cup of your delicious coffee."

"I'll bring it. When I get back I'll tell you about our delicious break-fast."

She returned with a blue mug on a white saucer. "I got you the big cup."

"Before we discuss breakfast..." Burton reached down and retrieved a manila folder from his lap. "You get lots of Appalachian Trail hikers around here this time of year, right?"

"Ah, sure, but earlier. We open at 5:30 and even that's too late for some. Same goes for our hunters and fishermen. Fisher people. Ah, you know what I mean."

Her eyes never left the folder as she spoke.

"I was wondering if you'd seen my son." He stuttered a bit on the "s" in "son." It was still hard to say out loud. He pulled a flyer from the folder and handed it to her.

Maureen held it at arm's length, although she had eyeglasses rest-ing on her hair. After a few seconds, she brought the flyer to her large chest, pinning it there with her hand, crinkling it.

"Your son is missing. I'm so sorry." She held the paper out again. "And you came all the way from Massachusetts. Oh."

She was not much taller standing than he was seated, but Burton still had to look up a bit. This suggestion of supplication gave him an unexpected impulse to cry. He leaned over his coffee cup and brought it to his lips for a sip.

"So many young, thin people come here in the summer." Maureen sighed. "Hiking will do that, of course. Make you skinny. Serious A.T. hiking anyway."

Burton felt in the folder for the larger, glossy photograph of Seb in shorts with backpack straps over his shoulders. He handed this to her.

She held this out in front of her.

"I'd like to put the flyer in your window," Burton said. "If you don't mind. With this larger photograph taped below it?" He only had a doz-en of the large photos but this seemed like the place for one of them.

"Of course," she said, bringing the photo closer to her face. "You know, he does look familiar."

Burton's heart quickened. He set the coffee cup down onto the edge of the saucer, nearly tipping it over completely, and spilling coffee onto the table.

Maureen stared at the photo. "I remember now," she said a few seconds later, in a flat tone which agitated him. Was it old-time, Mainer stoicism? What had taken away her cheer?

"Come with me." Maureen started walking towards the front door.

Where was she going to take him? There was a menswear shop next door that looked like it had been closed for years. Was Seb hiding there? That was a crazy idea, but he did not know what to think.

He followed her to the front of the cafe and out the door. She turned and pointed at the plate glass window. It looked like she was pointing to a faded green paper, but that was just a homemade ad for house-cleaning services. Next to this was a bulletin from the shelter showing dogs and cats with pleading eyes. Maureen flicked her finger upwards.

A missing child flyer. Seb's missing child flyer. An earlier version. Of course Maddy had sent it here, probably more than once.

"I'm sorry, sir. This is what I was remembering."

He nodded.

She looked unsure as to whether she should leave him there. He relieved her of this dilemma by going back inside.

At his table, he pulled out the itinerary he had emailed Maddy. The clerk at Pete's Motel let him print it out on the printer behind the desk last night. He was still staring at the itinerary when Maureen returned to top off his coffee.

"Our home fries are our specialty," she said.

He gave her a brave grin. "Coffee's all I need."

Later, she brought a blueberry muffin on a plate, and a small, white paper bag. "This is on the house. Take it with you for later if you don't want it now."

"Thank you. You're a sweetheart."

"I'll be sure to let you know if I see anyone who might be your son." She pulled the flyer from her apron and glanced at it. "Mr. Franck."

He sat for a few minutes longer, gazing out the window. Maureen never brought a bill. When he got up to pay, she shook her head.

Outside the Sunflower Cafe, Burton paused a moment on the sidewalk to look at the enormous vehicle he had rented. Its fat wheels were as high as his waist. He got this thing at a place outside of Bangor that catered to rich men seeking toys and, he guessed, leaders of secret paramilitary groups.

"*Massive Motors*" was the name of the place. The salesman who was helping Burton told him the only vehicle better for backwoods driving was classified. When the salesman paused, Burton suspected he was being offered the opportunity to bribe his way into an airplane hangar. A secret showroom of vehicles the government probably did not want civilians to own.

The morning sun blazed on the vehicle's shiny black roof. Its deeply furrowed wheels looked ready to chew up the earth and spit out rocks while its reinforced steel fender in front plowed trees out of the way. Burton climbed up and in. With a turn of the key, it roared to life. A man halfway up the block shuddered and turned around. The man gave a hostile, dismissive swipe of his hand. He reminded Burton of his grandfather Avo, who would make the same motion when impatient or dismissive, which was most of the time.

As Burton drove to the only other restaurant open that morning, he thought again about what Avo had done. What he said he had done. Leaving Burton's father to fend for himself for a whole week in the remote Berkshires. Avo's behavior was reprehensible, putting his child at risk like that, but there could have been a rational idea mixed up in there. It was possible he had been concerned that people no longer understood their place in the web of life and wanted to correct this disconnect in his son. Fifty years later, his great-grandson, Seb, had come to see just how disconnected from nature most people were.

Bentley's Diner did not have a Seb poster outside. Bentley did not seem to be concerned about catering to tourists, either. No photos of Katahdin on the wall. The black and white tiles on its walls looked like they had been there for fifty years. Squares of white linoleum on the floor were outlined with grime. Three speckled white tables with two chairs each lined either wall and there was a counter with a cash register at the back. The time was 10:30 in the morning and the place was empty.

A cook in an apron splattered with grease and ketchup came from a brightly lit doorway with no door. Presumably the kitchen. He stood at the register and looked at Burton without saying anything. Was this man the Bentley of Bentley's Diner? Perhaps not, but Burton ended up thinking of him as Bentley anyway.

He held up the flyer and set a glossy photo of Seb on the counter.

"Have you seen this young man? It's my son. He's disappeared."

Bentley leaned over and squinted at the photograph. A girl with the same black eyebrows and black eyes as him came through the kitchen doorway. She looked down at the photo.

"No, sir," Bentley said.

The girl put a cigarette between her lips and headed back to the kitchen. Some fool kid from the city, Burton imagined them thinking.

"Please call the number on the flyer if you see him or hear anything?"

"Uh-huh," Bentley said.

He held the flyer against the bulletin board near the register and secured it there with two thumb tacks. The bulletin board had a bunch of business cards, a five dollar bill, and a flyer selling fresh eggs.

Next to the register was a plate of round chocolate cakes with white icing in the middle. Burton thought Bentley might be more inclined to do something if he spent a little money, so he picked up one of the cakes.

"A dollar," Bentley said. "Want a bag?"

"No thanks."

The little chocolate cake was delicious. It was the first piece of food Burton had eaten that day. He could save the muffin he got from Maureen at the Sunflower Cafe for later. After that, he would be eating from the five-pound sack of trail mix sitting in the passenger seat.

He learned nothing at the campground, hostel, outdoor gear shops or hunting stores, although the people there were all a lot nicer than Bentley.

Burton could not bring himself to stop at the police station. Better they not know he was in town. They might interfere. Besides, he and Maddy had spoken to them many times. Maddy would probably call them again today.

As had happened throughout the morning, every time Burton turned a corner to face north, there was Mount Katahdin. It loomed so large relative to the small buildings of the town that it scared him. Not just the shock of its size, but the recurring thought of Seb being lost on this Godzilla. It was time to go there. Burton's heart immediately started pounding.

The road out of town headed straight at the mountain. It was the widest-looking mountain Burton could recall seeing. From certain angles, it seemed to take up half the sky. And then, the road would curve and Katahdin would be gone, blocked by a smaller, more near mountain. He imagined Seb going and up and down the Appalachian Mountains all the way to Georgia. His son getting tougher, feeling, perhaps, more able to take on the world.

Burton opted to take the quicker, non-scenic route to Baxter Park. For a non-scenic route, it was remarkably scenic. Mountains, fields, bogs, pines, birches, lakes. The recurring image of Katahdin's treeless peak and its green shoulders. With the windows down, and the rich, fresh air against his face, it was impossible not to have some moments of pleasure, to feel a bit more hopeful.

What Maddy said was true. He did like the thought of Seb being in a place like this. To calm himself. He liked that thought in isolation. In the full context of the situation, it was a nightmare. This was the wildest terrain Burton had ever seen.

It was a half-hour drive to the visitor center. Burton found Erin Casimir, the ecologist-ranger, behind the desk.

"Hi Erin," Burton said.

"Hi." A good sport, Erin smiled patiently, letting this dork stranger greet her like they were friends.

"It's Burton Franck. Seb Franck's father. The—"

"Oh, hey, Burton. Welcome. Any news about Seb?"

They shook hands. Erin waited for Burton to provide an update.

"Not really, believe it or not."

"I'm so sorry."

Between Maddy and Burton, they had spoken to staff at probably a hundred visitor centers. Burton wished he could spend more time in friendly banter with this woman who had been keeping an eye out for their son, but there was too much to do.

He would also have liked to learn a few things from the ranger. Dr. Casimir was not only an ecologist. She had extensive knowledge of the network of hiking trails in Maine. But Burton did not want to be talked out of what he was going to do.

Acid crept up his throat. This was not just the result of a muffin being overwhelmed by two cups of coffee. Being constantly on edge had him popping antacids for days.

The ranger waited for him with the wistful-hopeful expression Burton had seen on so many faces.

He swallowed his heartburn. "I'm going to the A.T. terminus to talk to people entering and leaving the trail."

He would not actually go to the famous weather-beaten wooden sign at the trail's end. He would stay in the parking lot so he could talk to anyone coming or going without getting too far away from his vehicle.

The ranger nodded. "Is there anything I can do?"

"The same as before. Tell everybody you meet. Do all the rangers know to keep looking for Seb?"

"We're on it. If he's in Baxter, we'll see him."

"My wife and I, my family, we really appreciate it"

"Bring your son by when you find him."

Burton took a look around the welcome center before leaving. A young couple standing in front of the literature rack, leaning on their retractable walking sticks. They, including Erin, were nothing more than objects that had to be walked around. His son was missing. They did not care. They were happy to be in this big, beautiful park. Erin was doing her job. Burton could have skipped going to the visitor's center altogether.

The drive to the trailhead parking lot took twenty minutes. Baxter State Park consisted of more than three hundred square miles with hardly any roads. If you got lost in there, on foot, you would be in serious trouble.

Burton took a lawn chair and a box of flyers from the monster jeep. He unfolded the chair and set it next to the entrance to the path from the parking lot to the trail.

The first people he met, two tall, muscular women in their thirties who could have been a formidable volleyball team, nodded and gave Burton their full attention as he explained the deal. They did not recognize Seb and seemed genuinely concerned.

Some time later, a woman whose hair was dyed watermelon red exited the trail. She had to be in her seventies. She looked on the verge of tears by the time Burton told her what was going on. The afternoon and evening went this way, more or less, until the sun set. Tomorrow, Burton would begin part two of his strategy. He had hoped it would not come to that, but he was not surprised.

CHAPTER FIFTEEN

REDNECK

WALKING MEDITATION. Focus on the bit of earth your foot approaches. Ignore, for now, the view from this ridge-top trail, the ravine off to your left. That movement is a squirrel. Who cares about a squirrel? You've seen jack-in-the-pulpits before. Not that waterfall, though. Let it go.

The ground before you. Someone's been here before. Some animal, taking this high road, this open space where low scrub grows. That last sentence was a poem. My toes where the low scrub grows. Now it is a corny poem. Just look where your foot would land next.

Walking meditation wasted good sights. The boy made a mental note to do walking meditation in a place he was familiar with, so there were not so many distractions.

The ridge trail moved down to a bog. Good. He was absolved from meditation. Don't want to fall into quicksand.

Before continuing, he sat on a log to zip off the lower half of his hiking pants, turning them into shorts. The lower halves went into his pack. Only an hour before, he was wearing his sweatshirt with the hood over his head. Cold mornings became warm mornings and hot afternoons, especially when hiking.

He took the compass and map from his pocket. North-West was that way. He turned in the direction of a forest so thick with pine trees that hardly anything grew underneath. Easy walking.

The chokecherry bushes ought to have warned him he was coming to a clearing. He had one foot on a dirt road before he realized it was a road. As a rule, he crept up to roads to check for parked or oncoming cars. This one, in any case, was clear. No dust in either direction. He ran across anyway. Once behind the cover of trees on the other side, he consulted the map and reoriented north.

This took him into a lowland of birches, the trees of reverse colors, surprisingly bright in the shade of the forest. It was like a scene in one of those vampire-hobbit movies his friends were crazy about.

The next marker to look for was a cluster of old apple trees. Trees in a forest could be easy to miss. So far, though, the printout from Trail Dude's blog had been perfectly accurate.

He was in the center of the apple trees when he noticed them. Most of their limbs were dead and leafless. They looked like trees planted upside-down with their roots in the air. Acorn-sized green apples dotted the branches that did have leaves. Were they left behind by a farming family a hundred years ago? Had a tribe of Native Americans obtained apple seeds and planted them here? Maybe hunters had tossed their apple cores into a clearing made by a lightning fire.

His destination should not be far. He thought he heard the gurgle of a brook mixed in with the wind and the creaking trees. In a few minutes, he discovered he was right. The brook he sought was still a long way down at the bottom of a canyon, but that was the brook he was looking for. He had to follow the top edge of the canyon, through dogwood and weeds that grew as high as his waist and cuts in the land made by rivulets of rain that merged before pouring over the edge and into the canyon. Eventually, the depth of the canyon began to decrease. Not long afterwards, the boy stood on a stone beach at the water's edge.

He took off his hiking boots and walked barefoot across the brook, slipping every once in a while when his weight caused a rock underneath to shift. The moment he stepped foot on the other side, he noticed the final marker.

A tower of flat, round-edged stones balanced one upon the other to an impressive five feet high. It was maybe twenty feet upstream. The cairn. He had arrived at the best place in the region to see otters, if *Trail Dude* knew what he was talking about.

The boy removed two self-inflating square cushions from his pack. He uncapped them so they would inflate, set one on the ground and the other against a boulder and settled in to watch. Hopefully, in a place as remote as this, otters would not wait until dusk to show themselves. He could not risk trying to get back to camp in the dark.

After ten minutes of sitting motionless with the crick in his back aching more and more, he put on his binoculo-glasses and took out a micro-printed copy of *Nuts for Nuts*. This book claimed to offer peace to agitated people by combining relaxation exercises with eating food you found in the wild. It sounded like bull crap but the title was funny.

A splash drew his eyes upstream. The expanding concentric ripples were too small to have come from an otter. All this to see otters. It was a beautiful spot, at any rate. From this side of the brook he had a good view of the smooth, gray and white rocks that made up the beach. Directly behind the beach was the dark forest, sloping up steeply. The boy had to lean back to see the bright blue sky above. When he looked down, he noticed in the water, the reflection of the tall cairn of oval stones. It looked even more precarious on the rippling sheet of the brook.

⁂

The loud crazy crow had to be standing on the downed tree right next to the tent. Like five feet away. There would be no going back to sleep. It was time he became a proper fisherman, anyway. Trout liked to eat early in the morning.

The boy crawled out of the tent. He was at the stream not long after sunrise. He tossed his fishing line out and settled in against a stump. Some time later he woke up when his chin hit his chest. After that, he was awake. The birds and bugs made sure of that. They loved the morning almost as much as the evening. Yeek-yeek-yeeking and cheeping, in rising and falling choruses, as if they egged each other on until they wore each other out. At which point they had woken every creature in the forest.

The boy reeled in the line, watching the hook bounce over stones through the clear water. He whipped his arm forward and let the line go again. As the hook and line sailed, something in the midst of the bug and bird chatter caught his attention. He let the bobber plop, held still, and waited. There it was. A voice. A human voice. His body tensed, sending his bony elbows into his ribs.

So as to not make any more noise by cranking the reel, he put a big rock over the fishing pole's handle and let the bobber drift. Again, the voice. Every few seconds, a word came through. Singing. A repetitive song.

The boy began to crawl up the hill to his left, like a soldier under the ferns. The song seemed to be coming from that direction. Near the top, he lowered himself down to his belly and crept, trying to avoid ferns that would sway and give his presence away.

He could see the creek. It had come around the hill he just climbed. Something was moving down there, something blue. It was a baseball hat, on backwards. That was the only thing visible of the person wearing it. The rest was hidden by a gigantic tree that had fallen into the creek. He, or she, cast a line out into the water. This person was fishing, too.

The words to the song drifted up:

"...knock it off.

"There's a skeeter on my peter, knock it off.

"There's a dozen on my cousin's.

"Can't you hear the buggers buzzin'?

"There's a skeeter on my peter, knock it off."

At this, the hat rose into the air, exposing a tangle of light, curly hair. The hat fell to the ground. The arm that threw the hat remained erect.

"Hey!"

The arm began to make a circular motion, a wave, perhaps.

"Hey. Up there. Catching anything?" A kid's voice. It sounded like a teenager. The kid leaned forward to retrieve the hat and put it on his head without looking behind.

A decision needed to be made immediately. Talk to this person or get lost, just in case? In case of what? The greeting was friendly. What was there to worry about a kid who sang, loudly, about a mosquito on his penis?

The boy decided to make his way down the embankment, holding onto saplings to keep his feet from being swept out from under him by the wet earth. He slipped and slid and lowered himself to the bottom.

The roots of the downed tree were massive. They extended out into the creek. One of the roots stood straight up into the air, at least fifteen feet high. It took longer to walk around the tree than it had taken to slide down the hill. Finally, after climbing under the last root, he came face to face with another boy.

This boy was wearing a white *Bruins* jersey with the sleeves cut off. The legs below his long skateboard shorts were tanned dark. Curls of blonde hair protruded from the backwards baseball hat. Attached to the hat's blue fabric was a white button with the word *"yes"* on it.

"I've seen you before, you know," the kid in the hat said. He put a worm on a hook. He looked up, and squinted. "You're kind of covered in mud."

"Nice song."

"Thought you might like to hear a real redneck."

"Hear" pronounced without the "r." Even less of an "r" than you got in Massachusetts.

It was probably never a good idea to agree someone was a redneck, so the boy said, "Your neck's not—"

"Oh, I'm redneck enough. But the song, that was just to mess with you."

"It's stuck in my head now. I'll probably wake up in the middle of the night with nightmares about...that."

The kid grabbed the handle of his fishing pole and cast the line with a flick of his arm. A bobber landed in the water. That was good to see, this local guy using a bobber, too.

The local, he certainly appeared local, guy removed his hat, scratched his head, and said, "I wasn't sure if you wanted to be alone."

So the song was an invitation. Okay. "No, it's cool. Are you catching anything with worms?"

"I can catch fish with a gummy bear." The kid pointed to a stringer tied to a branch that was dangling in the water a few feet upstream. "Two big brownies already. What about you? Hey, where's your pole?"

"Around the bend. Be back in a second."

When the boy returned, the kid in the hat had a bag of barbecue potato chips on his lap and several in his mouth. He lifted the bag and offered it to the boy. They smelled incredibly good.

"Thanks."

They were incredibly good. The boy sat on a flat rock a few feet away from the kid in the baseball hat. They shared the bag of chips for a minute without talking.

The kid re-cast his line without even looking to see where it went. "I almost never see people up here. Not this far in. If I do, they don't see me." He tipped his head back to pour the last crumbs from the bag into his mouth. "My curiosity got the best of me this time."

"It got me, too, obviously."

They grinned.

This guy came off as tough and confident, but it was hard not to see him as a kid, with his freckles and high cheekbones, and he looked like he was not tall, maybe five-foot-five. A faint shadow, the beginnings of a beard, at his jawbone and under his lip, confirmed he was not a child.

With teeth pink from the barbecue chips, the kid asked, "What do you do? I mean, like, when you're not fishing?"

Questions like this were why he should have run. People talked to each other, to their parents, for example. What had this guy seen already? His camp, his bike?

"Hike. Read. Chill out. I'm also trying to meditate."

"Never met anyone who meditated. What's the difference between meditation and just thinking?"

"Good question. It's like...less thinking. Make your mind a blank TV screen, clear of thoughts. So far, my TV screen is nowhere near blank. I suck at it."

The boy in the hat stared at him for a moment. "If you cleared your mind of thoughts, wouldn't you, like, shit your pants because you forgot to hold it in?"

The kid said this with a straight face until they both burst into laughter. Laughter echoed around them. The chattery creatures went quiet for a moment.

"Maybe that's why Buddha went off by himself under a tree," the boy said to the kid in the hat. "When he found a little surprise, he knew he was done."

They laughed again.

"I think I just offended a billion people."

It was great to talk to another person, a heady feeling, but that was also because it was dangerous.

The kid yanked hard on his fishing pole. He reeled in another trout. "Why, though? What do you need to meditate for?"

"It's complicated."

The kid pulled the fish off the hook, gave it a quick look, and tossed it back.

"You've seen my camp? Where I'm staying?" Taking the kid into his confidence might improve the likeliness he would keep his secret. It was also better to know.

The kid nodded. "Yeah. Don't worry. Not much chance anyone else has." He paused. "Pretty impressive, actually. Tying pine branches under your food bag to hide it before you raise it up. I liked that."

"Pretty impressive you saw my stuff, then."

"Well, there's no way to hide your tracks completely."

The kid liked to ask questions. Maybe it was time to leave. On the other hand, he had already seen the food bag and the camp and had not done anything about it.

The kid pointed to the boy's fishing pole. "You're totally roughing it? Only eating what you can forage? With lures like that?"

"I'm not that far gone. I'm not willing to croak out here. I have backup food. What's wrong with this lure?"

"It's good, if you know how to use it." The kid frowned. "You're not that far gone? How far gone are you?"

"Gone off the grid, if not out of my mind. No phone. No internet. No credit cards. Not that I had any."

"Well, like my father says, 'How do you know you're crazy if you're crazy? What if it's them that's crazy?' But he says it in French and it sounds a lot better. Fou, fou, fou."

It was time to change the subject.

"What's 'yes'?"

The kid reached up and touched the button on his hat. "It reminds me of a story I like. This guy goes into a funky art gallery. A small place, mostly empty. There's a step ladder in the center of the room. You had to climb to the top and look at the ceiling. The guy climbs until his face is a few inches away from the ceiling and there, in letters so small you could only read them when you were a few inches away, was a single word. Yes. It was a surprise, and it made the man feel hopeful. They got married later, this guy and the artist."

"Your parents?"

"John Lennon and Yoko Ono." The kid took off the hat and looked at it. "I've never told anyone what the button means. Most people wouldn't care. I only know because my Dad's a Beatles freak. Nobody my age has ever heard of Yoko Ono. They think I'm an oddball. But we all grew up together, and they're used to me. Besides, I'd punch them in the face."

Yoko Ono sounded like an alt-rock band or something. "I guess you don't live too far from here?"

"Pretty close. About four miles. Woods, logging road, and then the county road. Me, Mom, Dad, and my useless brother."

"No town, though, right?"

A laugh. "No town. Nothing. My parents used to run a lodge for fishermen, hunters, snowmobilers in the winter, but it went out of business. So, yeah, we're living at a big empty lodge on welfare right now. It was nonstop work when we had the lodge going, so I don't miss that but I feel bad, because the 'rents are losing it. I was in the woods all the time before I had to help with the lodge thing and now I'm back."

"I guess this is a good place. Four miles is a long way. I mean, your back yard probably looks the same."

"Four miles is nothing. I've done twenty-five. Close to it. There's some pretty radical caves out there, past the ponds."

"What you guys call a pond, I'd call a lake. Caves are cool."

The kid reeled in his line and clipped the hook to the lowest rung of his fishing pole. "I'm outta here now. Keep fishing around here if you want. I wouldn't think you were poaching my spot. I don't own this place either. Maybe I'll see you again."

"Sure. Good."

"I can show you these big ass otters if you want."

The kid stopped to put the stringer of trout into a canvas bag and walked away, holding the fishing rod by his side, as if he knew he would look too much like Huckleberry Finn with it over his shoulder.

Kind of disappointing that the otters were not more of a secret.

CHAPTER SIXTEEN

The Beast

THE JEEP'S LEFT WHEELS SLAMMED into a giant piece of granite which Burton had not seen until it was too late. His body was thrown against the seatbelt and then tossed hard to the right. The jeep began to tip. It was now flying down the hill on two wheels. Just as the airborne left wheels dropped back to the road Burton jerked his body in the opposite direction to avoid bludgeoning his head on the driver's side window. It worked, much to his surprise.

He thought the jeep was going to go over that time. There had been near constant lurching since he left the main road, but that last stretch was ridiculous. He stopped the jeep, grabbed the bug spray from where it had rolled under the seat, and got out.

Trees for ever. Dirt road and pine trees. He sat on the bumper, sprayed himself and tried to calm down. There was no guarantee the road ahead was not even worse, so he did not calm down very much.

"I'm coming for you Seb," he said. "Your father's hunting you down in a monster jeep."

This was day one of the intercept strategy. The intercept strategy, details of which he chose not to tell Maddy. There was no way she would understand. Today was two weeks. Two weeks. It couldn't be worse. Well, maybe it could be worse. Burton was not going to think about that.

Burton had expected it would be slow going on these logging roads but not this slow. *So get back in the vehicle.* He got back in the jeep.

After a short uphill climb, the road crested. As soon as it crested, it started going back down. There was no break, no flat ridge to ride along, to give his biceps a rest.

Burton brought the vehicle to a stop, rolled down the window, and stuck his head out. This was going to be the steepest descent yet and, somehow, there were even more boulders than the last, nearly fatal downhill.

"Just let her roll, she will right herself." That's what the guy at the rental place said.

"Which is good, because I'll probably be unconscious," Burton said to the forest.

At the outset, he thought driving slow would be best, but driving slow meant more time in between lurches, which meant more time holding your body tense, muscles aching, before being thrown into the next direction. Driving fast, on the other hand, was like rolling down a hill in a garbage can. If he relaxed, it was somehow less painful, if comical, the way his body flopped around at higher speeds. But he could not relax for long.

Burton looked down the hill with dread for a minute and then decided to get it over with. He tried "letting her roll" by riding the tops of the boulders like a mogul skier. Before he knew it, he was going too fast. He bounced off boulders like a pinball. A metal water bottle, which had flown out of the cup holder long ago, banged relentlessly in the back.

The jeep was very close to being launched off a boulder into a tree when the road suddenly became a little less steep. Burton jammed on the brakes. His head snapped forward and the seatbelt dug into his body, but he managed to slow the vehicle to a crawl.

The hill got steep again quickly. Burton managed to use only the left or the right wheels of the jeep at any given time to climb boulders and fall off of them onto the road. He wished that idiot from the place where he got the jeep, who told him to "let her roll," was in the back seat.

He finally came to a smooth stretch of road. He checked the topographic map against the GPS and was relieved to see that the steep inclines were behind him. It was a pleasure to hear the whirring of the deep-tread wheels over packed earth and sand. A bit of sun peered in through the trees. He rolled down the windows. The smell of pine was so strong he could feel it inside his nose.

About a mile later, the dirt turned to mud. The jeep was made for mud, but even this vehicle had its limits. This worry proved justified when the road ended abruptly at a lake with pine trees growing out of it. It looked as if he had arrived at the Everglades.

The GPS confirmed he was on the correct road. There was a lake on top of the road now. The monsoon spring rains had apparently collected here. According to his map, the terrain under the water here was pretty flat, and appeared to remain flat all the way to the foothills he needed to reach. He could actually see them at the far end of the lake. At least, he thought the pine-covered incline over there was the foothills he was after. Except that everything around here was pine-covered hills. He confirmed the settings on the GPS and his position on the map.

With a growl, he slammed his foot on the gas. The jeep entered the water. A wave broke and crashed onto the windshield, blinding Burton for a moment. He held his speed steady, and the water split, shooting off to either side. He could actually see straight ahead. It was just water but, still. The wake he created spewed out behind him like two fountains. Once in a while a blob of mud landed on the windshield. Fortunately, the mega-jeep had mega windshield wipers, and they got rid of the mud quickly.

He really hoped the GPS had not considered negligible some large boulder, or a jeep sized depression, because the only thing Burton could see was water and the trees standing in the water that he had to avoid. Every few seconds, a surprise boulder sent him bouncing off the seat. It was actually easier when he didn't know they were coming because he did not tense up.

At first he was not sure, but then it was certain. The jeep was coming out of the water. What a machine! In a few minutes he was out of the water entirely.

A half-mile beyond the lake, the road ended, but that was expected.

He got out of the jeep and sat on the bumper. It was relatively dry, but it didn't matter. He was sweating from head to toe. His shirt, his pants, pretty much everything was soaked.

The Appalachian Trail, and the shelter he sought, was less than a mile's hike away. But there seemed to be something else involved. He got up and walked until he was at the edge of a deep gulch. A gulch of yellow dirt about a hundred feet wide. Great. He tested the edge of the gulch with one foot. Clumps of earth broke free, rolled, and broke into sand. It was mostly compact sand. The gulch must have been created by a recent breach of some kind. Perhaps a spontaneous river of flood waters. Uprooted pine trees lay all around, some of them with their tops pointing straight at the bottom. They had been there for a while. Many of their needles had died and turned orange.

Burton locked the jeep, strapped on his pack, and searched for a climb-able place. He did not want to go around the gulch. A dead pine tree worked pretty well as a ladder, although, too late, he discovered its limbs were covered with pitch. Once free of the tree, the slope was a little less steep, and he climbed down by placing his hands and feet on the rocks that seemed least likely to pull loose. A few did, but never more than one at a time. Yellow sand stuck to the pitch on his hands.

Going up the other side was easier. He could test handholds and footholds before committing to them.

Once out of the gulch, he sat down in the shade of a tree. He got a bandana out of his pocket and wiped sweat from his face. It instantly became filthy. He looked down. His clothes, his arms and his hands were covered in yellow dust. And, apparently, his face.

The land rose steeply from here. Burton checked the GPS and was pretty damn proud of himself to see that it was a straight shot up to the A.T. He stuffed the bandana in his pocket and began climbing. He wedged his boots against tree trunks and hoisted himself up by the trunks and branches above. After a half an hour of doing this, during which he agreed with Maddy that he had officially lost his mind, Burton emerged onto the packed dirt of the Appalachian Trail.

The shelter was south of here, down the trail to the left. After only ten minutes of hiking, he came upon three thin men standing at a scenic overlook. Each of them was reaching into a small plastic bag and eating something. None of them noticed Burton until he was nearly upon them.

"Hi," he said.

They turned in his direction.

"Hey, there," one said. The other two nodded a greeting, then went back to looking out over the valley.

The size of their packs and their scraggly beards indicated these guys were doing a long hike. A view like this was one of its rewards. Burton felt bad for half a second about ruining the moment. Just a half-second.

"Sorry to bother you guys, but, well, would you mind taking a look at this?"

He pulled a flyer from the backpack and handed it to them.

"Whoa, that's rough," said the one who had spoken the first time. They could have been brothers, the three, but it was probably just the lean faces, beards and puffy, gray outgrown crew cuts.

The other two leaned over to read the flyer. "Give us a few more and we'll post them on the shelters, north of here," one of them said. He scrutinized Burton for a moment. "Unless you've been there already."

"No, I just got here."

The three exchanged glances. Then their eyes moved to his small pack.

He handed a dozen flyers to the man who offered to put them up.

"You're a champ. Thanks. Of course, if you see Seb—that's my son, Seb—would you call the number on the flyer? The next time you're in civilization?"

"Will do."

They stared at him with bags of peanuts and raisins dangling from their hands.

"Thanks again," Burton said. "Enjoy."

"Good luck to you," said the man who originally greeted him. The others nodded, each with their own version of the obligatory optimistic, empathic facial expression.

He met no one else on his way to the shelter. It was a lean-to and it was empty, as was to be expected in the afternoon. His family had seen A.T. lean-tos before, but Burton had forgotten how rustic and exposed they were. Three walls and a roof of logs with a plank floor. One wall completely missing.

This shelter had, on the rear wall, a chalk drawing of a smiling bear. A very good drawing. Burton took a thumbtack from a mint box and tacked a flyer next to it. Something gray scampered between his feet. A tiny mouse with big ears.

After tacking flyers on the outside of the left and right walls, Burton unrolled his sleeping bag and rather thin sleeping cushion in a corner of the shelter. He wrote WAKE ME in big letters across the back of one of the flyers, got in the sleeping bag, and placed the flyer on his stomach. It was probably three in the afternoon, but he was beat, and had nothing to do but wait.

"We're waking you," a woman's voice said.

Burton woke to a young man and woman just a few feet away, sitting cross-legged, side by side, facing him. The sky through the open front of the lean-to behind them had turned a deep blue. The two looked like they could not be more than twenty.

He sat up.

"Thanks."

The sleeping bag fell around his waist, revealing that he still wore the hiking clothes covered in yellow dirt. He smelled, too, like yellow dirt. Perhaps it had sulfur.

The young woman pushed a tear from her eye with a finger. The young man leaned over and kissed the finger. Why was she crying?

"Everybody's cool on the trail," she said. "Nobody's going to hurt your son." She whispered into her companion's ear, "Maybe I shouldn't have said that."

The two of them shifted, sort of waddled, to move a little closer to Burton without getting out of their cross-legged positions.

The young man stroked the scanty blonde scruff on his chin. "We're just doing Maine. North to south. Do you know where your son is headed?"

"I think the same direction as you. With some detours."

"Are you trying to catch up with him?" The young woman squinted as if unsure what detours Burton might be talking about.

"Trying, yes. I'm hitting some key spots to put up flyers and talking to people who may have passed him on their way north."

"Key spots?" the young man asked. Then he nodded as if he understood, probably just to be nice. You could not just "hit key spots" on the A.T. There were not any chair lifts or roads up to the best views. Except maybe for Mount Washington. You had to walk the trail for the rewards.

"Tomorrow," Burton said, to change the subject. "I'm heading back to the nearest town. I really don't know what I'm doing, to be honest. Our son's been gone for a couple of weeks and I'm trying every angle I can think of."

Each time Burton explained his plan, always vaguely, doubt and fear doubled down on him. He knew what he wanted but if his judgment was clouded by wishful thinking, it could come at Seb's expense.

What he wanted was for Seb to feel the least amount of threat possible. Burton would immediately make it clear that he was not going to tie a rope around Seb and carry him home. Although there were times when Burton wondered if that was exactly what he should do. Meeting Seb one on one was the only scenario Burton could envision that would not set Seb running into the woods. If Seb went, unprepared, into an area he did not know, he could get himself in real trouble.

The young woman wiped her right hand on her shorts and held it out. "I'm Simona."

Burton was about to shake her hand when he thought maybe he should clean his own hand as well. With nothing else clean nearby, he rubbed his hand on his sleeping bag before extending it out to her.

"Burton. Sorry. Had to hang onto some pines to get up a steep hill. I've got pitch all over my hands."

"It's all clean dirt up here." Simona said. "That's what I love about it."

The young man reached his hand out.

"Cletus."

The young woman snorted. "Stop with the Cletus crap, you dork."

"Also known as Alex," her companion said. He looked embarrassed for having joked with a man who had a runaway son.

"Hi Cletus." Burton said.

He stretched over to reach into his backpack and pull out some flyers. He set them on the floor in front of the young couple. "Keep a few in case you see him, so you have my number."

Simona nodded. Her eyes were misting up again.

"We passed a pack of teenagers," Alex said. "Two days ago. Boy scouts from Vermont. Maybe..."

"Yes, he's capable of infiltrating a Boy Scout troop," Burton said. "I'll have to check that out." He reached back into his pack again. "I have chicken salad sandwiches from this great diner. They won't last long, the way I heated up my backpack today."

Maureen had given him three Sunflower Cafe specials with a pickle wrapped into an outer fold of each sandwich's wax paper. He found the misshapen paper bag in his backpack and set it on the floor next to the flyers.

"May be a little scrunched."

The other two looked at each other for approval.

"I'm trying to make a good impression." Burton removed two sandwiches from the bag and held them out. "So you won't forget me. Go ahead, take them."

"Thank you," they said, together, and took the sandwiches. Simona took little bites, wiping the corners of her mouth after each bite with the napkin Maureen had folded around the sandwich.

"Is this really a rendezvous spot?" Burton asked. "A secret, for the 'in-the-know?' What I read online was kind of cryptic. Something to do with keeping a movement going. 'Passing Dropout's Torch?' Sound familiar? Are you allowed to tell me? Or am I too old?"

After swallowing, Simona grinned. "Are you kidding? This place is crawling with gray hairs. I love old people." She paused. "Not that you're, um, old. The only qualification is being an earth advocate. The torch is a message. Passing Dropout's Torch means doing something to preserve places like this when we get back home."

"Really?" Alex said. "I didn't know all that. I thought it was just an excuse to party together."

This movement sounded right up Seb's alley. Burton felt a rush of warmth. Seb could be hiding in the woods right behind this lean-to. Meeting all these cool people.

"You're not the only one, Burton," Simona said. "Most people don't know this is a special place. It's kind of new. They named it after a guy who wrote poems about the trail right here in this lean-to."

"Be cool to read one of his poems now," Alex said. "Especially now with the sun going down." He turned to look out the lean-to.

Burton and Simona looked that way as well. The land sloped upward from the shelter. Every inch of ground, every stump and every boulder was covered with thick moss. Little ferns grew in the crevices and spaces around the boulders. Only peeling birches and shaggy pine trunks interrupted the green. Any number of poems could be written about the greens and textures in the space framed by the opening of this lean-to.

"Is that why you came to this particular shelter?" Simona asked. "Is your son an environmentalist?"

"Oh, yes. He's many things, but yes."

"Everyone on the A.T. is," Alex said.

"Not all of us," Burton said. "Not enough, anyway."

Simona and Alex nodded slowly.

"Not enough of an environmentalist," Burton said. "I know I'm not."

The others nodded more enthusiastically now.

"I get you," Alex said. "No exaggeration. I don't know why I can keep forgetting about something so important. Like the most important thing. And I keep putting off being a vegetarian." He looked down at the sandwich wrapper on the floor in front of him.

"Oh," Simona said. "I *am* a vegetarian."

"Being mostly vegetarian is still really good," Burton said. "From what I've been reading. Our son has us scrambling to get up to speed on all this. If everybody ate less meat, that would really help turn things around, right?"

"Um," Simona said. "I think so. I think you're a better environmentalist than us. I just don't like killing things."

"Anyway, at least the chicken didn't die just to get rancid and dumped in the woods," Burton said.

He realized he was still sitting in his sleeping bag. He pulled his legs out, and sat on the bag, cross-legged, like the others. He was about to offer Sunflower Cafe cookies when he saw Alex holding out a greenish cookie to him. Burton took the cookie. It was raw, barely sweet, and tasted green.

They talked a while longer. Burton was distracted, hoping to hear more people arriving. The lean-tos were open to hikers on a first come, first served basis. No reservations.

No one else showed up.

An hour after sunset, the three of them agreed it was time to sleep.

Burton lay for hours, not sleeping. Several thoughts troubled him. Was Seb hiding from all hikers? Was he wearing a disguise? If Burton did come across Seb, would he run, and would Burton be able to catch him? Seb was a wiry kid with long legs. He might get away.

Several times, as Burton was on the verge of sleep, a creaking branch would pull him back. He held his breath to hear if the sound was a late-comer to the shelter, although this was unlikely, so long after dark. It was really dark out there. He finally gave up on sleeping and went over to sit at the edge of the lean-to. In the scant moonlight, the green mossy hillside had turned black and white.

He had not found Seb, but he had made it to his destination, and that was an accomplishment. A deranged accomplishment, perhaps. He could just as easily be lying unconscious down there in the endless trees, beneath an upside-down jeep.

But he, Burton Franck, was the beast. The unstoppable pale beast of the Maine woods. He was going to find his son.

CHAPTER SEVENTEEN

SKEET

THERE WAS SOMETHING OUTSIDE Seb's tent. He peeked under the door flap and saw two brown leather boots, their toes worn and shiny.

"Morning, bro," the voice above the boots said. The voice of the kid with the baseball hat.

"Morning, Skeet."

"Huh?"

Seb unzipped the tent and climbed out. The ground was cold on his bare feet. It was cold all over, since he was wearing only underwear and a T-shirt.

"The other day, walking home, I had that song stuck in my head. Peter, with a skeeter attached. I started thinking of you as Pete. Which meant I was calling you a dick. Literally. So, the next time that song ran through my head I thought it would be better to call you Skeeter instead of Peter. By the time I got back to camp it was Skeet. As in, *that dude Skeet shore wuz a redneck.*"

This produced a big laugh. "Well, your nickname is Bug Eyes."

"Oh yeah? Since when?"

"Since right now."

"Really? My eyes look buggy?"

"With that contraption on your head."

Seb had forgotten the binoculo-glasses. He had been reading in the tent and had pushed them onto his forehead when he heard Skeet's boots outside his tent. He pulled the binoculo-glasses off his head and hid them behind his back. "Redneck meets geek."

"That's about right."

"I had to pack light. So I printed all the books I need to study in microscopic print. I read them with..." He removed the binoculoglasses from behind his back. "These."

Skeet glanced down at the big eyeglass frames with the glass removed and binocular lenses attached. He then shifted his eyes from side to side, as if checking to see if he were alone with a crazy person. "You want to put on something other than underwear and go see that cave I was talking about?"

"I think I can fit that into my schedule."

The boy climbed back into the tent.

"And do you want to tell me what to call you?" Skeet asked. "If you don't want to be called 'Bug Eyes?'"

From inside the tent, the boy said, "Seb." There. It was done. His name was out.

"I got food."

Seb poked his head out of the tent. "What, you got food for both of us? You didn't tell your mother about me, did you? Who does she think the extra food is for?"

"Yes, every morning she packs me a peanut butter and jelly sandwich with the crusts cut off and puts in a little juice box with a little straw. So I said, 'Can you make another one for this runaway kid who's hiding out in the woods?'"

Running away had never been mentioned by either of them. But what else would you call a fourteen-year old living in a tent in the woods?

Seb came out with his sleeping bag rolled up, still in his underwear. "I have to get clothes out of the tree-bags. Do we need a flashlight?"

"I have one but we could use two. We can go a lot deeper with flashlights. And wear your muddin' clothes." Skeet laughed. "Muddin' clothes. I kill myself."

"All my clothes are muddin' clothes."

As soon as Seb tied the knot to suspend the bear-bags up in the tree, Skeet took off. He was tired of waiting. Seb jumped down from the tree, grabbed his pack, and followed. He had not gone in this direction before, and now he knew why. Twice they had to get down on hands and knees to pass under thorny raspberries. A little later, they crossed a swamp by walking along a series of half-buried logs with grass growing around them. A wall made by beavers, Skeet said.

The wet flats ended at a sparse incline. Sparse because it was too steep for most things to grow on it. Seb was not used to relying so much on finger and toe holds, and got a little scared. Fortunately he remembered not to look down. There were some sumacs, with their fuzzy bark, along the way, and he hung onto them gratefully for a moment before going after Skeet. The kid was like a mountain goat.

The terrain eventually leveled off and they were back under tree cover. Mostly tall pines and shorter maples.

Skeet suddenly turned right, onto a wide, flat rock. Seb followed. He stopped when he noticed Skeet standing at a precipice. There was nothing at all in front of him except for trees in a valley far, far below, and mountains even further in the distance.

The precipice was made of pinkish rock. At the tip, where Skeet was standing, it was only a few feet wide.

"Watch out." Skeet said. "It's probably a thousand foot drop from here." He sat down with his legs hanging over the edge.

Seb walked, hunched at the shoulders, with his arms out for balance, towards the far edge. He sat before he got too close and shuffled forward on his butt, before finally forcing himself to let his legs hang off. Skeet was good enough not to make fun of him.

All green. Mountain, valley, forest. All green, with the exception of rocky peaks scattered in the distance.

"See it?" Skeet asked.

Seb had seen it. A large raptor. It floated in a wide circle below them. It was near enough for them to see its tail shift, sending the bird in a new direction, into a new circle. Not a bald eagle. The white of a bald eagle's head would have been obvious from this vantage point.

"Know what it is?" Skeet asked.

"Golden Eagle."

"Nice."

Skeet pulled two plastic-wrapped sandwiches from his Army surplus pack. Seb smelled peanut butter immediately.

"PB and J for real. That turkey jerky is wrecking my stomach. And the farts are ridiculous. I actually put my head out of the tent last night. Of course a mosquito immediately bit me on the forehead."

"I'll get you some deer jerky. My Dad makes it."

They chewed and gazed into the center of the eagle's looping glide.

"What year were you?" Skeet asked.

"Eighth."

"Me, too. Did you think I was younger? I'm a short Frenchman but I keek your ass good."

"No, I figured about the same as me," Seb said. "This reminds me." He held up the sandwich. "Civilization is good for some things. Such as PB and J."

"I have a question."

Seb said, "Shoot," which sounded like "soo" because of the peanut butter stuck to the roof of his mouth.

"Are you in trouble?"

"You mean like a fugitive, hiding out from the law?"

"You're way too much of a geek to be a criminal."

The eagle tucked its wings and dove. They watched until it disappeared behind another outcropping.

Before Seb could reply, Skeet said, "At least tell me how you got here on a bike. All the way from wherever. I can tell you're not from Maine."

There were two reasons to leave Skeet in the dark.

Reason one: Skeet knew only enough to send a ranger snooping around. Seb could run from a ranger. Skeet would not be able to tell the ranger much else. Not even what state Seb lived in. Not who his parents were.

Reason two: telling Skeet the thought process that brought Seb to this place might make Skeet think he was not right mentally. *I'm probably not right mentally,* Seb thought, *but being here is what I need.* Skeet might not understand this, though, and feel obliged to go for help.

There were three reasons, actually. Seb did not want to come off as Chicken Little, hiding in the woods from the melting sky.

"It's kind of embarrassing..."

"What? That you'd rather watch an eagle, or walk for fifteen miles, than play video games?" Skeet bent his elbow and flexed his arm. "I got these bazookas so nobody messes with me, but I know what they say behind my back. Strange, inbred backwoods kid. I'm not inbred, by the way.

"They don't look down on me for being on welfare, though. Half the people are on it. No jobs unless you want to drive a truck or work somewhere far away and most people would rather be poor.

"You know, all us kids used to be out here when we were younger. We would spend the whole day swimming, fishing. Climbing cliffs. I'm the only one left. Some guys I know will fish up the road from their house but nobody spends all day out here like me. They might be right about the strange part." Skeet's voice trailed off. "It all sounds like kids' stuff, now that I'm saying it out loud."

Seb pulled his sleeve back and flexed his arm. His had been the skinniest arms in the eighth grade, since he was so tall and stretched out. His arms did not look much different when flexed. "I got these for the same reason, being the oddball." He looked at his arm. "No, I didn't. They're Muppet arms, I know it."

Skeet choked on his last bite of sandwich. "Muppet arms." After swallowing, he stood up, with tears in his eyes from laughing and choking. "You're a maniac. We need to get going."

"Don't be fooled. These are long arms. The muscle adds up."

Skeet crashed off into the brush. Seb took one more look at the valley and ran after him. There was no trail, just trees. How Skeet knew where to go was impossible to tell.

The canopy became so thick and dark that mushrooms and short ferns were the only things growing in the sea of pine needles on the forest floor. The boys walked side by side through the winding alleys of tree trunks.

"So, private detective," Seb said. "You're right. I'm not from Maine, but not everybody in Maine drops their 'ahs.' Do I look like city? I'm actually from the suburbs."

Skeet shrugged.

"You shouldn't be too impressed about the bike. I got here ninety-nine percent on gasoline. My parents drove me to Portsmouth, New Hampshire, to a monastery. See? It's getting weird already.

"It was an early Christmas present, the retreat at the monastery. I got hooked up with Buddhists in a meditation group. This monk who runs the monastery came to talk to us one night. I never met anyone like him before. The world was looking more and more crazy to me and he was the first adult who sounded like he had a clue how to deal with it.

"I kept emailing the monk and he kept answering. This guy was smart. He was an Ajahn. That means teacher in Thailand, which is where he's from.

"The Ajahn told me about a retreat they were going to have this summer. It wasn't until I was all set to go when he found out I was fourteen. I'm tall and, you know, old people aren't so good at figuring out what age you are. We knew each other pretty well by then, the Ajahn and me, and my parents got copied on all of our emails, so they knew he was cool. So they ended up letting me go to the retreat."

Seb stopped walking. He had never spoken these words to anyone. The closest he had come was typing some cryptic messages into a computer and hiding them behind a wall in a closet.

Skeet did not notice Seb had stopped at first. He turned to look back.

"What's up?"

"The Ajahn believed in me. I had no idea I was going to bail on him. Not when we first started talking. Things happened."

"They do," Skeet said.

Seb started walking again and the two of them continued, with Skeet a half-step ahead, since he was leading the way.

"You don't have to talk about it," Skeet said.

They came to a part of the forest that looked like it had been planted in rows. The trees stretched out ahead in straight lines. Seb wondered if it was possible anyone would plant a million trees in a row.

"Did you ever read *My Side of the Mountain?*" he asked.

"I think so. Yeah."

"That kid's father thought it was a great idea, for a boy to go live in the woods. He was even younger than we are. Now it's illegal and you have to worry about giving your parents a nervous breakdown."

Skeet cast a sidewards look at him.

"I know," Seb said. "And the kid in the book already knew a lot about living off the land. Still, I heard that people used to get married at our age. We can make a baby. What's the big deal if I need to be alone for a while? I told them I planned this out carefully and I knew what I was doing."

They came to the top of a rockslide. Thousands of broken-up gray rocks extended down a steep slope. A pile of dead trees up against the edge of a pine forest seemed to be keeping the rockslide in place. Sections of a creek showed through the forest further on. The landslide left an opening to the sky, and the sun cooked up a scent that Seb could only describe as hot rock smell.

"Sit?" he asked.

"All right."

They sat on a patch of grass just above the rockslide and Seb told Skeet what he had told no one before.

◈

"I left poor Ajahn Wattana sleeping that night," Seb said, "totally trusting me. He'd trust me if I stuck a knife in his forehead. After everybody was asleep I snuck out of there. I didn't even leave a note. I don't know if you ever went to one, but Buddhist monasteries are the quietest places in the world. I thought someone would hear me for sure.

"I ended up walking down the street in Portsmouth. New Hampshire. It was the middle of the night and I had a pack on my back, so I

228

tried to stay out of sight. Because I totally looked like a runaway.

"Any time I saw headlights, I hid behind a car. I had to walk five miles to the bike shop. It wasn't open yet. Up the street was a diner so I waited there until I saw a light go on in the shop. My bike and saddlebags were already paid for. I sent them a money order a few weeks before. They wanted to sell me more stuff but I got out of there before they started to ask questions and get suspicious.

"Getting to the bus station wasn't too bad except for riding my bike over the bridge into Maine. I went to Maine because I knew they would try to track me down at the Portsmouth bus station. The bus driver in Maine didn't want to put my bike in with the luggage underneath, but I was like, I know you're supposed to do it. He said it was too full. I said I was going to call the office. He threw the bike in and looked at me like I was lucky he didn't throw me in with it. Threw my bike in, literally.

"I had to take three different busses in Maine. The only thing I didn't have figured out in advance was how to get to Baxter Park once I got off the final bus. In the summer, though, there's always hikers who don't have a car and you can usually get a shuttle up to the mountain. That's what I read online and it was true.

"I was waiting for the bus out of Bangor, the last bus, when these four dudes showed up. They had some serious hiking gear. Backpacks that probably weighed seventy pounds. They didn't look much older than me. I got close and heard them say 'shuttle' a couple of times. When we got on the bus I made sure I got a seat across the aisle from them.

"People talk to each other when they see other people with hiking gear. These guys asked me where I was headed. I said to a friend's cabin for fishing and biking. They said they were going to check out the International A.T. That's the trail that goes on where the regular A.T. ends. This one goes way up into Canada. One of the guys kept staring at me, which made me really nervous, because I had a fake beard on.

"Yeah, I forgot to mention that. I put on a fake beard before I left the monastery. A trendy one, trimmed close and all, but they can come loose. The bus didn't have a bathroom, so I couldn't check it in the mirror. I had to just sit there and not touch it and hope it wasn't falling off.

"I asked if I could pay for an extra seat on their shuttle, if there was a seat, and they were, like, 'Sure, cool.' This one guy, Fro, he had this bush of red hair, took out a bottle of brandy, and I thought, *rut ro.* They passed it around and when it came to me, I held up my hand to say no. They didn't care. After that I pretended to sleep, in case they started to ask more questions about the college I was supposed to be going to in the fall. Everybody on the bus was sleeping.

"We got to town and just about everybody on the bus hiked down the road to the same campground. Most of them were going to hike the normal A.T., not the one that goes into Canada. I was definitely the only one not in college or older. Then these two hot girls started to talk to me, which was, like, incredible, but bad timing.

"One of them said how stoked she was, that she always wanted to come there. Was this my first time? I said, no, but I was stoked, too. What school did I go to? Rutgers, I said. They started laughing and I was, like, what? We'd have you over to our tent but we think you might be jail bait.

"I was so nervous I first thought they meant jail for running away and I didn't say anything. They started to laugh so hard they had to lean on each other. Then they felt bad and said it was because I was so cute. I got annoyed and told them I was all man and what did their tent look like?

"They stopped talking to me after that. I just needed to get to the campground. After we put our tents up, the guys whose shuttle I was going to ride in said they were going to town for dinner. I said I needed to crash. They said, 'Okay, we're meeting at the campground entrance at five tomorrow morning.' When they were gone, I sneaked back into town and bought every turkey jerky bar they had and all my other supplies. Then I had to get back to the campground and melt wax into the paint can.

"The college guys didn't get back until three. I heard them because I really couldn't sleep.

"Out in the parking lot the next morning, one guy had to lie on the ground because of his hangover. The shuttle was late. It was just a big, rusty van and a really old lady for a driver. We threw our stuff in the van. I squeezed my bike in the back. It was good luck they stayed up partying all night because they slept and didn't talk to me at all.

"I started to fill up the saddle bags when we got to the entrance to Baxter Park. I had to strap my backpack and my sleeping bag on top of the saddle bags. The whole time I was packing, the van was making these turns and throwing me up against the side.

"The college dudes started waking up because we were getting close. They were all watching me try to get all my crap onto the bike. The same guy who stared at me before was staring at me again. Right at my fake beard, I could just tell.

"Then this guy asked me where I was going.

"I said, 'For a long ride.'

"He said, 'Your friend can't have a cabin in here. It's a state park.'"

"They were all looking at me. I was sweating and that made me worry my beard would come unglued. I told them I wanted to see Katahdin first and then I turned around so they couldn't see my face. I checked my reflection in the window to make sure my beard was still good.

"They left me alone. They were pumped up for the hike, shouting, except for the really hung over guy, who didn't move. When it came time for me to get out, everybody was busy going through their own gear.

"I yelled to the driver that this was my stop. She said it wasn't a stop and I said, 'I know but, please?' So she stopped and I opened the back doors of the van while everybody watched me.

"I got out as fast as I could. Then I jumped on my bike and shouted, 'Have an awesome hike!' Fro, I think it was him, he was so easy-going, yelled, 'Rock on!' I didn't look back. My helmet was hanging from my handlebars bouncing all over the place. The first few seconds I got really scared and I seriously thought about stopping and yelling for the van. But I kept on pedaling, faster and faster.

"All of a sudden I realized I was on Mount Katahdin. Except I couldn't see what it looked like because of all the trees. I thought about stashing my bike and hiking up until I could see it but I had a long way to go still.

"There should be a prize for going *around* Katahdin, because that's what I did, and it's a lot longer than going up it. And more hills.

"Up a mountain, down a mountain, with all that crap on the bike. I'm in good shape but it was not fun. When a logging truck would pass me my tires would be wobbling. The whole bike was shaking but I think that was from nerves. I got so tired I had to find a place off the road to sleep in the woods for a while.

"Finally I came to the last road I was supposed to take and there wasn't even a sign. I wasn't totally sure it was the right road. First it was paved and then it was dirt and then it ended at the woods. I walked and pushed the bike the rest of the way with that mountain of junk piled on it."

"And that's how I got here from Massachusetts."

Skeet sat there blinking at him. "You planned to come to this place? I mean, where your camp is set up?"

"I did. Not that exact spot but in that part of the woods."

"It isn't that special. I mean there's a hundred other places, a thousand, like that."

"Maybe that's why I picked it."

A chipmunk, no, a red squirrel, popped out of the logjam at the bottom of the rockslide. It looked at them, scampered along a dead tree and dropped out of view.

"What did you say to your family? You didn't just disappear? I guess you left a note?"

"I sent emails. It's kind of complicated."

Skeet widened his eyes.

"I set up my computer to automatically send emails every day or two. After I left."

"Why not just one long email?"

"I wanted them to think about different things. Not all at once."

"What did they do, that was so bad?"

"Nothing."

"And you never talked to them? On the phone or anything, in all this time? Doesn't that kind of suck? For them?"

"Oh, yeah. It does. But if I called them..."

Seb realized the more he explained, the worse it sounded, but he was hoping it would make sense in the end. Skeet had to understand some reasons were private. If he stopped now, though, it definitely would not make sense.

"I asked my parents to answer my emails by making videos and putting them up on YouTube. I'm sure they did it but I haven't seen them. The one time I went into town, I could have watched the first one, but that would've made me feel worse."

"So you asked them to post videos that you were never going to see?"

Skeet had been staring ahead for some time now. The story he was telling had to be pretty disturbing.

"It's—."

Skeet interrupted. "I know. It's complicated. You must be some kind of genius, to send emails they can't trace. Are you having them make videos just so they feel better? Like you guys are talking to each other?"

"Maybe in the back of my mind I was thinking that. But the videos were supposed to make them feel better in a different way.

"The reason I had them do videos is that you really have to think hard. We made videos in my social studies class and the teacher said we should remember that once we make a video and put it on the internet, lots of people could see it. Somebody could even copy it. You could look really stupid. So we wrote everything down and made sure we didn't just make things up.

"Not that my parents would make things up. I just knew they would be all focused on finding out where I was. So I came up with this idea that they would think harder about my questions if they had to make a video."

"And then what did you want them to do?" Skeet asked.

"Just understand why I left. That I really had to do it. To save my ass. From my mind."

Skeet said nothing.

"You're probably thinking it's a miracle that some guy trying to get away from his mind could make it all the way the hell out here and still be alive."

Skeet had been squinting like he was deep in thought for a while. The sun reflecting off the rocks was bright but he could have looked somewhere less bright if he wanted to. Seb wondered if he had that look on his face because he did not like him anymore. Because of what he did to his parents.

"They were probably glad to get rid of you," Skeet finally said. A few seconds later, he glanced at Seb with a half-grin. "I'm not blaming you. I'm here, too, right?"

The thoughts began to go in circles in Seb's mind again. The thoughts he hoped he could meditate away, or forget, in this place without all the reminders of how insane the world was.

I had no choice. Yes, I did. I could have suffered at home instead of hurting everyone who cares about me. Did the emails and videos convince them I would go completely crazy if I stayed at home? Or did they make them worry more? The sky is falling, the sky is falling. Why can't I be normal?

Instead of saying any of this to Skeet, he said, "I believed I would get put in an insane hospital. And maybe go insane permanently. Or jump off a bridge. I don't know if you ever felt panic but it's the worst. There. That's the truth. Pretty pathetic, huh?"

"If it makes you feel any better, I think I would go crazy living in the city."

Seb opted not to interject that he did not live in the city. It would probably feel like city to Skeet, anyway.

"Well, you definitely hurt your parents bad," Skeet said. "But I think you wanted to hurt them for not dealing with the global stuff."

He lay back on the rock and put his arms over his head. "I love the sun. I could lay here all day."

Seb felt a huge rush of relief. Skeet had decided he had heard enough and he was still there.

"That story tired me out, just listening to it." Skeet's chest began to heave. He was laughing. "Fake beard. You're wearing that thing next time."

"Sure. With the binoculo-glasses."

Skeet lifted his head and set it back down. "No. I don't want to be seen with you wearing those."

"I guess it's possible we would run into somebody."

The squirrel popped up again, closer now. Seb threw a pebble in its direction. The animal did not move, just kind of looked at him like he was an idiot.

He leaned back and stretched out next to Skeet. Something pinched his shoulder blade. He pulled out a pine cone and tossed it away. There was no wind and it was hot, but as long as they did not move it felt good. Worth a little sunburn.

"All the people who want to get away from the city go to the Appalachian Trail. And you came to that patch of woods."

"The A.T. would be amazing, but I needed to..."

"Med-i-tate," Skeet said in a low voice, enunciating each syllable like Frankenstein.

"That, and chill and figure out what to do with myself. Not walk all day for six months, which is what hiking the A.T. means. They don't let you set up camp on the A.T. Just overnight. Besides, they'd find me there."

"Don't you get lonely? Sometimes I walk a couple of miles, and I think, I'm going to be alone all day. But I do it again the next day."

"Lonely?" Seb said. "I guess, but it feels worth it. That I got out before I totally lost my mind. I'm supposed to be meditating for at least a half an hour a day but I usually don't make it that long. Usually because I end up feeling guilty for what I did."

"You know," Skeet said. "You're not supposed to be camping where you set up your tent. There's places where you can, but I think they want a permit."

"Is there any place left in the world where you can just put up a tent?"

"Not for free, fool. And not when you're fourteen."

CHAPTER EIGHTEEN

FUTURE GENERATIONS?

BURTON WOKE IN BLACKNESS to the sound of the phone ringing. His knee bumped against hard plastic. It was the monster jeep's cup holder. He had climbed into the back seat to rest a little.

He sat up, shoved the sleeping bag to the side, and climbed over the cup holder to get into the front seat. The ringing was coming from the glove compartment. He opened it and saw Maddy's little picture on the phone's screen.

"Oh, Burt," she said after he pressed the answer button. "I was worried." She sounded it.

"I'm sorry, babe. It got too dark and I had to stop. I tried to call but there was no phone signal before. I don't know why the phone's working now. What time is it?"

"Five. In the morning."

"Wow. Really?"

"Yes. I've been calling all night. Where are you?"

"I'm at...GPS numbers that wouldn't mean anything to you."

"You're in the woods?"

"These roads take forever. I had a major delay when I got stuck in a mud hole. I didn't think I was getting out of that. This is ridiculous and I'm a fool. If Maureen, the waitress in town, didn't tell me how to use evergreen branches to get tires out of mud holes I'd be there still."

"Maureen? You sound strange. How far from the motel are you?"

"I told you about her—"

"Yes. Whatever. Listen—"

"I'm a long way from the motel."

"Are you lost? I thought the GPS Phillip picked out was the best you could get."

"Phillip got it right. A GPS doesn't tell you if the road on your map is flooded or should no longer be called a road."

"You're okay?"

"I'm okay."

"I've been calling because we got an email from Seb."

Strangely, this news did nothing but annoy Burton. He did not want another email. He was sick of Seb's demands.

"The same kind of message?" he asked. "Another canned email?"

"Looks that way. I forwarded it to you and Phillip as soon as it came in."

"Can you read it to me?"

The phone Phillip took apart and modified for Burton got better reception than any other phone in Maine, except maybe ones used by the military, but it did not get email.

Maddy did not answer right away. "I can read it. Of course." She stopped again.

The few seconds of silence unnerved him. "What's wrong?"

"He says it's the last message." Her voice quavered. "Whatever that means. Oh, Burton, I'm scared."

"Did he say...is he going to do something? Bad?"

"Nothing like that. I'll just read it to you."

"Okay."

"There's no greeting or anything." Maddy cleared her throat. "Okay, I'm starting to read now.

"I have one last thing to explain. But first, I'm really sorry about these emails and video homework, and sorry mostly for hurting you. I spent a long time trying to figure out if there was a better way to do this. You might not believe it, but this is what I came up with as the way to hurt you the least. It was supposed to help. Help you understand why I had to do what I did.

"In case you don't hate me, I want you to know that my plan is going to work. It's going to stop me from totally losing my mind.

236

"Looking over these messages, I sure do complain a lot. Maybe I am a spoiled, ungrateful brat. The thing is, I know I have more than most kids on the planet. It makes me feel more messed up to realize I could be starving in Africa with real problems but even realizing that didn't stop me from going crazy. I'm sorry.

"Anyway, here's the last thing. Of course you remember the article about global warming from when Dad was in college. Did you notice part of the article was missing? I cut it off.

"I want to tell you about the end of the article now. Maybe you should read it first. It's attached."

"Do you remember?" Maddy switched her tone from reading to questioning Burton. "What you wrote at the end of the article?"

He did not remember what he had written. He did not even realize part of the article had been missing. The old newsletter in the cedar chest was in bad shape, the paper wrinkled and ripped.

"I forgot all about it. Something extreme, I'm afraid."

Maddy's voice quavered. "I haven't looked at it yet."

"It's okay, babe. Let's read it."

"Okay. Hold on. I'm clicking on it. It's a picture. Well, damn. I can't read it. The letters are too small."

"You can—."

"Let me find the zoom button. Okay, here it is. I can see now. A thin rectangle. The bottom of the newsletter. It says:

"The title of this article is 'future generations?' What about them? They are at our mercy. Will we take care of them? The information, and the solutions, to global warming are out there, but nothing substantial seems to be happening. All I see is people focused on their own comfort and getting more stuff. If that's how we respond to an existential crisis, I don't think I would bring a child into this world. Not into a world that doesn't really care what happens to future generations."

Maddy stopped speaking.

"There's more, right?" Burton asked. "To the article?"

"I see the red stripe at the bottom of the page. It looks like the footer of the newsletter. Was there more? Something on the back side of the page that he didn't see?"

Burton sat there in the jeep, looking at the reflection of his face, lit by the phone, in the windshield. Besides this image, there was only the blackness of the deep forest all around.

"No," he said. "There was no back side."

"Oh my God."

"Yeah. Pretty bad."

How could he have forgotten this part of the article? An article he wrote himself? Psychologists would call it denial.

"Is there more? Is that the end of his email?"

"No, there's more:

> "Please believe me. I know you guys love me. I'm lucky to have the family I have. I didn't send this last part of the article because I was mad.
>
> "The reason I kept it until now is because it would have scared you too much. I wanted you to understand why I went away and the whole thing at once might have freaked you out. Maybe there was no good way to tell you.
>
> "So why am I showing this to you now? To finish the story of why I had to go.
>
> "When I finished reading Dad's article, I was in shock about how things had only gotten worse in all the years since you wrote it. Nobody had really changed what they were doing, even smart people. They just talked about it. Some tried but it wasn't working.
>
> "I felt like all the energy was leaking out of me. Like I would pass out right there in the attic with the article in my hand. But then I felt like I had to run. Drop the article and run and run. I didn't run because I knew I would get caught, and then I'd be stuck.
>
> "I was sitting there in the attic for a while, maybe an hour, not knowing what to do. Then I heard a siren up the street and it came to me. The reason I wanted to run.
>
> "It was people. So many people you need a siren to get your way around them. It was bad enough to think people were ig-

noring the most important thing in the world and making it worse at the same time. It was when I realized how many people there were in the world and none of them, not even the geniuses, were able to convince them to stop. That made me feel really crazy.

"Maybe you think I'm brave. A brave environment advocate. I'm not. I left to survive. I tried waiting for the panic to go away but it wouldn't. I felt so trapped.

"Then I saw that California was checking if oil companies knew a long time ago that the way we used oil and gas was a big cause of global warming and pretended it wasn't true. That almost made my head blow off.

"I couldn't tell you how crazy I felt because you would really keep an eye on me. Then I would have felt even more trapped. If I felt more trapped than I already did, I think I might have done something bad. To myself. And so, that's my story.

"I want to say to Dad, you were way ahead of people. You had the guts to say something before it was popular to talk about global warming. Before a lot of people ever heard of it. You tried. You're just one guy. And you were right. People don't care about future generations. They don't care about me. And I can't watch it any more.

"I know you must be scared and I'm so sorry.

"I won't be sending any more emails or assignments. I'm sorry about that, I really am, but I think I said enough. Just remember that I didn't do this to hurt anybody. It's true that I'm mad at humans but I did this to save myself.

"Jess and Mom, I love you.

"Dad, you're still my hero."
Maddy stopped speaking. Burton set the phone on the dashboard.
They finally had their answer. The answer they were afraid to know. Why Seb had not talked to them. During the twenty years the college newsletter lay hidden in the attic, his father, and the rest of the

humans, had not tried very hard to spare Seb what he felt the day he found it. How could he trust them now?

Burton checked to see if his boots were tied. As if that mattered. He wrapped his fingers around the door handle, opened the door, and looked out into the blackness.

"Burton?"

Maddy was the one doing the only truly useful things and she would find Seb.

"Burton!"

He avoided looking at the phone. What he saw instead was his own image in the windshield, his face lit by the phone's display. Dimly, but he could see himself. This man needed to get out and walk and just keep on going. It was what he deserved.

Maddy would not understand. Nor would Jessica. Or Seb. Seb.

He would have to deal with himself some other time. He picked up the phone and put it to his ear.

"Burton? I can hear you breathing. Listen. Those little college newsletters were meant to be provocative. And not to be read by children. For God's sake, they weren't read by anybody. If only Seb talked to us. If he talked to us, we could have helped him cope with this."

A few seconds passed.

"Burton?"

He did not know what to say.

"You don't believe that any more, what you said about not having children," Maddy said. "It was a mistake to have the newsletter around, but we never imagined..."

They fell into silence again. On top of everything else, this was the last email. Just when they were beginning to expect an email every other day or so it felt as if Seb had been ripped away from them all over again.

Of course it was not true. Seb had not been ripped away from them. They had known for a long time that he was gone and not actually in touch with them. The words Maddy just read came from a hole in a closet. Even so, it felt like Seb was finally gone. Left to wonder if he should ever have been born.

CHAPTER NINETEEN

TRAIL DUDES

THE PAIN IN SEB'S STOMACH made him pledge to get food for dinner, every day, before doing anything else. At least a bag of blueberries and some frogs. Why had he bought so much turkey jerky? He thought it would last longer and weigh less than peanuts, and had never imagined that eating it every day would hurt his stomach. All he could swallow was a cup of water.

He stood and felt his shorts hanging low on his hips. Anyway, his doctor once told him, "If people say you look too thin, it means you're healthy. You'll know when you're sick."

Out here, he moved more and ate less. His experiments with hunting had not gone well. He no longer believed he had good hunter genes from being part Puerto-Rican and therefore part Native American.

His micro-printed book on survival skills included instructions on how to make a bow and arrow. You first needed a young oak, maple or birch growing near a stream. Then you had to get deer parts. The deer was easy to find because there was a dead one off the side of the dirt road that stunk bad.

It took hours to make the bow and arrow. When Seb tested it, the arrow flew—no, "flew" was not the right word. It dropped three feet in front of him. He laughed so hard he had to sit down. Having turkey jerky in a bag up a tree allowed him to be cavalier like this. As did the bike, which would get him to a town if necessary.

His other insurance was the collapsible fishing pole, which he took everywhere. It was useful not just for food. Should he come across someone else in the woods, he could unfold the fishing pole. He had seen two different solitary men already, although Seb had been able to hide before they saw him.

The idea was that anyone deep in the woods would be a lot less inclined to be suspicious of a boy with a fishing pole. They would probably be happy to see a rare example of what a kid should be like. He tried to remember to prowl around like a Native American. He rarely did, though, and frequently spoke out loud to himself. Sometimes he sang.

But talking to himself in the woods was good for keeping the troubling thoughts away. He might walk ten miles before forcing himself to turn back, before he got too far from his camp and his food and water reserves.

He had another guilty pleasure. His daily ritual.

The ritual was basically a long bath. It was the height of summer, but the brooks and streams were still cold. For anything more than a quick cool-off, you needed to find still water that got sunlight. One particular pool, an eddy at the bottom of a cliff, got sun early in the morning.

He was in this pool the other day, talking to himself and scrubbing his armpits with clay, when he thought he saw a ponytail bobbing in the distance. Then the top of a fishing pole.

He would be the shame of his tribe, making all this noise, splashing and talking like a loon. He had been chanting a peace meditation, which was supposed to be felt by others, which he did not believe. Fortunately, the woman, or hippie, with the ponytail disappeared. He considered not going back to the spot, but it was just too perfect.

On this day, he put his mind at ease by getting dinner, a bullhead from the pond, before heading for his warm pool at the bottom of the waterfall. He stripped off his clothes and stepped in. A crayfish squirted away in a cloud of underwater dust. He was earlier than usual, and the water was not quite warm enough, so he did some laps. Very short, dog-paddle laps.

He stopped near a shelf that had been carved into the rock wall to the right of the waterfall. A thin film of water always flowed over this section and a funky world of moss grew on it. He counted four colors of moss. Yellow-green, golf-course green, dark green, minty green. It was possible some of these were algae. One patch of moss actually had flowers. Pink cups resting on thread-thin stems that looked as if they would dissolve if you touched them. A beetle with a white stripe down its back crawled between the flowers, which to the beetle must have looked like a grove of trees.

Primitive. Primitive life, isn't that what these things were called? Bugs and moss and algae and the microscopic animals swimming around him, and swimming inside him. What did that word mean, primitive? Been around for a million years or something like that. Or similar to things that were around when life began. Doing nothing but eating and making more primitives. Nothing close to emotions. Well, maybe the beetle had a little fear, but it never imagined itself dissolving in a bird's belly.

Seb wished for Ajahn Wattana to be as untroubled as a beetle in a forest of moss flowers. The monk deserved better than what he got from Seb. Then again, the Ajahn would probably disagree. About deserving. Peace of mind was everybody's own responsibility, no matter what was going on. He remembered the Ajahn saying something like that.

The Ajahn and Seb traded a bunch of emails about mindfulness, but probably not enough for Seb to be good at it out here on his own. Mindfulness took a lot of discipline and a lot of practice. Skeet did not think in terms of meditation or mindfulness, but he coped by being out in nature, too. And he noticed everything. That was mindfulness. Seb could not shake the thought that someone as smart as Skeet would think he was not a good person for what he did to his family. Had he seen Seb back in Massachusetts, balled up in the fetal position on his bed with the door locked, he might understand better.

The stretches of pleasure Seb had in these woods were much more than he ever thought possible. A calmer mind was all he was aiming for. He had hoped a calmer mind would also get rid of certain depressing ideas about people, but this had not happened yet. Would watching the videos his parents made help? He did not want to risk what he expected they would do: push him over the edge. How could they understand what was going on with him when he was not sure he understood himself? Maybe it would have been less painful to just leave a note that said: the seven billion dumb-assess on Earth are making me crazy and I need a break for a while.

Sometimes he came up against the thought that, even if his actions were justified, what kind of person could enjoy himself while his family was suffering?

It was not like he was enjoying himself nonstop. He felt really bad many times about what his family was probably going through.

But they made him. They put him in this world. Was he supposed to spend his best years watching the messed-up world they decided to put him in? He had done the best he could to explain and he really believed there was no other way. And he was a little bit mad at them, too. Maybe a lot mad. But not mad enough to like the idea of hurting them.

The thing was, this crazy plan of his was working. He felt better. Much better. He felt the panic return, frighteningly fast, every time he considered abandoning what he had found, however selfish it might be.

He would not be selfish forever. No, he was not selfish. He was saving his life. And having a good time? He could not let this confusing debate go on and on. The plan would not work, otherwise. He was supposed to learn to like life again, and be able to keep what he learned with him when he returned. Return. He did not want to.

If he did return, and if they forgave him, he would love to bring his family to this amazing place some day. To see the moss gardens and swim in the warm, sunny pool of the creek.

☙❧

The next morning, Seb found Skeet lying on a little patch of sand near the spring where he got his water every day. For some reason, in the mountains of Maine, hundreds of miles from the ocean, there were patches of beach sand, fine and light. Did it come from ancient seas? Or is this what happened to dirt when it was cooked by centuries of sunny skies? Maine was sunny.

Skeet sat up and brushed sand off his shirt. "I didn't want to ambush your camp. Be pretty sad to have no privacy after coming all the way out here."

"You can ambush."

"Off to work?"

Seb held his collapsible canteen under the rivulet of the water coursing from a groove in the rock. "Yeah. Read and think. And not think, if I can. Were you thinking of doing something?"

"You could still meditate and read your environmental science or whatever it is. I have my own book."

"I'm not ready to read environmental science. It stresses me. I'm still on what's it all about."

"Is that the name of the book?" Skeet did not wait for an answer. "I know a place where we can read, and when the sun starts going down, we might see river otters. Big, funny things. They're like water catdogs."

244

"Definitely."

They left the spring and followed the dirt road. About a quarter-mile down, Skeet jumped the roadside drainage ditch and headed into the woods. Seb recognized the path he had taken a week earlier, the day he tried to find the otters on his own, with directions from that guy's blog. When they reached the group of ancient apple trees, he figured it was not a coincidence.

"Did you find out about these otters from a website?" Seb asked. "A blog with tips about the Maine woods?"

"No."

They stared at each other.

"I've seen it, you know," Seb said. "The blog."

"I write it, you know."

How wild. Skeet was Trail Dude! The guy who wrote the funny journals about exploring the woods that Seb had read when planning his escape from Massachusetts. In Seb's mind, Trail Dude was a skinny man with an overgrown, half-gray beard who wore long sleeves in the middle of the summer. Seb chose his camp because it was one of the most remote places he could get to, but Trail Dude's information was probably the deciding factor. So, it was not a total coincidence they met, but still...

"I read your blog a bunch of times!"

"Really?"

"Yeah. That's how I knew about the spring. I never saw any otters, though."

"That's because you talk to yourself. But you are a computer genius. To find my blog. It doesn't exactly come up first on anybody's searches. My number one readers are from like Germany and Japan. At least the ones that post comments. I'm pretty sure they have no idea how hard it is to get to this place. They never actually come here."

"Yeah. Only me."

Skeet looked pleased. "I've been writing that blog since I was nine."

The stood there looking stupidly at each other until it felt awkward.

"I think I didn't see the otters because I was there too early," Seb said, to break the silence. "What if we have to wait until the sun starts going down for them to come out?"

"No probs. I know this forest. Mom goes to bed early, and Dad, well, he'll be asleep in front of the television."

"Ummm. And how do I get back to my camp in the dark?"

"I'll get you there before I head home."

Seb did not entirely believe Skeet could do all this. "Why don't we go some morning before the sun comes up? That way, if we get lost, we have daylight to get un-lost."

"I'm Trail Dude. We're good." Skeet held a thorny branch out of the way so Seb could follow. "Don't worry," he said over his shoulder. "I didn't post any blogs recently about a city kid hiding out. Although I do need some new material. Maybe a story about a Buddha-boy who wears binoculars on his face."

Seb laughed, but he wanted to get off the subject. He thought for a moment and then remembered a question he had been meaning to ask.

"Do you know anything about keeping off ticks? Like a leaf you can rub on your skin? I have a big jug of concentrated bug stuff and a spray bottle, but I don't love the idea of putting it on my body and clothes every day."

"Yeah, that sucks. You have to do it, though. My friend got Lyme disease."

"Mine too. So I guess there's nothing?"

Skeet began to run. "Workout time."

Seb accelerated to catch up.

"Maybe there's something for ticks," Skeet said, panting. "That could be my next blog post. For the three people that read it."

They were covered in sweat when they reached the brook. Without a word, they peeled off their clothes and jumped in. It was shout-out cold, even on a hot body. They ducked their heads under before climbing up the bank. They found a sunny, relatively flat boulder to lay on.

Seb closed his eyes.

He heard Skeet getting something from his pack a while later and opened his yes. It was a cushion with diagonal straps that kept it at ninety degrees when unfolded.

"Sorry, only got one of these," he said, and sat in the little chair, facing the brook.

Seb did not have his self-inflating cushions. He did, however, have a piece of canvas he always brought in case an opportunity like this presented itself.

He went off to break four thick sticks from dead branches on trees nearby. Three branches, he tied together at one end with twine. These formed a tripod. Next he lashed the remaining branch across horizontally. The piece of canvas got tied to the peak and to the horizontal branch.

He sat in the tripod. It was marginally more comfortable than sitting on the ground.

"Geek," Skeet said. He placed his backpack in front of him. It looked rather full.

Seb raised and lowered his eyebrows like an evil magician. "Un-natural food?"

"Mom made donuts. They're incredible. I almost just brought donuts. But I threw in chips, too. If you want something other than dandelions, I guess you could have some."

Even in the shade it was hot. They left their shirts on the ground and ate donuts.

Seb took out a micro-printed copy of *Siddhartha*. He placed the binoculo-glasses on his face and hung his front teeth over his lower lip.

"Hey Thkeet."

Skeet refused to laugh. He shook his head, but his eyes betrayed amusement.

"Just wait until I put my bookshelf-bra on."

"Your wha—"

The two boys read, ate, napped, and took a jog to a boggy pond to swim in something warm, which Seb did not enjoy so much, because he kept imagining leeches on him. He did, in fact, get a leech, and had to pull the slimy, spongy thing off with his fingers.

They went back to the brook and waited for a couple of hours, silently reading and napping, for otters. The stars came out. A thousand stars in that one hole in the trees above them. Several shooting stars flashed across. No otters came.

They jogged back to the spring with their flashlights on. After topping off their canteens they crossed the road towards Seb's camp.

Skeet stopped twenty minutes later. He swung his flashlight in a semicircle before them. Insects cheeped.

"Dude," Skeet said. "We're lost."

"Obviously. You have any donuts left?"

They sat where they were and ate the rest of the donuts.

Seb had a compass but he did not think he could figure out how to get to his camp without light and landmarks. He was tired. Skeet seemed unworried. The night was not cold.

They decided to push armloads of pine needles into a pile. Both were smart enough to have stashed ultra-light emergency blankets in their packs. They placed one blanket on the needles and put the other on top of their bodies. They slept until the damn birds woke them up. It was still dark.

But Seb liked waking up before dawn now. Groaning about damn birds was out of habit.

CHAPTER TWENTY

Don't Find Seb

Burton kept one hand on the steering wheel and bent down to reach the phone that had fallen on the floor. The vehicle lurched and its giant tires ground through gravel at the side of the road. It sounded like an avalanche. Once he got the thing back to the center of the lane, he pressed the voice control icon and said, "Call Maddy."

She answered on the second ring.

"No luck in the village, I guess, or I would have heard sooner."

"Zero. The granola and hemp store—."

"Do I know this place?"

"The General Store. You've spoken to them. I gave them a big glossy photo of Seb. The sheriff was hard to find. I think he was sleeping at the dump, but, no, he hasn't seen Seb either."

Maddy's clogs clunked. She was going upstairs.

"I need to talk to you about something," she said. "Seb's email was enough to deal with while you were stuck in the woods in the middle of the night."

"I'm sorry about that. Don't worry. I've given up on driving to A.T. shelters, even in this monster machine. It just can't be done. Is everything okay? It's not Jess?"

"Jessica is a trooper. She's outside right now, chasing the cat from the bird feeder. She keeps trying to take care of me. I let her do it. A neck massage last night."

He heard the door close.

"I wanted to talk to you about the videos. Have you been following the comments? People are...a lot of people are commenting. A lot."

"About Seb? Helping us find Seb?"

"I wish. There are people who make supportive comments. Then there's the rest."

"I haven't read them closely in a while," Burton said. "I just skim over, looking for posts by Seb. I'm depressed enough as it is without reading that crap. Calling Jess cute, making stupid jokes, injecting opinions which have nothing to do with helping us get Seb back home. I guess I've let you suffer through that."

"It's taken a strange twist. There's kind of a firestorm going on. Two camps have formed. One thinks Seb is some kind of hero. They're talking about it on their own blogs and driving all kinds of traffic to the videos we made. Not just kids. Serious people. Links to our videos are getting posted and discussed on Facebook and discussion groups."

"A hero for what? Parent-bashing?" Before Burton got too hot, a more rational idea came to him. "A hero for his ideas?"

"You got it. But the other camp, he's not a hero to them. They paint him as a brat for what he's done to us. Hold on. I'll read one to you."

There was a pause.

"Okay, listen to this: 'It really galls me that people are using this child for their own agenda, especially when he is a poster child for all that is wrong with America.'"

"Damn," Burton said.

"Some of it is nastier than that. But the real bile comes from the people who are afraid about the big positive response Seb is getting. They're using words like radical and dangerous. Just a sec. Liberal propaganda. All of which, by the way, they only know by inference. Nobody's seen or heard an actual word from Seb. All any of them know of Seb comes from our videos to him. I'm sure his mythic status adds glamour to all of this."

Phillip's home-made phone had painfully clear reception and Burton could hear Maddy's fingers clicking on the keyboard.

"Here's another one: 'Go ahead and listen to a young man who is old enough to know what pain he is willfully causing his family. He's an authority on nothing. If you're going to listen to what he says, listen to what he is really saying, and doing: stop supporting our businesses. And panic.'"

Burton found a place to pull over. A defunct gas station with a Bait for Sale sign in the window. All these bullies on the internet. What would this do to Seb?

"I want you to listen to this one, too."

He waited for Maddy to find it.

"Here:

"*This boy Seb stops and looks around and tells the truth. And so does his family. Here we have a fourteen-year old who finds himself trapped in a world of gluttons, and it was more than he could take. Which is a healthy reaction, if you ask me. We owe it to him, to all of our children, to ask some difficult questions, and not stop until we have some good answers.*"

Burton reclined the seat and gazed out the sun roof at clouds rolling quickly by. A drop of rain fell on the glass, then another.

"Have you really not been reading these?" Maddy asked. "This battle started several days ago."

"Not in a couple days. What I read, I took as grandstanding. Taking advantage of us for their own purposes."

"I guess there's actually three camps. The third one is people who know Seb and his family are watching. They know we are trying to get our child home safe. But that's boring. It's the debate that's taken on a life of its own."

"It's easy to spout off on the internet. From the comfort of their couch."

"I don't care what their deal is," Maddy said. "They're not helping us. But I don't think it's just a game for a lot of them. This has really struck a chord. Some of these people seem pretty well educated."

"If they're so smart, why don't they help us find our son."

"You don't think he planned this, do you? Being a martyr to get a movement going?"

"A movement for what?" Burton said, loudly, over the rain that was now drumming on the roof. "To protect the planet?"

"Maybe."

"It's possible, I suppose. But I doubt it. He must have had his hands full just orchestrating his getaway."

"I agree," Maddy said. "But I have an idea."

"Tell me."

"Both camps are riled up. There's major flack at the Seb fans for glorifying someone who's put his parents through agony. That's only riled the Seb fans more. They're telling people to spread the word to other websites and activist groups. I think we should use this momentum. Do a video that speaks directly to the people who are commenting and reading the comments. Ask them to help us find Seb. Tell them to find Seb."

"Well, yeah. Yes. That's a great idea."

"You should get home. I mean to your motel."

"Right. I'm going to read all the comments when I get there."

"Be prepared to hate humanity. And to love it, too. There's a lot of good people who stay out of the debate and just say how sorry they are about what we're going through. And people who are really concerned about Seb. There's one I wrote down." Maddy paused a moment. "Here it is:

"This is a good family. They're on your side and you need them, Seb."

"That's awesome," Burton said.

"Try not to post any replies to the haters."

"Or to the ones calling Seb a hero."

❧

The garbage truck out in the parking lot whined loud enough to make the motel window shake. A dumpster fell to the parking lot with a smash. Burton opened his eyes and realized his face was pressed against the coffee table. He sat up, barely able to move his stiff neck, and fell back against the couch.

The laptop lay on the floor, open, screen dark, but still running. He had a vague memory of knocking it off at one point. Yes, he had pushed it off intentionally, after reading a comment about "ungrateful children."

A note on the table caught his eye. Without bending his neck, he leaned over and picked it up. *You give me hope, Seb* was handwritten on a yellow notepad. Underneath was the screen name of the person who posted the message: *Girl Leprechaun*. Before Burton fell asleep on the coffee table he must have thought this was worth writing down.

He went to the bathroom and then called home. As the phone rang, he smelled himself. He had not changed clothes in two days.

"Dad!" How great to hear Jessica's voice.

"Hi, honey. Mom says you're taking good care of her."

"And Mom says you've been four-wheeling the mountains and swamps of Maine. And cliff climbing? I'm jealous."

"Be grateful you were not there. It was a waste of time. My whole body hurts. I am not a mountain goat. Okay, you would have loved it. Do you think Seb intentionally sent me on a wild goose chase?"

"No. Possibly. Can't I go on the next trip?"

Next trip. Burton did not know what the next trip would be. It was

252

looking like home.

"Dad?"

"Sorry, Jess. I'm not sure what our next move is."

He did not know if Jessica had read Seb's final email and he was not going to bring it up.

A click sounded on the line. Maddy's voice said, "Jess? Who's on the phone?"

"It's me." Burton said.

"You read all the comments?"

"All. It's incredible."

"It's viral," Jessica said. "Spreading like...a virus. Have you heard about the latest?"

"The latest?" Burton asked.

"The *Don't Find Seb* thing?"

Burton knelt next to the coffee table to get the computer off the floor. The carpet smelled like rancid grease. His neck really hurt from sleeping on the coffee table.

He could hear Maddy breathing hard into the phone as he was waiting for his computer to start up. She was probably on her way to get her own laptop.

"There's a new website," Jessica explained, breathless with excitement. "It's called *Don't Find Seb* and there's a really creepy image on it. Two of my friends texted it to me already this morning. It's a drawing, I mean an avatar, you know what that is?"

Burton thought it was a video game character. "Maybe."

"Like a symbol for a person. This one looks like a shadow of a head."

"A silhouette?" Maddy said.

"Yeah, a black silhouette of a guy's head with a circle around it and a diagonal line across, like a 'no smoking' sign. And the words *Don't Find Seb* across the top."

"That's ridiculous," Burton said. "Who would do that? They should be thrown in jail. Who's doing it?"

"We have to have it traced," Maddy said.

"Send me the link," Burton said. "Please. And Phillip Geer, too."

"All right." A bang as Jessica put down her phone.

"I'm looking at the YouTube comments now." Maddy said. "They're coming in fast about this *Don't Find Seb* thing."

"What's that supposed to mean? *Don't Find Seb?*"

"Basically that Seb needs an appropriate response to the environmental crisis. That Seb doesn't want to be found until that happens. Easy for them to say. Their son's life isn't in danger."

Burton could not believe what he was hearing. "Are they seriously saying a boy should be sacrificed for their cause?"

"Not exactly. Most of the commenters are being very careful if they say anything at all. Like this one here who wrote *Powerful*. I think they can tell this is getting dangerous. I think the *Don't Find Seb* faction is too controversial. Most of the environmentalists are keeping their distance from it. I bet they love the attention, though. It's a mess."

"You'll make sure the police look into the *Don't Find Seb* stuff?"

"Already on it."

Burton was not at all surprised. "Maybe the FBI or some big guns will get involved, with this irresponsible crap. Criminal."

There was a scraping sound. It was Jessica picking up her phone. "I sent the link to you Dad. Why are all these people so upset? They're not upset about Seb being lost. What's going on? Is something really bad happening?"

"Hon," Burton said. "Your brother's unusual methods seem to have gotten a lot of attention. It's a volatile subject. Now they're arguing with each other."

"They're so angry, so upset. It's kind of scary, having Seb mixed up in the middle."

After they hung up, Burton noticed his jaw hurt. He must have been clenching it hard, talking to Jessica. They could not keep doing this to their girl. Meanwhile, he was chasing Seb around Maine. Was there a limit to what they could do for Seb at the expense of Jessica?

CHAPTER TWENTY-ONE

Winter

"Dude. Dude."

Seb recognized Skeet's voice. He managed to open his eyes a slit. Still daylight. Still outdoors, lying face up on the forest floor. His back hurt. He turned his head to the side and vomited.

"What the hell?" Skeet exclaimed.

Seb felt a hand on his shoulder.

"Don't touch. Hurts to be touched."

"Whatever you puked up smells horrible. What did you eat? I'm gonna puke right next to it."

"A root."

"You ate a root?"

"Supposed to taste like potato."

"Did it?"

"Taste...root."

Seb gasped for breath. He could barely get the words out. He felt so tired.

"Could be the water you drank. You wouldn't drink water from a pond? The brook's not safe either. You know that."

Seb did not respond, or move, except to breathe, which hurt his stomach. He tried to remember what had happened. Thinking made his head throb, which in turn made him even more nauseous.

"How long have you been laying there?"

"Breakfast," Seb groaned.

He was lucky Skeet showed up. Now, if he would just leave him alone, it would be perfect.

"Feel better or worse?"

"Same. Don't make me talk."

"I'll stay here until you feel better, I guess. Maybe I should go home and call the hospital. My Dad could drive up the road and we could hike in here with something to carry you."

"No."

Seb heard Skeet move away, his feet crunching the pine needles. In a minute, the crunching got closer, and clanking metal along with it.

"I'm guessing this white mush in the pot is the root. They might want to figure out what kind of root it is. These leaves are the plant it came from?"

Seb opened one eye to look at the leaf in Skeet's hand. "Yeh." He closed the eye.

A long time passed, maybe hours, before he felt well enough to open both eyes. His stomach pitched. He turned and opened his mouth. Nothing came out.

"You should get away from that..." Skeet came closer and pointed his toe at the lumps Seb had vomited earlier, which were less than a foot from his head. "Never mind."

Skeet came back with a stone and used it to push the soaked pine needles away. He covered them with more pine needles.

Seb glanced down at his body. A sleeping bag lay over it. A real fire, not the paint-can stove, burned in the pit. It was about twenty feet away, too far for any of its warmth to reach him.

Skeet sat down on the short stump near the fire and looked over at Seb.

"How long have I been sleeping?"

"All freakin' day."

"Really?"

"Really."

It was getter darker. Seb tried and found he could sit up.

"Don't start about the fire." Skeet said. "I don't care if someone finds you."

Seb walked slowly to the fire with the sleeping bag around him like a cape. The food and supply bag lay on the ground next to Skeet.

"Yeah. I had a great day," Skeet said. "Eating your turkey jerky and watching you sleep. Tasty, mmm." He opened his mouth wide and stuck his index finger in. "Oh. Sorry."

Seb raised one shoulder. It must have looked pathetic, the half-shrug.

"You look better." Skeet said.

"I must be. I almost feel hungry."

"You want some—"

"No."

Skeet reached for his pack. "I think I have—"

"No. Thanks."

Skeet handed him a canteen. "You should drink, anyway."

The logs in the fire snapped and hissed. Pines, their sap boiling. It felt good and it smelled good.

"Dude," Skeet said. "What are you gonna do? Things change fast in September around here. At night, anyway. Do you even know how to fish when it gets cold? If you think you're going to bike all the way to town for supplies after it snows, you're not, and it's too far to walk. I don't know why I'm talking about snow anyway. You'll be freezing in that tent if you're still here in October."

"I know."

"What do you know?" Skeet tossed a stick in the fire and stared after it.

"I know winter's coming," Seb said.

"At first I thought you knew what you were doing, with your books and paint-can stove, but you ate that poisonous root. You obviously don't."

"Yeah, I know. But I just got here. Do I have to think about winter already? It's not even August yet."

"You're just going to get on your bike before it gets cold?"

"I can go south."

Skeet inched closer to the flames and Seb realized he was wearing only shorts and a sleeveless shirt. The temperature fell quickly out here some nights.

"You should head home before it gets dark," he said. "Before it gets too cold."

"I'm fine."

"Thanks for hanging around to make sure I didn't die."

Skeet stared into the fire a moment longer, then turned to look at Seb full-on. "I'm not your mommy but this place is serious, even in the summer. I've been banging around these woods my whole life and I don't know enough to survive out here on my own. There's two kids from my county a few years ago who never made it out of here alive.

And it was summer, then."

"Don't worry about me," Seb said. "When winter comes, I'm going to turn into a popsicle and never have to see the ugly world again."

Way to go, he thought. *Why don't you just start crying, too?*

"What do you mean ugly world? You ran away from home because your neighborhood was ugly? Did anybody, like, abuse you or something? In my mind, I see you in a nice house on a nice street. With your parents making videos for you that you were never going to watch."

That sounded bad.

"I told you I was crazy. But I'm trying. I'm working on an idea. I've been writing, not just meditating."

"What you need to do is talk to somebody. Since your only plan is to freeze like a popsicle."

Seb wrapped the sleeping bag tighter around himself. He was pretty sure Skeet would not accept it if he offered it to him. He was still shivering from the root ordeal, anyway.

"Having them do videos was probably a bad idea," he said. "And yes, I do live in a nice house. Nobody ever abused me. But it was like...Imagine you're in a nice house at the base of a volcano. Everybody on the island lives at the base of the volcano. Wise people, experts, try to get their attention, saying, 'although you can't hear the volcano rumbling, we have math that says it's going to blow.' Everyone thinks about it and says, 'why should we trust you? And we don't like math. We can't move. We can't give all this up. You just want to take our land.' And stuff like that. Then they throw their garbage over the fence, right into the volcano, like they are trying to convince themselves they don't believe the wise men. Then the volcano starts to bubble even more.

"I know you can't stop a volcano. But in our world there were things we could have changed and there are things we can still change. You know, I was in the Green Club at school. We wrote letters to the governor, and collected batteries to recycle, and signed a petition to close the coal plants. I started reading too, and what I read said none of this was going to be enough, by a long shot.

"I started smelling and seeing and hearing everything around me and all I could see was ugliness. Pollution. Garbage dump mountains and barges going out to sea with garbage on them. Pollution that makes people sick. Airplane, car, and lawnmower noise. We would drive down Route One and I would think, this used to be fields, and there used to be forests on those hills, and now it's all concrete and tar and metal. I saw a tree growing out the window of an abandoned factory and that gave me some hope, that man could never kill nature. At the same time I knew the tree was only growing there because the people had left."

Seb had to stop for a breath. Skeet was still staring at him. He felt stupid and confused.

"So your house is covered in garbage and smells terrible and there's loud noise all the time?"

"No. It's not."

Skeet blinked at him. Now Seb just wanted him to go away. It was humiliating. After a minute, Skeet shook his head.

"Hey, man, listen. I'm sorry. You looked really sick. I didn't know what I was supposed to do. Go get help or not. I was stuck here and I started to think you had a decent home. I got mad. I know you explained it all to me before but...I guess I don't really like to think about it. Global warming or any of that stuff. It depresses me."

Seb felt such a wave of relief that this guy didn't think he was an incredible jerk, that he had to turn his head, because his face was crumpling up like he was going to cry. When turned back to look at him, Skeet was leaning back on the stump. It wobbled and he almost fell off. When he righted himself, a strange look crossed his face.

"What's that look for?" Seb asked.

"Just an idea," Skeet said. "We're being honest, right?" He paused. "My cousin? He got put on medication for nerves and it really worked."

"I couldn't put the pills in my mouth. It would be like...giving up. But I guess that's not that much different than hiding out in here..."

"It's not giving up. It might make you able to do something to help, instead of being too freaked out to do anything."

"That sounds great but I don't believe there's a pill like that." Seb covered his face with the sleeping bag. Without removing it, he said, "I'm a loser."

"At least see a doctor and see what they say. Maybe you don't need anything. Nobody will know and you might not be a loser anymore."

"Thanks," Seb said from under the sleeping bag.

"I get nervous at school some times, if that makes you feel any better. Being stuck there."

Seb pulled the sleeping bag aside just enough to uncover only his face. "Confusing, isn't it?"

Skeet gave a dismissive shake of his head.

Seb let the sleeping bag drop around his shoulders. "You know how I'm always writing in my journal? Partly, it's to get thoughts out of my head by writing them down. But, sometimes when I'm writing, I want to yell it to the world. Except it's all too messy still. But it helps. I feel like I'm doing better now. I don't want to mess with it."

"Maybe you don't need pills," Skeet said. "Have a good time. Just admit that's what you're doing. Don't feel guilty about it. You're fourteen. You don't have to be an adult yet. These are adult problems you can't do anything about. Go a little wild, have fun. If you don't have fun while you can, you will definitely go crazy. My brother, you know he's a useless stoner, but there was one time in his life when he said something interesting: 'When you're an adult you'll wonder why you were in such a rush to get there.'"

Seb almost said, "I won't last until I'm an adult," but he was done spewing out his fears.

"This stump is not comfortable," Skeet said. He stood up and stretched "Listen, I'm screwed, too. I like it around here but I'm going to have to leave. Leave the county, maybe the whole state. There's no jobs here. The people who went to school with my brother, the ones who went to college, most of them don't live in Maine."

"I could survive in here, like you're doing." Skeet's eyes roved over the spot where Seb had lain all day. "Better than you're doing. But I don't think I want to. Not all day and night, day after day. It's too lonely."

"Let's do it then," Seb said. "Let's ditch this place and steal a car. Get a couple of girls. I'm tall. I could wear my fake beard. Change the plates. You're a redneck. You must have a few rusty cars in your front yard? We could use one of those license plates."

"Bite me." Skeet frowned. "I guess we could rob gas stations for money."

Seb nodded. "I went bad fast, didn't I? From saving the world to vigilante."

"Buddhist gives the world the finger."

They laughed.

"You're lucky," Skeet said. "Summer in Maine. People pay a lot of money for a week of vacation up here."

"Summer in Maine," Seb said, as if he were making a toast.

"No more roots," Skeet said.

CHAPTER TWENTY-TWO

To the Fans

An instant message box appeared on Burton's screen.

Are you ready?

It was Phillip.

Ready.

A little pen on the screen wiggled back and forth, indicating Phillip was writing.

Be back in five minutes. Wait for me.

Burton hurried over to the windowsill to bite into a hamburger from *Casey's Rolling Kitchen*, a hitch-trailer out on the main road. The burger smelled good, tasted incredible, and was going to make him sick. He had not eaten anything all day but a bag of peanut butter cookies from the Sunflower.

They were rushing to get a video done because Seb might not be a hot topic on YouTube for long. Maddy, genius that she was, had come up with the concept for the video they were about to make. Seb had not requested it. He would be hard-pressed to take umbrage to an unsolicited video, having finally left them with no instructions whatever. Even if the video did bother him, little would change. If anything, Seb might slip up, not expecting this change in script.

It was Phillip's idea for Burton and Maddy to record a message simultaneously, which he would splice together into a side-by-side video. Let Seb wonder why they were filming from separate locations.

Jessica suggested Burton get a moose painting from Goodwill to put on the wall so Seb knew his Dad was not home and was missing work. They had, however, decided to keep Seb in the dark about Burton being in Maine. Jessica accepted that Seb might be in Maine, but she still maintained he was on his bike.

Alone in a motel, dripping ketchup and pickle juice from a hamburger onto a carpet that already smelled, Burton felt like a character in a Raymond Carver story. The only thing missing was the alcohol.

A chime sounded on the laptop. Burton returned the burger to the windowsill and went back to the little desk with the lamp screwed to its surface.

I'm nervous.

It was Maddy.

Burton now had two instant message boxes open, side by side on his screen. He typed a reply to Maddy.

Me too. Helps to have Phillip, doesn't it?

That man is the best.

The best, for sure.

The little pen started wiggling in Phillip's box. His message appeared.

Ready to go. I'll edit the video later so it starts at the right place.

A third box appeared at the top of Burton's screen.

Allow PGeer to take control of your computer.

Burton clicked the *Yes* button.

PGeer now has control of your computer appeared in this third box, and then the box disappeared. The two boxes containing his typed conversations with Maddy and Phillip remained on the screen.

A tiny light next to the built-in camera in the upper frame of Burton's laptop turned green. His unshaven face appeared up on the right side of the screen. He was supposed to have shaved. He wiped mustard from his nose with his wrist. A second later, Maddy's image appeared to the left.

Her video seemed frozen, until she blinked. She was wearing the summer dress of white linen with the faint print of yellow irises on long stalks. His favorite. The only sound coming through his speaker was the fan in their bedroom back home.

Maddy looked tired, of course, but still beautiful, her eyes fixed and determined. Her lips moved, unconsciously rehearsing what she would say. Their task was difficult. Stating the truth while remaining hopeful.

262

In Phillip's text box: *Can you see each other?*

"I see Burton. Hi, hon."

"I see you, too. Love you. Where's Jessica?"

"In her room. She knows this is serious."

The little pen in Phillip's text box started moving again. *Just start talking when you're ready. If there's a problem, just say so and we'll edit it out.*

His message box disappeared. This was it. Burton liked it better when Phillip's text box was there.

"Shall we?" Maddy smiled as if they were about to jump off a cliff together.

"Yes."

As planned, Maddy spoke first: "Seb, we are one hundred percent here for you. We've done what you've asked because we take your concerns seriously and we respect your beliefs. Now that you've had your say, please hear us out. We have an obligation to make sure you're safe and we continue to believe the best thing you could do is let us help you. We will listen to what you need.

"I can't imagine you've missed all the activity around these videos. I hope you know your welfare has remained our priority. We're not distracted at all by the other emotions and opinions flying around here.

"Our request is simple. Please communicate with us. Any way you like. We won't force you to do anything."

This could turn out to be a lie, but they had not been able to come up with anything better to say. Which, of course, only gave more credence to Seb's fears. Theirs was an agonizing situation.

"We're not sure you're going to see this video," Maddy continued, "since you don't expect it, so I'm going to talk a little bit to whoever else might be watching."

Maddy paused to allow viewers other than Seb to realize she was addressing them now. It was her idea, to start off with a message to Seb, and then rope the other viewers in. She even lowered her gaze a bit to suggest a different audience and squinted to indicate warmth to these strangers. Warmth Burton knew she did not feel.

"If you know of any trouble or danger for Seb, please call this number." Her hand rose into view, holding a piece of paper. A toll-free number had been printed on it in thick black letters. Tall, narrow lettering done in Jessica's hand.

This was Burton's cue. "Seb, back to you. I'm talking to you, son."

Maddy kept the phone number visible and let it rest against her breastbone.

"We really wanted to splice in a clip from home movies. The time we went body surfing with your cousins at Popham Beach, but, well, we thought you might think that was too manipulative. Our motive was pure, though. Those movies reminded us how much our family means. Nothing else comes close. You're probably sick of hearing it, but we love you and we hope to see you home soon."

Maddy turned a bit one way and then the other. She was trying to simulate watching Burton, but did not know on which side he would appear in the video.

He continued. "To everyone else, this is about helping our son. We don't care about your campaigns or your opinions. We care if you can help us find our son. Seb, we will do everything possible to help make this world safe and right for you. Everyone else, this video is *our* video, which we created to enlist your help in getting a boy safe. Get it? Once he is safe, we welcome a conversation about working together on your very valid concerns.

"Now call us, please, and save a kid's life."

CHAPTER TWENTY-THREE

Doc Barlow Mountain

This was the day Seb would go to the top of the mountain. He had decisions to make.

The mountain was not Katahdin—he had to stay out of Baxter Park, with all its rangers—but a place Skeet told him about, a place that would be just as motivational, and easier to get to.

He packed the usual day-trip supplies and extra, in case he got stuck out there overnight. Enough food for three days. If he passed a gas station store along the way he could get sandwiches and a Coke, which would be awesome, but he was pretty sure there was not going to be a gas station along the way. It would be even better if it was true, what he heard. That they were putting Coke into biodegradable bottles made from corn.

Getting to the mountain would require the bike. He had not used it since his one trip back to town. The tarp covering the bike drooped with leaves and mud from the big rain storm the other night. He should have taken care of it earlier, because a person walking by could have noticed something odd.

Before setting out, he took one more look at the topographical map. The dirt road near the spring would bring him to the first of two county roads he would take. Then, another dirt road, and finally, a fire road up the mountain. The county roads were a risk, although maybe not too much. He doubted his photo had been on Maine TV news. Possibly on milk cartons.

In Maine, a pond was really a lake, and a hill was really a mountain. Mountain after mountain. He got a minute's relief coasting down, just long enough for his sweat to chill, before he had to grind up another mountain. Cars generally gave him a wide berth, but a few forced him close to the slippery sand and gravel at the edge of the road. A couple of times he found himself dangerously close to the ravines that dropped steeply down to his right.

Once, he heard a horn in the distance behind him growing louder and louder. A pickup truck passed, the horn still blowing, and it did not stop blaring until the pickup disappeared around a curve.

 Most of the time, though, he had to road to himself. It was hard work, but really cool. He liked the swamps a lot, for some reason. It was like the Amazon of Maine, plants and trees in the water.

He passed the time seeing how many colors were out there. Yellow and gold and tan depending on how the wind hit the marsh grass, white farmhouse paint, gray old gravestones. A one-room trailer as bright as a lemon with rusty streaks running down its front and a rotten black table in the yard. Tons of green, of course. Pine trees and crop fields. A really bright blue sky.

The flowers had every color. Blue irises. Red lilies. Orange trumpets that hung from vines on the trees. Spiky plants with purple flowers that had peach inside each one. Little fuzzy pink daisies in the dirt at the side of the road. All this just on the ride. The mountain would have a hard act to follow, to be more impressive.

The time came to turn onto the little dirt road. He tensed up a bit. Some dirt roads were private and some people did not like it if you drove up to their secluded homes. The bike's odometer read 24.4 miles, though. This had to be the road.

He saw that this lane of dirt and holes and rocks had a name. Not just a number, like on the map. *Doc Barlow Road* had been carved into a wooden board that was half-grown into a tree. The sign looked about a hundred years old.

Seb imagined people way back when taking their sick children or granny down this road. Did Doc Barlow remove Uncle Ned's leg with a hacksaw after it got gangrene from a run-in with a wild boar? Did they have wild boars in Maine?

Not a thing on this road. Not a house, a shack, a power line, a driveway, a mile marker, nothing. Nothing until the fire road, which was two ruts with grass and baby trees growing between them. Someone maintained the road once in a while or there would have been taller trees on it.

The fire road was stand-on-your-pedals steep. His rear wheel spun out in the sand of the ruts again and again, forcing him to keep at least one tire in contact with the grass on the median. Otherwise, he would have gone down. The sun was directly overhead and he was sweating hard, so he stopped to remove his helmet and cool his head. He got back on the bike and lasted about ten minutes before he had to stop. The road was just too steep. He would walk until the incline became a little less intense.

A few minutes later, a deerfly started zooming at his head. After slapping at it a hundred times, he fished the bug stuff out of his saddle bag and sprayed his head. Summer in Maine had its issues, like deer flies.

The road looked like it was never going to level off. Bike riding was over. He looked for a landmark so he could ditch the bike and get it later, on his way down. Rock? Stump? Downed tree? All recipes for not ever finding his bike again. He shoved his empty soda bottle onto a little pine tree and pushed the bike into the woods. It would be bad luck for someone like himself to come along and put the soda bottle in her pack to recycle.

He walked up a road so steep he could not imagine any vehicle traversing it. Eventually, the blonde sand became more plentiful. The land started to flatten. He was near the top.

As he walked through short grass full of tiny yellow flowers, the sky before him lowered. A valley appeared. A valley of lakes. Ten lakes, maybe more, a mixture of blues and white where the sun glanced off waves and ripples.

Skeet had done well. The sight struck Seb hard. He stood for several minutes scanning the valley and then lowered himself to sit on the grass. Oxygen rushed to his head.

His plan was to start by meditating, his own kind of meditation. To begin, he kept his eyes open and let them go where they wanted. He let his head and neck rest on his shoulders, like an apple in a bowl, as the Ajahn would say. Instead of touching his index fingers to his thumbs, he leaned back and supported himself with his palms on the ground behind him. The sun shone from a cloudless sky, but the breeze, rushing up from the valley, made the temperature perfect.

Seb listened and fantasized that the wind, being such a natural force of nature, would carry an answer, a whisper, in the sound it made. You have to ask the wind a question if you want an answer, he could hear

Skeet say.

Seb had prepared a mantra the night before and would start with that.

"My family knows I'm okay," he said, out loud.

He repeated the phrase over and over again.

His eyes wanted to close. He stopped the chant and let them close. The sound of the wind could be his "Om." It was a very cool sound.

After a time he changed his mantra.

"Please let my family be okay."

Who was he asking? God? Wasn't God going to do what God was going to do? Did God need Seb Franck to say, *hi there, I'm this young confused dude on a mountain, I need help?* If God had the power to help him or his family, wouldn't he already be doing it? He wouldn't keep them suffering until Seb offered up a prayer, would he? Unless something prevented God from giving help until it was prayed for? Who or what could stop God?

And if humans were making a mess of the world, would God stop them? If they didn't care enough about God's world to stop destroying it, would God clean up their mess just because they said some prayers?

This did not feel like meditation. Seb tried to remember what the leader of the meditation group suggested they do when thoughts got dark and swirling. Was it to focus on his breath? It was always to focus on your breath, but that was not the only thing.

He could not remember, so he decided to go back to focusing on something positive before letting his thoughts float free.

"Thank you for this valley filled with oxygen and heat and life."

Seb could honestly say he was grateful for this.

But the point of coming here, he remembered, was not to get all warm and fuzzy. Dark feelings were inevitable. He came here to get energized and get woken up and be motivated and get his mind clear. He came here today specifically to get clear about what to do about his parents. He had done the worst thing a son could do: rejected them and kept them worrying constantly.

It was obvious he was not going to meditate. Not yet. Maybe after more thinking.

Should he go back home? That was the question. He was no longer paralyzed by panic. The woods had chilled him. He was even writing again. The losing of his mind had really slowed down. But would that change when he got home?

There. A stab in his chest. A real physical pain from the mere thought of going home.

Nothing else would make his parents feel better. If he got in touch with them, they would find him, and come get him.

His chest hurt and he felt dizzy. He hated himself. Maybe that was what he had to feel. He tried to meditate again.

When he opened his eyes, the valley looked so amazing that all his thoughts, hating himself, his worries, kind of fell out of his head. If a place this awesome could exist, and exist so far and so wide, there had to be enough good in the world to stop his parents' pain. And his own pain too. His family was good. They were really good people.

Unfortunately, even the rush of that valley could only last so long. The world might be full of good, but you had to find it. Or use it. Seb was getting confused again.

Skeet said he needed help and he was probably right. What adult could he trust? May there was a hotline. An anonymous person to help his mind get clear. Maybe Skeet could lend him his phone.

Otherwise, what? Was it going to take winter and hunger and shivering cold to force a plan out of him? Losing a toe to frostbite? That might cure his fear of home. This was an immature joke, he knew. He really did need to have a plan.

He would never forget how the world looked from the top of Doc Barlow Mountain. There was goodness out there. A lot. Why couldn't he see it when he was living in Massachusetts? His parents were really good people. Was it just panic? It could have been panic. But what if it was something else? Something his parents couldn't fix? He remembered how he felt in the days before he left. He never wanted to feel that way again.

*

CHAPTER TWENTY-FOUR

CALIFORNIA AREA CODE

"BURTON?"

"Yeah, hon. What time is it?"

He looked for the clock, then remembered he had unplugged it the other day, when the alarm would not shut off. A call in the night was a call in the night, whatever time it was. Almost never good.

"Eleven." Maddy whispered. She sounded strange. "Listen, I don't want to wake Jess. I have a boy on the line. On hold. He wants to talk to us about Seb."

Burton held the cell phone to his face with both hands to make sure he did not drop it as he sat up, shaking.

"Okay. Okay. Talk to him. Don't lose him."

"Hold on. I can patch him in."

"Don't lose him! Just talk—"

The line went silent. A second later, a bit of static.

"Hello," Maddy said.

"Hi," the boy said in a deep voice. Not, Burton suspected, his natural voice.

"Hi. I'm Seb's Dad."

There was bluesy guitar music playing in the background. The sound suggested a small, confined space. Burton was not sure what to say next. He was barely awake. They had to get this right.

A chime came from his laptop. There was a message from Maddy: *I sent boy's # to Phil and police. I am recording call.*

The boy spoke. "Seb would really think I ratted him out if he knew I was calling."

"You must have a good reason for calling?" Maddy asked.

The boy did not answer. Burton pulled aside the curtain. A raccoon on the dumpster blinked, lazily, its eyes solid white and blazing in the parking lot spotlight. Their boy had been out on nights like this for weeks. Nights meant for feral animals. They had to handle this phone call perfectly.

"Seb's okay," the boy said, his voice trembling.

Maddy let out a faint moan. This sound, and the news, brought tears to Burton's eyes, but he made no sound.

"He told me he wished you could know he was okay."

The boy was speaking slowly and making only short statements. Burton got the sense he wanted them to guess, to ask questions, so his having called would feel like less of a betrayal. He could blame whatever happened on the persuasive powers of adults. Burton did not want to pry too much, though. The boy seemed very skittish.

"He needs..." The boy took a deep breath. "He needs to go somewhere safe. I'm just not sure home is going to make him feel safe. The problem is...I think he might get hurt."

Burton began to speak quietly, enunciating each word, evincing a calm he did not feel. "Is he planning something dangerous? Or was it something he said?"

"The thing is, it's hard to tell when he's joking. It's not like, I don't think..."

They waited.

"He talks about plans for the future but none of them are realistic."

"We're concerned, too" Maddy said. "We know he's worried he'll be trapped here, but we get it. We can take a break from school, travel, figure it out together. But we can't do any of that if we can't communicate with him."

After a couple of seconds, the line went dead.

Burton groaned. "No. No."

"Ohhhh." Maddy, he could tell, was starting to cry.

"All right," Burton said. "Let's just deal with this. We have the phone number. I'm going to call Phillip."

His phone made a ding. It was a text from Phillip Geer.

I am on this. Should not take long. Hold tight.

"Mad, did Phillip text you?"

"I got it."

Thoughts raced through Burton's mind. They needed to plan what to say if the boy called back.

"Burt?" Maddy asked. "Do you think the boy saw the video we made for all the YouTube commenters?"

"I don't know. Probably. Our number was up there and it got a lot of hits. Or, he could have seen a flyer."

"I thought for sure he would keep talking," Maddy said, choking back a sob. "That's a lot of responsibility on his shoulders. I shouldn't have said that bit about needing to communicate with Seb. Damn it."

"There was no way to know what would keep him on the line. It was a poker game."

Burton held the phone to his ear with his shoulder and typed the boy's area code into his computer. He might get lucky and find something Phillip could use.

A message from Phillip arrived at the center of Burton's screen: *California. San Jose.*

Burton typed back: *And?*

Will let you know ASAP.

"You saw from Phillip?" he asked his wife. "San Jose? I got the same result on my computer."

"I saw."

"What do we say if the boy calls back?"

"Follow his lead. We have to find out where Seb is but we can't push. Better if he feels comfortable calling us back later if necessary."

"Hopefully Phillip can get an idea where the boy is calling from. It's not necessarily California."

They had been in touch with Duranne's parents every day since Seb left but they had pretty much given up on California. Duranne's family was living south of Los Angeles, which was far from San Jose, but it could mean something.

"Burt," Maddy said. "What do you think the boy meant when he said he was worried Seb might get hurt?"

"Go to jail for hacking into a super-polluter's website?" Burton asked. He thought this unlikely, although he would not rule it out. The only reason he said it now was to stave off panic. Maddy had to be thinking what he was thinking. Had Seb given the boy the impression he might hurt himself?

He pictured Maddy at the big desk in the basement. Down there so Jessica could not hear, trying to hold it together. He was about to message Phillip for a status on the phone number when Maddy shouted into the phone.

"I'm getting a call from the same area code! Hold on. I'll do a conference call."

A moment later, Burton's phone beeped. He touched the answer icon.

"I'm sorry about hanging up," the boy said. "I got a little freaked."

"It's okay," Maddy said. "We understand. We know our son. He's a little intense, huh?"

The boy did not reply.

"Don't tell us anything you're not comfortable telling us. We're just glad that you care about Seb. Really, really glad."

"I saw your videos on YouTube," the boy said. "All of them. Seb doesn't know I watched them. The last video, where you told people to shut up and help you find Seb? That really got me thinking. You're nice people. Good parents. I wanted to tell him not to be afraid to go home. I almost did, but I think he would run off if I told him that."

"What do you think about all this?" Maddy's voice was barely above a whisper.

"I think it's like claustrophobia."

Smart kid.

As they were talking, another message from Phillip appeared on Burton's computer screen.

Area code does not necessarily mean that much about where the caller is located. People move around and keep phone # for years. But phone # can be traced back to a person. Getting trace results now.

"Again," Burton said, "don't tell us anything you don't want to tell us. But, it would be a tremendous help if we knew where you are. Even if it's just what state you're in."

"If you ambushed him, I don't think it would be good. He could get lost in the woods."

"We're not going to ambush him," Burton and Maddy said at the same time.

"If Seb saw your videos," the boy said, "he would feel better. But—"

"He hasn't seen the videos?" Burton asked. He had not been able to completely stifle the agitation in his voice.

"Um. No."

The line was silent again. Burton decided to wait. Maddy was quiet as well.

"You didn't know, did you?" the boy finally asked. "I wasn't sure, but the way you talked on your videos, I kind of figured."

In slow, steady words, Burton asked, "Do you know why he hasn't watched the videos?"

"He had you make them to help you understand him. Something like that."

Burton waited to see if Maddy would speak. After a second of silence, he asked, "But didn't he also make the videos so we could help him?"

"I think he won't watch the videos because he doesn't want to be talked out of what he's doing."

"Did he have us make the videos just so we felt better? So we believed we were helping him?"

"He says no. Just to make you understand what he did was the right thing to do." The boy paused. "I'm not sure I should talk about this any more. I'm going to get it wrong."

"That's fine." Burton scrambled to think of something more encouraging to say.

"He does feel bad about not watching the videos."

Maddy and Burton were being tested. A test of their ability to keep the boy on the line while they absorbed the incredibly disturbing news that Seb never watched the videos.

A new message from Phillip popped up on Burton's screen.

This is a computer-based phone number. Some kind of app or website most likely. A company I am not familiar with. The call could be coming from anywhere.

The boy's voice came on the line again. "I saw Seb's last name on one of his papers. Your videos were easy to find once I knew his last name. It kind of shocked me, how many people were watching the videos and making comments. Seb should probably read those comments. It would be good for him to know how many people take him seriously. Not everybody, but a lot."

"Yes." Maddy's voice trembled. "Do you think—"

Burton cut her off. "It sounds like Seb is a friend of yours. We understand you want to be a good friend and I get the feeling you can see that Seb is kind of stuck. That's what's hard about being a friend. You're supposed to keep secrets but when your friend is stuck in a dangerous place, you have a difficult decision to make.

"Just so you know, we never...there was never any, you know, harm done to him by anyone here. His home is a safe place. And legally, he's supposed to be here. We're actually pretty good parents."

"We don't think he should come back just because of the law, of course," Maddy said. "We're worried about him. Like you are. And we miss him so much."

Another instant message from Phillip appeared: *Called phone # boy is using. Generic recording gives company name only. No way to leave message. I did send message thru their website.*

Oh, come on! Burton wanted to say out loud.

He heard, through the phone, the sound of feet on a creaky floor. Then springs. The boy had moved, perhaps, to his bed. The bluesy guitar music that had been in the background was no longer audible.

The cursor on Burton's screen started to move again. Phillip was composing another message.

Requested company to identify caller location. Still searching for other ways to reach them. Police might speed up. Uncertain how long.

The boy spoke again.

"I said too much. If he got forced to go home, I don't know. He's really scared of what would happen if he got stuck at home again. Scared enough to do something bad, maybe. Besides, your videos were good but I'm not sure it's enough to stop him from freaking out about global warming again."

Burton tried to come up with a response. Maddy must have been doing the same. There was silence on the line.

"I have to go now. I'm sorry."

The line went dead.

CHAPTER TWENTY-FIVE

THE SPRING

BURTON WALKED A DIRT ROAD with about as many plants as could possibly be crammed into the land on either side of it.

A bird chirruped, waited, chirruped again. The air was thick, damp and strong with the scent of earth and pine. This road would be a great place to go running. He had not been running since the one time in the county park when he remembered what Seb said about Katahdin. The mad hike the other day, down the yellow ravine and up the side of the mountain to get to the A.T., had probably burned more calories but it was not running.

The boy who had been with Seb, who telephoned them last night and hung up abruptly had called back an hour later. His name was Matt, although Seb knew him as Skeet. Matt said Burton and Maddy could call him Skeet. He seemed to like the name.

Skeet made them promise not to tell Seb he had called. Seb would most likely figure this out on his own, but they agreed. Skeet then told them all he knew.

Seb had been living the entire time in the woods. Somewhere in the thick trees surrounding the road where Burton now walked. He had supplies and was off the grid. The woods calmed him.

They pressed Skeet for information, to be sure it was their son, and to judge for themselves how well he was doing. Hearing about the binocular lenses attached to eyeglasses, the morning baths, the failed bow and arrow, brought Maddy and Burton their first real comfort in weeks. Their son may have had a hard time but he was alive and well enough. Enjoying himself, too, apparently. It was hard for them to be angry that Seb could enjoy himself, such was their relief. Skeet did say Seb was rather conflicted about it all.

After the final phone call with Skeet, Maddy broke down sobbing. Jessica got on the phone and assured Burton she was hugging her mother, although Jessica was crying, too. They had more hope than at any time before but their son was still not home and still not safe.

Seb had learned enough to get by, but the wild woods of Maine could be harsh. Even experienced hikers got lost or hurt. More disturbing was Skeet's comment about Seb getting hurt. Both Buron and Maddy thought this could mean hurt himself. A couple of his emails had alluded to this, his fear that the panic would become too much to tolerate. For intance, if he knew people were closing in on him.

They learned from Skeet that Seb had indeed initially planned to hike the Appalachian Trail. In the course of making these plans he realized he did not want to spend all his time hiking. He also realized the A.T. was too much exposure. So he looked for the place with the least possible risk of being found. The best he could do, with the time and money he had, was to take himself to remote, swampy land in the Katahdin Valley.

There was no mention of Seb's childhood thoughts of Katahdin. Seb probably did not even remember his comment about falling off the end of the trail into uninhabited Canada. Still, Burton remained certain that Seb's early ideas about Katahdin had played a part in where he ended up.

Burton had said it before and he said it again. His wife was a genius. The video demanding the spectators on YouTube do the right thing, and Maddy, the missing boy's mother, holding up the phone number to call, got through to Skeet.

Now everything rested on this boy. Another unusual boy who was drawn to the woods. Burton was to meet him in less than an hour.

A white boulder came into view. The marker for the trail to the spring. The time was eight-thirty. Burton was a half-hour early. His car was a couple miles back, at the only place wide enough to allow another car to pass.

After sitting on the white boulder for a while, he grew uncomfortable and sat on the ground. 8:45 came and went. At 8:50, he stared down the road. He was in full worry by 8:55. This was cutting it close, when you had four miles to walk.

A boy ambled around the curve at 8:59. He wore a gray T-shirt with a big, red B at the center. Skeet had told them he would be wearing a Red Sox shirt.

Their fate, Burton saw, was in the hands of a boy even younger than he expected. When the boy got closer, Burton could see from his face that he was older than his height originally made him appear, as did his muscled arms, which he held away from his sides a bit like an ape, probably to look more masculine, in compensation for his height.

"Hi, Skeet."

"Hi, Mr. Franck."

They shook hands.

The boy's black cargo shorts looked ironed. Had he dressed for the occasion? This was a big deal for the poor guy. Something he was probably now regretting.

A troubling thought occurred to Burton. A grown man and a child should not meet in a remote place like this. Nobody, probably, should meet in a remote place like this. It was not something he should have asked Skeet to do. Burton's reluctance to involve the police, for fear they would scare either boy away, had clouded his thinking.

It was done. Skeet was unlikely to ever be presented with such a situation again.

The boy looked Burton in the eye, surprising him with the boldness of his stare. He may have sensed Burton's hesitation.

"You ready for this, Mr. Franck?"

"I'm ready. I'm sorry, by the way, for putting you out like this. I shouldn't have. My wife and I, if we can make it up to you and your family, we would like to."

Now why had he mentioned Skeet's family? They would not be happy to hear of this meeting in the woods. Burton was just trying to make the boy feel comfortable. Best to be honest, anyway. Too much was at stake.

"Everything go okay last night?" Burton asked.

"Yeah." Skeet glanced up the road in the direction from which he came.

This must be where Seb would come out of the woods and cross the road.

The plan, as Burton told it to Skeet, was for Seb and Skeet to meet at the spring to fill their canteens. Burton would be waiting nearby, out of sight. He would say, as soon as Seb noticed him, that he was there alone and only wanted to talk. Whatever happened next would be based on Seb's wishes.

It was pretty much a lie. Burton did not plan on only talking. He planned on leaving with Seb. They would start by talking.

The real danger would be if Seb ran. He would not have clothing, food or gear to be safe and warm later on in the forest. Burton was a runner, though, and he was wearing trail running shoes. He also had gear and food for two. Wherever Seb went, Burton would be there.

"Do you want to walk with me to the spring?" Burton asked. "That way you'll know where I've stationed myself when the two of you get close."

"All right."

Skeet led him into the woods. Before long, the sound of water splashing onto stone could be heard. In a couple of minutes, a steep, algae-covered mass of rock came into view. Water rippled over its surface. Some of the water gathered into a stream and coursed through a groove to splatter on a shelf of rock below. Burton moved closer and placed his mouth under the stream. The cold hurt his teeth.

Skeet, he could see out of the corner of his eye, was staring at something. Burton took a step back and followed the boy's gaze.

A piece of paper was attached to the rock wall at eye level, held in place by two sticks that had been wedged into a crevice. As Burton got closer, the paper began to look familiar. At first he thought it might be an announcement, like the hundreds of announcements he had seen on bulletin boards and storefront windows while distributing their flyer about Seb's disappearance. It was something he had seen before, but not on any bulletin board.

The paper featured a crude drawing of a male silhouette inside a circle with a diagonal line through it. It had been drawn with a simple black pen. In large letters across the top read the words: *Don't Find Seb.*

❦

Burton and Skeet ran through the forest. Skeet glanced at him several times, looking scared, as if he had screwed up. Perhaps also scared that this all-out pace would give Burton a heart attack. If anything was going to give him a heart attack, it would have been that wet piece of paper by the spring with those cold, desperate words on it.

Seb would not stop running, no matter the cost. The reason, Burton knew, underneath it all, was his old newsletter article, the part about bringing children into a world that could not care for them. If only Seb would give his father a chance to help him come to terms with this, not try to explain it away but learn how to move past it. Together, and with whatever other help was needed.

Skeet eventually slowed down. Burton watched him jog in a twisting route amongst some trees. When Skeet stopped, Burton came over to where he stood. They looked down onto a charred stick at the bottom of a hole. The look on Skeet's face told the story. Seb was gone.

"Your son's a dick," Skeet said.

Burton said nothing. The area looked remarkably devoid of human presence for a place where someone had lived for weeks.

"Did he stay other places, or is this it?"

"This is it. He kept the hole covered. He kept his food and gear in two bags that he hung up in that tree every night." Skeet gestured with an imprecise wave to his right.

Burton shifted his eyes back to the hole. The two boys had been good buddies. Skeet did not deserve this.

Skeet went off to look at a few other places. A crinkling sound came from the direction of a huge fallen tree. He returned with a plastic bag in one hand and a book in the other. He threw the book into the fire pit and sat down.

It was a copy of *The Hitchhiker's Guide to the Galaxy*. Seb's favorite book. A slip of paper protruding from the center of the book had handwritten words: "I'm sorry."

Burton looked over at Skeet. "My son has a lot to be sorry about. You don't. We are so grateful to you. We know you were watching his back while he was out here."

"Your son's not a dick. I get to come here any time I want. He doesn't. This place meant a lot to him. It's complicated." After all that, to still stick up for him. Burton felt even more grateful that this boy had been the person to discover his son. Another kind heart in the world. With all these good people around, you would think mankind could take care of its planet.

Burton took a squashed granola bar from his shorts pocket and offered it to Skeet. He accepted it, but kept it in his hands, turning it over and over.

"How do you think we can help Seb? If you don't mind me asking?"

"I guess I don't know. I screwed all this up."

"You tried to save his life. You did save his life. We're going to find him. He must be on his bike?"

"It's gone, so, yeah."

It was nearly noon. Burton did not want to make Skeet feel worse, but he needed information.

"How did Seb know we would be at the spring this morning?"

"Pffff." Skeet said. He interlaced his fingers and started squeezing his palms together like a beating heart. "I'm a bad liar."

"Any idea which way he might go?"

"Not really. I don't get how he found out about the *Don't Find Seb* thing. I never mentioned it."

They stared into the fire pit.

"What are you going to do when you find him?" Skeet asked. He was still turning the unopened granola bar over and over in his hands. "If you said, 'you're coming home, and that's that,' would he go with you?"

"My guess is no."

"Have you figured out what you're going to say?"

"Maybe. Something like: *go easy on yourself. It's not your fault.*"

Skeet nodded. "That's what I said."

"We...I should be looking for him. It's a little strange to say, 'Go easy on yourself,' and then chase him down. But what choice do I have?"

CHAPTER TWENTY-SIX

RUN

Seb pushed his bike around a clump of poison ivy, giving it a wide berth, before stopping to compare the compass to the map. He might be lost, and he could not afford to be lost. There was no telling how long it would take to get out to the road. But he was stuck with this plan, having had only a few hours to put it together.

A few hours in which a lot happened.

It started the day before. Skeet was acting strange. Smiling too much. Seb almost asked him what was wrong. So, he was already suspicious when Skeet screwed up.

Skeet was complaining about the amount of time his father spent watching television.

"I get this picture of the Franck family reading books or working on their computers. Never watching TV."

"Are you kidding? The TV is on a lot."

Franck family? Seb was pretty sure he had never mentioned his last name. In any case, what Skeet said sounded an awful lot like "Franck Family Video." He must have checked out the YouTube videos Seb told him about. Seb would have probably done the same. But to be acting strange and to say that particular phrase at the same time meant something was up.

When Skeet suggested they meet at the spring at nine the next morning to go swimming at a pond with no leeches, Seb did not have any reason to be suspicious. They laughed, recalling how Seb got two leeches in a pond and hopped around frantically to see if he had any more on him.

They were having a good time and Seb figured he was wrong. He must have told Skeet his last name at some point and didn't realize it.

A little later, though, Skeet called Seb by his full name. Seb knew the jig was probably up then. Skeet was definitely acting weird. He would not be that nervous just because he watched the videos. He must have done something. Seb was pretty sure his father or the police or some ranger were going to be near the spring at nine the next morning. His house in Massachusetts was not so far that his father could not be at the spring by the morning.

Seb was now the only person who had not seen these videos. It literally made him sick to think about it, but he needed to know what Skeet knew. He had to watch the videos.

When he was studying maps before he left Massachusetts, Seb had noticed a bed and breakfast a few miles north of where he was now. This bed and breakfast was on the same road as Skeet's house. In fact, to get there, Seb would have to pass his house. Which meant he had to start biking to the bed and breakfast as soon as Skeet left his camp and headed back home. Seb had to get beyond Skeet's house before Skeet got there and saw him riding by on his bike. He could sneak past the house in the dark on his way back if he had to.

Everything happened so fast. It was late afternoon when Skeet finally left Seb's camp. Seb threw a few things in his pack and started running while he pushed his bike at a diagonal towards the little dirt road Skeet took home. He had to get on that road far enough ahead of Skeet so he wouldn't see him.

When he found the road, he started riding like a maniac. He was soaked with sweat by the time he got onto the county road. The Skeet House came up pretty soon afterwards.

Seb knew it was his house because of the long, wooden building next to it. The outdoorsman's lodge that his family had to close down. There was a porch extending the entire length of the lodge, with six sets of steps and six doors. A sign leaning against the last set of steps said: *West of the Mountain*. Paint was missing from a few of its letters.

Skeet's house looked like a lot of the farm houses in the area. A tall rectangle of two stories, painted white with black trim and black shutters. It was in great shape compared to the lodge next to it.

He got to the bed and breakfast not too long afterwards. It was a surprisingly small yellow house at the center of a big field. A yellow sign hung from a weeping willow near the road, with the words Caitlin's Inn done up in stylish, dark green letters.

Seb left his bike on the lawn and climbed the porch steps. The porch was covered with clay pots of flowers and some of them smelled really strong. He rang the doorbell. A chime of hollow wooden tubes clunked somewhere.

The front door opened almost immediately. A woman with super-short blonde hair stood looking at him through the screen door. She had both a smile and a frown on her face. Seb had meant to prepare what he would say as he was riding up here, but forgot. Which was bad, because there was no other place to go.

"I'm sorry to bother you," he said. "Would it be okay if I used your computer to check some messages from my parents?"

She stared at this boy who showed up in the middle of nowhere on a bike. "Sure."

Somehow, he had said the right thing and technically, it was the truth.

"Thank you so much."

"Take your time. No guests until the weekend."

The frown disappeared. Now she looked like she wanted to offer him cookies and milk.

"There's the computer, right there."

A computer sat on a writing desk to her right. The only other things in the tiny foyer were a coat rack and a plant stand on which rested a glass bowl of water with pink roses floating in it. They smelled even stronger than the flowers out on the porch.

Fortunately, she left him alone in the foyer, although she left the door between the foyer and the rest of the house slightly ajar. He waited for the squeak of her sneakers to grow quieter.

He turned the volume knob to low. In less than a minute, he was watching the first of his family's videos. He watched one after the other, with his hand on the mouse and the cursor poised to close the window if the woman returned.

After the last video, he sat there staring at his hands. They were filthy. He felt sick and dizzy, like the time he gave blood and they put him on a cot for a half an hour.

Something flashed outside. A cloud must have moved and uncovered the sun. The flash had come from his red bike, which he deposited on the grass near the foyer's only window. His family claimed to still love him in those videos, but how could they? He realized suddenly that the bike and his stuff back at camp were all he had for sure in the world.

His parents looked so tired in those videos. Doing what he asked. The worst part was the begging. He got choked up when Jessica dumped her bag of garbage and tried to be mad at him. He laughed when Grandma Rosa jumped in there to make her speech. But she made him cry, too. Seeing his little dog Myro. All of it hurt to watch.

They found the computer in the closet. What a nightmare.

There were an unbelievable number of comments underneath the videos. Page after page of them. He skimmed through, looking for a comment from Skeet. Looking for signs his parents were on their way to get him. He saw no sign of that.

No proof, but he knew what happened. When he saw his mother hold up the phone number and beg people to help them find their son, he knew. Skeet had seen the video and called the number.

The *Don't Find Seb* stuff was a major curveball. Did those people really want him to stay out there so the climate movement could get more attention? At least they were not pretending that the volcano wasn't bubbling in their back yard. But they made his family furious and his parents made that incredible video telling them off.

The ones who called him a shame and a brat didn't bother him. There were bigger problems in the world than that. His parents seemed to be ignoring those people, too. He could hear his father say they were just a bunch of losers blabbering.

Seb never intended, never imagined the videos would go viral. He never imagined anyone but his parents would watch them. He ran off to pretend all this crazy stuff was not happening and to stop himself from going crazy. Not to make people talk about global warming. He was very glad they were but that was never his plan. He had been too freaked out to think about anything other than getting away and he barely managed to do that.

His head was spinning from all the comments under the videos. A lot of people were talking about the same things that made him feel crazy. Some of them talked about what they were doing to fix the problem. That was really cool.

The comments were one thing. But watching the videos was torture. His parents trying so hard. It made him sick. Having them make the videos had been a really bad idea. He tried to remember if he had other reasons besides getting them to truly understand how freaked out he was. That he had to go where he could pretend global warming wasn't happening.

Did he also ask them to make the videos because he was mad and wanted them to feel as bad as he did? Maybe at the back of his mind, but he never thought about that when he was planning all this. Still, he was stupid for sure for not realizing how crazy and mean it would seem to his parents when they found out he never watched the videos.

Then he had a really awful thought. As bad as he felt about what he did to his parents, he wanted more than ever to get away from them. To get away from the people who loved him so much.

If his parents found him, they would not let him out of their sight until he was eighteen. They saw how sneaky he was. They would keep him in the middle of the flushing toilet of the world for the next four years.

And they were definitely coming. Soon. Skeet's slip-ups that morning had made this obvious. He had watched the videos and told Seb's parents where he was.

Seb felt worse than he ever felt in his whole life. He was ashamed for abandoning his family so they had to deal with the things that scared him while he hid in the woods. Sure, he was writing and trying to come up with a plan but that was in the future. That was a dream. It felt like pretending. He felt like a big baby. But more than any of those things, he felt like a cornered animal.

He stood up from the computer in the B and B's foyer and knocked on the door to the main part of the house.

The woman appeared a minute later. Her expression immediately changed to one of concern. Seb's crying and agitation must have shown on his face.

Before she could speak, he said, "It was great to hear from them. Thank you so much. I love being out here with my cousins but it gets lonely sometimes." This lie was quick thinking but then he realized a problem with it. "Especially since they don't have internet."

An unlikely scenario but not impossible. Nonetheless, he needed to get out of there as soon as possible, before he really slipped up.

The woman nodded. She looked even more concerned than she had before. Seb disturbed people everywhere he went. He felt like dirt.

"Do you have a piece of paper and a pen?"

"I do. Do you need an envelope, too? A stamp?"

He did not need either, but he said, "An envelope would be great. I have money for the stamp."

"Don't be silly." She paused. "The paper is right here in the desk drawer."

Seb stepped back. She opened the drawer, took out several pieces of printer paper, a pen, and laid them on the corner of the desk.

"I'll be back in a minute," she said, leaving the foyer again to give him privacy.

He quickly drew the *Don't Find Seb* sign he would put up at the spring, folded it, and tucked it into his pocket.

The woman came back with the envelope and stamp. He noticed for the first time the jeans stained at the knees from gardening, the blueberry festival т-shirt, the sunburn on her cheeks. He thought he might love her.

"Thanks again."

He took a couple steps to the front door and opened it. The woman looked surprised, probably expecting him to write the letter on the paper she gave him before he left. Holding the door ajar, he said, "Thank you very, very much. I've got to get going. Long ride still."

"Enjoy," she said with cheer, but there was a catch in her voice. Concern. Or love back for him.

He let go of the screen door and it banged shut. Without looking back he walked to his bike in the grass and was about to take off when the door creaked open. He gripped the handlebars, to be ready to ride off if necessary, before turning around to look.

"Is everything okay?" The woman stood on the roofless porch amidst her collection of potted flowers, keeping the screen door open with her thigh.

"Uh. Sure."

"I suppose you know this, but there's nothing for miles around here. Especially to the North. It's so beautiful here, people get carried away sometimes and want to explore. I'm only telling you this because you'd be surprised how many people underestimate how far it is to the next gas station or store. People get stuck up here every year."

He tried to look like a person who knew what he was doing. Smile and nod knowingly. She was probably thirty years older than him and he loved her. But he had to leave.

"I appreciate it." He patted one of the bike's saddle bags. "Compass, which I don't expect to need." He smiled to show confidence. "And I always take food, water and a jacket. A repair kit for the bike, of course. And a phone."

"That's good."

She had been standing with the screen door open, propped against her thigh the whole time. She moved out of the doorframe to the edge of the porch. The door slammed.

What was the problem? Why wouldn't she let him go? He had erased all traces of the videos he watched.

"Okay, just one more thing. South of here? Where this road merges with another paved road?" She looked to her right and lifted her chin in that direction for emphasis.

Seb gave a nod although he did not know what intersection she was talking about.

"If you turn right, you'll be heading towards Milltown. A couple miles further there's an old man who sells junk out of his garage, pretending it's a store. He does sell some useful things, though. Drinks. Peanut butter and cheese crackers. Maybe a little stale. And just between you and me, he has a short-wave radio. If for some reason your bike broke down and you had no signal on your phone. Or something like that."

She held up her hands. "Don't be insulted. I tell everyone that comes here. You'll recognize it by a dirty old sign that says David Raymond's Dry Goods. He's crotchety but harmless. Anyway, it's a gorgeous day. You have fun now."

"I will. Thanks again for the internet." He was going to add, "I'll tell my parents…," but he did not want to sound too much like a kid. "I'll tell my friends there's a great B and B up here."

"Well, thank you."

She waved. He rode away and did not look back.

One rule he could never forget: even the most well-meaning adults would turn him in, because not turning him in would be some kind of crime.

Just before he reached Skeet's house, he heard a lawn mower. He rolled to a stop behind a tree and peered around to get a look. The front lawn had been cut already and the mower sounded pretty far off. Skeet told him more than once that his brother never did a damn thing around the house, so Seb knew it was Skeet doing the mowing out back and would not be able to see him cycling by.

He stopped by the spring to put up the *Don't Find Seb* sign he made at the bed and breakfast. Back at camp, he packed everything but the tent and sleeping bag onto his bike, and looked over his maps with his flashlight. The birds would wake him before the sun was up and then he would head out.

❧

Seb finally broke through to a dirt road. Hopefully the right road. He let the bike fall to the ground. Vines and sticks were wedged into various places on it and the whole thing was covered in mud.

He had been pushing the bike with all his gear on it through the woods since daybreak. Longer than it took him to ride all the way to the B and B the day before.

He was exhausted but could not stop. It was almost ten in the morning already.

Skeet and Seb's father or whoever showed up at the spring to see the *Don't Find Seb* sign would go straight to his camp. Once they saw that all of his gear was gone, they would go back to the road and get into a car. Seb needed to be as far away as possible, as soon as possible.

At least the bike was lighter now. He had ditched his cook-stove (the paint can) after the first big hill. A half-gallon of wax weighed a lot.

The bike, and most of his body, was splattered with mud. There had been a giant, mucky section of the forest and he chose to go through it rather than take the time to go around it. He found a stick and when he reached out to clean mud from the gears he saw blood all over his arms. There must have been thorns out there, although he had not felt them at the time. He probably had blood on his face, too. They were just scratches, but he must have looked like a psycho, with all the mud, and the blood, and the bike piled high with crap. And he was about to get on a county road.

At least it was roads from here on out. Today, anyway. The road in front of him now was not much of a road, packed dirt worn badly by the rain, with enormous potholes full of water. Up ahead, it was completely under water as far as he could see, at least to where it curved off to the left. No worries. It would be like a car wash.

Depending on where he had come out of the forest, he had only a mile or two to go before he reached the county road. All he needed was an hour, possibly less if he pedaled really hard. Then he could get off the road and lie low. There was still plenty of turkey jerky left and he had his water filter.

He would wait at least a couple days before getting more food from the guy who sold things out of his garage. The one he heard about from the woman at the bed and breakfast. After looking at his maps, he was pretty sure he could find the store, although he could not remember its name. If he did not find it, he had enough supplies to make his way further south, to where there had to be some kind of store.

There were other nature preserves closer to his old camp, places he could have gotten to without so much bushwhacking, and with less time exposed on public roads, but he needed to get out of the area altogether. A search party would search far and wide around his previous camp site. They would start with roads first, though, and hopefully chose one of the many small, dirt roads nearby, some open to the public and some not. He could have used one or two of these roads to connect up to the county road he was headed for now, but he took the road-less route through the woods, hoping they would expect him, in a rush, and with so much gear, to get on one of the nearer roads, and search for him there. They would also have to decide to look for him heading east, north, west or south.

The reason he was risking as much as an hour on this county road was that it would take him to a big forest. To the south there was a large tract of land owned by the state of Maine and kept wild. This forest was connected to more forests like it and he could make his way under cover of the woods almost the whole distance to Greenville. It would take a while pushing a bike through the forest but he could not risk being out on public roads. There were probably some dirt roads in there he could use, too. He would hear a pickup truck or a jeep kicking up gravel before they saw him and he could pull his bike off into the trees until they were gone.

He was not sure how long he should wait before he went into Greenville. At least he still had his fake beard and a baseball hat. He really did not want to leave his bike behind but he would be much more recognizable trying to get on a bus with a bike. Busses had to stop in Greenville, at least once in a while, in the summer.

CHAPTER TWENTY-SEVEN

CALL THE POLICE

THE MONSTER JEEP GLIDED DEEPER into the valley. Such a long, straight road. No boy on a bicycle. Just trees, trees, trees, trees.

Seb had been gone for hours. Possibly gone since the night before, after Skeet went home, although it would have been difficult to move his bike and all that gear in the dark.

Burton phoned Maddy.

"Hi," she said.

"It didn't work. He wasn't there."

"No! What happened?"

"Somehow, he knew we were coming. He ran off. I'm looking for him now."

"Do you know which way he went?"

"All I know for sure is he left a note saying he was gone. I'm sorry, babe. This is not our fault. There's something wrong with him."

Disappear Seb, Burton thought, *into the trees. Don't come back. I don't want to see you.* Then, his anger having been vented, the cruel thought slipped away.

"What are you going to do?" Maddy asked.

She sounded oddly calm. Maybe it was the phone. It was unnerving, though. Burton could have used a little lift. He was still jittery from the sight of the sign Seb hung up at the spring.

"I'm checking the local roads," he said. "Even if he left last night, he couldn't have gone far with a bike full of gear in the dark woods."

"How's the boy? Skeeter?"

"He's okay. He isn't that mad at Seb, believe it or not. I just dropped him off. At least we know where he lives, in case I need to go back and talk to him again."

"That's good."

"I'm on the county road now. There's a dirt road up ahead that connects to a whole network of roads hardly ever traveled. Really rough roads. Not too rough for this jeep, don't worry. I think he would have gone that way, to stay under the radar. Otherwise, the only road that goes anywhere is this county road I'm on now. I can't imagine Seb would stay on this road for long. He would be easy to spot."

Burton was pretty sure Seb was heading towards an entirely different forest than the one he just left. A forest Skeet did not know. Some place he could lie low. Burton wondered if the forests north of here were too big for a search party to cover. Maybe they would use dogs.

To get to one of these new forests, Seb would have to still be on his bike. The jeep could travel in a few minutes a stretch of road that would take Seb an hour, especially the steep uphill parts. Burton would catch him.

"Have you had a chance to call the police?" Maddy asked.

"This is the first I've had phone service." Burton paused. "Just let me find him. I've come this far."

"Burton, you can't cover every road. The clock is ticking. He could ride his bike a short way and then go back into the forest. We need more cars on the road."

"I don't think we're going to get police cars out here soon enough. If they came at all, it would be too late."

Maddy did not reply right away. "Even one car would help. We have to try. If you pick the wrong direction, you might never see him. What direction are you going, anyway?"

"North."

"I'll tell Phillip. He can try to connect to your GPS. But you need to call the police."

"Say the police do come. What are they going to do? Chase him through the woods and tackle him?"

"Maybe they should. What are you going to do?"

"I'll do the tackling."

"Please, just call them." She paused. "What did the note say?"

Burton had hoped to avoid upsetting her, for the time being, about the note.

"It was a drawing of the sign. The silhouette with the line through it. *Don't Find Seb.*"

"I hope those...I hope they're happy."

"They should see the sign I'm going to make for them."

Burton's eyes were drawn by a glint up ahead. It turned out to be nothing. A piece of glass in the road.

"Okay," Maddy said. "Phillip's going to send something to your GPS. I've got a map of the area on my screen now if that doesn't work."

"I'd better go. I'm watching out for Seb and trying to read this GPS."

"Well, be safe. I don't know from what, but be careful. And call the police now before you lose the signal again."

She hung up.

Burton scanned the sticky note of phone numbers stuck to the dashboard, looking for the state police.

Seb was fragile enough as it was. A showdown with the police would be bad.

"Forgive me, Maddy."

The valley was so damned beautiful. Flowering plants everywhere. Stalks of what looked like giant asparagus grew in rows through the wetlands on either side of the road. Beyond these were miles of yellow grass.

The phone rang. Burton answered without looking at the number.

"Hello?"

"Dad!"

"How's my girl?"

"I'm flipping out. My crazy brother is getting chased through Maine on his bike. Are you okay?"

"I'm not yet flipping out but it's been wild."

"Can you believe it? My brother is stupid brilliant crazy. You know what I mean?"

"Sorry, but I don't. How about just stupid?"

Jessica laughed. "I guess I'm excited that we might actually find him. That he's so close."

"We're going to find him."

With Seb almost home, Jessica was able to romance her brother's adventure once more. It must have seemed impossible to her that they would lose him now. It was still possible.

"Can you hold on a second, Dad?"

Muffled sounds followed. Jessica had placed her hand over the mouthpiece. Burton could hear the lilt and whirls of her speech, but no words.

"Mom says I need to leave you alone. Go, Dad!"

"I'm glad you called. I needed some Jessica power. I have to get off the phone, anyway. I just saw something."

"What? What?"

"A bed and breakfast."

"You think he's in a bed and breakfast?"

"No, but they might have seen Seb go by. I have to run, Sugar."

"Bye, Daddy."

He pressed the brakes and coasted to a standstill. Before he was out of the jeep, a woman with short, whitish-blonde hair came onto the porch. She used a hand as a visor over her eyes. He parked, hopped out, and went straight up the steps to greet her.

"Hello. This might sound strange, but have you seen a teen-aged boy on a bike go by here this morning?"

"Oh, no. I thought something like this might happen. Oh, I should have...It's your son?"

"Yes. My son."

She mumbled something to herself that sounded like chastisement. "Not today, but yesterday. A young man on a bike asked if he could use my computer to check messages from his parents. He seemed fine. Except it's unusual, of course, for someone to show up here on a bike." She glanced from side to side, in case Burton had not noticed there was not another building in sight. "He was so much taller than me. I'm not good at telling ages any more. I should have called someone."

She started to hyperventilate.

Burton wanted to put a hand on her shoulder, to reassure her. Mostly for selfish reasons. He needed her coherent. He ended up with his arm partially raised, with the palm open, reluctant to scare the poor woman by touching her. He closed his fingers. She looked at his hand and blinked.

"Did he give any indication where he was headed?"

She shook her head from side to side. "Did he not show up where he was supposed to?"

"Nothing like that. I'm trying to catch up to him. He's, let's say, a bit rebellious."

The woman glanced at the door behind her twice, wishing, perhaps, to go inside before she was found liable for aiding a runaway.

"You didn't happen to see what he looked at on your computer? Maps, maybe?"

"No. I gave him his privacy."

Burton did not ask to see the computer. Seb would most certainly have used a private search or erased the history.

The woman took a step forward, knocking over a potted geranium. "We did talk a little."

"Oh?"

"I suppose it was only me doing the talking. I was concerned he might get lost. There's really nothing around here for many miles, especially if he were to go north. So I told him what I tell all my guests. There's a store, well, a grumpy old man who sells supplies out of his garage, about twenty miles south of here, not far from where this road intersects with the road from Millinocket."

"South? On this road?"

"Yes, south. All the way until this road ends, and then right."

"Thank you. Thank you."

The woman looked doubtful.

"If—after you find him—would you let me know he's okay?" She shook her head. "Only after you're rested and everything. If you think of it." Her hand slid into her front pocket and came out with a card. "And please call if there's some way I can help. If you lose this card, just look up *Caitlin's Inn*."

Burton took it. "This is good to have. Maybe we'll need a place to stay. If you have a vacancy. Thank you. Very much."

"We have a vacancy."

Burton turned to go.

"I sat by the phone after he left," the woman said. "Wondering about calling the police. I couldn't think what to say. A young man on his bike. A kid who contacted his parents using my computer. I still should have called."

"No. No. Thank you again. I've got to run, though."

She put a hand to her breastbone. "Of course. Good luck." She said this doubtfully, as if it might be the wrong thing to say.

⁂

The GPS beeped. The blinking dot was the jeep, about to begin the efficient itinerary through the forest service roads uploaded by Phillip. The first turnoff was less than a mile away.

The next thing Burton knew, he was guiding the jeep onto a patch of sand at the side of the road. He rolled down the windows and looked out over a pond.

A smell of swamp water mixed with fresh air blew in. A black-capped chickadee, just like at home, appeared on a cattail a few feet away. "Hee hee," he sang, high note to low note. "Hee hee. Hee hee."

Maddy was right. Everything depended on choosing the right route. Burton picked up the regional map which lay on the seat next to him. A thick blue circle indicated the location of the spring where he was supposed to meet Seb. The amount of green surrounding it, indicating nature preserves and parks, was awful to see.

He put his finger on the blue circle at the spring and slid it over to the county road. The road he was on right now. His finger wanted to go north. South meant more cars and more people. It was not yet August. Plenty of time for Seb to go to warmer places later.

The largest block of green, east of his finger, was Baxter State Park. Skeet said Seb would not go to Baxter, because it was too well patrolled. But there was another cluster of green quadrants, plenty big, directly above his finger, accessible by the network of dirt roads Phillip had mapped out for him.

Things were different now for Seb. More difficult. His sources of food and water, which he planned for in advance, and those he discovered, were no longer available. Seb would need to find clean water soon.

Burton moved his finger south on the map. He found the intersection, the only two major roads in the area, that woman at the B and B had referred to. He found something else as well. A very large patch of green. It was twenty miles away, but it had one distinct advantage. Emergency food and water in the old man's garage, just outside the boundary of the preserve.

Burton tossed the map to the side. The chickadee flew off. He hit the accelerator and spewed sand into the pond as he pulled out.

The road was flat and straight here. Burton got the jeep up to maximum speed in a few seconds. Its gas tank showed half-full. In this part of the world, if you were driving a gas-guzzler on half a tank of gas, you needed to be headed towards a gas station. However, by the time Burton ran out of gas, he would either be with Seb or have lost him to the night. No use in thinking about gas.

The phone started to ring. It was on the floor and he could not see who was calling. It went to voicemail. Shortly after came the beep of a message. Maddy would have to believe he had lost service again.

He could feel his heart thump. Pushing the jeep as hard as he could as he took a sharp curve, he thought of the time he went up on two wheels on the logging road. Cornering was not the jeep's forte.

Another straightaway, a downhill. The jeep was shaking. It felt like it would lose its grip on the road if Burton pushed it past 85 MPH.

The downhill tapered off and the road soon began to climb again. Something flashed in the distance, a half mile or so ahead. The sun was shining directly in Burton's eyes so he could not tell what he had seen. It was a steep hill and the sun was reflecting right off of it into his eyes. Then, he saw another flash. This time Burton was closer and he could see what it was. A bicycle moving slowly up the mountain.

Burton tried to accelerate but the pedal was already on the floor.

He could see now that this was a very fully packed bicycle. The young man riding it looked so thin. It was Seb.

The bicycle had no rear-view mirror. Burton slowed to thirty, then to twenty miles an hour. Seb gave no indication he knew a vehicle was approaching. Burton drove slowly, not to sneak up, but to avoid shocking him. He rolled the passenger window down.

The jeep's bumper came astride the bicycle's rear tire. Seb's helmet turned briefly, to verify a vehicle was passing. Burton slowed until he was riding at the bicycle's speed, alternating glances between the road and Seb. The helmeted head turned again. Tears streamed down Seb's face.

CHAPTER TWENTY-EIGHT
DOES ANYBODY NEED A PINEAPPLE?

A LOUD "CAW" JOLTED Burton awake. It sounded like the damn bird was sitting on top of his tent. A different bird had prevented him from falling asleep the night before. That bird kept saying "weee-oh-weeeeel" over and over again. In the irrationality of near-sleep, the high-pitched "weeeeel" every minute or so kept him in a state of agitation. It was as if the thing was saying "something's wrong...something's wrong." Fortunately, the bird shut up after about an hour.

Burton saw through the triangular vent at the top of the tent that there was a little bit of brightness in the sky.

"Caw!"

It was probably five in the morning, but he knew he would not be going back to sleep.

He dressed and unzipped the door. The wings of the bird that had woken him flapped loudly as it took to the air.

Seb was sitting at the edge of the same hole Burton and Skeet had been sitting around the day before. A pot hung over the hole, suspended by a branch, and Seb was stirring its contents, metal clicking against metal.

The temperature had cooled enough to warrant a jacket, but Burton figured he would be warm enough at the fire. He sat on a stump near Seb.

"It's fascinating to see you this early."

"I know."

In the twelve hours since Burton found him, Seb had spoken only when addressed and only in one or two word phrases. He surprised Burton now by handing him a plastic bag of blueberries and looking him in the eyes for first time since the jeep pulled up next to him on his bike the day before.

Burton poured a pile of berries onto his hand and rolled them into his mouth. They were delicious.

His plan for today was to rest and let Seb take the lead.

It felt unreal, sitting in a forest with Seb. And Maddy had gone along with the idea so easily.

When Burton came up alongside Seb on his bike the day before, he stopped pedaling. There was no shoulder, so he stopped the jeep and put it in park right where it was in the road. Seb, without saying a word, got off his bike, went to the back of the jeep, lifted the hatch, and put his bike in. He came around to the passenger seat, climbed in, lay against the door, and gazed blankly ahead.

Before Burton could figure out what to say, his phone rang. It was Maddy. He answered and slowly started driving.

"Seb is here with me."

"Oh my God. Oh my God. Just like that? He's okay?"

"Skinny but fine. Won't talk to me, though."

With every movement of the jeep, Seb's body rolled against the door, as if he were already asleep.

"I have an idea," Burton said. "Yes, another spontaneous idea, but hear me out. We need a rest and some kind of transition. If Seb will go for it, I was thinking of joining him in his camp for a few days. Neutral territory, of sorts. And see what happens."

Seb let his face touch the glass of the jeep's window and closed his eyes. This was the first he was hearing of the idea.

Maddy took a couple seconds before responding. "You'll be out of communication the whole time?"

"Yes."

"Do I have time to think about this? How close are you?"

"Of course. I'll think about it too. We don't have to decide for a while. I have to go to the motel anyway to get my stuff. I think there's a place still open where I can get a tent and some supplies. If we do go back to the woods."

Seb now had his elbow on his knee and his chin in his hand. The jeep entered a sharp curve and his arm slipped off his knee. His head lunged forward, stopping a few inches from the dash. He returned his chin to the cup of his hand, leaned against the car door, and closed his eyes.

Burton heard Jessica saying something in the background.

"Not now," Maddy said. "And don't pick up the other phone."

Burton weighed his options. He was not sure there was enough time to drive back to town, buy the tent and supplies, and return to Seb's camp. But the other two choices felt all wrong: go to the bed and breakfast, or spend the night in the crappy motel. They could, he supposed, drive back to Massachusetts.

"I see where you're going with this," Maddy said. "Diminishing the chance he panics, and runs again." She paused. "Can you check in with me tomorrow? Maybe from Skeet's house if your phone's not working?"

Burton expected a long dialogue with methodical Maddy. Not such quick agreement with his spontaneous camping plan. He looked down and noticed he had unconsciously pushed the jeep up to a rather high speed.

"I'm not sure Matt, Skeet, wants to see Seb," Maddy said. "But if I don't hear from you, I will be calling him and his parents. And the police."

"We'll check in with you. Phillip has the GPS coordinates for the campsite, too."

Seb flinched when Burton said this.

The sun was almost down by the time Burton parked the jeep in the same spot he had parked before meeting Skeet at the spring. Seb removed his bike, full of gear, from the jeep. They headed into the woods, with Seb in the lead, pushing his bike beside him.

When they arrived at the camp site, Seb set up his tent and got inside. He either did not care if the bear bag got torn apart by animals or assumed Burton would hoist it up a tree, which he did.

❧

It was not a dream. Burton was at a campfire with his son.

Seb lifted one end of the branch over the fire and used a rag to slide the pot off.

"Licorice tea," he said. "Sort of." He poured steaming liquid from the pot into two metal cups. There was a speck of friendliness in his voice, only enough to communicate, "I might not hate you but don't make me talk yet."

"Smells good," Burton said.

"It's the only backwoods recipe I know. The only edible one."

Burton had heard about Seb's misadventure with the root, but he took the cup in solidarity. The drink resembled green tea and tasted like a minty licorice. It was actually quite good. Not the "best you can do in the woods" flavor he expected.

They ate blueberries and trail mix and stared at the flames in the pit.

"If you want to meditate," Burton said, "go ahead. I'll do the same."

"Okay, we can meditate."

Seb got up and started to dig through one of the big bags from the tree. He removed a laminated map and a compass.

"I've got a good place for meditation."

After walking side by side for a long time without speaking, Seb and Burton came to a wall of shoulder-high grass. Seb turned, following alongside the grass and suddenly turned again, onto a path on a narrow ridge of raised earth. The only thing they could see besides grass was the wide crown of a tree ahead of them and the branchless tips of a dozen or so dead trees in the distance. They were heading towards a bog.

Seb stopped and Burton bumped into him. At their feet lay the dark water of the bog. Fluorescent green dots of duckweed rolled in time with the slow current underneath. Nearby, a large swath of grass lay on its side, having taken the brunt of the wind.

The tree they had been walking towards turned out to be a double-trunk birch. From the bare earth in front of it, Burton could see this was a favorite spot. He could see why. Hidden and quiet it offered something flat to lean against, and the bog-world to watch.

"Hey, Elephant Legs," Seb said to the birch. He lowered himself to the ground and leaned against the smoky-white bark of one of the tree's two trunks.

Before Burton could take his place against the other of the tree's trunks, Seb tossed him a flat, floppy square of plastic.

"It's self-inflating. Just open the valve."

With this cushion under him, Burton thought he might be able to sit in this spot for a long time, as Seb had undoubtedly done before.

He had not meditated in years. Not since he and Maddy went to that poetry festival. They tried to keep serious faces as the group was instructed to sit on grass full of acorns. The only thing he could remember was, "Focus on your breath."

To un-focus on what was before him, though, would be a shame. The greens and browns and sounds and smells and gust-borne wrinkles spreading across the bog. The bullfrog croaking. The high-pitched chorus of unseen insects.

A gray bird with a blue stripe on its wing shot past, skimming the water just in front of them. It dipped up and down, almost touching its reflection. Just before it ran into a stand of reeds, the wings flashed, and the bird zipped upwards, and sped off.

Burton's eyes lingered on the place in the sky where the bird had disappeared until he noticed, in the periphery of his vision, a massive brown blotch. He lowered his eyes to see, on the other shore of the bog, a huge, hornless deer. No. A moose. He leaned over to tap Seb's shoulder. Seb opened his eyes and followed where Burton pointed.

The animal, even at fifty feet away, looked too big. It would be more plausible as a statue in front of a general store. A store which had been swallowed by the bog. For a moment, the moose did nothing to dispel this image. Then it bent a knee and lifted a hoof. The hoof descended slowly, never pausing, into the water, revealing the animal's confidence in its ability to stand on the invisible, and certainly soft, bottom of the bog.

Her head and neck stretched forward. The long face sunk below the surface. She removed it and blinked while water streamed out of her mouth and over her whiskers.

A miniature version of herself stepped into view, thinner, with more leg than seemed practical. The calf began to see-saw its body into the water, splashing, and stopping when its belly became submerged.

"I've never seen them before," Seb whispered.

The animals chewed and ignored them.

⁊⁊⁊

Burton thought for sure they were lost on the way back from the swamp with the moose and calf. There were no trail markers. Seb did not seem to be paying much attention to where they were going. Only when they came to the dirt road with the white rock near the spring did Burton relax. Seb had to know his way back to the camp from there.

Now they could talk. It would be easier to talk while they were

305

walking. No need to look at one another.

"Would you want to stay in this place, if you could?" Burton kept his gaze to the roots and pine needles on the forest floor.

"I can't stay here."

There was no need to discuss the reasons. They both knew what they were: winter, trespassing, the law, worried parents.

"I know it's been hard," Burton said. "Very, very hard. But I think, together, we can figure out a way to make our home feel safe for you again. No miracles, of course, but something that works? Something creative?"

They walked for nearly a minute before Seb responded. "I'm not being stubborn. It's just that there's nothing you can do. I can't live back there any more. Being there makes me not want to live. But it doesn't have anything to do with you. Maybe I should never have mentioned the article you wrote. It's not because of you or your article. It's because of the truth."

Burton nodded. "But one thing all of us do, all animals, including humans, is adapt."

"Adapt to what? How crazy we are?"

"I—"

"But you're not expecting me to adapt out here. A fourteen-year old can't make it on his own, right?"

"You might survive. You've shown you're pretty resourceful. But I believe, I really believe, it would not be good for you to be without your family at this stage of your life. It's also possible you would not survive."

"It's been weeks," Seb said, his voice tinged with bitterness. "And that place—"

"Our home?" Burton asked.

"It scares me more than ever."

The coldness in Seb's voice reminded Burton of his father in the days before he died. His father's attitude at that point seemed to be: *I've already let go, don't pull me back and make me live through letting go again.*

Seb was shutting down. Maybe he had already shut down. The purpose of his elaborate scheme of emails and videos was to tell his family he was letting them go. Seb's fear that his family would not let him go was accurate, but what he did not understand was that it did not have to be the nightmare he envisioned. They would figure something out.

Burton was about to broach that subject, when Seb spoke.

"When I came here, the only thing I hoped for was to stop going crazy. To at least not be reminded all the time that global warming was happening. I stopped reading things on the internet but I still saw all the busses at school, parked around the circle, shooting out carbon dioxide, when they could have turned their engines off, and all the stores full of junk, and the cruise ship advertisements on the TV. Those really got me. They put a whole city on a boat and then push it around the ocean while these gigantic smoke stacks shoot out black smoke. I mean, the warm ocean and the warm weather and the palm trees and you want to eat at the same restaurants and shop at the same shopping malls you have at home?"

Seb pulled a dead branch from a pine and snapped it in half. He threw it aside and glanced over at Burton. Their eyes met, and the look in Seb's eyes scared him.

"I started to feel good," Seb continued. "I didn't expect that. It made me feel guilty because you guys were going through hell, but it was such a relief. Then I told myself, you gave birth to me and you knew what you were getting me into. So I let myself have my time up here. There's so much nature. The animals and the plants, they made sense. I don't know. I think it just calmed me down.

"After a while, I started writing. I really didn't plan on writing much. The crazy thing is... Don't laugh. I wrote a manifesto."

Burton nodded so Seb knew he did not think this was laughable.

"It started out at first as a website."

"A website you made in the woods?"

"Yeah, a website in the woods. In my head."

Seb did not smile but the words came out with a bit of a laugh behind them. Just a bit.

Burton waited for his son to continue. It seemed he had not expected to be talking about the manifesto just yet.

"I ended up writing a manifesto but it started out as a website. The address of the website was going to be: *The Ugly World of Stupid Humans*." Seb paused. "*Dot-com*. At the top of the page it was going to say, *I guess maybe climate change will take care of things since the world looked better before we showed up to ugly it with strip malls, stink it up, make it poisonous, and fill it with the ugly noise of our machines. And then change the atmosphere until eventually it gets too hot and nothing will grow.*"

Burton thought about this for a few seconds. "I get you. But don't forget, without civilization, you have to worry about being eaten by wolves. That used to stress the old cave man a lot, you know."

"I think I'd rather be eaten by a wolf."

This was easy for a fourteen-year old to say. There would come a day, though, when wandering the forest would not be enough for him. He would go into the ugly city. Not just because of hormones. Society. Possibly, too, for comforts and distractions. Seb loved his computers, after all.

"Some people prefer cities, you know," Burton said. He had been looking at Seb and switched his eyes back to the ground, to lessen the accusation. "You won't win those people over by promising a life in the woods. Some of them hate the woods. I also think that cities might be more efficient. For things like food distribution and energy. Besides, there are beautiful cities. You've said so yourself about Boston, looking over the Charles at night."

"I know." Seb's voice had, until then, been growing stronger. Here it sounded rather weak. "Anyway, I ditched the website. It was over the top. Sometimes I think the problem is not the world or people. It's me and my brain. I'm just too sensitive for this world. And there isn't any other world. Or any other brain."

"Oh, no. You've got a champion brain. Yes, you're sensitive. That's real. But that's something we can help you with, too. Avoiding all people by living in the woods...I'm not sure how long that is going to work for you. If it's even possible."

Except for the time their eyes met at the very beginning of this conversation, Seb was not looking at Burton. He did not look in his father's direction at all. Instead, he kept his eyes focused on the ground right in front of him, as though he needed to take great care where he placed his feet, although the terrain was flat and soft with a layer of pine needles.

"I know I need people," Seb said, shaking his head. "I know cities are probably the greenest option, if you do it right." He sighed. "I just don't think I can handle all that...all those people and their stuff. Not right now. People confuse me too much. Remind me of too much."

Their feet crunched on pine needles. Burton waited for Seb to continue, watching him in the periphery of his vision.

"I couldn't stop writing. I did another manifesto. A real one, not just a sentence and a name for a website."

Seb looked up. Without altering their pace, he pointed a finger to the left of a tree with a trunk as wide as a barrel and covered with scars. A landmark, apparently. Burton followed Seb down a row of evenly spaced trees stretching out diagonally to the left of the big tree.

"Does anybody need a pineapple?" Seb asked.

Burton assumed this was rhetorical, and said nothing.

"That's the name of the manifesto. Does Anybody Need a Pineapple?"

Seb swung his backpack around and zipped it open. He dug through it, apparently looking for what he had written. He zipped it up without having taken anything out.

"It's up in the tree. I pretty much know the whole thing by heart. Besides, it's a manifesto with an asterisk."

"Does anybody need to eat a pineapple with an asterisk." Burton gave Seb a glance and a half smile. He could not tell if Seb noticed.

His son put the pack back on. He resumed walking, a little faster now. "The title's goofy, I know." He kept his eyes cast down. "I think it might sound too much like a joke. It's not a joke."

"You can always change the title. Will you tell me? What the manifesto says?"

Seb lifted his head to stare before them as they walked. He seemed to be trying to remember his manifesto.

"Just so you know, the asterisk means some of the examples I give might be wrong. I'm in the woods without a library or a scientist.

"Humans survived on Earth for a long time without eating pineapples. A few people need them, wherever they are, wherever pineapples come from, so they can go on eating them. Maybe they grow in California now. See why I need an asterisk?"

Seb paused and used his hand to wipe sweat off the back of his neck. He rubbed it into his shorts.

"We're so spoiled. We think we need and deserve all the stuff we have. Pineapples and a new phone every year from halfway around the world. A hundred other things. Filling up our houses with stuff that never gets used. Meanwhile the world is getting sick. Right now. For what?

"It's not just pineapples. I noticed the apples at the store were from New Zealand. They had to come 10,000 miles on a ship. There are probably other kids who think we're out of control. Maybe a lot of us are getting freaked out. I guess they are better at hiding it than me. Maybe they really trust whoever runs the world? I guess they do. I think you're allowed to do that when you're a kid.

"Not me. I think we are in real trouble. We have this huge problem and still the only thing that happens is blaming the president or the Democrats or the Republicans or the atheists.

"Then there's people like Grandma Rosa, who told me to pray. It helps that she loves me and is trying to help me, and praying might help me survive feeling crazy for a while, but I don't think it's going to do anything about what's making me upset in the first place. Don't you think she should ask me to help God instead of asking God to clean up our mess?"

Seb was walking even faster now, feet flopping on the pine needles, sucking in breaths between sentences.

"Ajahn Wattana is such a great person. I don't have my emails but I remember a lot of the things he said, and that really helped me write the manifesto. He helped me." Seb threw his arms out to the side. "And I screwed him over."

He shook his head a couple of times, trudging ahead. Burton had to increase his pace yet again to keep up with him.

"One of the things the Ajahn used to talk a lot about was balance. I realized what messed me up the most was that things seem so out of balance. Why don't people take just what they need? They could even take more than they needed if it didn't put the planet out of balance. Balance ourselves! Come on! What a bunch of ass wipes!

"I know if people hear me say we have to balance ourselves they're going to say we have to balance our budgets first. Sorry, but do both. Figure it out. It *is* possible. I don't believe any of them. Governments, companies, even the charities or whatever they're called. They can balance their budgets *and* deal with this. I think some of them are trying but they have to try harder. We waited long enough. We have to force them. Make a big stink and not leave them alone."

Seb took a couple of deep breaths before continuing.

"So," he continued, "the manifesto calls for a strike."

"When I'm ready, I'm going to get people to join me on this strike. We're gonna say no. No more. You got enough. We're sitting in the road and that truck with your fifth television set is not getting through.

"To the people that say 'it's a free country and I'll pollute all I want,' I say: 'I'm at war with you. I'm not letting you do that to me. I'm not letting you go around saying we can't do better because we'll go out of business.'"

Seb, deep in thought, continued to stare at the ground ahead of him, and Burton began to wonder if he had lapsed into automatic pilot. If they got lost, so be it. Burton could not interrupt what was happening.

"I'm with you," he said. "I am definitely with you. Maybe this is where I could help, with some strategy I've learned the hard way from living longer and making mistakes. If you're saying no pineapples, you're probably saying no to a lot of other things that are imported. Like coffee. We've got to have a really good plan if we're going to try to take coffee away from people."

"Coffee?" Seb barked. "So what? What do I care about coffee? Did people live without coffee for like forever, until they brought it over from Africa or wherever. If you want coffee, show me how to do it and keep the world in balance.

"And I say no to out-of-touch people making plastic messes like babies throwing food around their highchairs. No more air that makes you sick. Not when it doesn't have to be that way.

"How about this?" his son was yelling now. "Let's be conservative! I'm not the first person to say that, but it's true. There's no backup planet. I can't, I really, really can't, understand why we don't try as hard as we possibly can to make sure we don't destroy our world."

Burton's son had taken on so many difficult thoughts for a boy his age. And then kept them inside. It was awful for a father to hear but at least it was coming out.

"The manifesto says two things have to happen," Seb shouted. "First: nobody, no way, don't you have kids unless you can explain what is going on. And second: if you believe there is even a small chance we are ruining this world, stop right now! Find a way to live that makes sense! Find a way to make money, to feed people, to have a good time. You can even have your pineapples if you can do it without ruining the world.

"Pineapples or balance? Stupid! I'm going to freaking take your pineapples away from you until we get balance."

Burton was a couple of steps past Seb when he realized Seb had stopped moving. He turned back to see his son squatting with his head between his knees and his arms around his shins. Burton ran over and knelt beside him. He put his arms around Seb and rested his cheek on his son's back. He could feel Seb's body shaking.

Seb flinched and jerked his arm back, pushing his father's arm off.

"Why did you have me?" Seb kept his eyes towards the ground. "If the world didn't care about future generations, why did you have me? Why did you do this to me, when you knew?"

Seb closed his eyes. He sunk closer to the ground. Burton put his arm around him. Seb did not push him away.

His son began to sob. Burton's body absorbed every sob. He wanted to answer Seb's questions but he knew no answers. All he could do was squeeze his son tighter.

They crouched for several minutes, until the sobs dissipated and Seb's breathing became slower. His body started to lean heavily against Burton's arms. For a moment Burton did not know what Seb was doing until he felt him slide slowly through his arms to lie on the ground.

CHAPTER TWENTY-NINE

THE YOWLING WIND

THE BOY STARED AT THE GREAT MOUNTAIN with the stone pyramid on top. Cracked stone, nothing but stone, sloping down until there were a few hedges holding on for life. Tumbled pieces of the mountain, blocks and sharp chunks, lay in piles on lower ledges still above the tree line. Future avalanches.

This rock extended a long way in several directions until it finally went down below the pine trees. You could not really understand how huge the mountain actually was, because most of it was buried by trees, just like most of an iceberg is hidden by water.

Any Martian who landed on that stone pyramid, with only pine trees and lakes to see, would know nothing of humans, would not know a human ever existed.

The boy took a red ski hat from his pocket and pulled it over his ears. He slid back deeper into the crevice. The wind yowled around him, just like on Mars.

❧

Seb was shivering on the forest floor when he woke up some hours after spewing out his manifesto, collapsing, and sobbing in his father's arms. He did not know how long he had been sleeping but in the mountains of Maine, even in the summertime, it got cold fast when the sun went down. As it turned out, this first day with his father in his corner of the forest, his camp, the little world he had discovered and explored, was to be the only day they spent there together.

He remembered the pine needles under his back and his father looking down at him. How his father leaned forward and kissed him on the forehead. At that moment, Seb felt thoroughly embarrassed and disgusted with himself.

They were back in Massachusetts not long after midnight that same evening.

His mother and sister were in the foyer to greet them. They hugged all at once, the four of them. His mother and sister blubbered. Seb did not cry, but he probably would have, had he not cried so hard only hours before, in the forest with his father.

The next day, his parents had only one thing to say: he could talk to them if and when he felt ready.

He told them not to worry if he slept a lot.

Nobody in the family did much his first few days home. It was still summer break. Frisbee in the back yard. Yard work. Movies on TV. Seb was around, but mostly sat and watched. Otherwise, he was in his room sleeping.

When, a few days after coming home, his father looked him in the eyes and said he did not think the things Seb spoke of in his emails were the product of any psychological problem, Seb knew he was about to visit a psychiatrist. His mother said that his concerns were very understandable. They asked if he would go see a psychiatrist. He felt he owed them this, although he did not like the idea at all.

They took him to a Doctor Kelly in Cambridge. Then to a Doctor Coots in downtown Boston for a second opinion. Both doctors encouraged Seb to pour out his story, the whole thing, starting with the first time he felt trapped. He told them everything, and caught himself being fascinated, almost proud, by what he heard himself saying. How he betrayed a monk, tortured his family, had a nervous breakdown and passed out with his face in pine needles.

Each doctor reserved the last ten minutes of the session to say the same thing: he was a fine, smart young man. Growing up was difficult and perhaps more stressful than ever before. And he should take pills.

Seb liked Dr. Coots more.

The first thing Dr. Coots said to him was, "There's nothing wrong with you. Except that you think there's something wrong with you."

So Seb agreed to see him again. The second time they met, the doctor assured Seb that the kind of pills he was talking about would make him no less aware of the world and could actually make it easier to meet the challenges of life. It did not mean that Seb would have to take them forever. Seb came to the conclusion that if the world was as mixed up as he believed it was, pills were not going to be strong enough to prevent him from understanding what he needed to understand. So he took pills.

He had been feeling like a zombie when his parents brought him back from Maine and he felt like a zombie after he took the pills. He really did try to do things differently, though. He admitted to his parents that he felt like a zombie. He told them this was a lot better than the panic. His parents said they were really happy about that. If he felt like a zombie for a long time, then maybe they might have to try something different.

After several tolerable, sometimes enjoyable days as a zombie, a rather big fact started to bother him. School was only a few weeks away. The students must have heard about him. He told his parents about this worry. His mother said they might want to consider another school.

That night, he had trouble falling asleep for the first time since he came home. The panic, he realized, could come back. It might actually already be worming its way in. He did not tell his parents.

≈≈≈

Wind whistled around the boy in the crevice. He watched the pointed tops of the pines as they swayed and how nothing moved on the bare rock mountain peak across the valley.

Another boy appeared in front of him with the hood of his sweatshirt pulled tight to his head.

"No garbage, no art, no pizza, no bikes, no people." The boy in the crevice yelled at this other boy, over the noise of the wind. "Is that what I wanted?"

The other boy said, "Don't go crazy on me again. Besides, I heard there's a guy who makes bikes out of cardboard. Get a grip."

With that, the other boy was off.

Even with the shelter of the crevice and the red ski hat, the boy was soon cold. He placed his hands against the sides of the crevice and lifted himself up. Sage-lichen came loose in his fingers. Wind lifted the dust and flakes and tossed them in his face.

Seb sat in one armchair and Dr. Coots sat in the other, facing him. This was their third visit. He did not want to be looking at the psychiatrist for a whole hour but there seemed to be no other choice.

"How has it been, being home?" Dr. Coots asked.

"Okay. I knew it would be weird at first. It's definitely better than before I...ran away. I was starting to think what happened was over but now I'm not sure."

"Are you worried about school coming up?"

"Well, yeah. Everybody knows. I feel like a freak."

"I think your parents and the school are—"

"That's not really it."

Seb shifted his eyes from the doctor to an owl sculpture on the book-shelf next to the doctor's chair. It was made of metal parts that looked like they came from a junk yard, in a good way. He hoped the doctor would let him keep looking in the direction of the owl while he spoke.

"Remember how last time I said I used to tell my parents every-thing? I still think that way. This idea pops into my head and I'm about to go down to the kitchen to tell them about it. Because my parents are cool. It used to make me feel smart, too, that I had these brilliant ideas.

"But now I always end up thinking it's a bad idea to say anything to them. They're worried enough. If I say more, I don't know what they'll do. Honestly, it just seems better for them to not know things. You have a lot of patients my age. The less our parents know, the more we can get away with, right?"

"Some times," Dr. Coots said, smiling. "What do you mean, 'say more' to your parents?"

"After the all the videos and talking, I'm still not sure my parents understand why I left. Nobody else understands. My friends, teachers, most of the people making comments on YouTube. They think some-thing bad must have happened to me. Something I'm not telling them. Like abuse. It doesn't make sense that a kid would scare his parents like that and give up everything, just because of global warming. I think that's because they don't really know seriously bad global warm-ing is. They have no idea that they're screwing up."

Seb was getting upset. He had not gotten upset in a while, even though he had been home more than a week. That was interesting. Home for a whole week without getting upset. Maybe it was because of the drugs and Dr. Coots. Or maybe he was just tired and allowing his brain a vacation.

He glanced at Dr. Coots for a moment and immediately felt nervous again. He went back to looking at the owl sculpture on the shelf before he continued talking.

"There are some people who do know how scary global warming is. They seem to be doing okay. At least not abandoning their lives. Maybe some of them get drunk, but they go to work. But I can't do that.

"I guess that's what I'm not telling my parents. I'm thinking that I might start to go crazy again. That there's nothing they can do to help me. Nothing really. I can't tell them that."

Dr. Coots seemed to be waiting for Seb to look at him before he responded, so Seb did look at him, but not in the eyes. He looked at the doctor's shoulder. He might get away with that.

"You're crazy," Dr. Coots said, with a little smile, "but it's healthy, and unavoidable in this case. When grown people—the ones you are supposed to learn from—don't act rationally, your mind blames itself. It's still used to thinking a kid can't know better than an adult. You would think grown people confronted by even the possibility of global warming would get the facts, right?"

Seb was not sure if he was supposed to answer. He nodded just in case.

"That's hard for a kid your age to deal with, but it is what it is. The good news is that you've done a lot of the hard work already. You lived through this disorienting experience. You had some bad anxiety. You panicked and put yourself in danger. But that was temporary.

"My patients are all young. That's my specialty. At some point we usually talk about the first time a kid sees an adult struggling. It often comes as a shock. It's scary because you have been counting on them to be strong and capable. When it's really scary, they panic and do what you might call crazy things.

"In your case, it's more complicated. You're right in there with them, dealing with one of the most difficult things adults have ever had to deal with. I'm a fifty-year-old man whose job is to understand people and it's been a challenge for me to understand the way the people react to global warming. You're one of the people whose reaction I actually understand."

Dr. Coots glanced over at the clock.

"That was a lot. I should have timed this better but we're almost at the hour and I've got someone waiting. We're going to see each other the day after tomorrow but I can fit you in sooner if you want."

Seb thought about it for a second. "It's okay. I actually feel better."

"Great. You can also call me whenever, if you feel like it. There's one more thing, though. Something I'd like you to try.

"You can have your secrets and you can sneak around some, but check in with your parents every day. Just a check-in. If you have something really embarrassing on your mind, don't tell them. Pick something else. Can you do that?"

"I think so."

"It might help you break out of keeping thoughts to yourself that are hard to share. Think of it as an experiment your wise psychiatrist came up with. I'm not asking you to give up your private thoughts. They know you want your privacy.

"You can even bail out on this plan if you want, but I'd like you to keep talking to me. I can't make you do anything, so it's totally safe to talk to me."

A few hours after that appointment with Dr. Coots, Seb knocked on his parents' bedroom door. His father opened it.

"Come on in."

He could hear his mother opening and closing drawers in the master bathroom. It looked like they were getting ready to go somewhere. His mother came out of the bathroom in a bathrobe with a towel wrapped around her head. His father tucked his shirt in. Seb thought it would look better hanging out.

"No tuck and no belt," Seb said.

"Someday, maybe," his father said, with a half grin. "Should I sit here with your Mom?"

"Okay."

Seb felt a little weird standing there with both of them sitting on the bed, watching him.

"So, I only came to say I realize I used to go around here acting like I was more intelligent than you. And that sometimes I still kind of believe it."

His father's smile grew bigger. "We've known that for years."

"You may have a bigger brain than we do," his mother said, "but less practice using it."

"That's all," Seb said.

"Okay," his parents said in unison.

"I'm going outside to rest my intelligent head."

"We're going to dinner with the Becks," his mother said. "You okay?"

"Uh huh."

Seb went out to the patio and sat in the lounge chair. He watched red finches hop between the coneflowers that grew in the middle of the ivy out back.

The next thing he knew, the aggravating questions came flooding into his mind. The questions had probably been waiting until after he had done his assignment for Dr. Coots (talking to his parents) and they left him home, alone.

"Am I a crazy, selfish, monster? A massive wimp? Am I smart like Dr. Coots says? Or just too sensitive? What am I supposed to be doing? Maybe I just suck at life."

A clacking sound interrupted his train of thought.

Jessica came around the back of the house, riding her bike on the grass. The clacking was a bent fender. It had been bent for months. She was clueless about that kind of thing.

"Hey," Seb said.

Jessica let the bike drop to the ground. She walked towards him, adjusting the shoulder strap of the bathing suit she was wearing under her jeans shorts.

"No swimming?" Seb asked.

Jessica stared at him for a moment. "Nicky wasn't home."

Seb stared back. "Why are you looking at me like that?"

"You didn't even get punished."

"I know. They don't want me to leave again."

"Yeah, well things were pretty cruddy around here."

"I'm sorry."

His sister climbed onto the lounge chair next to him. "You didn't even watch the videos." She gave him her favorite look, the one that said she really had better things to do. He had overhead enough of her conversations to know she took great satisfaction at already being cooler than her older brother.

"You don't want to hear any more about that do, you? I really am sorry."

After a couple of long talks with his parents, the three of them had done their best to explain to Jessica what happened. She said she knew already.

"Were you scared?"

This question surprised him. His sister seemed genuinely concerned. She had been upset, of course, when he first got home, but she seemed to get over it quickly. Seb realized this might have been wishful thinking on his part. Just because she pretended to be okay did not mean he hadn't hurt her pretty badly.

"It was definitely scary some times. I would be in my tent and it would be incredibly dark and I would think I am *so* stuck. Then I told myself it didn't matter, I had to get up and run the hell out of there.

Except I didn't because I would only end up in some other part of the woods in the dark without a tent or any of my stuff. Being eaten by mosquitos and ticks. So I laid there and it was terrible but eventually it just went away. A couple times I dreamt that a bear was licking my toes and I woke up covered in sweat. After the first few nights, though, I was so tired I just fell asleep."

His sister was staring at him now, probably trying to picture what he had just described.

"I can't think of a suckier thing to do," she said.

"What thing?"

"I don't know. Walk around the woods for a month."

Seb just smiled at her.

"Boring with a capital B."

"I did get bored, even a tree-hugger like me. And lonely."

"Dad says you could have easily died out there. I thought he meant bears but he meant you could get lost and starve, it's so big."

"That definitely could've happened. I'm a genius and all but..."

"What?"

"I didn't know what I was doing and then I did it alone, with nobody knowing where I was. They found a lady's body a half a mile from the A.T. last year. Her journal said she just went a little off the trail to go to the bathroom and got lost. There was a huge search party and they didn't find the body for two years. I could've figured out a better way to go somewhere peaceful. Mom and Dad would've let me."

His sister narrowed her eyes at him. "Are you better now?"

"I think so." This was basically a lie, but what else could he say?

"My friends think you're going to be put in a...hospital."

"What do you think?"

"I think maybe. You're not the same."

"The doctor says I'm mentally exhausted."

Jessica scrunched up her nose. She did this when she did not understand what had been said.

"I really am sorry for what I did to you guys."

Jessica bent her legs so she could lay on her side, facing him. "I guess. But I think you might do it again. Was it really better there, than here?"

Seb sighed. "I don't think I can explain it."

Jessica pulled an ant off of her arm and tossed it away. "Send me an email."

Seb glanced over and saw that she was laughing silently.

"Here's an instant message." He lifted his cup of water and flung it onto her.

She screamed and wriggled on the chair.

⚜

The boy left the shelter of the crevice and walked across the stone outcropping. He slipped between two pines and entered the forest, leaving the wind behind.

He took off the red ski hat. As he was stuffing it into his back pocket, his attention was drawn to a noise up ahead. It was a man, fighting his way through a thicket. Strange, because there was a well-worn path only a few yards from the man, the same path on which the boy walked now.

Dark skinned, wearing a white, v-neck sweater, this man looked a lot like a deer. He was lucky it was not yet hunting season, although the commotion he was making, breaking branches out of his way, probably have saved him.

The man saw the boy and immediately veered his way.

"This place is a bit scary," he said. "I think I saw a wolf."

"I've never seen a wolf. Anywhere. What are you doing out here by yourself?"

The man pulled a black device from his pocket. "I have satellite imagery and GPS coordinates."

"But you know you've got to bring a compass and a map, too, in case that thing stops working."

The man patted a bulge in his pocket. "I have them but I may as well have brought nothing."

"You need a lesson. Tonight."

"So warm today. I'm sweating from walking the dirt road in the sun. Why are you wearing a sweatshirt?"

"I was on top of the mountain."

"There is the brook! Watch this!" In a series of twisting movements that would have injured most people, the man pulled the sweater over his head and flung it away. It landed in some ferns. He pulled his boots off without untying them and hopped out of his pants and underwear. His naked, brown body took off towards the stream.

"No! Phillip. No! It's—."

Splash.

"Freezing."

Phillip's body shot straight out of the water like a supposedly drowned killer making his last attack at the end of a horror movie. A scream followed.

The boy ran for Phillip's backpack. He found a towel inside under a bag of dried apricots. He pulled the towel out, ejecting the fruit and sending it flying.

Phillip snatched the towel. Shivering, hopping from foot to foot, and lifting his knees high, he rubbed the towel over his body.

⌘

After Phillip dried off and dressed, they began walking together. Wherever Phillip had been going, he decided to turn back and walk with Seb. The trail was wide enough for only one person and Phillip let him lead. He seemed to sense that Seb did not want to talk and they walked without speaking.

The world on top of the mountain, now that summer was fading, was such a strange combination of peaceful and awful. The green trees in the sun going on forever, the harshness of the wind. Which was it? Friendly or deadly? Not knowing stressed him out sometimes, but knowing everything would most likely make for a boring life.

He certainly never expected, after everything that happened, everything he had done, that his father would be the one to apologize.

On the tenth day after returning home, his mom and Jessica went to a movie, not trying very hard to disguise the fact that they were leaving Seb and his father alone. Grandma Rosa had gone home earlier that afternoon, after a big lunch prepared by Maddy. His father made a speech to thank her and they all raised glasses of ginger ale to give her a toast. Then they ate the slightly raw cake Jessica had baked.

Seb and his father watched the Sox game on the couch that night. The Sox were down by five runs when his father picked up the remote.

"Can I turn the game off? So we can talk?"

"Okay."

Seb thought they would talk again about school. The panic swelled up.

"I have to apologize," his father said. "I never apologized."

Seb shook his head. "I'm too sensitive. If it wasn't your newsletter, something else would have freaked me out."

His father shook his head in return. "It didn't have to be that way. You know, I realized I wasn't much older than you when I wrote that article. Young enough to think I knew more than I did. Irresponsible with my anger."

"It helped me. To finally wake up. And what you said about having children? You were scared. You were so scared for the kids of the future. Your kids. Me. Isn't that why you wrote the article? To wake people up? It hurt, but—"

His father held his hand up, trying to get a word in. "That's just it—"

"It doesn't matter! So what if I hurt? Life hurts."

"It matters because your welfare, and your pain, is going to be the most important thing to me, always. Always."

"I know."

"I'm not sure you knew that right after you read my article."

His father had a strange look on his face. Not blinking at him, like he was going to get emotional. It made Seb feel a little squirmy.

"You are not a mistake, Seb. It is not a mistake for you to be here in this world. Far from it. You are a gift to this world. I gave the world a gift."

This took Seb by surprise and the next thing he knew, he was feeling choked up. He tried not to cry. Then he felt annoyed for giving in to the *guys don't cry* thing, but the impulse had passed.

"Okay." He shrugged.

"Does that seem like a big responsibility?"

"I don't know. Not really. Maybe Jess will grow up and finally do something helpful."

His father laughed and then they were both laughing.

"There's something else," his father said, when they had stopped laughing and were sitting there with stupid grins on their faces. "When I wrote that article, I couldn't imagine bringing a child into a world that had pain and danger. But to prevent your child from experiencing pain or danger is to never give them a chance to live."

"You didn't know your kid was going to give the pain and danger back to you, did you?" Seb grinned.

"Actually, that, I expected."

His father's smile went away, then. He did not look unhappy but he was staring at Seb, in kind of a weird, serious way.

"You need to know," his father said, still with that serious look. "No matter what, even if we're deciding the fate of humanity, you will still matter most to me. You and your sister and your mom. Being your father is a part of me. It's not everything that I am. I'm a citizen of the world. I have to take what I need and not more. And to care about people I am never going to meet. That's my religion, if you will. But you and Jess and Mom will always be number one. I can't help it." Here, his father broke out into a smile again, an even goofier one than before.

Then his father sat more upright and stretched his arms towards the ceiling. Like you do when you realize how you have been keeping your body too tight. Like during an intense talk.

"You know what's also true?" his father said. He stopped stretching and let his arms fall to his sides.

"What?"

"You're a good guy. And a brave guy."

"If you say so."

His father lunged forward and tackled him.

"I say so."

CHAPTER THIRTY

Find SEB

Seb laughed into his pillow. Phillip's clueless leap into the chilly brook. His scream. Hilarious.

He rolled onto his back. There was enough moonlight coming through the space between the curtains to see the paper he had taped to the wall. The only decoration in this bare, pine-paneled room.

"A souvenir from our 24 hours in the Maine woods," his father had said, handing him the paper, the night before Seb left home for a second time.

This paper on the wall was dirty and wrinkled from having been soaked, dried, and stuffed into a backpack.

When Seb woke up after having his meltdown on the forest floor, he and his father packed up camp. They stopped at the spring for water on the way back to his father's all-terrain monster. The sign Seb had hung on the rock wall by the spring was still there, but it looked different.

The words *Don't Find Seb* had been crossed out. Underneath, with multiple holes from where a pen had gone through the wet paper, were new words. *Dumb Bastard Found.*

Skeet had forgiven him. The first thing Seb did when he got to this room was put that dirty paper sign on the wall.

He was living in the Skeet family's old lodge, room number two, the one with no mice or leaks in the ceiling. It still smelled like a barn. Of course *Skeet* was not their real name but Seb amused himself by referring to them that way, to himself.

As the old pamphlet Skeet showed him said, his room was *Designed for the True Backwoods Experience.* It contained only two pieces of furniture, both made of pine. A twin bed and a dresser without a mirror. Paneling of a darker wood pattern covered the walls. The place did have its own bathroom, done entirely in light blue stick-on tile, including the floor. Even the toilet was blue. Only the tub and the ceiling were white.

Seb was pretty sure he did not deserve this. His parents should have sent him to military school. Not only did he scare them to death, Jessica said they had a huge fight and their mom left the house. The fight was about blaming each other for spoiling him or something like that. Their Dad had argued with Grandma Rosa, too.

His parents had also become more touchy-feely-lovey than normal. Cutting flowers from the garden. Kissing. It was embarrassing. Not really. It was nice. As long as they didn't act that way all the time. As long it was not fake.

He had been worried about his parents but more worried about himself, which made him feel like a selfish loser. Dr. Coots said adolescents had to think about themselves. It was programmed into them. Seb tried to believe this, except that none of the other kids he knew were doing what he was doing.

It was okay after they found him and brought him home but he always felt like it was not real. The cars and bad news and plastic crap were still around and he never knew when they might become too much, just like they had before.

The only reason he was not in military school, or locked inside a mental hospital, or worse, was the fact that he decided to tell on himself one night.

He decided to give his family the chance to help him. They already knew he was crazy, anyway. He didn't believe they could help him and he was pretty sure he would break their hearts again, but he gave them a chance.

It was midnight, a few weeks after he had been home.

He knocked on his parents' bedroom door.

"Yes?" His mother's voice asked. She sounded a little too cheerful, like she was afraid and trying to cover it up.

"I've started thinking again. Like I was before. Maybe I shouldn't do it alone."

Light appeared in the space under the door.

"Come in, hon."

He opened the door a crack. Myro used his jumbo hot dog body to push the door further open and slip into the room.

His parents were sitting upright in their bed, puffy-eyed. Myro clawed at the bedspread.

"Take the puppy out of here, all right?" His mother asked.

Seb scooped up Myro, set him on the hardwood floor, his claws clacking, and closed the door before he could get his nose in it again.

"You heard what I said? About thinking?"

"We did," his father said. "What's on your mind?"

His father looked like he was going to cry from happiness that he decided to talk to them.

Seb told them he could not stay in Massachusetts.

⚜

This is how it happened.

Maddy called Seb's school, the board of education, the Massachusetts Department of Elementary and Secondary Education, and the U.S. Department of Education. Seb, his mom and dad met with a whole team at the high school. The students knew everything. Seb's photo had been on the local news for weeks, and then there was the whole ruckus surrounding the YouTube videos.

It was his father's idea to contact colleges in Maine about the possibility of a research project. More than one professor had heard of Seb. Incredible.

They came up with an educational program that was part independent study and part traditional classes. The independent study part of Seb's program covered biology and social science. His main project for the semester was to do a report on the history of government and citizen action to protect the environment.

Credits for physical education and health would be earned if he emailed photos of himself hiking and did a report on the safety measures necessary for journeys in the deep woods. Journeys he was not allowed to make alone.

Skeet's mother had been born in Quebec and she would teach Seb French. For English, he had a pile of Twentieth-Century novels, each of which he would have to write about. Algebra II, he would get to experience through an online class.

One or both of his parents would come get him and bring him home every four weeks. He would stay with his family for a week and meet with teachers and take tests at school. And see Dr. Coots.

An environmental science professor, Judith Marie Smith, became part of the plan. She told him to call her J.M., not Dr. Smith. J.M. had a very active mind. She kept Seb and his parents on the speakerphone for an hour talking about getting serious about a carbon fee and dividend and building an advocacy group from the ground up.

Seb's project would dovetail perfectly with J.M.'s research into the effectiveness of new ways to *Get Done What Needs to Get Done*. That was the name of a book she wrote. Once a week, she would spend a night at the Skeet family lodge to serve as consultant and mentor for Seb's independent study project, paid for with money from her grant.

J.M. took Seb aside after they met in person and told him with a wink that part of her motivation was to experience the beautiful part of the country where he was staying. They could take hikes while she mentored him. He couldn't tell if she was serious.

One night during the time they were planning all this, Seb was in his bedroom, not sure if their wild plan was going to work, and not sure if he might still go crazy, when he heard a noise out on the patio. He was already in bed. He got up and looked through the screen of his window.

It was laughter. He could just barely see the top of his parents' heads. They were standing on the patio. Then his father began speaking. Seb's bedroom was pretty far from the patio and he would not have been able to hear if he was not standing at the window.

"We were never going to let him out of our sight and now he could be living in another state?"

"What were the other options?" his mother asked. "Heavier drugs?"

It was almost midnight. His parents were usually in bed by now.

"I don't know," his father said. "I've never been a parent before. What's Jessica going to think?"

"She's going to try to get something out of all this. But she's a homebody. She'll just stay here and torture us." Seb's mother paused for a moment. "We really do need to do something special for her, though. Seb's gotten all the attention for a while. We have to make that a priority."

His parents went quiet again. Seb could hear the ice in their glasses. That's how quiet it was that night. He knew he should not be listening but he couldn't stop himself.

A minute or so later his mother spoke again. "What do you think your parents would have done?"

"Punished me. Now that I think about it, they were not that much different than your mother. They provided a good home and if their kid didn't appreciate it, it was not their fault."

"Rosa once threatened me with Catholic school. I didn't want to be separated from my friends so I did what she said for a while. And got sneakier."

"We should probably give them a little more credit," his father said. "If my parents had a kid like Seb, they would've tried to understand him."

"Do you ever wonder what you would have done if what happened to Seb happened to you?" his mother asked. "If you learned the kind of things he learned at his age? I mean, we worried about nuclear weapons and nuclear power plants. But the climate stuff is not a possibility. It'll come to a bad end for sure if we don't get it together. Our response has been pretty baffling."

"Adults have probably always baffled kids," his father said. "Except now it's so easy to find the most awful information. How is anyone, especially a kid, supposed to put it in context? If I saw all that stuff, I would've been a lot more selfish than Seb. I would've gone out and had a good time."

Seb's parents got quiet again. He hoped they were done. This was getting serious. But his father started up again a few seconds later.

"I guess the real question is how to be a parent in this weird new world."

"With our unusual child."

His father let out a little laugh. "The way we parented him might not have made any difference. Seb was going to revolt against the world's b.s. anyway. We're certainly not the only parents worried how their kid is going to make it through adolescence."

"There's probably something we could have done differently," his mother said. "I'm not sure what, though. Sheltered him more? Is that possible? Maybe we did allow his busy brain to get too much information too soon, but how could we have stopped that? Home schooling? With no internet? Our kids would have hated us."

Suddenly, his father's tall body came into view, walking across the yard. If he had looked up he would have seen Seb in the window. He let his body drop, slipping on the hardwood floor as he fell out of sight. He waited there, hoping they had not heard him. After a minute, he stood up slowly. His father was back over by his mother. The way he was speaking, it sounded like he had not heard anything.

"Maybe our kids hating us would have been worth it," his father said. "At least Seb understands he's lucky to have made it out of the woods alive. And lucky we trust him again."

"I think we have to trust him." His mother made the same kind of little laugh his father made before, like it was something she should not be laughing about. "Principal Jordan doesn't trust him any more, that's for sure. Seb's lucky the superintendent is such a tree hugger."

Dr. Jordan, Seb's principal, used to like him, before he caused all this trouble. But the superintendent, a guy Seb never met before, seemed to get why Seb was so upset. And he was Dr. Jordan's boss.

He was about to stand up, to listen at the window again, when he heard his mother's voice. She sounded strange this time.

"So, I wanted to talk to you about something else, actually. I need to apologize. You may have been right. I probably was a little jealous of you and Seb. I don't know if that had anything to do with how I behaved, but it was not good that I couldn't control my temper when he was in such trouble."

Seb had no idea what his mother meant by jealous. Or her temper.

"I'm sorry I get so intense," she said. "The whole thing's left me with some serious doubts about myself."

"It shouldn't," his father said. "You saw what was happening to Jessica. To all of us. Were you supposed to be in love with Seb? It scares me to death to think of how much time I wasted on the wrong things. And then to throw it all in your face, at a time like that."

"You don't think you were right? That I get blinded by anger? That I'm too defensive because of my genes or my childhood?"

"I didn't say that."

"I think you did. Maybe not all at once. But we can talk about it another time. Seb's home. That's what's important right now."

"I was a disaster," his father said, kind of loudly. "I left you here to deal with reality while I was doing...I don't know what. Distracting myself like Seb, maybe. I take back everything I said. Don't pay any attention to it."

"That would be stupid. I shouldn't have apologized now. We can work on being better people another time. I really wanted to tell you something else. Just let me say it."

"Okay."

"You're not more responsible for what happened with Seb than me. So, it was your article Seb found. At least you wrote an article. What did I write? And Seb was reacting to something much bigger than what his parents did or didn't do. I think we handled this as well as anyone could have. Better than most."

His mother's voice faded out. Seb was not sure if she was whispering.

"Come here," his father said.

The chairs scraped on the patio. Seb smiled, thinking how Jessica would say they were being disgusting down there.

He left the window, lay down on his bed, and closed his eyes. It was weird to hear his parents talk about themselves like that.

Then he started laughing. Out loud. He put his hand over his mouth so his parents did not hear him through the open window.

Stupid, disgusting, hilarious human beings. Where had he gotten the idea that humans were smart and did the right thing? From adults who lied and hid things from you, he supposed. He should have stuck to doing brainless kid things.

He wondered if it would actually be better if kids knew from the beginning that everybody grew up to be stupid and disgusting. He had tears in his eyes from laughing into his hands. Why did he think any of this was funny?

At least people weren't boring. You wouldn't want to get out of bed if the whole world was controlled by Eagle Scouts. And they did have some good qualities, humans. They made the Appalachian Trail. He supposed animals, even rocks, and streams where you could take a bath, were better than humans but there was nothing he could do about that. It was a good thing he had an appointment with Dr. Coots the next morning.

Knowing about his appointment with Dr. Coots must have calmed him down because the next thing he knew, it was the next morning and his mother was knocking on the door. They had to leave the house in ten minutes for his appointment with the doctor.

Seb told Dr. Coots what he heard his parents say. How confusing it was to start laughing about how disappointing people were. Dr. Coots said it was probably a good thing that kids did not find out right away how infuriating and hilarious and strange humans could be. It was too much information.

Then Dr. Coots asked him if there was anything he did like about people. For some reason, Seb started crying really hard. For like ten minutes. He tried to talk and he couldn't.

"It's okay," Dr. Coots said. "You don't have to admit you like them."

The next day, Seb, his mom, dad, and Jessica went to spend the weekend at *Caitlin's Inn*. The place he went on his bike to watch all the videos for the first time. That nice, beautiful woman's в and в just up the road from Skeet's. His parents wanted to meet Skeet's parents before they would let him do the education program they had cooked up. They also wanted to make sure his mom and dad knew what they were getting into, including all the details about Seb running away. The Buddhists, the emails and videos, his secret camping spot, how he tried to run away again on his bike, having a psychiatrist. Mad about global warming. The whole deal.

If she had not gotten an invitation, his mother probably would have hinted around enough to get them invited to dinner at the Skeets. She wanted to make sure the food was okay. Fortunately, Mrs. Michaud invited them over for venison stew the very first night they got to Maine. That was their last name, Michaud. Seb continued to refer to them as the Skeets, but not out loud. Mr. Skeet, Mrs. Skeet, and Skeet. Only Skeet's brother was left at Larry. Larry, as Skeet had claimed, truly was a couch-lump.

The Michauds spent the last two weeks of August getting the lodge back into shape, with some money from Seb's parents to help.

They would never have gone for this plan, he was sure, if Phillip Geer didn't get involved. They loved Phillip. His father wanted to buy him a better car. One with a GPS in it.

Phillip got involved when Burton asked him to find out about internet options for doing homework and research where Skeet lived. They were surprised to learn that Seb's disappearance had affected Phillip profoundly. He had not been able to stop reading about the human impact on the planet and had joined a group that was showing the government what needed to be done. He only told Seb's parents about this after their son was safe and home. When Phillip said the words "Motha Uuuuth" over the speakerphone in his Boston-British accent, they tried not to laugh out loud.

Only one day later, Phillip provided information about internet options at Skeet's house and a proposal outlining other ways he wanted to help. This included living full-time at the Skeet family lodge. He wanted to put all his energy into caring for the planet. He could afford to do this with income from his internet detective agency, which he could run from his room in the lodge.

Everybody Seb cared about was helping. It was fun for them to come up there to see the hiking trails and the awesome mountains and forests and to be a part of his adventure. But they also wanted to do something about global warming.

Aunt Terrie was coming up to fix the other motel rooms for the Skeets. She was not charging except for the cost of materials and free lodging in one of the rooms while she was there. His father said it was too much time and lost income for Terrie. Seb's parents were already giving the Skeets money for his food and rent. But Terrie insisted.

Even the Ajahn was doing something. He sent Seb an email about a new program he was trying to get started in the Portsmouth schools. Loving-kindness meditations for the earth. Working with the school system had the Ajahn meditating even more on forgiveness and patience.

Seb had expected that being back in the woods was going to be what helped him the most. But what helped him most turned out to be working on the project with Phillip, Skeet, the very excitable Dr. J.M. Smith, his mom and dad. Even strangers on the internet.

⁂

Skeet suggested he and Seb build a retreat in the old greenhouse behind the row of hedge-apple trees in a far corner of the yard. Its cinder block and steel frame had survived the Maine winters, but a lot of the glass was cracked or gone. They replaced the missing panes with plywood for the time being.

The greenhouse was a huge mess. The two boys had to start by dragging four collapsed wooden tables out into the woods. The mounds of dirt covering the greenhouse's concrete floor had to be shoveled into a wheelbarrow and carted to the garden. Skeet's father let them have a pair of stuffed armchairs which had been in room number four, the room with the leaky roof. The chairs were covered with spotty mildew and smelled disgusting. Seb and Skeet scrubbed the chairs and left them in the sun to dry. Skeet's mom donated worn blankets to cover the bleach-stained fabric.

On a September afternoon, Skeet connected three orange extension cords and stretched them from the house to the greenhouse and plugged in his music player. Even though it was nearly October, the building was too warm to sit in until the sun stopped shining directly through the roof.

The boys leaned back in their blanket-covered armchairs for the first time, with guitar-band music playing in the background.

"We're still going to see that band in Bangor, right?" Skeet asked. "Percy's Brass Ass or something like that?"

"I can't. They're trusting me. I can't stay out all night with your pot-smoking brother."

"What I was going to say is that Phillip will take us. Besides, your parents are worried you're not going to have any fun anymore."

"Really? Phillip's going to drive? Then we should go for sure."

Skeet nodded. "Are you going to wind up staying in the woods your whole life?"

"I like having the excuse that I'm too young to know the answer to that. I feel good right now and I don't want to mess with it. I know I'm lucky I get to cool my head here."

"Are you, like, going to try to get everybody to start living in the woods?"

Seb shook his head. "No. No. Probably most people would hate living here. Dr. J.M. knows this stuff better than me, but we need people in cities. Cities are better for being green anyway. And somebody has to go talk to the politicians and force them to make sure polluting isn't free. And all the other reasons I can't remember."

After this exchange, the two boys just sat there bobbing their heads to the music and admiring the work they had done on the old greenhouse.

When a quiet song started to play, Skeet asked, "Your mother's coming for a whole week?"

"Yeah. Next Friday. She wants to help with the project and do some hiking."

"And then your whole family for Christmas. That'll be cool. Except for me getting stuck helping your Aunt fix up two more rooms."

"Jessica wants to see the otters."

She did not know Seb had not seen them yet himself.

"You're doing a lot more than you need to do for this school project, aren't you?"

Skeet kept staring out the grid of rectangular windows that made up the top half of the greenhouse walls, not looking to Seb for an answer, not even when Seb didn't answer right away.

"The homework is what I need to do to get an education. The project makes me feel good. Did you read what I gave you?"

"Some of it. I agree with the main idea. Taking care of this planet has to be number one. Which doesn't mean you can't still have a really good life."

"It's all about..." Seb felt a little childish prompting Skeet to say the word.

"Balance." Skeet jumped up from the chair and stood stiff. In a voice like a soldier's, he said, "Find Self/Environment Balance. Find SEB."

"Too cute maybe." Seb laughed. "But it hooks us in with everybody that was going back and forth on the YouTube pages. At least my name isn't Zach or something like that."

"Did I hear your mother got a lawyer? Isn't that expensive?"

"We're going to raise money to pay the lawyer. If not I think it's my

Christmas present for the next ten years. She wants to make sure my ass is covered."

"Your ass is exposed big time."

"The whole thing is exposed. It could get sabotaged or screwed up. None of us knows what we're doing."

Seb lifted a brown paper bag from the floor, the bottom half of it darkened by butter.

"Vous de popcorn?"

Skeet took the bag. "You're going to fail the French test. Too much time on that independent study. But really, what are you trying to do?" He put a handful of popcorn in his mouth and finished chewing before continuing. "How are you going to do it? Get people more balanced? Scare them?"

"I don't know. Maybe we should scare people more. We're working on it. I'm following some blogs, and reading piles of stuff J.M. is giving me. A lot more is happening, even since the time I read my Dad's article. I'm just not sure it's enough. If people really know how big a problem we have.

"There's this one blogger J.M. said I should follow. He has ideas that could really work but they're kind of complicated."

Seb took back the greasy bag of popcorn which Skeet still had sitting on his lap.

"Okay, so what's this blogger's big idea?" Skeet asked.

"Something about how it's not real capitalism or good capitalism to put your own company out of business by putting life out of business. This guy is really pro-USA. He says the U.S. is a country full of inventors and business, um, starter-uppers who can figure out what to do."

Skeet frowned. "I don't really understand capitalism."

"I don't either, but it's what we've got. I asked Dr. J.M. what we could do about people who won't let us make the changes we have to make to keep the earth healthy. I told her about my dream. People lined up on a sidewalk. The line went for miles and miles on the sidewalk from city to city to city. They were going to stay in the line until the government got serious. They had chairs for people with disabilities and even some beds.

"And in my dream the president of the U.S. had to get on TV every night and tell them what he did that day to deal with global warming.

"J.M. said I was right. Then she winked at me and said it can start anywhere."

"You got your work cut out for you," Skeet said. "I don't see people giving up watching their favorite TV shows to oppose anything."

"What about only watching half their TV shows?"

"Don't see it happening."

What Seb was trying to do was hard. He knew that. But he felt good. Sometimes he wondered if it was too good to be true, or too good to last.

"People are going to worry," Dr. Coots told him before he left for Maine. "If you're worrying all day and night, give me a call."

A song both boys liked came on the radio. They listened while staring out the greenhouse windows at the pointed caps of the pines in the distance, edged in orange from the setting sun.

"Did you say you talked to the monk?"

"Yeah."

"He forgave you?"

"It would be pretty sad if a Buddhist monk didn't forgive, right?"

Skeet shrugged.

"He told me he forgave me so long ago he forgot what he forgave me about. We're emailing each other again.

"I asked him what he thought of an army fighting for Self/Environment Balance. You know what his answer was? I gave the answer to that question the day you ran away."

Skeet laughed.

"I swear, half of Buddhism is stop asking questions you know the answers to already.

"Still, I need to figure out something to call it other than an army. We're going to do the Gandhi thing."

"Are we talking about people our age?" Skeet asked.

"I wasn't thinking about a particular age. Maybe. Okay, say it is people our age. People our age who are scared or fed up or confused or angry about the way the world is going?"

Skeet thought about this for a moment. "If that's what young people are feeling, they don't talk about it."

"We could call them the silents. Not silence but silents. No, that's a pun. I hate puns."

CHAPTER THIRTY-ONE

KIDS

This is an automatic reply from Find SEB.

Yes, they found me. I'm OK but it's a good thing they found me. I almost croaked out there.

Go out and swim or hike or make some music. After that, <u>click here</u> to learn more about Find SEB.

Get hooked into our network of really incredible people. People who know we have to deal with global warming now, right now, and are willing to stand up for it. So many of us will be standing, it will be impossible to ignore us.

If you're already doing that, awesome. Email us about what you're doing. We take money, too; click the button at the bottom to give it to us.

I wish I could answer your message personally but I'm busy working on some really cool things. Thanks everybody. Keep the good ideas coming.

A picture of an otter with a crayfish in its paws occupied the space beneath this paragraph. Below the otter picture, the text continued:

I'm trying to do the right thing. But I'm still young. What do I know? Maybe I won't end up doing very much to protect this amazing world. Did you?

But maybe young people like me will make the difference. Maybe that's what's been missing.

THE END

ACKNOWLEDGEMENTS

Jim, true to his word: there for me. For the peace and strength I had, knowing you were there for me. Not always an easy job, but think of the things we have seen and done together, and will do! Bob and Judy Bonney for teaching me to care about people, the most important lesson of all, who took me from the tundra of Orono to...Buffalo, and many places in between, an adventure, building your lives around us, so that we could have happy childhoods and enter this big wide world as strong men. And who still give so much to us. Mark Bonney and Dave Bonney, my brothers, two guys with the biggest hearts, for all the great times and for the kindness you've shown me, and for bringing Erin and Simone into my life. My nieces and nephews, who inspired me to write this book and who make my life so rich, in order of seniority: Kelly, Cait, Jordan, Liam, Mya, Matthew, Quinn.

My Hermit Island people!!! From the sand to the woods, for the best times of my life. All my aunts and uncles, grandparents and cousins. Maureen and all of Jim's family, who I love.

Anthony Bachus and John Stanicki, the truest friends, even if they never read anything I wrote. But they read it all. Do you know it was you who kept me writing? I would have been happy if you two were my only readers. Terry Wallace for loyalty that's hard to find and leaning on each other and for feeding me. Tommy Southall, who is more generous than he will ever admit, who built my beautiful website, and for decades of friendship. Mr. Bertrand, for love withstanding an ocean (and a great name). Chris Hudson for listening, any time, which helped me more than you may know, and the huge laughs, and starting our lives over together. David Woolwine; thoughtful, hilarious and kind. Thom, I'm not sure where I'd be without your ever-present Thom-ness, thank you and all of QC. Matt Ruther, because you make me happy.

339

All the big C's in my life:

Citizens Climate Lobby—*www.citizensclimatelobby.org*—for saving my life. Let them enrich yours.

Cincinnati Writer's Project, for the tough love, generosity, and big, obscene laughs.

Cancer and Blood Diseases Institute at Cincinnati Children's Hospital, who employed me while I wrote this book and surrounded me with heroes.

CB3, crybabies who are tough as hell and will actually show up when you need them—whatever you need them for. I love you guys. A lot.

Roberta, George, Arthur, Buddha and Buddhists! All the helpers of the world. You make life possible.

ABOUT THE AUTHOR

Robert (Rob) Bonney was born in Rumford, Maine.

He has a degree in English from Rutgers University and a Masters in Public Policy from The George Washington University.

Hide is his first novel.

You can contact Rob through his website:
www.rjbonney.com

Hide is set in Gandhi Serif and Gandhi Sans. Gandhi is an "open-source" type family designed by Librerías Gandhi S.A. de C.V., Mexico. According to the designers, it "does not distract the reader with ornaments or unnecessary flourishes." It *is* an exceptionally fine typeface.

Book and cover design by
Thomas Rae Southall Graphic Design, LLC

CPSIA information can be obtained
at www.ICGtesting.com
Printed in the USA
LVHW051530070519
616953LV00001B/133/P